The Pretty Sister
Leila Hilkmann

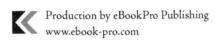 Production by eBookPro Publishing
www.ebook-pro.com

THE PRETTY SISTER
Leila Hilkmann

Copyright © 2024 Leila Hilkmann

'*The Pretty Sister*' is a work of fiction. All the names, characters, places and events mentioned in the plot are products of the author's imagination. Any resemblance to actual persons living or dead or to locals is totally coincidental.

All rights reserved; no parts of this b ook may be reproduced or transmitted in any form or by any means, electronic or mechanical, including photocopying, recording, taping, or by any information retrieval system, without the permission, in writing, of the author.

ISBN 9798329534719

CHAPTER 1

Tall and slender with long legs balancing on stiletto Manolos, she scouted her surroundings like a tigress on the prowl, sauntering towards the canopied doorway with swaying hips. Adding an air of mischief to the exquisite silhouette, her blond spirals brushed lightly against the bare shoulders. A diamond-studded Rolex, the only jewelry she wore, dangled loosely over the slender wrist.

"He can wait…I need a drink before I see him," her thoughts raced.

Moving seductively in her strapless black dress with fingers curled around the Hermès purse, she glanced at the dazzling flower arrangement set as a centerpiece at the Le Château lobby with its Spanish styled ceramics and wooden décor.

To onlookers she resembled a cross between a goddess and a whore, the fulfillment of any man's dream. Stepping into the elegant bar room with its dimly lit settings she took the time to adjust her frame on the tall stool.

"How are you, Harry?"

"Carlene… Carlene the beautiful!" The burly built bar man returned her smile.

"The usual, Hun," she pouted, tracing her upper lip with the tip of her tongue.

"Right on…it's been…what…two weeks?"

Her eyes focused on his hands mixing the drink.

"Enjoy!"

Harry smiled as he placed the tall glass in front of her, wondering what was going through her mind. Nine years at New York's Waldorf and the twelve that had followed at Le Château made him feel like something of a people expert. Harry's theory recognized two types: Those chatty ones that unraveled their life's story during and after the first drink, and the bottled-up ones who suffered from chronic emotional constipation. The latter were usually loners who took to drinking as an escape. Here and there he'd run across an exception that was difficult to categorize, like Carlene, who was all smiles yet with an unsettling air about her, an added flicker of something wild, an unfamiliar tinge which Harry couldn't quite define. He had to admit she was the most beautiful woman he'd ever seen, but was careful not to overstep his boundaries. Her very generous tips were well appreciated.

Her mind wandered as she sat fondling the drink. She thought of her so-called chance meeting with Glen, her husband of two years, whom she preferred to call Presch. It was carefully planned but far easier than her first encounter with Tierry, the man who was now waiting for her in the executive suite.

Carlene tried to guess how long it would still take to finish what she had set out to do.

Looking at Harry she asked.

"How many of these do you fix a night?"

"Difficult to say…I'd guess…not too many… not many people drink it," pointing to her glass.

Her eyes kept focusing on Harry but her mind darted back and forth trying to recall her last conversation with her husband, Presch, only hours earlier.

She had called him from the airport just before taking off from New York on her way to Dallas.

"I'd like to spend the weekend with Margie, if that's ok with you Presch?" her voice a near whisper.

"Well…if that's what you want…but don't forget to use plenty of sunscreen otherwise you'll burn …like the last time …"

"Oil, Presch… I'll dip myself in oil…would you like to smear it over my body?" in a raspy whisper that drove him crazy.

"Carlene, you're making me …"

"Yeah, me too …" she rolled her eyes then whispered again.

"Presch…it's Thursday, but I promise to be back on Sunday… please…" pouting her words in that special way.

"Of course… I'm sorry…of course I want you to enjoy yourself with Margie."

Carlene hung up.

She'd calculated the price she'd have to pay for lying but decided it was worth it.

It was now time to meet Tierry.

Carlene got up, took a green note out of her clutch bag and smiled in Harry's direction.

"See you next time."

Harry smiled back. He had just earned himself an easy buck.

Crossing the grand lobby on her way to the house phone, Carlene stopped momentarily next to the beautiful bird-of-paradise bouquet, the flower that reminded her of the divinity of human creation. She eyed the elongated stalks, stiff and erect, each boasting a concaved extension in deep crimson then shifted to the daggered shaped petals. Lingering momentarily on their pointy beaks, licentious little tools in bright orange and blue, she smiled and proceeded to the phone.

Within seconds Tierry was standing next to her with glowing eyes.

"I waited for you upstairs…why didn't you come up?" he asked after kissing her lightly on each of her cheeks. "I missed you… oh, I missed you so much… if you don't want me to make a scene you better follow me upstairs…"

She smiled.

"Later … right now I'm hungry."

"Where's your suitcase?"

"George took care of it." she glanced at the front desk, "I'm really ravished."

"Yeah, me too…I missed you…"

"No…I mean…I'm starved… for real food…"

She loved tantalizing him.

"Where would you like to go?"

"My favorite…"

Tierry was only too happy to oblige.

* * *

She had met Tierry only four months earlier after having hired the best help money could buy to ensure the success of her plan.

"I need to see you," she had called the detective.

"I'm on Wilshire and…"

"Name another place as long as it's not your office."

There was a second's hesitation before he answered.

"D'you know Larry's Diner?"

"I'll see you there tomorrow at six."

She hung up.

The following day she sat opposite him wearing dark sunglasses and speaking in a tone that didn't leave any doubts as to who was calling the shots.

"What exactly would you like me to find out about him?" he looked at the card Carlene had given him.

"His favorite color, what he eats for breakfast, how often he farts and fucks his wife …d'you get the picture?"

"I'll need a retainer of ten grand plus expenses."

She couldn't care less about the costs involved.

"I want it within a week," she crushed her cigarette.

The detective handed her back the small card.

"Find someone else. I need at least two …if I'm lucky. I'll need to tap the phones and …"

"Ok. Two. But not a minute longer."

"You're gonna have to be flexible on this…" his eyes didn't leave her glasses.

"Call me when you've got it all," she shot back.

"Can I ask you something?" a curious look on his face, "What's the interest?".

"An old sweetheart."

"And you don't know his favorite color?!" he grinned.

Carlene stood up.

"I'll expect to hear from you shortly!"

She turned around and left.

When they had met again, two weeks later, Carlene knew not only the man's favorite color but also that of his wife and child.

She had brought along a thick envelope.

"You can count it later. It's all there," she placed it in his hand and walked away.

She had all she needed.

It took her a while to set things up.

The Annual International Banking Gathering held in May at the luxurious Crystal Hotel in Dallas, Texas, was the most sought after event of the year across the international financial community. Top-ranking bank executives from Europe and Asia met with their American counterparts for an enriching brainstorming exchange of strategies pertaining to the promotion of the lucrative commodity shared by all: Money.

The gathering, known as the A.I.B.G., scheduled to last four days in the city's extravagant setting, allowed for a loosely balanced mixture of business and pleasure, with one representative from each institution.

Carlene had set things up carefully ensuring the smallest of details were well placed. It took her some time to find just the right dress but when she finally did, at the end of the Blakely Elite fashion show, she had handed an open check to the person in charge with an attached note:

"Fill out the amount and deliver immediately."

Once the parcel was delivered, she was ready to proceed with her plans.

She arrived in town a day earlier, and had checked into the Royal suite, the hotel's most luxurious room reserved for those able to pay its exorbitant price. She enquired about the entertainment available within the hotel itself, clarifying she did not wish to exit its splendorous comforts.

"Well…the only thing we're currently hosting is the A.I.B.G… it's in the Carlisle Wing," the front desk manager explained.

Carlene moved her eyebrow.

"It's for international bankers. They come from all over the world. Not exactly your everyday entertainment…"

"Au contraire! How interesting! I read about it in the paper but didn't realize it was being held here. Is there any chance…?" she left the sentence in mid air.

Her voice, somewhere between the roughness of a man's unshaven face and a woman's velveteen charm, compelled men to imagine the feel of her soft skin.

The young man eager to please the amazingly beautiful and obviously affluent guest, was only too happy to oblige.

"I'll try. We're not actually the organizers, but…I'll do my best…"

"If it's a matter of…" she stretched out her hand.

"No…oh no…no need for that, Mrs. Wilmore, the hotel is honored to have you with us."

She smiled.

He blushed and quickly moved away.

"Fool!" Carlene muttered behind clenched teeth. "Just like the rest of them."

Moments later the front desk manager returned.

"I've got one!" his face beamed as he held out the invitation.

Taking it, Carlene placed a folded bill inside his stretched hand.

The young man lowered his head slightly.

"Thank you, Mrs. Wilmore…thank you."

Wearing a long evening gown in blue lavender silk trimmed along its deep side slit and bare back with silvering rhinestones that made it impossible to ignore, she entered the grand foyer with the style of elegance and the know-how of a professional. Holding a wine glass in her hand she circled the large room, enjoying the stares and the head turnings, looking for the one person that was important to her. When she spotted him within a circle of delegates, she took a long sip from her glass and waited patiently for the right moment.

The crowd, almost exclusively male, filled the room with the best suits money could buy. Carlene kept moving in small circles careful not to lose sight of him. The fact that the gathering excluded wives only made it easier to near her target.

The casual chitchat and circulation of drinks were soon replaced by long speeches, introducing the 126 delegates and their respective institutions. Carlene loved the atmosphere. She could almost feel the massive power of money, which had a smell all of its own. No one spoke in terms of millions. It sounded too insignificant in light of the billions gathered in that one room.

Her seat gave Carlene an open view of the table she wished to observe. As she neared it, all seven men stood up and tilted their heads in her direction. In return she gave them a dazzling glimpse of her pearly teeth and luscious lips. She moved slowly, spending precious seconds finding just the right angle for the comfort of her body inside the tightly fitted dress. Fourteen eyes stared at her every move unable to relax in the company of the glamorous blue-eyed beauty.

The man to her right kept staring at her. Without as much as a smile or a word of introduction, he extended his hand.

"Nigel Factor. London."

"Fuck off," she wanted to reply but knew it would be the wrong thing to say. Instead she smiled.

"Carlene Wilmore. New York."

She kept smiling wishing to say as little as possible.
"Oh! And you're with…?"
"Myself."
The men laughed.
"Aren't we all!"
More laughs.
Carlene's head moved to the left.
"I'm Dean. Dean Trevor. Banker's Choice."
"Nice to meet you," she concentrated on the young man's nose wanting to spit out.
"Howdy woodpecker!"
But a tiny voice inside her head echoed.
"Shut the fuck up!"
Shifting her eyes to his lips she said.
"Carlene Wilmore, New York."
"Whereabouts in New York?"
Carlene faked a coughing attack.
"Are you ok?" both her neighbors inquired, offering water and help.
The master of ceremony saved the situation.
"I would like to call the first representative… Mr. Frank L. Majors of Regents Bank Madrid Spain."
The room was a busy beehive with executives rotating back and forth among the tables, shifting chairs and striding up stage then back again. More applause. More of the same questions. More wine. More names called up stage. Carlene kept her eyes focused on the table across the room.
"Mr. Nigel Factor Brock's Bank London the UK."
There was a sudden movement to her right as her neighbor pushed himself away from the table and walked briskly to the podium. Carlene's foot tapped nervously. It was dragging longer than she had hoped for. Sitting in one place was getting to her. She felt her skin begin to crawl and knowing she had no choice only aggravated the situation.

Another name. More hand clapping. Then all at once.

"Ralph T. Huber of Franco Swiss Credit Bank… a local Dallas-ite."

Carlene's eyes followed him as he made his way up stage.

"We're situated right across from this room," he pointed to the tallest skyscraper in town, "Flew here directly," he flexed his arms flapping them sideways.

The room roared.

Carlene studied him carefully concluding she could tolerate his presence. He wasn't bad looking. She only hoped that her plan would prove successful. Somewhat edgy, she waited for the speech parade to end.

Three hours later the room had finally resumed its earlier activity with background music played by a live band and the re-circling of delegates. It was time to act.

The stiletto heels, added to her five feet seven inches, enabled Carlene to scout the crowd and move closer, carefully closing the gap in his direction. She had only one chance. Now inches away from him she took a deep breath. Lifting her foot under the long gown, she slammed down forcefully the previously-loosened heel of her shoe propelling herself into Ralph T. Huber's astonished face. Her well calculated step landed her in his arms with a broken heel and a glass full of white wine splashed over both of them.

"Oh…I'm… so sorry…please…allow me…this is so embarrassing…" she squeezed herself into him.

There was a small commotion as someone picked up the heel and rushed forward to help the elegantly dressed woman who had accidentally landed in the arms of a total stranger.

"Please forgive me… Mr. Huber…" she looked into his eyes.

"Do I know you?"

"Your name tag…" she quickly lowered her eyes as if shying from her own admission.

"It's Ralph… please call me Ralph. And you are …?"

"Carlene. Carlene Wilmore."

She noticed the change in his face, from anger to pleasure and knew she was going to get what she had set out to do. It was now only a matter of time.

She had trapped Ralph T. Huber in her net.

"I'm really sorry…I…I don't quite know what to say…"

They were standing in the middle of a growing crowd. Having rehearsed the scene countless times, Carlene was able to act out her part in a very convincing way. Her shiny eyes were filled with tears just waiting to roll down. Taking out a silk handkerchief, she steadied the fingers of her left hand on his shoulder while carefully dabbing the remainder of the wine from his face. Well aware of his gaze, she moved her tongue over her upper lip taking in his scent.

Ralph T. Huber didn't flinch. Dumbfounded and totally transfixed he felt hot all over. He looked at the perfect skin and the lips smoothed over by the tongue, registering the eyes, near lilac in color and bright as diamonds. He'd never seen such sparkling blue stars. He couldn't move his eyes away, noticing that she kept lowering them trying to avoid his stares.

He swallowed hard.

"It must be…so embarrassing…I'm really…" she spoke hesitantly.

"That's ok…don't … don't worry…I'm sorry your heel broke…I can't imagine …please don't…" his hand kept moving in her direction wanting to wipe off the tears.

"Is there something I can do…" his face looked pained.

She lowered her head brushing the hair strands against his nose. He smelled her perfume. When she looked up their eyes met for a split second, long enough to make him feel as though he'd been hit by a low voltage current.

"Would you like me to…? I can walk you to your room…I mean…your dress…it's wet…"

Again she lowered her head and in a voice thin as air replied.

"You don't have to…"

"It's no trouble…. really…"

She fixed her eyes on his lips.

"Thank you…that would be very kind…"

Inside the elevator Carlene leaned on his arm.

"I'm sorry…I don't want to fall again …"

As soon as they walked into the suite, taking in the soft lighting and music, Carlene knew it was a matter of minutes before they'd reduce the distance between the front door and the bed in the adjacent room.

"I'm…" Ralph managed but Carlene had placed her finger on his lips. She shut her eyes and kissed him. He couldn't help himself. He felt totally out of control as if he was no longer master of his own thoughts or actions. Shutting his eyes he let his hands caress her shaking body.

"I'm so…"

Wanting to accomplish what she had set out to do, Carlene moved into him and placed her lips on his. She felt him harden and moved in the direction of the bedroom. Their clothes were off before reaching the bed. Carlene eased herself onto him, holding his head towards her with both hands. Her sunlit mane infused with copper streaks, created a sensuous curtain around their heads, a tropical island in the midst of the wide bed.

"Oh… this…this is…oh Carlene…" he sucked her breasts then groaned and pushed himself inside of her.

Following their frantic love making, Ralph buried his head in her hair.

"I…I don't know what came over me…it's never happened to me before…I'm a married man…"

Carlene traced his strong jaws with her fingers while staring at the large, brown eyes.

"It's ok…it's ok…" she brushed her leg over his.

Ralph sat up covering his face with both hands.

"I can't believe this is happening to me…"

Placing her hands over his shoulders, she whispered in his ear.

"It never happened to me before, either…I …I'm …I don't know…"

Her fingers moved gently over his naked torso.

Ralph got out of bed.

"How can I face my wife? She's at home with my daughter…I can't do this…"

Carlene's voice spoke quietly as she helped his guilt-ridden conscience rid itself of the acute pain. Ralph felt trapped. As though they had a will of their own, his hands kept touching Carlene, drowning in a frenzied passion he had never known before.

They spent the rest of the night in bed unable to keep their bodies apart.

At one point Carlene had asked him.

"What does the 'T' stand for?"

"Tierry. It was my grandfather's name… he was French."

"How is it pronounced?"

"It's like tee-ye-ry…but smoother…like your skin…" he moved his fingers along her inner thigh.

"I like your middle name. It turns me on," she wrapped herself around his hardened body whispering his name over and over.

Her hands were everywhere, touching and soothing and fluttering over his skin, dizzying him like a butterfly. He couldn't control his own hands as he held her luscious breasts, sucking on them hungrily. With his face buried under her velvety skin, he let her hands roam freely over his body, playing hide and seek on his rib cage, each move getting lower and closer to his hardened core, craving for her to touch him and lead him into her. He tried to hold off the explosion he felt coming. Letting go of her, he moved his fingers along the hidden trail craving the splendors below, a smooth downhill path to the heavenly secrets of her womanhood.

She groaned. Enjoying his touches and taking in his manly smell, Carlene felt giddy and for a split-second lost control. She held his manhood firmly in her hand and used soft airy touches to stroke its length and make him groan again. His hardness was beautiful, like a lighthouse towering above his handsome torso. Lingering along its surface with her tongue, she licked his firmness, inching her way to its tip, circling his ripened corona and wetting it with her drooling.

"Carlene…" he moaned.

Clasping her lips over his beautiful bloom, she made her tongue dance around forcing him to sound again,

"Oh…Carlene…Oh…"

She loved tantalizing men's dicks. It made her feel totally in control and in charge of everything a man really cared about. His groaning grew louder.

She kept moving her tongue in tiny circles licking the velvet-like tip around and around and..

"Oh…I can't…"

Reaching its wet tip with her tongue she tapped it gently again and again like a bird lapping dew off a leaf…

He drew in his breath.

"I… I can't…"

Moving her hands swiftly she guided his hardness into her.

* * *

Now eager to satisfy Carlene's wish, Tierry drove to Chez Henri, Dallas' most prestigious French restaurant located on McKinney a short drive from Le Château.

The place was packed, as usual, but Tierry didn't see it as a problem, rather as an opportune moment to enjoy preferential treatment. It was his choice restaurant for the selective clientele he handled at the bank, and the one place he felt owed him gratitude for the sheer number of seats he'd occupied over the past years. It was not unusual for him to appear at the lucrative establishment without prior notice accompanied by clients.

"For you, der iz olvayz a ples," Henri would say in his thick French accent and at once order the waiters to rearrange the tables.

Henri twitched his thin mustache and snapped his fingers as he approached them.

"A voila, mon ami…nice surpriz Madame," he bowed his head in Carlene's direction while shaking Tierry's hand.

She smiled back. He moved closer and kissed her right cheek, then her left then right again as was expected of a true Frenchman.

A new table appeared from nowhere and placed in a quiet corner near the window overlooking a small patio.

"Iz ok?" Henri pointed to the table.

"Merci, Henri," Tierry patted his shoulder pronouncing his name the French way.

"Avec plaisir."

They took their seats. Carlene leaned towards the single rose in its spindly vase.

"You like?" Henri gestured to the red flower.

"It's lovely."

Tierry held up a Champagne glass.

"To you, my love."

Carlene's eyes glowed.

"I love you so much."

"Would you like the usual?" he asked.

"Mmmm. I'd love the …"

"Peppered steak with French fries …and an extra large house salad…" Tierry grinned.

Carlene laughed.

"You saved me having to order."

"I love you," he looked into her eyes, those maddening diamonds that forced him to stare at them.

He took her hand and kissed it.

Following dinner accompanied by a fragrant deep wine and a perfectly delicious crème brûlée, they hurried back to Le Château to consummate their lovemaking. Giddy with drinks and the plans that lay ahead, Carlene stumbled into the room, her lips glued onto Tierry's. With eyes still shut she let his hands roam her body until they found each other and satisfied their hunger.

They fell asleep immediately failing to notice the flashing red button next to the phone.

The phone ring awakened her.

"Yeah?" Carlene's eyes were still shut.

Margie's nervous voice forced open her eyes.

"Glen's already called twice. Why didn't you return my messages?"

"When? When did he call?"

"Last night. I left you three messages. Where the hell have you been?"

"What did he want?"

"To speak with you! What d'you think he wanted?!"

"Ok, ok. I'll call him right now…"

"Yeah! I'm sure you will. What are you gonna use this time? The movies?! Why don't you fill me in on where I was yesterday? Eh?!"

"Cool it, Margie! You've got to help me on this one!"

They went through the usual routine coordinating their stories.

After hanging up Carlene dialed New York. In her special voice she left Glen a message.

"Hi Presch…hope you're not working too hard…I wouldn't want you to over- exert yourself…I could use a massage on my back and …" she moaned while moving her hand along Tierry's abdomen.

Her lengthy message touched the most delicate corners of her lover's body.

After hanging up she turned to face Tierry.

"What was that all about?" he asked in a drowsy voice, his eyes still shut.

"That moron! I swear he'd enjoy watching us right now."

"What?!"

"He once asked me to do it with someone… said it turned him on to hear about it…"

"Did you?!"

"Of course not! Who d'you think I am?"

"I sometimes wonder…" he answered, only half joking.

Carlene tickled him.

"What do you mean?"

Tierry felt strange and for a split moment tried to imagine Carlene with another man. With her husband. The idea sent shivers down his spine.

Carlene had given him a plausible explanation. At least a partial one. She told him that her husband was a possessive man, incapable of holding a relationship for long, that he made her feel worthless and his touch sickened her. Using fragments of her own imagination she elaborated the truth, adding lies and creating visions which she knew would make Tierry take her side and feel sorry for her.

It worked. Tierry was convinced that Carlene was truly suffering in her marriage.

But he was less sure of how she felt about their relationship.

* * *

They spent Friday shopping at the Galleria then returned to the luxurious hotel for the ultimate in pampered care at the private spa. Now back in their suite, Carlene's body tanned to perfection and well saturated with aromatic oils, felt velvety and sensuous. Every inch within her screamed to be touched. Tierry obliged vowing to love her forever.

His hands were constantly on her face, circling her breasts then lowering his fingers contouring her stomach and thighs below. His body shook with excitement.

"Slowly…" she kept whispering in his ear, "I like it slow and smooth…yes, like that…" her fingers cupped his, touring her softest spots that felt feather-like to the touch.

"Oh…oh Carlene…" he groaned once more.

Later that evening, seated opposite her lover at the Sea Fest Restaurant, Carlene smiled.

"You're so handsome…my Tierry," her long leg sneaking its way under the table and into the sleeve of his pants, brushing against his skin, knowing only too well what it did to him.

"You're the fairest of them all," he answered with glowing eyes, "and right now you're giving me a hard-on…"

She smiled in that special way of hers that made Tierry reach over with his finger and touch her lips.

"I want us to be together more often…I feel I'm losing you every time you return to New York to that husband of yours."

"But we set the rules from the beginning…" Carlene knew Tierry felt trapped.

"To hell with rules! We made them and we can break them. I can't go on like this, Carlene. I can't stop thinking of you…"

"But what about your wife?"

"I've decided to tell her about us…I don't want to waste my years …you and I are meant for each other…"

"Hush," Carlene reached over and placed her forefinger on his lips. He shut his eyes to her touch.

"Let's not spoil this delicious meal. Want to help me with these?" she tried prying open the lobster.

Tierry forced a smile. He felt heaviness in his chest.

"Oh… look," picking up the thin fork she pulled out the white meat. "It's delicious! I've never had such a tasty one," she sipped again from the dry white wine.

"I'm glad you like it."

Carlene was ravished. Following the appetizer they had shrimps and calamari, but her thoughts skipped elsewhere, far removed from the luxuries she had learned to take for granted.

Deep within her was rooted the young girl, the one who'd escaped long ago the white walls of Cedars Home.

***

She picked up the phone on the first ring.

"I've missed you, Presch," Carlene whispered into the receiver.

"Where were you? I called Margie and left messages…"

"Didn't she tell you?"

"She said something about an accident…and that I shouldn't worry. I don't understand…"

"Presch, I love you for not panicking. I simply adore you. I can't wait …"

"What happened, Carlene?"

"Well…we were driving along this smooth trail …just outside Dallas. It's… sort of farmland, with cows and horses, and …there's even a small lake for fishing. There was only Margie and me in the car and lucky for us she was the driver… because when that steer came face to face with the hood of her car, she was so cool. She pushed on the brakes and the car went dead… I mean …dead. The steer was hit in the lower chest and kind of to the side. His legs buckled under and they had to scrape him off the hood. I didn't feel a thing… not until Margie saw the inflated cushion and pulled it off of me. Nothing happened but I was so scared. I tried calling you but couldn't get through. I wanted to hear your voice and…"

"So did Margie finally take you to the hospital?"

Carlene wasn't sure what to say. She was always so good at remembering the detailed lies she'd made up but now found herself groping for help.

"Didn't Margie tell you what happened?"

"Yeah, she said they took you to a clinic and that the paramedics checked you…"

She felt relieved.

"That's right…they did. Oh boy …did they check every part of my body… I wish you could have checked me, Presch…I miss you… as soon as I'm back home I'll show you the places they checked…" her voice had turned husky again.

"I want you Carlene... I miss you."

"I'll see you tomorrow night, Presch."

She hung up.

Letting her bathrobe fall to the floor, she joined Tierry inside the Jacuzzi.

* * *

On Sunday afternoon they drove to the airport.

"Promise me...promise you'll soon come again...when can you make it?" he cupped the beautiful face between his hands.

"We need to slow down...I think Glen's getting suspicious...after today I'll have some explaining to do..."

"I love you Carlene... I want to share the rest of my life with you...I don't care what he thinks. Why not tell him about us?"

Carlene felt a tinge of panic.

"No...not yet. We need to plan it...do it carefully. Let's wait a while longer."

"But it seems like we've been together forever ... I don't want to wait any longer. I want you with me for the rest of my life."

"Give me just a little more time. Please, Tierry, please..." she let her hand slide carelessly to his thigh as if by chance.

"Don't...not now...please Carlene..."

His breath came fast. Carlene opened her eyes and saw his face. She smiled.

"I better leave now. I've got a plane to catch."

"Promise me...promise ..." he held her tight and whispered into her thick mane. "Promise me you'll come next week..."

"You know I can't make such promises," she laughed, "I'm a married woman."

"Don't laugh." He looked her straight in the eye. "I want us to be together."

He kissed her deeply.

"I promise… I love you… I'll give you a call as soon as I can."
She got out of the car and into the terminal.
Once inside she walked briskly to a quiet corner and dialed.
"Hi…it's me. Did he call again?"
"No, not since yesterday."
Margie sounded her usual, nervous and edgy.
"Good. I just spoke to him. Now listen carefully. There's one more thing you need to do…move some stuff for me…"

CHAPTER 2

Abigail was born in Emmeth on the outskirts of Brownsville, Texas, on a dark October night with only a friendly neighbor to assist her birthing. But her entrance into the world only added to the sorrow and heartbreak of her grieving parents. Five years earlier they had known the loss of their first baby, followed by a second boy born a year later, just as ashen colored and dead as his older brother. Their baby girl born prematurely two years later had died only hours after birth.

Her mother Mable was inconsolable. A devout Christian, she tried to find solace in her daily prayers held in the small town's church. Guided by the local priest she practiced charity and good deeds to soothe her soul, while finding hope and purpose in life.

When she realized she was with child again, she hurried to the priest and was quick to take on his words of counsel. She chose Biblical names and repeated them in her prayers to strengthen her chances of a healthy birth. With God's will and powers she was hoping to deliver the joys of fatherhood to her husband, Jasper, by blessing the name Abigail, in case of a baby girl, and Abbot in case of a baby boy.

At the first contractions Jasper hurried over to the neighboring farm and returned with the farmer's wife who was quick to prepare for the delivery. Jasper stayed in the kitchen next to the brass spittoon, chewing tobacco and cradling a bottle of whisky. His head was empty of thoughts. He'd already given up on fathering a boy but was willing to compromise on a girl as long as she was as beautiful as his Mable. It was her beauty that made him decide to marry her in the first place. Heck, with his good looks he could have chosen any girl but her eyes caught his young heart and had stayed with him ever since.

Jasper kept drinking. He couldn't face another small grave or more of Mable's tears. Darn! Why couldn't they just have a normal baby, a healthy little baby to hold and cuddle, but the more he thought about it the worse his fears, and the more he drank.

By the time the baby's first cry sounded, Jasper was lost deep in his impassive world.

He was lucky in a way, having bought himself a few hours of refuge, unlike the neighboring farmer's wife who was forced to face it the moment the baby took its first breath of air. She stared at the face trying to figure out if it was human. When she realized it had a gaping hole in place of a mouth she froze. She'd never seen a newborn monster. She shot Mable a quick look.

Mable's tearful face looked horrified.

"It's the Lord's way of speakin' to you …sayin' you don' need to keep it, love."

Mable was paralyzed, unable to touch the little thing.

"Should I call your hus…?"

"No, it's ok… I'll…"

Mable shuddered as though she'd snapped out of something. Then she stretched her arms and collected her newborn baby, holding the tiny parcel to her heart.

"Of course I'll keep her! And tomorrow I'll go see the Doc."

"You ain't got enough money for that, love…"

Shocked and confused, Mable was overwhelmed by what had emerged from her womb. She tried to place the little baby on her breast but there was no way for it to suck. With its gaping hole for a mouth, the baby was unable to clamp on to the nipple.

The neighbor remained in place, appalled at the sight of the tiny distorted face. She stared at Mable who was cuddling the small bundle. After making sure that Mable was ok the neighbor went in search of Jasper and found him snoring on the kitchen floor.

"You need to come see this," she rattled his shoulder.

By the time Jasper dragged himself off the floor, the neighbor was sorry she'd waken him up. Unsteady on his feet and reeking of alcohol Jasper followed her into the bedroom only to be shown the newborn.

"What in fuck's name is this?" he croaked, unable to focus with his glassy eyes. "I'm not havin' that…that thing stay here! It ain't human! Get rid of it!"

"Don't look! But keep your hands away from her!" Mable countered.

It was the start of Abigail's life and a vision of what her future was to be.

* * *

The next morning Mable forced her sore body out of bed and went to see the local doctor. Jasper kept his eyes on the road refusing to look in her direction.

The doctor examined Abigail.

"It's what's called a congenital anomaly… a birth defect … she has a cleft lip with a cleft palate… happens in one out of six hundred births or so… yes, they usually occur together… she'll require several surgeries… yes, from what I can see it also involves the nose and ear, as you can see here," his finger moved gently across the baby's face to the strange looking ear, "but no need to worry about it…most of it is cosmetic …it'll be done later on… what's important is the first surgery on the lip and the second one on the palate…"

"Hold it! Hold it, Doc!" Jasper interrupted, "We ain't got that kind of money. We're simple folks, you know, I'm just a farmer and I can't pay…"

"Oh…no… not to worry, charity care will pay for it. The first surgery to correct the lip is something she'll absolutely require in order for her to eat properly…and like I said, it'll be done and paid for. Later on she'll be hospitalized again for the second surgery …then the hole will be stitched from the inside to repair the palate. See?" he pointed to it, "that too will be taken care of in the same hospital."

Jasper was repulsed by the distorted face. It was hideous, didn't even look human.

The doctor went on.

"But no need to worry now. Her condition definitely qualifies for charity care at the Children's Center in Brownsville, so no need to worry about the costs. They'll start with the lip surgery and then the palate…"

"But how can I feed her 'till then?" Mable asked.

"We'll go over that in a minute but you should know that we can only operate on the lip around three months of age… she needs to gain sufficient weight, at least ten pounds to undergo such major surgery…yes, it's done under general anaesthetic," he then went into great detail explaining how the baby should be fed.

"Like I said, it's no use discussing the cleft palate surgery at this stage because it'll only be done around the age of nine months. It's two separate surgeries."

"And what about the scars and…"

"Well, some repairs are considered cosmetic, of course…because they're not a must. But the final aesthetic repairs are done much later around the age of eighteen once the face has fully matured… the main concern now is getting the baby to suck so she can gain weight to undergo the surgery…"

"But what about them scars? Will she have 'em here?" Jasper moved his finger around his own face.

"I'm not the one who'll perform these surgeries. Like I said she'll be thoroughly evaluated at the Children's Hospital but we'll help you with the paper work and do the interim follow ups. As for the scars…it's too soon to know, but…yes, she'll probably require some rhinoplasty over here," he again pointed to the baby's drooping piece of flesh where the nose was meant to be, "I prefer that the surgeons explain everything to you. Right now we should focus on the surgery on her lip… I can tell you that the second surgery on the palate doesn't leave external scars because the stitching is done from the inside. The only surgeries that might involve costs are those elective procedures…the ones that can be done when she's much older…."

"So you're tellin' me she'll be ugly with a face full of scars?"

Jasper couldn't accept such a baby, not after having lost two baby boys and another angelic looking baby girl. No! It wasn't right! He could never bring himself to love such an ugly creature. Heck, he couldn't even force himself to look at her now. No! They should definitely give her away…get rid of this…this thing…this ugly looking monster.

Mable refused to hear of it.

"You ain't takin' my little girl away. She's my girl! The Lord's already took two of my boys and my little girl. I ain't givin' her to no one!"

But even as she spoke the harsh words, Mable found it impossible to kiss the tiny face, especially when it was screaming to be fed. Whenever she could, she'd avoid touching the baby's face and fed the gaping hole with the special bottle the doctors had recommended. She attended to Abigail's needs using her hands, but refused to involve her heart and soul having already experienced the pains of loss. She wasn't about to cope with another loss, not even if it involved something as monstrous as Abigail.

There was only one marvel the baby could claim for herself: Her beautiful eyes which were identical to her mother's.

"What a waste," Mable thought, "what a waste on such an ugly thing."

Jasper kept to himself and refused to come near the baby. The only time he voiced his discontent was at the last meeting with the pediatrician right before the scheduled surgery.

"So… are you ready for the big day?" he asked both parents.

Mable held Abigail in her lap. Jasper kept his eyes on the floor and snarled.

"That thing ain't fit for life."

The pediatrician's eyes bulged out.

"You're her father, right?!"

When he met with silence, the doctor added.

"Shame on you! As a father you should comfort her!"

Mable entered the hospital on a Tuesday holding three-month-old Abigail in her arms. By Friday the two were back home. According to the doctors, surgery on the lip was successful.

"We had to detach and reposition the muscle of the lip to recreate the circular muscle over here," the doctor pointed to the precise place then went on to answer other questions, "No need to worry about the scar…yes, it's crimson now and very pronounced …but as time goes by it'll fade and the swelling will subside…it's gonna look less obvious…it takes time so no need to worry about it …"

It was now a matter of waiting for the second surgery on the cleft palate.

* * *

Abigail's pains began the day she was born and continued throughout her first two years of life setting the tone for the years that followed. Beyond her physical pains and the complexities derived from her congenital medical condition, baby Abigail was experiencing another kind of pain: A constant ache of estrangement, lacking the feel of belonging or being claimed by someone, a sense familiar to babies who come into the world unwanted and unloved. The long years of accumulated emotional neglect would ultimately scorch her heart and mind and leave an impression of rejection known only to discarded little humans left at the mercy of heavens or strangers.

Given her birth defects, Abigail was unable to comfort herself by sucking a finger, using a pacifier or placing anything else inside the open gap of her face. Her little soul was forever in search of something soft, a small thing to cling onto and make her feel loved and wanted. As an infant she cried a lot. Her small voice sounded distressed and unhappy, much like the cast-off wailing of a deserted pussycat or stray dog imploring to be noticed and petted. When she was older, Abigail would notice how they'd meow and yelp, wanting to be held and cuddled and the longer time passed, the more eager they'd become willing to put up even with abuse as long as they'd win a lick, a blink of attention, a casual stroke, or a momentary curl up.

Abigail's existence throughout her early life resembled that of a stray creature, a loveless little something that no one liked or wanted. Recognizing her baby's need for something soft and soothing but unable to make herself love her, Mable used a leftover piece of velvet cloth to sew a small pillow which she placed inside Abigail's tiny hand. Lacking compassion, Mable didn't even grasp the significance of the piece of softness she'd given her baby daughter or appreciate how important the little velveteen pillow had became. Abigail held on to it as though her life depended on it.

Having missed the small gestures of a baby's earliest communications with his surroundings, Mable totally ignored the clues and details hidden within the shattered face. She assumed there was nothing more to Abigail than her ugliness and deformity, and was completely blind to what lay inside her baby's little heart and soul.

Mable's thoughts, like those of Jasper, didn't stretch beyond the baby's face. Neither of them ever considered its soul, or mind or anything else that might be hidden inside. They labeled their first surviving baby as "damaged" without searching further. It never occurred to them to enquire what thoughts churned inside their baby's head or what lay behind Abigail's damaged face. They shared a deep belief that all was dictated and pre-ordained from above. The fact that the baby thrived despite all odds was the Lord's way of testing their spiritual strength. It was useless to try and out-guess the heavenly blessings and waste time over things unknown. In a way, ignorance was blissful for those willing to follow the Lord' scriptures without raising any doubts; after all, things were clearly stated and the less one asked the better.

Both failed to recognize that baby Abigail was blessed with a strong spirit, a bright mind, and a sharp innate intuition. She lay all alone in her crib crying for attention, but was quick to grasp as if by osmosis that she must help herself in order to survive. This realization reflected her mental acuity and changed the course of her thinking and behavior forever. When she'd smile at her mother, she'd barely get a response. So after a while she stopped smiling and tried crying, screaming and other means of getting attention. She learned from the start to make do with very little, and was forever willing to satisfy people even at the expense of her own needs. She could feel momentary happiness with a meager smile, a little finger holding or a split-second soft touch. Over the years she'd used her sharp mind and found additional survival mechanisms, emotional patterns of behavior that could help her cope with the deeply rooted scars of rejection she'd known since birth. She'd learned to exploit people and situations for her own benefits, and use them as shields or weapons as she saw fit. But despite all, her needs and wants for a mother's love were never fulfilled.

Over the years Abigail's deep emotional deprivations only intensified. The rejection she had felt by her parents and its cumulative affects seeped through the pores of her baby heart and continued scarring her as a teenager, and by then she was convinced that she was indeed a loathsome creature. No one wanted her. No one loved her. She was less than a drop within the ocean of humanity, a worthless ugly thing that should be cast aside and forgotten.

As for her father, who rarely, if ever, bothered even to look at the crib, it was obvious that he wasn't interested. He'd sit as far away as possible from her, aim his bottle at his mouth and shut his eyes. That way, he could ignore her existence altogether.

By the age of two, Abigail stopped trying to get the attention of the man who kept disregarding her. And by the time she turned six and was forced to endure a daily Via Delarosa to and from school, Abigail had come to resent the people who'd given her life.

Mable tried loving Abigail but couldn't bring herself to be kind or patient with her. In her own mind Mable referred to Abigail as 'a creature' unable to accept her presence as that of a human being. There was something solid and enduring about the child, a mighty strength with a fiery temperament fortified by an inquisitive sharp mind. But the combination angered Mable who was unable to cope with it all. She felt that it would have been so much easier had Abigail been born with a feeble mind to match her looks. Mable could have then felt sorry for her, treated her differently and even cradled her out of pity. It could have strengthened her sense of motherhood, awarded her the pity of others which she enjoyed.

As a young girl Mable grew up thinking that the way to love someone was to pity them. Her own mother used to say.

"I pity you for not havin' smarts… so I'm tellin' you this… you need to sharpen up girl and make a man pity you if you wanna marry one day…"

Mable had to think about it. She was a bit confused initially but then she learned to equate pity with love.

Yes, people liked to pity others. It made them feel stronger. They also liked to feel sorry for the poor and innocent who couldn't fend for themselves, the priest explained to her. He told Mable she should take comfort knowing that the good church-going women felt sorry for the bad luck that had befallen her. Knowing that others cared about her and commiserated with her own misery should pacify her need for love and give her a soothing feel of comfort.

Following the loss of her three babies Mable had come to know the meaning of pity which the priest referred to as empathy; and now with her damaged child, she longed to feel it again, but Abigail simply refused to comply.

"That devil of a girl is sharp and swift as a whip!" she told her neighbor.

Mable went as far as dismissing all of Abigail's aches and pains, and even found it hard to feel sorry for some of the medical procedures she was forced to endure.

Why was Abigail so accepting of everything? She never complained and she'd even stopped crying. She didn't bother Mable or demand attention. It was so annoying! She was supposed to look miserable and act the part, cry for help, ask for pity, but instead she was always agreeable and went along with everything that came her way.

Why was she so willing? And always trying so hard to please everyone?

Mable looked for other words that could best describe Abigail but fell short of the word ingratiating, realizing it might very well muddle up her thoughts. Yes, Abigail was definitely a freak of nature, an ugly thing that wasn't supposed to live so maybe she wasn't human in other ways, too? And maybe…well, was Jasper right after all? Maybe they should have placed her somewhere and…

The thoughts churned inside her frail mind like a wheelbarrow roiling downhill without giving thought to its return journey uphill.

Perturbed and unable to be comforted by Jasper who was a man of even fewer words than her, Mable turned to the priest.

"This baby is the Lord's way of strengthening you as a mother," he smiled at her deadpan face. "The Lord's ways are mysterious and it's the lesson he's chosen for y'all…"

Tearful Mable whispered back.

"But I don't feel I can love her."

The priest blessed her once more promising to serve as a comforting source for her future doubts and difficulties.

"We can never give up hope."

But Mable had already given up hope of loving Abigail. The damaged creature that was left in the crib for hours on end was proof of her own worthless motherhood. Mable had convinced herself that a divine power was responsible for the deformed baby and was forcing her to pay for ancestral sins committed in the past. She found proof in the priest's words who'd explained all this to her following the death of her first son.

"We are all a human chain connected to one another in mysterious ways …" When her second baby boy died the priest dug deeper.

"Those who choose to break away from the human chain that connects us all shall be cursed and punished by the Lord almighty …"

Mable assumed that her mere questioning of the Lord's ways, those she'd dared entertain inside her head, were perhaps responsible for breaking the divine human chain and had caused the death of her second boy.

Mable's spirits were beaten and her heart broken. Throughout her pregnancy with her third child she had been very careful, making sure to dismiss any thought that brushed through her mind, staying on track and refusing to discuss any possibility of a mishap. The priest took it to heart. Every Sunday during his sermon, adamant to prove his theory right, he released a hint reminding her of the divine human chain.

But Mable ended up losing her little girl, a beautiful blue eyed angel that blossomed overnight then shut her eyes forever. Jasper had disappeared for three days. Upon his return, Mable noticed his eyes. They had turned black. And angry. And ugly. He couldn't utter one word as he stood near the small grave site. His arms seemed longer than usual as if trying to catch the culprit responsible for the death of his beautiful baby girl.

Mable remained in bed for several weeks, unable to eat, to sleep, or to keep her eyes open. When she finally got out of bed, Jasper relaxed.

"Praise the Lord."

Within days Jasper seemed to regain his strength.

He spoke some. Mable listened. He spoke again. Mable made him dinner but didn't smile at him. It was a sign they had between them. Mable's smile meant she wanted his company for the night. A month went by, then two and three until Mable released her smile. As far as Mable was able to calculate, nine months later, to the day, the creature was born.

As for the priest, he was never proven right.

Nevertheless, he continued serving Mable as a well-deserving wise man with a divine knowledge of the Lord and his perplexing ways.

＊＊

Jasper's world tilted away slightly from that of others. Born and raised on a farm by a father who barely smiled, if ever, and spoke even less, and a plain looking mother who lacked thoughts, reason or wants, Jasper was a straightforward thinker who avoided all questions.

"What you have is what you got!" was his motto. "So no need to bother with what aint in front of your eyes."

He knew farm work from an early age, liked working the land and using both his hands and had set his mind to become a farmer. As a child he'd already declared that he'd like to follow in his father's footsteps. He was a strange little baby and an even stranger boy and remained such throughout his youth. It was as though he'd been born with written instructions on how and when to do things. At the sight of anything out of the ordinary, an unexpected move or remark, or any other form of spontaneity, Jasper would become rattled. He'd keep silent, turn his head and walk away. Not because he disagreed with it, but because it would jeopardize his set rules of conduct to the point where he wouldn't know how to react. Feeling uncomfortable he'd keep walking until he was sure he was out of harm's way. With very little tolerance for anything or anyone out of the ordinary, he liked to keep things as simple as possible.

When he realized that schoolwork was way over his head, he decided he could do without it. Keeping matters straightforward, he approached his teacher and confessed he'd reached his maximum capacity for learning. Initially the teacher thought Jasper was joking but when he realized it was no joke, he was dumbstruck and kept his mouth shut.

It was Jasper's pure honesty that helped him solve most annoyances, but not all.

Things got confusing around age sixteen when his testosterone levels began fluctuating capriciously. Unlike the rest of his classmates who chose to quit school at an early age and go work the fields, Jasper was in a deep jam. He'd fallen madly in love with Mable and her beautiful eyes. Robustly built and handsome he had the choice of the entire flock of school girls, but he chose Mable for her glances, for her height and for her smiles. He knew that her father expected her to stay in school until the end of the year, so he made his choice right there and then and stayed along. It wasn't easy for someone who could barely read but he knew what he wanted and whom he wanted it with and Mable was it. Nothing less, nothing more.

The end of school was approaching. He picked a day and at the end of that school day walked over to Mable, looked her in the eye and said,

"Will you marry me?"

Mable blushed. All the girls were losing sleep over Jasper, the head rooster of the entire school if ever there was one. But Mable being Mable, she simply listened to the chatty girls and smiled. Not once, not ever, did she dream that Jasper would propose to her when he did, or the way he'd done it. Not ever.

Mable stood there agape.

"Ah…ah…" was all she managed.

Jasper was hoping to hear a Yes, but he understood her hesitation.

"Should I speak to your dad?"

Mable blushed. She was speechless. Jasper was simply too perfect for her.

"I'll walk you home if that's ok with you," he told her, to which she replied.

"It's more than ok. It's perfect."

And off they went in search of Mable's father.

The deal was a short and straightforward one. Mable's father consented and the young couple declared their upcoming marriage which they scheduled to take place within the next two weeks.

On their wedding night, Mable was nervous. She'd never been with anyone before, never dated, never felt someone else's skin on hers or even kissed other lips. Never. She was scared of not knowing what she was supposed to know or do.

"Not to worry," was all Jasper said.

Mable chose to believe him, and let him take the lead.

Unbeknown to the bride, Jasper had never been with a woman before. Despite his good looks and reputation, all he'd heard were mumblings from his drunken father and older brother. But he didn't have a clue.

The small wedding took place at the local church with a few neighbors and even fewer friends. Jasper's parents came to meet the bride's family and thereafter returned to their own home a couple of miles down the road.

The bride and groom were given a short break before the night when it was time to get acquainted with each other.

Jasper made sure the lights were out and Mable was well tucked in bed under the summer blanket before approaching her. Lying in bed next to each other, he stretched his arm in her direction. Mable remained as still as a statue waiting for whatever it was a bride was supposed to wait for. Jasper moved his hand and touched her long hair but made sure not to utter a word, not wanting to embarrass her. It would be best if he could do it in silence but he wasn't sure exactly how to go about it. He'd heard talk about tearful brides and such and he didn't like it. He loved

Mable too much to cause her tears, so he kept stroking her hair until he felt a slight tingling inside his night pants. He recognized it and moved closer to Mable who remained utterly frozen in place with both arms clasped on her chest and eyes tightly shut. She was waiting. Jasper moved closer and kissed her cheek and from there on things moved faster than the wind, finding Jasper on top of Mable.

"Will it hurt?" she whispered.

"Nah," he answered and moved into her.

Mable let out a hushed squeal followed by small sobbing noises. Jasper quickly backed out and away from her.

"Did it hurt?" he asked.

"Not much…I'll be ok," she sounded between snuffles.

Over time Mable got used to it as part of her wifely duties but she never really enjoyed his touches. Or smell. Or the stench of his breath.

The following day Jasper set out to plan the construction of their family home next door to that of Mable's parents.

But the Lord had other plans.

Shortly after the wedding, Mable's mother began having problems breathing and died the following month.

"Cancer," the doctor told them, "it was cancer."

It didn't take Mable's father long to follow in his wife's footsteps. A heavy smoker and drinker, he'd joined his late wife five months later at the ripe young age of thirty-eight. The orphaned Mable was left with an older brother who was living not too far with his own wife and child. A decision was made that Jasper and Mable remain in her late parents' house and work out the farm.

When Mable found out she was pregnant, there wasn't a happier man than Jasper. All he ever wanted in life was to farm the land and father children. He really enjoyed making babies and shared his joys with Mable who complied in her subservient manner.

"Do you pity me?" she asked him during a romantic moment.

"Not sure," was his response.

It left Mable wondering if he loved or pitied her. Or both.

***

Following the birth and death of their first baby boy, Jasper exhibited near stoic behavior; unable to verbalize his emotions he chose silence and retreated into his shell, disappearing from the farm. Three days later he returned home reeking of alcohol with eyes glazed over.

He repeated his performance following the birth and death of their second baby boy, but this time he chose to stay away for a longer period. When he finally made it back home, Mable wasn't sure he'd remembered how to speak. He kept his mouth shut for nearly a month.

After the birth and death of their little baby girl, Jasper lost his wits. He crouched on the kitchen floor and refused to eat. The following day, after the funeral, he went out to the fields and drank himself sick. He felt his life was doomed. Why were they cursed again? And who was cursing them? Surely it wasn't the Lord if only for all the prayers and devotions that Mable granted him daily in church. Maybe the devil himself did exist, after all? Or was there another kind of devil?

It took him an entire month to return home and check in on Mable. He couldn't look at her disappointed face, convinced that he was to blame in some way. Deep inside his head he tried to figure things out, but somehow all reason eluded him. But Jasper wasn't about to quit and being the stubborn mule that he was, he continued carrying his tallness wrapped with pride and hope. He kept debating whether or not it would do him good or do him harm to talk about the things that filled his head and hurt his heart but decided to play it safe and stay away from church and home.

Mable, meanwhile, was broken hearted. The priest and some of the women came to comfort her and went out of their way to try to soothe her aching heart. By the time Jasper had returned indoors, she was more than ready to welcome him back.

"Me and Jasper …we know it how to communicate with silence," she told her neighbor.

It took them a while to settle back into their daily routines and silences.

It was the silences that comforted them both, and served as thin cobwebs to weave afresh their intimate relationship.

The night Mable had finally asked him to share her bed, was one of the happiest and most satisfying nights Jasper could remember. It took them a while to readjust to the mechanics, but pretty soon Mable was with child again. But unlike her other pregnancies when Jasper had stayed away from her, this time he was adamant to guard Mable from any harm and convinced her they should copulate nightly in order to strengthen the unborn child inside her womb.

Mable agreed, of course, raising no questions or objections. Things continued until Mable was too large to comply with Jasper's theories at which point he declared that by now things were going well and there was no need to reinforce the unborn baby.

But as soon as Jasper saw Abigail for the first time he referred to her as Mable's baby.

"She's your flesh and blood. That thing ain't right an' it ain't mine!"

All his wants and wishes were brushed aside by the monstrous baby that wouldn't quit crying or trying to catch his attention.

"Can't she tell I ain't interested? Make her shut the fuck up!" he'd roar whenever Abigail cried or tried to get some attention.

Mable knew what she needed to do so she moved ahead and did it.

When Abigail was a year-old Mable found herself with child again, though it was difficult with Abigail's second surgery only months away.

Whenever Abigail cried, Mable was forced to confront emotions she'd never known before. On the one hand her heart was crying to love the little baby but when she'd look at her twisted face she'd be repulsed. Torn between the natural emotions and unconditional love expected of a mother and her inability to fulfill them, caused Mable's heart to overflow with a deep sense of failure and guilt, well aware of the fact that she wasn't acting as a good mother.

Abigail's pleading eyes stared at Mable at all times begging to be cuddled and loved. On one particular occasion she had smiled inadvertently at Abigail and was immediately ingratiated by her smiley face, a monstrous ugliness that forced away Mable's eyes. It only pained her more and felt like a stab inside her heart.

Mable's heart was broken and confused.

The second surgery to repair little Abigail's cleft palate went by uneventfully except for its final stage, when the surgeons had to work very slowly and extensively so as to align the precise stitching on the inside of the upper gum. Baby Abigail's surgery lasted longer than was initially planned and she remained hospitalized for three days. Mable was told the stitches would need to be removed after some additional days.

Once the stitches were removed, Mable felt that she had done all in her power for Abigail. It was now time to prepare for her next birth and, with the Lord's blessings, a healthy baby would soon join them.

CHAPTER 3

Presch, the nickname reserved for Carlene's husband of two years, was Prof. Dr. Glen Wilmore, one of New York's most celebrated psychiatrists who simply adored his gorgeous-looking Carlene for making him feel taller than his five feet two inches. Convinced that Carlene was the closest thing to a miracle that had ever happened to him, Glen was willing to pay whatever price Carlene demanded. With her at his side he was able to look in the mirror without averting his eyes.

Born and raised in New York, Glen had learned to live with disappointments as a child.

"There goes that fat ass," the kids would point their fingers at him.

"Hey Wilmore, how 'bout shortening your nose 'fore it scrapes the ground?"

Unlike his brother who inherited the tall muscular figure of his father, a teacher at the local elementary school, Glen took after his exceptionally short mother, a nurse by profession who was known for her good deeds rather than looks. From a young age, Glen was determined to prove his worth to the world.

"I'll show you!" he'd say to the short kid in the mirror. "I'll show all of you!"

Though his early years taught him to stay away from the bullies and the beauties, his appetite for the latter remained unquenched.

He liked to imagine himself the master of a beautiful woman who'd appreciate him for his amassed wealth, convinced that women could never favor him for any other reason.

Glen's outstanding grades finally got him into Columbia on a full scholarship, and from there on to the podium he longed to stand on, but his journey uphill was a bumpy one.

At one point, Glen began dating a lady friend but was soon struck by anxieties that impeded him from performing the manly duties expected of him. Shame and humiliation rattled Glen's core. Looking for momentary relief and wishing to mollify his ego, the bright-headed student journeyed to Greece where he was immediately captivated by the culture with its deeply rooted mythology and gods.

Still haunted by his failures within the realm of Eros, the god of carnal love and passion, Glen decided to look elsewhere and soon found solace in Cupid, the Roman counterpart of Eros and the god of affectionate love and romance. Cupid's kingdom was more flexible than that of Eros, offering practical solutions that happened to coincide with Glen's traumatic experiences. It also fortified his intention of specializing in psychiatry, allowing him to dedicate his professional life to healing men's worst nightmares and freeing them of nuptial misfortunes. Cupid's consoling qualities were softer, allowing for amorous words and affections to set in motion a chain of intricate actions, alternating between soothing and arousing men's most fragile organs. It proved a sure way to manipulate situations and overcome drooping spirits and body parts.

Glen put his understanding to the test several years later, when he opened an exclusive practice for the revival of withering organs and even went as far as researching the precise mechanisms and complex processes involved. His laborious work awarded him momentary relief in the form of intellectual climaxes, brief experiences only he himself was able to enjoy.

As a young man Glen was troubled by his failed sexual attempts involving women and at one point began thinking about men. Not that he was particularly drawn to them; but then he wasn't strongly drawn to women either. It took him a while to sort out his likes and dislikes and even longer to admit certain facts to his therapist.

"I simply enjoy the playful part of sex…the physical… kinky sort of stuff, you know… that involves… well, some level of pain, but not too much… just … casual spankings …to a low degree, of course…"

"Do you enjoy being strapped to a bed and flogged?"

Glen's eyes shone.

"Yes!"

"Well then," the therapist exhaled, "If that's what you enjoy…"

"Yeah…but is it ok?" Glen's eyes were big and wide.

With his head tilted slightly sideways and not daring to blink, he stared at the therapist convinced his life depended on the latter's words.

"As long as it's consensual and practised with other adults, of course…"

Glen exhaled. He puckered his lips and released a strange smile.

"Yes, of course, of course…I would never…you know…"

It was the greatest relief for Glen's ears and the last time he'd brought up the subject with anyone.

Glen had known long years of self-flagellation and was insecure with his own sexual preferences and relationships. Every time he'd stare at the mirror he'd admit the ugly guy didn't merit more than pain and humiliation. He deserved to be flogged and punched and mistreated, it was part of who he was, but it was so painful he couldn't even admit it to his therapist.

As for his sexual ambiguities, there was no simple way to explain them. He wasn't even sure about his preferences and at times tried to imagine what it would feel like sticking his penis inside another man's body, but for whatever reason, the vision always unhinged him at the last minute. He was hesitant about the mechanics and the feel and…oh, he could never unravel his deepest emotions to anyone, it would…no, he couldn't…not yet…in the future…sometime in the future…

Glen kept things bottled up and stuck to his one ritual: after dressing up for an event, he'd stand in front of the mirror and repeat out loud.

"When we'll meet, my love, I promise to share with you my ugly little secrets!"

He preferred to leave his sexual orientation dangling in mid-air.

Now aged forty-six with an envious practice and a formidable career as one of Columbia's most distinguished lecturers, Professor Dr. Glen Wilmore was only a step away from realizing his dream. He wished for a wife, someone beautiful who'd be willing to stand by his side and make him look something other than what he was used to seeing in the mirror.

Relying on his own experiences and beliefs, Glen had become an expert on the subject of unconsummated marriages.

"No two people share the same wants and results…" was his opening line for the many patients who turned to him for help.

His ending line was designed to pacify:

"There is not one curative prescription for all…"

But despite his extraordinary intelligence and sensitivity, Glen Wilmore didn't know how to realize his own dream.

Luckily for him, destiny crossed his path in the shape of Carlene Ridge.

* * *

He had walked into a dinner party expecting the usual crowd when his eyes fell on an exceptionally beautiful woman. From the distance he noticed the hostess approaching his way.

"Darling, I'd like you to meet a dear friend of ours," Denise's arm hooked into Carlene's, "He's the sweetest man you'll ever meet."

Carlene offered her hand.

"This is Professor Doctor Glen Wilmore, *the* Professor Doctor Wilmore everyone is talking about," she released a short chuckle.

Unable to avert his eyes from the stunning face, Glen held onto Carlene's hand.

"I'm flattered," Carlene lowered her head shyly.

"Why?"

"Excuse me?"

"Why are you flattered?"

"Oh…it's just…well…you know…new people…new city…and you're so famo…."

"Are you from New York?"

"Well…actually…" she glanced at Glen's hand.

"Oh…I'm sorry…I'm so sorry…sometimes I forget…" he released her hand.

"That's ok…really…"

"It's just…"

"Don't worry about it…it's fine…I'm sure your life is so interesting. Please tell me about your work, Professor Doctor Wilmore."

"It's Glen…please call me Glen."

"Glen…I love the name…it has a…a 'gling' sound to it…So what do you specialize in…Glen?" showing off her tiny dimple.

"I'm a psychiatrist.…"

"Oh, how exciting!"

"Is it?"

"Sure… just think of all the people that come to you for advice."

"But that's what…"

"And you get to help them …"

"I try to…at least …but …"

"You're probably so good at what you do, Glen…"

"Thank you, Carlene."

"I've always thought psychiatrists are the smartest amongst doctors."

"Why's that?"

"Because they must be able to understand what's going on inside the brain…and heart…lots of guessing work and…"

"How observant!"

"Well… thank you, Glen."

"It's not easy, sometimes…"

"I'm sure it's very demanding. Denise had mentioned something about Columbia…"

"Yes, I'm chairing the department."

"Oh…my…" she looked into his eyes hidden behind thick lenses.

"Yes, I've been there for …let's see…I got my doctorate eighteen years ago then…"

"That's a lifetime," she touched his shoulder lightly with her hand.

"Yes," Glen smiled turning red around the cheeks.

"And what do you enjoy doing when you're not working, Glen?"

"I…don't laugh…I…."

"I would never laugh at you," she held his gaze.

"Thank you."

"So…what do you do after working hours, Glen?"

"I've got this stamp collection…it's… quiet extensive…"

"Oh! I assumed you collected beautiful women…"

"Oh no! No! Absolutely not…I wish I did…but…"

"Wouldn't you like to collect me?"

"I… Carlene," he lowered his head.

"Yes Glen?"

"You're teasing me, right?"

"Never. I would never tease a man like you."

Carlene watched him move, as if swaying sideways his head moving slowly left to right then back again.

"Did I embarrass you?"

"Yes…you did…"

"I'm sorry… I didn't mean to…please excuse me…I'm so sorry…."

"Ok," Glen shook his head, "Ok… I'm ok…"
Carlene felt she had said the right thing.
"Any other hobbies?"
"I love classical music so I have this collection…"
"Oh, my favorite…"
"Who's your favorite composer?"
It was time to recite the article she had read.
"I love Verdi…and Bizet…"
"Me too!"
"Do you go to the Met?"
"Sure! I love it. Do you?"
"I love it too," her tongue circled her lips.
Glen sighed.
"What a pleasure, Carlene. What a beautiful…name…"
"Would you like to approach the table?" Denise announced.
"Shall we?" Carlene offered him her arm.
Glen held it proudly.
"Any preference?"
"Yes…close to you…" she squeezed herself slightly into him.
"Carlene, dear, your seat is over here," Denise moved among her guests like a butterfly.
"Great! I'm over here…right across from you," Glen smiled.
"I…I'm glad I met you."
"Yes, me too."

They were now seated across from each other surrounded by a roomful of smiling guests who were busy enjoying themselves and contributing to the noisy social hum. Sliding off her shoe, Carlene brought her bare foot to rest inside his crotch. Glen felt a bolt of lightning hit him. His eyes bulged as he stared at Carlene in utter disbelief.

By the time the dessert arrived, he was madly in love with her, willing to do anything in his power to make her want him.

Carlene's special talents awarded Glen a deep sense of conquest, matched only by Carlene's equal feelings for Glen.

It took Carlene less than four months to get the wedding band on her slender finger and even less time to find her first lover. Twenty months later and following several other lovers condensed into her twenty-five stormy years of life, Carlene ended up with her current lovemate whom she liked to call Tierry.

"I like your middle name. It turns me on," she had told him when they were in bed together for the first time.

CHAPTER 4

Now on her way back to Presch, her husband in New York, after having spent the entire weekend with Tierry in Dallas, Carlene was hoping for a peaceful flight.

"Can I offer you a drink?" the flight attendant asked.

"I'd like to move over there," pointing to the seat closest to the cockpit.

"I'm sorry, Mrs. Wilmore, it's occupied."

"Can you perhaps try to make the exchange?" her eyes piercingly cold.

As though reading her mind, the flight attendant, having experienced seventeen years of serving customers like Carlene, was adamant to cut it short.

"I'm afraid that's impossible," she spoke quietly, "Those seats are reserved. Maybe…"

"I'm not interested in your maybes, miss…?" she eyed her tag, "Leslie. Is it Leslie or do you prefer Ms. Slater?"

Leslie Slater looked Carlene in the eye.

"Ms. Slater is fine, Mrs. Wilmore. I was only trying to be helpful."

"I can see that! I'd like another of this bloody thing," placing her glass on the tray.

"Right away, Mrs. Wilmore."

Carlene leaned back in her chair disregarding the man sitting to her right. His eyes were glued onto her long legs, elevated and stretched all the way to the seat in front of her.

"Enjoy it, Mrs. Wilmore," Leslie placed the fresh drink on the laced doily.

"I'd like some nuts, Ms. Slater,"

"Right away, Mrs. Wilmore."

"Good girl!"

Carlene shut her eyes.

A moment later Leslie returned with a plateful of mixed nuts.

"Enjoy it," she smiled.

Carlene opened her eyes, picked a few nuts then glanced at the man to her right.

"Jim Parson," he said, extending his hand in her direction.

Carlene didn't respond.

"Mrs. Wilmore, right?"

Carlene moved her lips then changed her mind. She was in no mood for small talk: there was a lot on her mind. She shifted again in her seat fully aware of the eyes following her.

"D'you always travel first class?"

"D'you always ask so many questions?!" Carlene shot him an icy look.

She shut her eyes. Her thoughts were elsewhere, staring at a large bedroom with floor to ceiling drapes in navy blue sprinkled with tiny colorful tulips identical to the pattern of the nearby bedspread. Standing at its entrance, Carlene looked at the lush white carpeting and canopied bed then scouted the lavish furniture throughout the magnificent room overlooking the park, and knew it spelled luxury.

The room was, of course, hers and her husband's.

She shut her eyes tighter, and once again went over the price she'd have to pay for the time spent with Tierry over the weekend.

"Anyone ever tell you how beautiful you are?" the man to her right insisted.

"Can't you tell I'm not interested?!" her eyes still shut.

The man never spoke to her again.

***

Her uniformed chauffer, Larry Baldwin, was waiting at the airport.

"Mrs. Wilmore," tilting his hat in her direction he trailed behind with both her suitcases.

With the door held open, Carlene slipped into the Mercedes.

"Thanks Baldwin," she said with a casual flip of her hand, never looking at him.

Servants were part of the landscape like all her other permanent fixtures. Now seated, she reached for a drink while Larry loaded the cases into the trunk and took the driver's seat.

"Is he home?" Carlene asked matter of fact.

"No, Doctor Wilmore is dinning at the Ritz. He asked that you join him."

"Crap!"

Larry shot a quick look in the rear view mirror.

As Professor Wilmer's chauffer for the past thirteen years, he had learned to read the new mistress from a distance, wary of her fast changing moods. He now realized this was one of those dangerous times and decided to say as little as possible.

Their eight-bedroom Château-like apartment located on Fifth Avenue was known for its exceptional décor exhibiting contemporary art handpicked by Carlene alongside French originals and Old Dutch paintings which Glen loved. Each room was decorated differently allowing for a well-balanced mixture of antique furnishings with modern art creating a cohesively aesthetic experience for their guests. Only too glad to appease Carlene's wishes, Glen took pleasure in spending a near fortune just to hear her say.

"I want you to fuck me."

They dined out every night, and drank with those whose business it was to make things happen in the city. Using her looks to her advantage, Carlene performed her wifely duties as sparingly as possible. Glen didn't mind. His once-a-month nuptial conquest satisfied and gave him the sense of worthiness he desperately yearned for. As an experienced psychiatrist, Glen had learned to accept his meager sexual drive having treated several of his patients with similar afflictions.

Now sprawled on the fawn-colored seat with her legs stretched over the soft leather cuddling a fresh drink, Carlene distanced herself from the chauffer by the push of a button and the tinted glass. Then she picked up the phone and dialed.

"Do you miss me?" her raspy voice spiced with sweetness.

"Do I?! Where are you?"

"I just landed…on my way to the Ritz."

"We can't go on like this…"

"I know… I miss you terribly."

"I can't think of you with him…"

"I know…it's killing me too… I'll try calling you tomorrow."

"When?" but Carlene had already hung up.

Tierry was getting desperate. She smiled and licked her lips.

The car came to a full stop. Larry hurried out and opened the door.

"Enjoy your evening, Mrs. Wilmore."

Carlene didn't bother answering.

Larry knew it wouldn't be too long before the doctor and his wife came out.

* * *

"Darling…" Carlene entered the elegant restaurant wearing that sensuous air about her. She knew how it made Glen feel. He stood up at once joined by the other four men. Closing the gap between her body and Glen's, she lowered her head and glued her lips onto his. Glen beamed.

"I missed you, Darling," she said in a voice meant for everyone to hear.

They all smiled. She circled the table lending her cheeks and hands and was soon seated at her husband's side.

"I missed you so much," she whispered quietly into his ear licking its lobe with her tongue.

"What would you like, honey?" he smiled at her.

"A drink! I need a strong one…" she placed her hand under the table, and let it rest on Glen's thigh.

She was eager to get home. Only too familiar with the shortcuts to her husband's passions, Carlene was anxious to leave as soon as possible and get it over and done with. Moving her hand up and down Glen's thigh was a sure way to shorten their stay at the Ritz.

A short hour later with a mouthful of excuses, the Wilmores were inside their limo and on their way home.

* * *

"Don't move!"

She was naked except for a black push up bra and stringy laced underwear that barely covered her pubic triangle.

"I said don't move!" she ordered him again.

Glen loved the game. Carlene forced him down on the bed.

"Keep your hands to yourself…otherwise I'm gonna have to punish you!"

As expected, Glen grabbed her breasts with his thick fingers. Carlene repeated.

"I'm warning you! Don't touch!"

Moving his fingers to the lace below, Glen ripped off her panties. Carlene responded in the raspiest of voices.

"You've asked for it…now you're gonna get it!"

Glen's face beamed.

From the bedside drawer Carlene produced a set of handcuffs. With one smooth movement she placed her body over Glen's and dragged him towards the headboard. He played a short game trying to struggle out of her clasp. Carlene complied, rolling over him as he groaned and asked to be saved. It was all part of a well-rehearsed game one that Glen adored.

"Don't… please…" he whimpered smilingly.

Carlene slapped his face. His eyes sparkled.

"Please…" he begged again.

She held the handcuffs and, grabbing both his hands, attached them to the loop set within the headboard. Lying handcuffed on his back, his upper torso naked and wearing only underwear, Glen waited anxiously for the next scene. Carlene towered over him staring down at the glowing face. Fondling her breasts with both hands, she let out small sounds of a hungry animal. Slowly, very slowly, she took off the bra and let it fall on Glen's hairy chest. Still staring at him, she cupped her luscious breasts with her hands then continued slowly towards the dark triangle below. Glen moaned. Carlene lowered herself and placed both knees on each side of his waist.

"That's for touching me!" she slapped his face again.

Glen flinched. Saddling her nakedness on his stomach, she rode his chest up and down until he felt like exploding.

"Give it to me…give it…"

She stared at his tearful eyes.

"You should have kept your hands to yourself…" again she slapped him then pulled the hairs on his chest.

He groaned.

"That hurts…burns…" the tears kept trickling down his cheeks.

Carlene lowered herself and licked them as her hands kept plucking the hairs. She reached for the small bowl prepared in advance and placed conveniently on the night table. Holding the spiky ice cube she raked Glen's chest with its sharp nail-shaped endings. Glen let out tiny yelps. Sealing his mouth with her lips, Carlene moved the freezing spikes over his abdomen inching them in circular movements towards his pelvis. Glen sucked in his breath. Carlene pulled down his underwear with one hand.

"Don't hurt me…don't …" he kept pleading.

"I'm ordering you not to move!"

"I ...can't...you're... touching me..." his breathing was choppy and heavy.

"You'll love this..." she kept her knees saddled on his hips, balancing herself teasingly above his growing hardness, barely touching him. It drove him crazy.

"Oh...I can't... can't stand it...please..."

Carlene slapped his face raking both sides of his ribs with the icy spears.

"Fuck me... fuck me now..." she slapped him again and again.

He let out strange noises somewhere between cries and laughter.

The icy spears were now circling below rounding his scrawny cock with tiny movements.

Flattening her body she pushed her legs back and leaned herself on her elbows, dangling above him and rubbing herself against his stalk.

As Glen was about to explode she spread her legs wide, grabbed the lanky cock and using her fingers, shoved its shriveled scraps inside of her.

CHAPTER 5

Lydia came into the world in late November when the threatening sky turned gray and the temperatures plummeted below freezing. Her birth came in the midst of difficult times, just as Abigail had come down with fever followed by a bad cough. Abigail couldn't get warm despite the layers wrapped around her smallness. The days dragged on with even longer nights and still Abigail wasn't getting any better. Mable was becoming nervous. Jasper turned angry.

"Let her be," he scolded Mable. "No need to fuss over her".

"She ain't gettin' better with that cough of hers and the baby's comin' any time now."

The snow kept coming down as Abigail's fever raged and her cough worsened.

"You better get over this real quick. The baby's comin soon… any day now," Mable scolded Abigail.

For some reason those words stayed with Abigail, though it made no sense. She was only two at the time but she was sure she'd heard her mom say those words. She didn't know how to get rid of her fever or stop her throat from hurting and coughing but she knew not to fuss. She was feeling miserable and very cold. Left in bed with her eyes shut she tried to disregard the faces that kept coming at her. They neared her then backed away swaying back and forth. She covered her eyes with her small hands thinking they'd go away but they moved into her face then backed out of focus. Her throat burned like fire and she didn't know how to quit hacking and wheezing.

Mable got out of bed and warmed another cup of onion water adding a touch of honey to prevent Abigail from retching. It was the best remedy against colds and infections and the only one they could afford. A second onion crushed earlier and wrapped in several layers of gauze, was placed as compress on Abigail's small chest. Mable sat on Abigail's bed and held her in her arms. Very slowly, a few drops at a time, she poured the warmed up stench into her mouth disregarding the retching.

At some point during that awfully long night, a morbid thought had crossed Mable's mind and for a while she actually thought she might lose Abigail. But then a second thought passed by and confused her even further: Losing Abigail meant the loss of a fourth child. The thought saddened her. Mable didn't want to lose Abigail but she also didn't know how much longer she could take care of her.

Looking at her pale face, Mable mumbled.

"Is this the end?" muttering mainly to herself since Abigail kept coughing and whimpering and couldn't really hear her, "Is this the end?"

Jasper woke up.

"What?!"

Mable was in her own world, chanting her words of despair.

Jasper sprang out of bed, neared Abigail, lowered his head and screamed into her teary-eyed face.

"Shut the fuck up you ugly thing!"

"Oh…it's here…it's comin' now," Mable called out just then.

"Who's comin'?"

"The baby. It's comin' now."

Jasper got dressed and hurried out to get the neighbor.

Abigail didn't quite remember what happened next. But she did recall seeing her tiny sister Lydia for the first time and staring at her pretty little face that looked like a perfect little petal.

"Don' touch her head and stay clean away from her," Mable warned her.

Abigail's fever had already broken by then. She lay in bed as white as the snow outside and felt her heart fill with something she'd never known before. It was a soft kind of feel, a petal-like softness of something so sweet and tasty, something… something loveable. For the first time in her life she felt love for love's sake. Abigail smiled. Mable smiled back then shut her eyes.

The next several weeks were so sweet, despite Lydia's nightly awakenings and cries. Abigail felt that her heart was opening to the freshness of life. She adored her little sister, her perfect little sister and loved to move her small fingers over Lydia's soft skin. Her fingers and toes were so tiny and so cute, perfect little hands and feet.

The changes that followed Lydia's birth came swiftly and abruptly sending two year old Abigail into utter confusion. Most of the time she wasn't allowed near Lydia. Jasper, who had never touched or held Abigail in his life, kept picking up Lydia and holding her in his arms over long hours. He'd smile at her then look at Mable.

"An angel. Beautiful like you."

Then he'd kiss little Lydia.

It was made very clear that the two girls were unequal and were to be treated accordingly. Abigail, once again, was made to feel the pain of rejection only now it was worse. Lydia was getting all the hugs and kisses that Abigail never knew, the soft words, the quiet times spent with her mom and dad, who absolutely adored their beautiful daughter. Jasper would play with her, tickle her and smile and kept calling her 'my angel beauty'.

Abigail was cast aside, barely spoken to and mostly ignored.

There were times when Abigail would cry herself to sleep, hoping she wouldn't wake up to another day of feeling so alone and totally ignored. Being kept apart from her little sister was the worst. Abigail didn't understand what she'd done wrong. But she'd given up on asking why or why-not, and was soon curled up deep inside her own world like a cocoon.

The only happy times she knew were those spent in the hospital or at the doctor's office during her follow-up checkups. Inside the hospital's white walls and long corridors surrounded by smiley faces of doctors and nurses, Abigail felt protected. Jasper insisted on waiting outside, a fact that added to Abigail's sense of safety. It was during those times that she was allowed to sit close to her mom with baby Lydia in her lap. She loved the soft feel of her baby skin. It reminded her of the tiny velvety pillow her mother had once sewn for her. She'd smile at Lydia's beautiful face and move her fingers gently over her tiny hands. It felt so good to be able to touch Lydia and feel the warmth of her little fingers. Abigail would shut her eyes and hum lullabies.

The sweet smell of Lydia's hands accompanied by the softness of her little velvet pillow stayed with Abigail throughout her life. She'd shut her eyes and recall the feel and smell of Lydia's small hands. It soothed her heart. The doctors and nurses were always so gentle and encouraging and Abigail loved the feel of being touched by kind hands that spoke softly to her. Her entire childhood was dotted with momentary splashes of seconds-long episodes that pained her heart, reminding her of her yearnings for the love she never knew.

"Here comes smiley Abigail!" the doctor would smile at her as she stepped cautiously into his room. "How are you, Abigail?" he'd always ask her then wait for her response.

She wished her own dad was as gentle and patient.

The best part always came at the end of each visit.

"See you again soon," he'd say and she'd move closer waiting for his hug.

It felt so good and caring.

"Can I come again?" she'd always ask the doctor.

"Of course! We all look forward to seeing you next time," he'd again smile at her and she'd smile back.

The doctor always smiled at her, despite her ugly twisted face. Abigail loved him for it.

* * *

There were only a handful of stores in their small community located a mile down the road, with a school in the center of town. Abigail remembered the first time she'd seen the school. They'd gone into town to replenish their supplies huddled together inside the cabin of the old truck driven slowly by her father. After parking next to a tool store, her father stepped out of the car leaving her mother with her and Lydia. Mable was carrying Lydia in her arms. She turned around and said,

"You can join if you want…." she then crossed the dirt path to its other side.

The school consisted of one large room that catered to the entire community with a small annex that housed a toilet and a sink next to three long shelves with books, lots of them, Abigail thought. The teacher, a spinster by the name of Miss Dines, just happened to be there rearranging the desks and chairs for the opening of the school year.

From the moment Abigail saw the books, she fell madly in love with them. They were the most intriguing things she'd ever seen and all she wanted was to understand the signs drawn on each one. Miss Dines explained that they were words, printed words that told stories, lots of stories, that anyone could make up in his head and then turn into signs for others to enjoy.

Miss Dines took to young Abigail immediately. She listened to her questions, recognizing the brilliance of her mind, and decided to lend her a book. It was the first book Abigail had ever held in her hands with many others that followed. Abigail had never forgotten the feel of that first book and had promised Miss Dines to return it as soon as she'd read all the words.

Abigail looked up to Miss Dines as a savior and loved the fact that she paid attention to her. With little help from her mother, Abigail was soon able to decipher the signs and began reading words shortly before her fourth birthday.

Miss Dines was enthralled, and remained a close mentor to Abigail.

Jasper took pride in his younger daughter's beauty nearly as much as he enjoyed bullying Abigail. Whenever he'd get angry or frustrated he'd holler,

"Don' give me no back talk! You was born ugly 'cause you're stupid!" his hands on his belt.

She hated him. Hated his smelly, foul breath after he'd drunk himself to oblivion, hated his voice, his filthy hands and the trails of mud he'd drag into the house. She hated her mother just as much, for standing there and watching her being punished for something she didn't deserve. She didn't ask to be born this way and it wasn't her fault that she came out looking the way she did.

Mornings were the worst. She'd go to the bathroom shared with Lydia and find herself staring at the mirror.

"Mornin' Abby," pretty Lydia would greet her sweetly.

Abigail thought Lydia's face was beautiful because of its well chiseled frame and the overall plainness of her undistinguished features. There was nothing out of the ordinary in her sister's face which Abigail found to be beautiful. Lydia's face looked soft as were her voice and movements and everything else about her that seemed fluid and gentle fitting nicely with her almond shaped eyes and matching color identical to those of their father's.

She tried to avoid the morning bathroom routine by rushing in and out without brushing her teeth or combing her hair, but it only added to her problems.

"You smell bad!" her mother would say.

Abigail wanted to explain but knew her mother wouldn't understand.

Instead she tried other ways.

"Look mama… look at my eyes… it's the same color like yours…"

"But color ain't the only thing that counts," her mother snapped.

Abigail couldn't find any other nice thing to say about herself and neither could her mother. With no one to offer a kind word or a soothing hug except for Lydia who tried to befriend her, Abigail grew up hating herself and the world around her, alternating between a sense of worthlessness and deeply rooted jealousy. Convinced she wasn't worthy of anyone's love, Abigail rejected Lydia's approaches.

"I hate you… I hate your stupid face and I hate the way you pity me. I hate you and one day you'll live to regret it…" Abigail screamed into her sister's face.

* * *

By school age Abigail was used to hiding behind walls and bushes spying on people and listening to their private conversations. It was something she'd learned from a young age when there was no one around to help her fend off the teasers and the bullies.

"Let's get her…she's over there," they'd point in her direction.

She'd find a tiny space even if it meant fighting her way into a bramble bush. It was better than being caught by the kids and hearing their words.

"She's got a monkey's ass for a mouth!"

"Look at that snout of hers!"

On the way home from school she'd pretend not to see them huddled behind the red bushes whispering and giggling. Sometimes, though, she couldn't resist and then she'd poke them with a stick.

"Stop it! That hurts!"

She'd stand and watch them run like mad, a crooked smile on her strange looking face.

She grew up knowing she was ugly and took it for granted that people looked strangely at her, turning their heads away with disdain.

But she couldn't understand why they shied away from her. And the harder she tried to befriend them, the worse their reactions.

Her parents' words didn't help.

"You just need to get used to it… it ain't no one's fault you was born this way."

She felt bad. And ugly. And always so alone. Ugly and alone.

She'd lie in bed with her head under the blanket and hear her parents' words.

"No use complainin'…just learn to live with that messy face of yours…"

There were long teary-eyed nights spent trying to figure out how to remedy the situation. At one point her parents told her.

"You was born this way… and we ain't rich… and there ain't no money for us to fix it."

Hearing those words changed Abigail's understanding of her situation. If her face was fixable, she could now hold on to hope. Realizing it was only a matter of money, she came up with the idea of fixing it herself. She went into the shed, picked up the tool, placed her face sideways on a flat surface and hammered its side to line up with her mouth. But it proved too painful leaving her black and blue for several days.

The older Abigail got, the worse her face looked. It seemed to change and grow misshaped tugging at her nose and making it even longer. By the time she was brave enough to stare at herself in the mirror and study up close the twists of her face, her soul had become as warped as her face.

Money became Abigail's obsession. She saw it as the only solution to all her problems, the one thing that could help change her deformed face, and the sole barrier to her salvation. There were times when she'd wonder why she was born at all with such a face, or if it was some form of punishment. And if so, why? And who exactly wanted her punished? She couldn't help wonder what it was that she'd done wrong to deserve such a terrible affliction.

Lacking any explanation or reason, and having been treated over the years as a shameful creature not to be seen in public, Abigail began blaming herself.

A very clever little girl, who taught herself how to read at an early age, Abigail spent her days reading, trying to understand people and the world around her.

* * *

The passing years only added to Abigail's confusions and to her sense of deprivation and misery. She understood there was no one she could count on, not one family member who would be supportive of her in case of need. If they didn't show her kindness as a child, they surely wouldn't do it when she was older.

A decision began fermenting in her mind.

She would forge her own way, erase all sentiments from her heart and detach herself from her entire family. To reach her goals meant she'd let nothing come in the way of her dreams. From now on her life would center strictly around her own needs and her own wants.

Over the years Lydia tried to befriend Abigail but it was too little too late. The barriers enforced throughout childhood by their parents proved stronger and thicker than blood, and all of Lydia's attempts to forge a friendship with her sister, failed. As a child, growing up the way she did, made it virtually impossible for Lydia to understand Abigail's perspective. And by the time she'd matured and was old enough to see things differently, she'd lost her chance of ever gaining her sister's trust and friendship.

Time was not on their side. It was as though the Gray sisters had each grown up in a separate household with two very different sets of circumstances and parents.

Both would live to regret it.

CHAPTER 6

Abigail had plotted everything very carefully and had watched Lydia from inside the shed across the house. Now she waited to see her plan at work.

"Mama?"

Lydia entered the kitchen.

She stood still trying to penetrate its darkness. A small neon lamp hung above the wooden table like a broken limb, releasing a bleak light that reminded her of the old, soggy train station in winter. It was early afternoon, a sure time to find her mother at home, busy folding laundry, or ironing, or standing next to the old stove range preparing dinner. She'd tried the front door first but it was locked. Looking for the spare key she picked up the flowerpot next to the window overlooking the front yard. The key wasn't there. She cut through the porch and around the back garden making sure not to trample the fresh seedlings. The kitchen door was wide open.

As she stood inside the silent room, Lydia wondered where her mother could be at this time of day. It wasn't like her to simply disappear.

Winter was nearing its end but the cold was still trapped inside the brick house and spotted along its walls with black moldy shapes like dirty foot prints. A strong musty smell mixed with what seemed like meatballs in tomato sauce filled the small kitchen with its tiny window overlooking the tall rose bushes. It had rained for the past several hours. The half filled bucket stood to the side of the oven. Out of habit Lydia's eyes searched the ceiling for drops. Two simmering pots rested on the stove range.

She again called out.

"Mama?"

This had never happened before to ten-year-old Lydia.

Their small town consisted of 29 families. Each owned a large acreage with horses, cows, chickens and enough crops to feed and sustain them throughout the year. They were all hardworking folks, dedicated to their land and its rich soil.

Lydia's birth witnessed the lush farmland in its finest days, despite the fact that the original house that had once belonged to her grandfather had remained unaltered. Lydia's mother was a practical woman who took pride in spiritual empires rather than earthly ones. Known for her rigid mind-set and stubbornness she insisted on retaining a simple lifestyle, clinging to her strict and frugal upbringing.

"There's only them two girls," Mable told Jasper, "we can manage with the house as is."

So the house with its three small bedrooms, living room, kitchen and the tiny bathroom shared by all and added only a few years earlier, remained the same.

As Lydia now stood inside the kitchen she found herself thinking out loud.

"How strange …mama would never leave a flame burning."

She stepped outside.

Standing on the porch she again called.

"Mama?"

She noticed the straw broom in its usual corner behind the tall climber with the red flowers. Plants of all sizes and shapes huddled together in pots and scattered on the open spaced porch, created an inner garden that covered the bare floor. Lydia walked over to the lemon tree and touched its leaves.

The licking sound of water drew her attention. Following the path to her left Lydia reached the aerial bridge formed by the roses their necks tilted from the kitchen window to the adjacent living room.

"Mama, where are you?"

The wooden ladder was sprawled over the newly planted flowers. It took Lydia a second longer to recognize her mother, next to the hose with its running water. Her head was red except for the blue eyes that remained wide open as if staring at a ghost.

"Ahaaaaaaaaaa," Lydia's shriek pierced the air.

At once Abigail appeared at her side.

"Oh God! What have you done?!" she screamed into Lydia's face.

Lydia didn't move.

"Call the police. Can't you see mama's hurt?"

Lydia remained glued to the ground.

"Move it!" Abigail shouted again.

"What?" Lydia looked at her sister.

"Call the police… I'll stay here with mama."

Lydia went back into the house and sat on a chair unable to remember what it was she was supposed to do.

Abigail's face appeared in the window.

"What are you waiting for little sis?!"

"Ah!" Lydia let out.

"Did I frighten you?"

Lydia moved her head.

"Get used to it! Now move your fingers and dial!"

Lydia shook so hard she kept missing the dials.

"My mother…she's …she's by the roses…her face …it's full of blood…"

Standing behind the open window Abigail listened in.

"I…I don't remember…we live in…in…in Emmeth…my name is Lydia Gray…" she hung up.

"Can't you even remember your own address?!" Abigail's face appeared through the window.

Lydia burst out crying.

By the time the ambulance and police cars arrived, Abigail had cleaned off some of Mable's blood leaving the white face void looking as if the open mouth was about to reveal the way in which she had found her death.

* * *

The funeral, attended by some of the town's people, took place the following day. They all tried to be supportive and give comfort to the heartbroken Jasper and his two daughters. Lydia, too overwhelmed and shocked, didn't cry much. She stood quietly, holding her father's hand as they listened to the eulogy expressed by the local clergyman. Abigail read from a page she had prepared earlier and kept wiping her tearless eyes. Two neighbors helped the devastated Jasper place the bouquet of red roses on the gravesite.

Four days after the funeral the police report was concluded and shared with the family. The chief of police seated in Jasper's small living room spoke quietly, his eyes shifting between Jasper, Abigail and Lydia.

"Given the evidence at the scene…the broken ladder with the pruning shears and so on, Mable sustained a grave basilar skull fracture…" his hand motioned to the back of his head, "right here… at the base of her skull. Must have been the bed rocks 'cause we found the large rock with the blood…and the conclusive report finds it to be an accident."

Lydia's eyes met Abigail's and for a split second it seemed as though she was about to say something but then she shifted her eyes and looked at her devastated father. The once robust chest and wide shoulders now looked hollow and thin.

In a raspy voice with tearful eyes Jasper asked.

"Did she suffer?"

"No!" the officer said, "definitely not! Her skull…she fractured it from the fall… didn't feel a thing…"

Officer Krause lowered his head then pushed with both hands against his knees and stood up. Placing his hat on his head, he shook Jasper's hand then turned to Abigail and Lydia tipping his hat in their direction.

* * *

The days that followed were long and sad. Jasper no longer laughed or joked. He didn't seem to care if the soup was cold or the meat dry. His unshaven face and teary eyes only added to his severe-looking expression.

"Dad, can you maybe help me with this?" Lydia approached him with a bagful of fresh corn that had to be shucked, but Jasper's eyes were elsewhere, staring into a faraway distance.

"Would you like a cup of tea, Dad?" Lydia's voice sounded like a tiny whisper.

Jasper's hand went up and down as if swatting a fly. Seated on his dead wife's favorite chair Jasper shut his eyes and rocked back and forth. Lydia bent, kissed his head and left the room.

"Would you like a cup of tea dad?" Abigail mimicked Lydia.

She was standing in the corridor blocking its passage.

"He's not only your dad!" her face inches away from Lydia's.

"I'm not …"

"Smarty assed little Sis!"

Lydia knew better than to reply.

"He'd never take a cup of tea from me… but then I'm not as pretty as you, am I?" she smiled.

Lydia felt the tiny hairs on her arms stand up.

"What's wrong, Abigail?"

"What's wrong?! Ah! You're asking me what's wrong?! Don't you know by now what's wrong?!"

"I just want…"

"I don't give a fuck what you want! I also have wants and no one ever asks me about them! How 'bout that, pretty Lydia?!" Abigail's face was furiously red.

"Abigail …please…"

"I'm done pleasing the world little sis. From now on it's Me! Me and My own self! And My wants! And My decisions!"

Lydia knew that any reaction would only aggravate the situation and turn Abigail into an explosive hurricane.

"Lost for words, Sis?"

"I …"

"Shut the fuck up!" she screamed into her face. "Ever thought of me wanting a cup of tea…or something sweet…or maybe another face that looks like yours?! Just 'cause my mouth is twisted doesn't mean I don't deserve to be asked!" the veins around her neck were bulging.

"Maybe …"

"Oh… Miss Pretty has something to say! I should be grateful someone in this fucking house even speaks to me! Did it occur to you that I also lost a mother? Just 'cause my face isn't as pretty as yours doesn't mean I don't feel the way you do! You're dumb! If it wasn't for your pretty face, Lydia dear, you wouldn't have gotten this far. But smarts don't count in this backward house with two fucked up people for parents, one already croaked and the other isn't far behind. I'd say that's not very smart, is it, pretty Lydia?! Do you even understand what the fuck I'm trying to say? This family is fucked up! Our parents are fucked up! We're fucked up!"

Abigail's voice continued late into the night, battling her demons with vengeful anger.

Jasper felt he had no choice but to consult with Dr. Spores.

"I can't control her no more. Last night she raved on like a mad woman. It ain't good, Doc. Sometimes she gets real bad… causes real trouble…"

"That's why I'd recommend Cedars Home. It offers, among other treatments, controlled medications with behavior modification …"

Jasper shut his eyes. He kept seeing Mable's face, tears running down her cheeks.

"I'll do whatever you tell me to do, Doc. I've got another daughter to worry 'bout … a younger one."

"I'll take care of the paperwork, Jasper. We'll let you know as soon as we're ready."

By the time Jasper returned home, Abigail was gone. She stayed away throughout the night and following day.

"Do you know where she is?" he asked Lydia.

She shook her head.

When Abigail finally returned, three months later, she was 40 pounds heavier and dirty with wild hair and sores over her arms and legs. Jasper shot her a quick look and said,

"Get in the shower. You stink."

Too tired and bruised to argue, Abigail did as she was told.

The next day Abigail went to school as though nothing happened. It seemed to Jasper that Abigail had finally learned her lesson.

"Being away did her some good," he told Lydia.

Lydia, who had hoped to see a change in her sister, noticed the eyes. They remained bright blue and sparkly but with an added wild ingredient infused into them. The strange face with its oddities and melancholy expression looked enormous screwed on the heavy body.

Jasper never got around to asking Abigail where she'd been or why she'd left home. He paid little attention to anything but Lydia and his memories of Mable.

"Doesn't anyone care about me?" Abigail kept asking herself though she already knew the answer.

Aware of her need for attention and always in hope of a miracle, Abigail was willing to do whatever it took to gain her father's focus. If she wasn't getting it peacefully, she was going to get it forcefully.

***

Shortly after Abigail's return, Lydia began having nightmares. In her dreams she saw Abigail standing above her head with a strange tool in her hand. She'd scream and wake up drenched in cold sweat followed by an odd sensation that someone had actually been in her room.

Life seemed unchanged in the small house with Abigail's ups and downs and her unpredictable eruptions. Lydia was the one who cooked and cleaned and took care of Jasper and the house.

One evening, while Lydia was standing in the kitchen preparing dinner, she noticed the blue and red marks in the twilight sky.

"Oh…it's so beautiful…and peaceful…" she said out loud staring at the fiery sky.

Something behind her sounded. She turned around only to find Abigail inches away from her.

"Ah! You scared me…. I didn't hear you come in…"

"I hate you! I hate your sight and smell and the way you look. I hate you!" Abigail's face was inside Lydia's.

Abigail knew her father was due back any moment and was hoping to see him. She didn't care if he got angry with her, at least she'd get a reaction. Ignoring her was the worst. She could still hear her mother's silences, those angry hours stretched into days and weeks, held on for so long that she finally couldn't remember what brought them on in the first place.

Abigail had once rummaged through her mother's room and had found a photograph of a baby's face. It looked so horrid that she couldn't tell if it was real or not.

"What's this?" she asked her mother.

"Where did you get this?!"

"Inside this drawer."

Her mother snatched it away.

"It ain't for you!"

It only made Abigail want to see it again and try to understand who was photographed. But the picture had disappeared as if it never existed. Weeks later, one late afternoon, while Abigail was hiding in her usual corner trying to eavesdrop on her parents, she overheard her mother say.

"She found the picture…the one before the surgery… I told you not to put it there…if she'll find out it's her, she'll start askin' questions…"

"It's your fault. You wan'ed to keep her. I wan'ed to put her away," Jasper said.

"I couldn't bring myself to do it…not then…"

"She's no good…can't look at her…and she's got your eyes. Shame!"

"But…"

"The only thing good 'bout her is the brain …but it's wasted on her ugly face."

Abigail stayed in her hiding place long after her parents had gone to bed. She never got the courage to ask them about the photograph, but she also never forgot her parents' words.

Now standing in the kitchen staring at Lydia's perfectly normal face, with its well-defined features and almond colored eyes, Abigail remembered the photograph. It made her wish her parents would have let her die. Why was she deprived of a normal face, just an ordinary-looking face with clear features that wouldn't cause others to stare or shy away from her? She'd be happy looking plain-faced or having a long nose or…anything besides the awful face she now had. How she wished to be like Lydia…

"Why do you hate me so much?" Lydia's eyes welled with tears.

"'Cause you always get everything you want. Can you understand what I'm trying to say, smarty doll?"

"It's not my fault…"

"But did you ever stop to think what it's like for me?"

Lydia kept her head down. It was one of those crazy times again with Abigail out of control. She was hoping it wouldn't last long.

The door suddenly opened and Jasper walked in. His eyes moved from Lydia to the gas range.

"You hungry, Lydia?"
Abigail blocked his path.
"I'm also your daughter, your own fucking daughter! Take a good look at my face. It resembles your fucking brain!"
She stormed out of the house.

* * *

Nothing much changed during the three years following their mother's death.

Abigail continued to feel rejected and unloved, spending hours inside her small room, toying with her books and secret dreams. When all alone, in the dark, she'd reach for the small velvet pillow, hidden away inside the box she'd kept; she'd move her fingers along the black cloth imagining Lydia's tiny baby fingers. Then she'd shut her eyes and smell it and at once her soul would fill with the sweet smell of long ago memories and her eyes would well up and force her to sleep.

Lydia tried having as little contact as possible with her, fearing Abigail's explosive temper. Jasper continued living in the past with his memories of Mabel, worn down by sadness and bad health.

One afternoon just before dinner Lydia entered her room looking for the tortoise hairclip given to her by her mother. She scanned the room with its neat bookshelf, checked inside her chest of drawers and desk. The clip was nowhere. Standing in the center of her room Lydia shut her eyes trying to recall the last time she'd used it. When she reopened them, Abigail was staring at her.

"Looking for something?" she asked in her bittersweet voice reserved for teasing.

Looking at Abigail's hair Lydia noticed the clip pinned sideways creating a grotesque looking head.

"Give it back to me, it's mine!" she cried, grabbing at it.

"If you touch me, you'll never see it again!" Abigail's strong fingers plied open Lydia's. Her eyes resembled two metal circles.

"Ouch, that hurts!" Lydia let go and looked at the deep bruises on her hands then shifted her eyes to Abigail's head.

"There's no one to save you now," Abigail beamed.

Lydia didn't dare move. She knew her father was outside watering the garden and couldn't hear them.

"So what's gonna happen now, precious Lydia?"

She could tell Abigail meant harm. She looked into her eyes and followed her thoughts all the way through as if staring at a nightmare.

"Suppose I rearrange your pretty face... turn you into something the boys won't like, what d'you think little sis, eh?

"Pick someone your own age and size!" Lydia quoted her mother's words and tone.

But even as she mouthed the words, she knew no one could save her. Not this time. Not now with Abigail holding the long garden scissors clutched against her stomach. Out of habit, Lydia ducked and covered her head with both hands. The scissors grazed her hair. She watched them land next to her feet, two cold metals pieced together.

"What are you doing?" Lydia screamed. "You could have hurt me."

"Sorry I didn't," Abigail sounded an ugly laugh.

"That thing can kill!"

"I know! That's why I'm holding it!"

Her words sent Lydia into a spin of terror. She kept her hands in preparation to grab Abigail's long, chestnut colored braids, but just then, as if he'd heard his young daughter's prayers, Jasper walked into the house and called out.

"That you, Lydia?!" his words a statement more than a question. Lydia ran to the front door.

"Daddy, Daddy..." she held him tightly, "It's Abigail..."

From the corner of his eye he spotted a sudden movement.

"Now... now," he kissed Lydia's head, "What's she done now?"

Jasper held her to his chest. Lydia burst out crying but before she had a chance to respond, Abigail framed the door looking as gentle and as smooth as Mable.

"I missed you, Daddy. How was your day today?"

"What you done to your sister?!" Jasper demanded.

"Nothing she didn't deserve… Daddy!"

"If you keep this up you'll find yourself in jail or the hospital. They lock up people like you!"

Abigail smiled sweetly.

"Daddy, why would anyone want to lock me up?"

* * *

"I can't …breathe…I…" Jasper's voice was barely audible.

Lydia was sitting in her room studying. She dropped everything and rushed into the kitchen, grabbed the small dropper and ran back to the living room. With trembling hands she sucked up the liquid into the syringe and injected the needle straight into Jasper's stomach. Lydia watched him with a child's fascination, knowing only too well how crucial the shot was.

Watching them from behind her bedroom door, Abigail wished she could be the one to offer help and take care of the father who'd never held or kissed her. Why couldn't he see some good in her? She could be funny and entertaining or anything else he'd want her to be…she's been practicing in her room…one day she'll show them…they'll be sorry they treated her like shit…she'll make them feel sorry for what they've done.

Jasper's diabetes had worsened after Mable's death. He'd gained weight and neglected to care for his chronic illness. Within a span of three years, what had previously been a manageable medical condition had spiraled into a life-threatening one burdened with additional heart problems. Jasper no longer went out to the fields as before. He stayed in bed until lunchtime, immersed in his pain over Mable's death, unable to tend to Lydia's needs. Jasper's sorrow drove him towards oblivion.

* * *

Realizing how dangerous Abigail had become and at the insistence of the school that something be done to taper her unruly behavior, Jasper revisited Dr. Spokes.

"That's it, Doc! I can't handle her no more. She's got to go."

"What happened?"

After listening to Jasper, Dr. Spokes recommended, once more, that Abigail be hospitalized at Cedars Home.

"Until we feel she can function without causing harm to self and others."

Fifteen-year-old Abigail was about to enter Cedars Home.

"A home for bad children" was its second name used by mothers to threaten their misbehaved children, avoiding any direct reference to a mental institution.

Three days later, when they came to take her away, something snapped in Abigail.

"I'll show you… mother fucker!" Abigail screamed and spat in Jasper's face as she was held by two paramedics and forced into the ambulance.

Jasper stood to the side his face motionless thinking about Mable who was spared the heartbreak of seeing her daughter institutionalized.

It marked the end of Abigail's schooling and the beginning of her two-year hospitalization. Lydia couldn't stop crying as she listened to Abigail's screams and threats promising never to forget:

"Just wait…just wait 'till I come out…you'll be sorry for the rest of your life!"

***

The two years spent at Cedars Home left their permanent mark on Abigail though she now seemed calmer than before. She continued her daily treatment program, visiting her therapist and working in the cafeteria twice a week. Jasper took it as a good sign.

But Abigail saw things differently.

She kept quiet, yet inside she was furious at the world and feeling worse than before; but she'd finally learned how to hide it. Her soul and heart were stormy, filled with a gush of mixed emotions. At times she felt sore or sad, and sometimes angry and frustrated, with a deeply rooted loneliness that threatened to make her want to cry forever.

She had never felt so alone in her life.

She began going out at night and when Jasper, too weak to react, didn't comment, she stretched her curfew time to meet the rising sun.

Abigail sought the company of men willing to give her the one thing she craved: Love. She'd known rejection for so long and from so many, that the mere notion of being physically close to and touched by someone, made her feel alive. It was as though she was part of a group, touching and being touched by other humans providing her with a sense of belonging she'd never known. She had finally learned what it took to win attention, a hug, a kiss or just a soothing word even if it involved acting deviously or offering a sexual favor in return. She'd play coy, a shy girl with bright fiery eyes who always kept a light shawl over her face as a playful gimmick or teaser. Using her glorious womanly body as a lure, she'd easily manipulate them inside her playful rose garden with its seductive feminine nectars, though she seldom enjoyed their company or touch.

Abigail rationalized that their acts were a dual sided deal and chose to see them as proof of caring enough about her to shove their cocks into her while applauding her own successful manipulation of them. She had never met a man who refused her offerings and had not kept his part of the deal. They all ended up entrusting their tool to her talented hands. Abigail viewed it as an act of goodwill spiced with the sweetness of revenge. She'd smile and cry with each penetration; it was the only time she'd feel wanted, if only momentarily, but at the same time was overcome with shame. Her mind was able to process the pained needs of her aching soul while her body paid the price of its sacrifice. The physical feel of someone else's proximity was the most important element in her life. She couldn't get enough of it. Once she'd got her fill, she'd let her hidden tears roll down her deformed face. They felt warm and silky like the little velvet pillow and in some pervasive way made her feel alive. Wetting her face with her own tears was like fresh rain that brought with it the deepest and saddest of memories.

It didn't take long for Abigail to acquire the reputation of a loose girl, someone lacking moral boundaries. Her once shabby looking outfits in blacks and grays, loosely draped over her weighty figure, were now replaced by excessively short and tightly fitted clothes which showed off her splendid body. She no longer went to the library to exchange the books that had previously kept her mind occupied. Instead she sought the company of anyone willing to give her what she was after. When Jasper tried to inquire about her whereabouts, she lashed out at him, cursing and swearing obscenities.

Lydia realized that her father was getting weaker and sadder by the day. She tended to his needs, making sure his medications were always close by and concentrating her efforts on managing the farm with Sid, the handyman in charge of the other workers. It left little room and time for social gatherings or any after school activities. Fifteen-year-old Lydia was terrified of losing the one person who cared for and loved her.

One night Lydia was awakened to strange noises. She lay in bed trying to figure out who the speaker was. She stood in the darkened corridor behind Abigail's door and listened.

"Hear that, Mama? Daddy told me he's done with Lydia… can't stomach that face of hers… you think she looks like you? Think again! I've got your eyes… eat your heart away, Mama dear! Your special eyes! Dad promised to take me with him… yeah, just the two of us… what d'you say to that, fucking Mama? Are you jealous? I don't give a shit! I hope the worms do a good job on your heart, Mama… this is hilarious! Are you listening Daddy? I hate you Mama! I hate your voice and I hate your smell! You stink! You fucking rotten woman!"

Horrified, Lydia ran into her father's room only to find him weeping uncontrollably.

* * *

A year later on a beautiful late summer afternoon, sixteen-year-old Lydia was in her room busy studying. Jasper, who had recently recovered from a complication following a severe case of pneumonia, was feeling better. He stood in the doorway.

"How 'bout a sundae?"

Lydia loved the local ice cream parlor.

"Thanks, Dad."

She was glad to get out of the house with its somewhat melancholy atmosphere, occupied now only by her Dad and herself. Abigail, who had been gone for over a month, had planned her time away to coincide with her upcoming eighteenth birthday.

"I can do what I want! I don't need your approval!" she stood next to Jasper's bedroom door chewing gum, her shapely figure squeezed into a tiny black skirt with a red blouse open all the way down to her nipples.

Now seated next to the window overlooking the main street, Lydia was looking forward to her favorite ice cream at Bell's Ice Cream Parlor the only place in Emmeth that sold sodas and cold licks.

Jasper sat quietly across from her.

"What?" she smiled at him.

"Nothin'...I...I just..."

The large portions arrived.

"What is it dad?" Lydia asked again.

Jasper looked at her for a moment then spoke.

"Ok, Lydia, there's somethin'...I need to tell you somethin'. It's about the farm...our property..."

Lydia listened as her father explained the situation. The farm with its large plot of land had appreciated in price over the past ten years and was now at its peak. Too sick to work the land, Jasper was thinking of selling it and buying a small house for himself and for Lydia.

"Somethin' that'll give you a head start...in a good neighborhood...we might even get more and keep the rest..."

Though saddened and somewhat embarrassed to talk about it, Lydia listened very carefully noting the serious tone of her father's words.

"What's gonna happen to Abigail?" Lydia asked softly.

"We're not gonna talk 'bout her!"

"But..."

"She's crazy. No need for you to get mixed up with her. Just...stay away..."

They were silent for a while then Lydia spoke again.

"And what about school? Can we wait 'till I graduate?"

"Sure. I spoke to the men and they're willin' to stay on the farm and help out. We can move next summer once you graduate."

By the time they had concluded their conversation and had finished the ice cream, Lydia felt much more at ease than she had before. She knew her father had made a decision to secure her future financially.

It was her intention to see to it that Abigail's future also be secured.

Determined to graduate with good grades, Lydia worked hard immersing herself in schoolwork and leaving even less time for socializing with friends. Abigail's absence, though mingled with a sense of loss, had its blessings.

Jasper set about closing the deal on the farm.

The new family had already been to the house and approved the land. It was now a question of negotiating the final price, something Jasper proved good at. The following day he'd worked out a deal promising an even larger settlement than previously anticipated. With both parties' agreed terms and conditions there was only one more thing left to do: Sign the final papers.

Bill McKinney, the only attorney in Emmeth was out of town and expected back the following week.

"I'll have Bill change my will when he returns to the office…I've left him a message and explained it all…"

"Please Dad, don't speak about it…"

"I wanna make sure you'll be ok. More than ok."

Though she trusted her father and knew he wanted to ensure her future, Lydia was concerned about Abigail. Her recent disappearance, no different from her previous ones, had made Lydia realize that Abigail was the only person in the world she could still claim as family, aside from her father.

* * *

By the third week of September, the weather had turned cold with lashing rains and howling winds that threatened to blow away the barn roof. Jasper caught a cold that progressed into a severe case of pneumonia. He was rushed to the hospital and sedated.

"We need to consider his heart condition, your father is not a well man…" the doctors told Lydia.

She was scared. Sitting at her father's side, Lydia refused to budge or go to school. Ten days later, having survived a mild heart attack followed by a miraculous recovery, Jasper was placed on a strict diet and given additional medications to stabilize his heart condition.

His return home was a happy occasion for Lydia though she couldn't stop thinking about Abigail. She wished that things had been different and that she would have had a real sister with whom to share her life.

Before leaving for school the following morning, Lydia placed a glass of water on the small table in the living room next to the pillbox and adjusted the pillows on the couch.

"I'll be back by three thirty. No later. I promise."

She kissed her dad once more on his forehead.

"Study well," he hugged her.

Standing by the front door with her backpack, Lydia smiled and waved goodbye.

"Are you sure you'll manage without me?" she asked for the umpteenth time.

"Yeah, yeah…I'm ok! Now beat it! I don' wan' you late on account of me. I'll be fine."

Lydia ran outside to catch the school bus.

Jasper sighed and thought of Mable. In a way, he felt relieved that she was spared the last few years of Abigail's ordeal. He wasn't sure she would have been able to contain their sick daughter or watch her deteriorating condition.

Jasper watched TV, flipped some magazine pages then snoozed off. He thought of checking in again with Bill McKinney but then decided against it.

"Eh…I'll give it another day," he thought.

Again he eyed the clock. Nearly three. Lydia would soon be back. Suddenly he felt very tired.

Leaning back, he shivered shaken by nausea, the kind he'd known in the past. He reached for the water but his hand trembled so much it knocked over the glass. Jasper panicked. Reaching for the phone he stretched his arm but was unable to reach it. He tried getting up by pushing both hands against the back of the couch but his body refused to obey him. He tried again and again, but the more he pushed the weaker he felt.

The front door opened unannounced. Framing it was Abigail wearing a tight blouse and skirt, balancing on tall thin heels. Her long hair was stringy and yellow. Inhaling deeply, she held the cigarette between her fingers and winced at her father through a cloud of smoke. Jasper's forehead was wet and his tongue felt big and swollen. He tried to say something but the words wouldn't come out.

Abigail hiccupped.

"Hi Daddy," her body swayed sideways. "Aren't you gonna ask me in?"

Jasper tried to breathe normally but it was difficult. He remembered the small bottle and tried to signal Abigail, but she just stood there, watching his face contort and change color.

"Have you sold the fucking farm?!" she shrieked into his darkening face.

Jasper again pointed to the small bottle on the side table.

"Answer me and I'll give you the pill!"

Jasper's eyes looked ready to pop out of their sockets.

"Have you already sold it?!"

Jasper shut his eyes.

"Answer me!"

Jasper moved his head up and down.

"And you never said a word about it!" Abigail screamed. "I had to hear it from the neighbors!"

Jasper gasped for air, his twisted face the color of ink. Abigail took another deep puff. Moving closer she exhaled a mouthful of smoke into his bluing face. Jasper gagged then opened his eyes for a split second. Turning around Abigail left the house in search of Bill, and found him in his office smelling of beer and smoke.

By the time they'd found his body, Jasper's face had turned ashen gray.

CHAPTER 7

Glen's Mondays and Thursdays were the busiest. His lectures scheduled from nine in the morning until three in the afternoon with a two-hour break in-between, enjoyed a reputation of excellence. The odd-looking Prof. Dr. Glen Wilmore, who always seemed to be on the move, was credited for his humor and brilliance spicing up the complex *Introduction to Psychiatry* with dramatic innuendoes. Stepping onto the podium with its added inches made all the difference in the world. Life, for Glen, was a continuous struggle between his mirrored self and his strive for self-acceptance. The elevated platform helped him tilt in favor of the latter.

During his two-hour break Glen ate, met with students and colleagues, corrected papers and caught up with whatever needed catching up.

His other days were spent in private sessions at his plush clinic within the Timber Towers, a five-minute walking distance from his apartment. His patients, exclusively from New York's social elite, were very demanding when it came to comforts and extravagance yet equally generous when asked to compensate for Prof. Dr. Wilmore's precious time.

It was Monday, the day following his stormy game with Carlene.
Glen smiled and eyed his watch. It was nearing two with his lecture due to start in ten minutes. Time to wake up Carlene.
"How are you darling?" he called her.

"Sleepy!" she yawned, "You were such a great fuck last night... I wish you were here now..."
"I love you," he whispered.
Glen loved Mondays.
"That's when I have time to re-think the weekend," he told Carlene when they first met.
Carlene spoke softly giving him another reason for liking this particular Monday. Her voice, barely audible and drowsy, made him think of her naked body. He put his hand inside his pants pocket and scratched his balls. It felt good.

During their first sexual encounter, it had taken Carlene less than five minutes to size up Glen. They were in his apartment sprawled fully clothed on the king sized bed. Carlene had tried to arouse him but Glen was quick to say.
"Wait...I need time..."
Carlene had understood even before Glen had confessed.
"I...I'm...I sometimes...I can't... I can't get it up..."
She kissed him gently, took off his thick glasses and touched his near hairless face with the tips of her fingers, those long elegant extensions known to work wonders. Carlene suggested getting help, but Glen had refused to discuss it. Not that she really cared, but for the sake of saying something nice she added.
"I want to make you happy."
"Oh but you do, my love...you do. It's enough if you let me listen to you...I love it when you say those words..."
Carlene obliged.
"I'm so wet...I need to taste you...I'm so ready... right now... fuck me now...fill me...I want your cock...I...need it now...inside of me...now...fuck me now...now..."
The dim light from the living room allowed her the view of Glen's hands as they flung into the air then disappeared accompanied by moaning and cursing. From the minute Glen had revealed his secret fantasies to Carlene, their sexual encounters took on a set frame.

Now still tucked under the bed covers, Carlene sounded the words Glen loved to hear.

"I'm naked…touch me…fuck me…oh…I'm wet…I want to feel you inside of me…your dick…give it to me…I want your fuck… now big cocky…now…"

"You're making me…I can't … I…" Glen shut his eyes and for a moment felt a strong urge to rush home. But force of habit, logic and responsibility got in the way of spontaneity.

"Darling… I've got to go…" Glen swallowed.

"I'll wait for you," Carlene added softly and hung up.

All she wanted now was a long soak in the tub.

Moments later the phone rang again. She pressed the speaker with her wet toe.

"Hello?"

"Ah…"

"Hello? Who's this?"

There was a pause before Tierry's voice sounded again.

"I had to hear your voice."

"I told you never to call me here," Carlene whispered.

"I know…I know…I'm sorry…but… I've got to see you…"

"I can't talk now."

She hung up and smiled.

It wasn't as though she couldn't really talk; it was simply a way of controlling Tierry and the situation at hand. Having planned it down to the smallest of details, she was unwilling to veer from her original plan, even by a hair's breadth.

Carlene loved soaking in her luxurious tub, a circular pool skillfully decorated with ceramic tiles to resemble a mosaic rug. She wiggled her toes and laughed then shut her eyes with a sigh.

From a distance she looked like a beautiful queen submerged in a thick layer of perfumed snow, her hair crowned with a clip.

"I could sleep here forever…" she spoke out loud, allowing the white froth to cover her chin.

* * *

Following her long and restful soak, Carlene got up and dressed. Things were working out better than expected. It's been just over four months since her plan had begun to take shape and Tierry was already losing his grip.

"He can't stand the silence...the silence... the fucking silence... he can't stand the fucking silence..." Carlene sang out loud releasing a wild laughter.

She had calculated it would take longer than a few months but now she doubted it. He sounded desperate which was precisely what she had hoped for. She smiled at herself in the mirror.

"You look good... yeah... real good... real fucking good..." her face was against the mirror. She stared at her eyes then moved her face sideways sizing up her perfectly sculptured nose.

""Mmm... not bad...and what about you, lucky lips?" she shut her eyes and left red marks on the cold surface.

"Lip prints...beautiful lip prints..." she concentrated on each veined line, trying to recall names of different men.

"Fuck you! So many... so many fucking lips...so many fucking pricks..."

At once she turned away, picked up a lipstick and wrote 'I love you' next to the red mark. She repeated it over and over until the entire mirror was a messy scribble.

"Fuck you!" Carlene screamed then burst out laughing, "fuck you all, screw heads! Here comes the queen. Queen fucked up head..." she couldn't stop laughing.

Moving towards the large window and her dresser below with its wide mirror and lavish assortment of makeup, she reached into one of its drawers below and took out the box. She opened it carefully, shut her eyes and, holding the small velvet pillow to her face, inhaled deeply.

* * *

The reservation was for six.

"Two hours to kill… how can I kill time… how the fuck can someone kill time… just smash those hands… stop the fucking time… make it stop… oh, make it stop…" she placed both hands over her ears keeping her eyes tightly shut.

She let the tears trickle down her face.

After calming down she picked up the phone, punched in a code to ensure her number couldn't be traced then dialed.

"Hello?"

"Tierry my love. Why did you call the house?" she sounded like a schoolgirl.

"I'm sorry…I didn't…it wasn't…"

"I already told you… he sometimes shows up unexpectedly…he likes to surprise me."

"I'm sorry…please forgive me…I had to…"

"I know…me too. But don't call me at home again."

"Where are you now?"

"I'm out, calling from the drugstore…I've got to see you…I miss you…"

"When can you come?"

"He really gave it to me on last night…yelling and screaming … said he'd never let me go again…" she sounded sniffles with tearless eyes.

"Would you like me to come to New York?"

She made a snorting sound.

"No…no…he'll get real mad…."

"I can't stand the thought…of you and him…"

"I love you Tierry. I need you."

She glanced in the mirror and retouched her hair.

"I want you so much…"

"I promise to call you in a couple of days…"

Carlene allowed a few farewell words before hanging up.

* * *

Carlene dreaded spending an evening in the company of Glen's colleagues. It meant being on tiptoes the entire evening. Especially with Kalb. Carlene had never known fear of men, not until she had met Kalb Gales, Head of the Psychology Department. It was the most amazing thing, as if he could see right through her. During their first meeting and following the casual introductions, Kalb had asked her.

"Who are you, Miss Carlene Ridge?"

It was the one and only time that Carlene had felt her blood gush up to her face and down to her legs all at once. She sat with legs folded over, like a grand lady waiting to be called to the floor dance. Glen was sitting at the opposite end of the room conversing with his colleagues. Kalb's eyes penetrated her own. Lowering her head she answered shyly.

"I'm sorry my presence bothers you."

Kalb hadn't expected such a reply. He was simply being his cynical self making small talk and weighing newly acquainted people. He had not meant anything other than a small tease and did not wish to offend Glen's fiancée. Carlene's response had put him on the spot. He apologized.

"I'm sorry… I didn't mean to offend you in any way…"

Carlene smiled.

"Neither did I…"

Trusting his instincts, Kalb felt there was more to Miss Carlene Ridge than met the eye.

He was intrigued.

* * *

An athletic-bodied man in his forties, six feet four inches above ground level, with penetrating gray eyes that made women feel shy and smile without any reason, Prof. Kalb Gales was any women's dream of a catch. His smile, a perfect white sparkle framed by a set of strong jaws and a dimple in chin gave the impression of a very masculine and powerful face that possessed a gentle personality, a winning combination in the eyes of most women. As one of The Apple's most sought after bachelors, Kalb enjoyed the reputation but not his life.

Having been born and raised on a farm in a remote town in Illinois, Kalb preferred the company of farm animals and pets to that of people. He was a shy little boy rarely pampered by his four older sisters, all of whom had married into farm life and remained in Illinois. Though obedient and helpful, Kalb was frequently reprimanded by his father and had tasted the pain and humiliation of his thick belt.

"I love you son… that's why I'm doin' this," he'd tell Kalb just before flogging him senselessly.

Kalb's mother and sisters never thought of interfering, except on one occasion when Kalb had been very late coming home from school and had missed milking the cows on time. As soon as he walked into the house, Kalb's father, a big man with heavy hands and legs, dragged him outside and, forcing down his pants began flogging him with the belt. Kalb's shrieks echoed for miles around, but there were no neighbors to hear them. His mother and sisters waited a while before rushing out of the house.

"I'm sick and tired of you," his father screamed, "You look like a bum and you act like one."

"Please, Rufus," his mother eyed his father.

"Hush, Woman!"

"You'll damage the boy!"

"He's already damaged!"

It wasn't until Kalb's sisters had burst out crying, that their father had released him and by then he was semi-conscious.

Kalb never spoke to his father again, except in compliance with farm chores but he never forgave him, refusing to attend his funeral, five years later or offer consolation to his mother and sisters. Kalb swore that he would never follow his father's footsteps, but found himself unable to keep the promise during his marriage to Anne, his first wife.

He had met her at the State University of Illinois. A beautiful but shy girl from a town as small as his, Anne tried to appease Kalb. Like him, her own childhood was not free of violence and humiliation, but unlike Kalb, she had chosen to retain some contact with her hateful father, a fact that aggravated Kalb to no end.

"I've learned to accept him the way he is," she cried, trying to make her new husband understand.

"How can you accept his violence and abuse?" Kalb screamed.

"Maybe they didn't teach you respect!" Anne shouted back.

"Respect?! You call that respect?! You're still afraid of that son of a bitch, that's why you still talk to him. It has nothing to do with respect! Or love, for that matter!"

"How would you know anything about love? You claim you never had it!"

It was as though she had slapped his face with the truth. Unable to control his overwhelmed sense of humiliation, Kalb's hands grabbed Anne's hair and from there it was a short way to knocking her unconscious.

Kalb couldn't forgive himself for what he'd done in a moment of anger. He received initial help from his psychology teacher, and later sought intense professional help but it was too late.

Anne divorced him after a short marriage that lasted less than a year.

Kalb's second wife, Emma, a Norwegian beauty he had met nine years later at the age of thirty-four while on a visit with her family in New York, seemed the perfect match. A year older than Kalb Emma had experienced two stillborn births during her six years of marriage. The loss of both babies only accelerated the end of her broken marriage. Her arrival in New York, two years after her divorce, signaled a fresh start. When she'd first met Kalb at a coffee shop they ended in bed that same night and remained there for the next two months until her tourist visa was about to expire.

"Please stay with me… I've never felt this way before…" Kalb had begged her.

"I want to but…I can't…I've got to leave by next week."

"How can I convince you to stay?"

"Marry me!" Emma had answered and Kalb had burst out laughing.

They married two days later.

By then a professor of psychology at Columbia, Kalb was ecstatic. Emma, too, felt as though life was now worth living. She applied and was accepted to the PhD program at Columbia's art department. The couple was overjoyed and made plans to purchase a house. Three months later, while grocery shopping at a nearby store, Emma fainted and was rushed to the hospital with what seemed like an acute case of the flue. But it proved to be a malignant brain tumor and within two months Kalb was again a bachelor.

A devastated one.

He spent his days inside the apartment consoled by alcohol and self-pity. It took him five months to sober up and return to a less than happy life. Now aged forty-seven, widowed and without a family to call his own, Kalb was bitter and cynical. Women adored him; he could tell by the way they eyed him and the manner in which they spoke to him. But he couldn't bring himself to trust another woman and another relationship.

Feeling too vulnerable to chance it again, Kalb chose the path of loneliness instead.

* * *

Now in her boudoir, putting on the last touches of make up for her six o'clock meeting with Glen and his colleagues, Carlene remembered Kalb's words spoken only weeks earlier.

"You'll be sorry you ever met me!" he had said.

She had felt threatened then; but now she smiled thinking about Tierry who was more important to her than Kalb. Carefully choosing her outfit for dinner from among rows of clothes neatly hung and arranged within the enormous dressing room, Carlene picked out the white leather suit Kalb had liked.

She hadn't worn it since their last encounter.

It was now six o'clock. Carlene summoned the chauffer and shortly thereafter entered Tony's and joined the small crowd.

"Hi Presch," she kissed Glen then offered her cheeks and hands to the others around the table.

Kalb's eyes were icy as he greeted her with a kiss on each of her cheeks.

"Nice to see you, Carlene!"

It was pleasantly cool inside Tony's, the upscale Italian restaurant not too far from Glen's clinic. Wearing the white leather suit, short skirt and jacket, with a strapless violet top under it and matching stilettos, Carlene looked striking.

"You look beautiful, Carlene," Orin Tinker, lecturer on bi-polar syndromes commented.

"I love your chignon," Susan Finns head of administration at the medical school touched the thick bun, "I don't think I've ever seen you with your hair up."

"I usually leave it down," her blue eyes danced laughingly.

"You can always put it up in a ponytail," Susan said in admiration, still holding onto it.

"Or in a horse's tail for that matter," Kalb added as he picked up his drink and saluted in her direction.

"He's only teasing, honey," Glen smiled.

"Teasing is the only thing he does well," Carlene laughed out loud.

"I'm not sure about that," Ruth Warding, clinical psychology and the oldest lecturer in the department winked and took a long sip from her drink. Everyone joined the laughter.

"Kalb?" Carlene caught his eyes, "Is there anything besides teasing that you do well?"

As she said the words, Carlene realized she'd made a mistake. But it was too late.

"Funny you should ask. Don't you know by now?" Kalb shot back.

Carlene felt hot all over.

* * *

Her affair with Kalb started out as a casual encounter, prompted by Glen's insistence. An avid opera lover and a supportive patron of the Met, Glen made sure not to miss a single performance.

Bumping into Kalb one day, at work, Glen said.

"I'd like you to join us, Kalb…Carlene and I are going to the opera and we have an extra ticket."

Kalb was initially hesitant. Though he had seen Carlene on several occasions, his first impression of her was still fresh in his mind. He'd found her intriguing, but there was something else that cautioned him not to want to get any closer. He sometimes wondered about Glen's marriage and the long hours he spent at the office and the clinic, and about Carlene's flirtatious behavior.

As head of the psychology department and the founder of The Center, a well-established private clinic employing twelve psychologists, Kalb was an admirer of Glen's work and research. When asked to recommend a psychiatrist he'd always say.

"Glen's the best shrink in town."

As he sat at his desk, Kalb wondered whether or not to take Glen up on his offer. By evening he had opted to join them and, a few hours later, found himself standing in the grand foyer in the company of Glen and Carlene waiting for the start of the second act of La Traviata.

"I'll be right back," Glen left in the direction of the men's room.

"They should have named you Carlene the Beautiful," Kalb looked admiringly at Carlene.

"Coming from a handsome man like you, I'd say that's a compliment."

"D'you really think I'm handsome?" a mischievous smile on his lips.

Carlene stepped forward and whispered in his ear.

"Handsome enough to fancy."

"Do you fancy all handsome men?"

"Only those that turn me on."

Looking straight into her eyes Kalb knew she had meant it.

Just then Glen had rejoined them.

"How about a late nightcap over at my place?" Kalb asked.

Glen looked at Carlene who had moved her shoulders up and down as if she couldn't care less.

"Fine by me if it's fine by you," Glen spoke in Carlene's direction.

"Sure… sounds like fun," her eyes met Kalb's.

The bell sounded reminding the audience to return to their seats. The second act was about to begin.

Despite the darkness in the upper box seats, Carlene was acutely aware of Kalb's stare. His eyes penetrated her light-colored chiffon dress causing Carlene to shift slightly in her chair. Slowly, as if not wishing to disrupt his stare, Carlene's hand, well hidden under a loosely sprawled shawl, moved to her right and came to rest on Kalb's thigh.

Glen seated to her left, was busy holding onto his binoculars and focusing on the stage below.

Following the performance, Glen insisted on returning home to complete a report leaving Carlene in Kalb's company.

"No, darling…I insist you go… I'm afraid it's my fault…I must finish the report. Besides, you deserve to have some fun."

"Are you sure you don't mind leaving me here with Kalb?" she smiled and kissed Glen's cheek.

"The report is due tomorrow. I've got to finish it tonight. Would you mind taking care of my special lady?" Glen turned to Kalb with a smile.

"If that's your wish, Glen…"
"Only if the lady wants."
It was almost too easy, as if Glen had pushed them together.

Kalb's apartment, a short distance away by car, was spacious and well kept with a distinct masculine air to it. Magazines and books sprawled randomly over the table, with a loose coat and a pair of sneakers next to the couch.

Carlene took in what seemed like hundreds of books on long shelves, overlooking two love seats in rusty colored leather with a low glass made coffee table in between.

"A drink?" Kalb asked.

Carlene smiled.

"Did you actually read all of these?" she pointed to the books.

"Yeah. Even enjoyed some."

Carlene laughed and moved closer to read their titles.

Kalb put on soft music and walked in her direction holding two glasses. As soon as Carlene turned around and met his eyes, she knew what was about to happen. Kalb kept his eyes on her while extending the drink.

"To us," Carlene held up the glass.

"To Carlene the beautiful," Kalb's eyes remained fixed.

"How about dancing?" she asked with a smile and a voice that reminded him of how much he missed the company of a loving woman.

Kalb felt cornered. Afraid to touch her yet wanting it more than anything, he stood still like a bashful teenager. Carlene closed the short gap between them. Now inches away from his face, she traced her lips with her tongue, moving her fingers along his arms and shoulders, barely touching him but knowing only too well how it made him feel.

Kalb's breathing became shallow. He felt the situation get out of control.

"I like your muscles," her fingers moved in tiny circles over his biceps.

Kalb couldn't hold it back any longer.

He kissed her hard on her lips. Carlene groaned and moved into him. With his eyes half shut and still holding onto her, Kalb maneuvered her into the next room.

"Careful," she said in a husky voice, her eyes slightly closed, "careful with the dress."

Slowly, very slowly, he removed her dress and let it fall to the floor. Carlene unbuttoned his shirt then dampened his nipples with her tongue. Kalb groaned.

"Maybe we shouldn't..." she half teased before placing her mouth on his.

She liked the feel of him. Moving her hands skillfully, she unzipped his pants. Kalb got a whiff of her perfume and felt a momentary dizziness. Holding her slender body with both hands he placed her on the bed, flinging off his shoes and the rest of his clothes with one swift move. Staring at her naked body with admiration, he used his fingers to roam the valley under her lush breasts tracing it downhill to the perfect triangle below.

Her welcoming smile urged him on.

It was curiosity that had first brought them together and infatuation that kept their bodies aching for each other during the next several weeks. If he noticed anything, Glen hadn't mentioned it, making it seemingly easier on Kalb and Carlene. But in fact, it only made it harder on Kalb causing him to feel like a traitorous liar. Glen would smile and ask Kalb about his outings with Carlene.

"So how was the movie last night? Carlene said she enjoyed it."

Kalb felt like shaking Glen by the shoulders and shouting.

"Don't you know that I'm fucking your wife?!"

But instead he'd say.

"It was ok."

Kalb felt a deep sense of shame. How could he lie to a colleague of his? And especially to Glen?

Two months into their relationship, Kalb was madly in love with

Carlene willing to do anything in his power to keep her at his side. He felt helpless without her, missing her scent and the touch of her skin against his. He believed she was amazingly beautiful and equally smart. Her willingness to accept him with his faults and complexities meant she had granted him the biggest gift of all: unconditional love.

"I love you Carlene." Kalb held her tightly in his arms.

Carlene did not return the words. As far as she was concerned, their affair was just an episode, a pastime to spice up life, brew up some excitement and break the daily monotony.

"You're sweet," she replied with a smile.

It was on the tip of her tongue to say out loud.

"You're as stupid as the rest of them!"

Two days after his confession of love, Kalb had noticed a change in Carlene followed by her statement:

"You're starting to bore me."

Kalb was unprepared for Carlene's sudden disinterest and was quick to respond.

"Any suggestions? I'll do anything you want…"

But it only made Carlene shy further away from him.

The following day, looking especially ravishing in a white leather suit Carlene entered his apartment and announced.

"It's time out. Don't call me anymore."

"Is this a bad joke?"

"Am I smiling?"

"You can't do this," Kalb felt his heart sink.

"Did you really think that I loved you?"

Kalb felt sick.

"I love you, Carlene. Doesn't it mean anything to you?!"

"You must be joking!" she turned in the direction of the door.

"If you walk out of here…"

"It's not an if!"

"Don't do this, Carlene. Please…don't walk out on me."

"Are you threatening to tell my husband about us?"
Kalb was silent.
Carlene turned around and headed out the door.
She heard Kalb say.
"You'll be sorry you ever met me!"

CHAPTER 8

On the day of his death, Lydia had returned home to find Jasper sprawled on the couch. She assumed he was snoozing but seeing his color she touched his face and at once realized that her father was dead. She sat next to him cradling his head and thinking her world had come to an end. Wanting to stay with him for as long as she could, Lydia waited until the sun was about to disappear before calling for help.

Doug Stoke the town's sheriff came immediately and summoned the ambulance.

"Why don't you come stay with us for a while?" he said after checking and confirming Jasper's death.

"I'd rather stay here …or maybe go to Holly's …" Lydia replied.

"Is Abigail back?"

Lydia shook her head.

"We'll have to locate her."

Lydia didn't respond.

"D'you have any idea where she might be?" he asked gently.

Again she moved her head.

"Ok, Lydia. Let me worry about it. Can I drive you over to Holly's?"

Lydia packed a small bag and left the house.

***

It was Sheriff Doug who had called Bill McKinney, Jasper's attorney.

"Hi Bill. This is Doug. How are you?"

"Couldn't be better. What's up?"

"Jasper Gray just passed away."

"Serious?"

"Yeah!"

There was a sudden noise with muffled voices in the background. Then all at once.

"Hey Doug, Abigail's here. She wants to know when it happened."

"I thought she was out of town?"

"She…was, but now she's back."

Doug heard more voices and giggles.

"Can I talk to her?"

"Hold on."

A second later he replied.

"Nah! She doesn't wanna talk to anyone. She only wants to know when it happened."

"Lydia came home from school and found him dead on the couch. Heart attack."

"Fuck!" Doug heard a woman's voice.

"As Jasper's attorney, I guess… you've got the will…"

"Yeah."

"Then you should take care of the funeral arrangements. I dropped Lydia off at Holly Quince's. Let Abigail know in case she asks…"

"Will do."

Doug hung up.

***

Had Bill McKinney Jr., a man in his mid-thirties, very tall and very stocky, not been the sole attorney living in Emmeth, he probably wouldn't have been Jasper Gray's choice of an attorney. But the convenience of proximity played an important role in the daily lives of the hardworking farmers who trusted him with their legal affairs. Slovenly looking and often reeking of alcohol and cigarettes, Bill enjoyed the reputation of his beloved father, Bill McKinney Sr., who had served as chief prosecutor for the district of Corpus Christi until his death two years earlier. Despite Bill Jr.'s physical resemblance to his father, they couldn't have differed more, character-wise. Though he tried not to veer in the wrong direction, and had graduated from the University of Odessa as a fully qualified attorney, Bill McKinney Jr. suffered the heavy burdens of two addictions: alcohol and women.

From a young age, his robust body and handsome features attracted the girls, followed in later years by hordes of women. His chubby cheeks and round brown eyes stamped the cherub like face with a permanent look of amazement, arousing in women the deepest emotion of all: motherhood. By his late teens, Bill was already able to claim countless would-be-mothers.

His office, a messy place on a back side strip only doors away from where the main street cut across the railroad tracks, was set in an old building that had once housed the jailhouse and sheriff. A mountain of files heaped on top of the single filing cabinet transformed the smallish room into a sloppy looking barn, its floors, chairs and desk flooded with loosely strewn documents and newspapers stained by moldy leftover coffee and cigarette butts. Standing in the entrance of the narrow bathroom with its filthy toilet and sink reeking of empty beer cans, was an overflowing trashcan.

Bill's clients, all of whom had admired his father, remembered an honorable family that had long since dispersed with both parents deceased and his only sister married and gone. They had remained faithful to the McKinney name by force of habit. By electing to ignore his heavy drinking and sudden disappearances, considered as an eccentricity of a well-educated man, his faithful followers enabled Bill to maintain his habits.

But it was Kayla, to everyone's amazement, his sweet wife of eight years, who, for reasons comprehensible only to her, had remained in love with Bill despite everything and everyone. A small and cheerful young woman with honey colored hair and a permanent smile on her lovely face, Kayla was born and raised on the farm next to that of Bill's parents. In later years she chose to raise their only son by herself, knowing her husband was incapable of contributing to his education. The town's people sided with Kayla and whenever the occasion was called for, helped her.

"Lord only knows what she finds in that good for nothing piece of shit!" was the usual comment made by all.

Kayla's father, Jimmy Basel Scones known to all as J. B., had inherited not only the small Scones Bank, but also his father's managerial skills which assisted him, within the short span of four years, in acquiring Banker's Best, another small and well reputed bank. Five years later, and with two additional acquisitions, J.B. Scones had become a very rich man. He continued to expand and acquired an insurance company, adding an extraordinary distinction to his already well-established name.

J. B. didn't really care for his next-door neighbor's son and didn't trust Bill McKinney Jr., not even at the age of eighteen when he first set eyes on Kayla.

"How are you Bill?" he'd greet him with less than enthusiasm.

"Fine, sir," was Bill's only reply, his face a bewildered iceberg.

J.B. knew of Bill's escapades but at the time it was easy to brush off Kayla's interest in Bill as mere teenage infatuation. J.B. was consoled by the fact that Kayla was readying herself for the prestigious University of Texas in Austin.

It was pure luck that parted their ways and sheer coincidence that brought them together again four years later.

Bill had just returned home following his graduation from the university of Odessa with well above average grades while Kayla, by now a beautiful young lady with a long trail of admirers, had returned for a brief two-week visit eager to ride her favorite horse and meet with friends. She had one more semester to complete her finals before graduating.

Entering the stable she walked over to Anan, the Arabian thoroughbred given to her by her father as a special gift two years earlier. Saddling herself proudly on the horse's back, Kayla rode him into the surrounding fields of their acreage.

It was a hot day with a merciless sun. Wishing to reach the creek faster, Kayla took a shortcut through the McKinney property heading towards the creek that marked the borderline between the two farms.

"Wow!" the tall young man stood at the edge of the water holding up his hand.

Kayla pulled tight on Anan's reigns and stopped a foot away from Bill McKinney Jr.

"Well I'll be darn if it ain't the beautiful Kayla!" Bill called out with a wide smile.

"Bill!" Kayla jumped down from the horse and ran into his arms.

The minute she felt his arms around her, Kayla knew she was madly in love with the man who had once been just a teenage infatuation. Holding each other in a warm embrace for what seemed like longer than was called for, Bill released his grip bent down and kissed Kayla hard on her lips. Somewhat stunned though overjoyed, Kayla returned his kiss with ardent passion.

Moments later, with Anan as their only witness, they made love on the soft grass next to the creek. Following their lovemaking they splashed naked in the quiet waters and caught up with the years that had separated them.

For Kayla it had marked a new beginning of love. Bill saw it instantly as an opportunity to combine his newly acquired law degree with the affluence of Kayla's family.

It took J.B. only a couple of days to notice the distinct change in Kayla.

His fears were confirmed later that evening when Kayla announced she was going to meet Bill.

"I forbid you to see that good for nothing …"

But the more J.B. insisted, the more persistent and stubborn Kayla became.

J.B.'s only consolation was that Kayla would soon return to Austin.

The two weeks went by quickly for the young couple. Bill spoke of his future and his want of a private practice. Kayla voiced her long-lasting love for Bill and dreams for a family of her own.

"Let's elope," Bill suggested.

Blinded by love and unable to think clearly, Kayla agreed.

The two got married the day before Kayla's scheduled return to Austin. Unbeknown to either of them, at the time, their son had already been conceived.

Furiously angry and too shocked to even speak to Bill, J.B. asked his attorney to deliver the longest marriage agreement ever drafted in the county of Cameron. Spread over sixteen long pages J.B. detailed the accommodations he was willing to provide for Bill as a young attorney, agreeing to settle him in the small office previously occupied by the sheriff, and set aside a special fund for his new wife and future children. In return J.B. had demanded one thing of Bill: to remain faithful to Kayla. He then elaborated on the definition of *"faithful"* which was immediately rejected by Bill. J.B. had no choice but to redefine the term within the agreement, but refused to budge as to the specific clause detailing Kayla's inheritance.

Bill had become a prisoner to Kayla's money and fortune.

Over the years, Bill had learned to circumvent that specific clause and had even gone as far as telling Kayla about it.

"I don't need a policeman for a father-in-law!" he hollered and stormed out of the house.

It was the first time Bill had left the house, but it marked the beginning of his frequent disappearances. Staying out late and returning home in the dawning hours of morning became a routine, one that Kayla was willing to accept.

She had found solace and reason for her existence in her pure love for her husband and child. Bill continued his unruly but tolerated behavior. With J.B. still at his heels and forever waving the marriage agreement in his face Bill knew where to draw the lines and how to maintain a balance acceptable to Kayla. With her agreement, he was safe. But it kept Bill on his tiptoes.

"I love you Bill, and I'll put up with a lot, but don't flaunt it in front of me," Kayla had warned him.

Bill made sure to exercise his ex-marital relationships out of town, in the larger city of Brownsville. But every so often, whether out of laziness, stupidity or a simple wish for some hairy excitement, Bill reached out for a young girl within the town of Emmeth.

It just so happened, that Abigail Gray was there for the taking.

CHAPTER 9

Bill's unruly behavior was precisely what attracted Abigail to him in the first place; she liked his messiness and lack of respect for order and rules, though as an attorney he was obliged to follow both inside the courtroom.

After leaving her father's house, Abigail stormed into Bill's office unannounced.

"Sober up you big cocky hunk!" she thundered into the room reached his chair and grabbed his crotch.

Bill admired Abigail's wild behavior. He grew up hearing stories about the-weird-looking- girl, but after seeing her a few times he didn't really mind the strangeness of her face or the untidiness of her clothes and hair. Though much older than Abigail, they got to chat on several occasions while crossing paths along the main street in town or around school. Bill soon learned to admire her brightness of mind and the way with which she handled the bullies and teasers.

But their first serious adult conversation took place at the local diner shortly after Abigail's release from Cedars Home the year before. Abigail had staggered in after having spent a couple hours inside a stranger's car, a passerby whom she'd met briefly at the gasoline station. After a short exchange of words they sat in his car and played some then fucked but mostly drank up the one bottle they shared. Tipsy and unstable on her feet, Abigail got out of the car wobbled to the side and threw up more than just the drink. She was sick to her stomach and crying. With her head swirling and aching all she wanted was to reach the diner up the road and sit down to a hot cup of coffee.

Bill was having his habitual late night cap when in swayed Abigail with a stained shirt and a filthy face. She settled three stools away from him and said with her eyes still shut.

"Coffee please."

Bill took a wet napkin and moved next to her.

"You ok, Abigail?" he cleaned her face gently.

She squinted at him.

"Sure thing, Bill."

Bill paid for the coffee.

"Let's go sit over there," he helped Abigail off the stool and guided her to a side table. After settling her down on a chair he asked if she'd like something to eat.

Abigail smiled.

"Haven't eaten a darn thing in a while."

Bill paid for a sandwich and stayed with her.

Over the next three hours they conducted what Abigail liked to refer to as the most intoxicated and sobering adult conversation she'd ever had with anyone. Bill proved to be a great listener and a gentle spirit at heart. He showed true compassion and understanding regarding her difficult circumstances in life. It felt so good to be able to share her aches and pains with someone who truly took an interest in her.

After a few more cups of coffee and feeling somewhat relieved at having found a kind friend, Abigail listened to Bill's soft voice.

"You know, Abigail, you could do so much better. You're smart… you're real sharp, but you're also wild and unruly. People don't really care about someone else's problems…or the things they've been through in life… so don't expect pity from anyone. People will always tell you stories and try to take advantage of you… but with your smarts you can do things that'll really challenge you. You may not realize it, but you're strong, Abigail, and you can do anything you want if you put your mind to it. Heck you can even grow stronger but only if you learn to hold back… tame yourself. You need to learn to control whatever it is that you wanna have real bad. Don't grab it. Let it go… control yourself and then you can have it all! Big time!"

Abigail ended up spending the night on the torn love seat in Bill's office and the following day she returned to the silence of her home. But Bill's words stayed with her and proved to be the best advice she ever got and carried them in her heart and mind throughout the years to come.

Abigail enjoyed being touched by Bill and feeling his skin against hers. His tall and masculine body was what turned her on and aroused her. His face and brain didn't faze her but as soon as she neared him she'd feel a tingling between her legs. She'd then grab his hand and shove it inside her panties. His touch was irresistible to her. She melted as soon as she felt him and was willing to go along with anything he wanted. He was the one man who could turn her on instantly and satisfy her over breakfast or dinner. She could never tire of his touch or his manly smells. Sometimes, during evening hours, if she felt like it, she'd leave the house and walk over to his office. If she'd see a light she'd knock on the door step inside and reach for his hand. Bill was the one person who never pushed her away and always welcomed her inside which was why she'd chosen to disregard everything else about him that wasn't related to the one thing she craved: The physical feel of another human being who accepted her for who she was and cared about her.

Bill McKinney made her feel like a normal person and a desirable woman.

So it was not without pleasure that Bill now let Abigail grab him by his balls. It felt good. Reaching with his hands, he joined the game, tossing off her blouse, tearing down her skirt and entering into her full force.

Although the two now seemed satisfied, Abigail asked for more. But Bill, too tired and spent, lay quietly on his back.

"I've got a preposition for you, hunk," she moved her hand over his flattened cock.

"I'm dead… finished…" Bill exhaled.

"How about an easy buck?"

"What d'you have in mind?"

"My dad sold the farm. You can have a crumb."

"What the fuck are you talkin' about?"

"My old man's dead."

"What?!"

"Yeah… died in front of my eyes."

"When?"

"Just before I got here."

"Are you fucking me?!"

"Sure am!" she grabbed him again.

"Cut it out!"

"What's wrong?"

"I want the truth for once! Is your old man dead?"

"Would I lie to you?" she twirled his pubic hair with her finger.

"Cut it out, Abigail! D'you call the police?"

"I left that pleasure to Lydia. Don't look mortified. He probably had a heart attack or somethin'."

It was at that precise moment that Sheriff Doug had called Bill to tell him about Jasper's death.

After hanging up Bill was silent. Abigail went on.

"Well…he told me he'd sold the farm…never even asked how I felt about it… I know he wanted to give it to his favorite…the farm was probably sold between three fifty and four hundred grand. I'll make it worth your while."

"Why would you wanna do that?"

"I'll need to see my dad's will before anyone else sees it."

"I can't let you do that."

"You can and you will. I might need you to make a small adjustment…" she went on to tell him of her plan.

"You're out of your fucking mind! I can be disbarred for it. No way!"

"Look…I didn't kill him, if that's what you're thinkin'. But don't ask me to lie and tell you I loved him."

"So?"

"So I'm just tellin' you the man's dead."

"What exactly do you have in mind?"

Abigail repeated her request for a change in her father's will.

"No way!"

"J.B.'s a pretty good listener and you know he hates your guts. I can have your cute ass thrown to the dogs on account of raping me here… but I'm sure you're not gonna make me do that…" she held his thick cock in her hand and bounced it around like a piece of play dough.

"I don't believe you!"

"Try me. It'll be interesting. You've got till tomorrow."

Abigail crossed her leg over his. Bill didn't budge.

Though Bill had initially rejected her plan, he was soon forced to oblige. Abigail was careful not to tell him about her father's last moments of life.

Several hours later, and following Abigail's unrelenting probing, Bill switched on the light and moved to the large cabinet in back of the room. Opening the drawer, he picked out Jasper Gray's folder. A yellow note attached to it read: "Change Jasper Gray's will in favor of Lydia (savings and estate proceeds)."

It was then he'd remembered the messages left by Jasper. He'd listened to it two weeks earlier upon his return to the office but failed to follow it through.

Now seated at his desk he read the will. It had spelled out an even split of the estate, fifty percent to each of his daughters. Abigail's request could easily be attained by simply disregarding the yellow note, but it was something Bill was unable to conceive. He sat with the folder for a while trying to figure out a way of getting rid of the yellow note.

The help came from Abigail. Watching him from the darkened corner of the room she got up and moved next to him.

"Why don't we simply get rid of this," she plucked off the yellow note, tore it into tiny shreds and stuffed it in her mouth, "Lydia won't know the difference …it was only a little yellow note telling you someone was lookin' for you …"

"What if Lydia suspects …"

"Why would she? With you as her dad's attorney there's no need for it."

"What if she…"

But Abigail was now beaming at the document Bill was holding in his hand.

"I trust you'll make this work," she smoothed her hand over the document that had been hand-written and signed by her father next to Bill's signature then picked up a beer bottle and swallowed the remains of the shredded note.

After taking care of business it was time to resume the fun.

"Come on, big sucker, give it to me …give it to me now…" Abigail pinched his butt and forced him down. They rolled in a frenzied passion on the floor. Abigail held his red hot penis with one hand as she latched onto his neck with the other, brushing up her body against his and forcing him to groan.

"I want you…I want you…I want…I want…"

"Fuck me…oh mother of god… fuck me…Bill…fuck me…"

Drowning in a fervent lust they ignored the ringing phone and the occasional cockroach that dashed across the floor. After being satisfied, they burst into uncontrollable laughter.

Bill grabbed Abigail's tit and sucked on it.

"I want to fuck you again!" he said, "I love fucking you…"

"Let's see you big fellow!" she rolled onto him.

They continued toying with each other until the room was as dark as the night outside.

* * *

Abigail sat next to Lydia as both listened to Bill read out their father's will relinquishing the proceeds of the estate equally to both his daughters.

"It's wrong," Lydia said as soon as Bill had finished reading it.

"What are you getting at?" Bill turned his head sideways as he asked the question.

"It's a mistake!"

"It's your father's one and only will, Lydia. Look," he pointed to the signature, "Your dad signed it."

"But…but he was going to change it. He told me so."

"Well… he may have wanted to… but he didn't."

"What's going to happen now?"

"Stop moaning just 'cause Dad favored me too," Abigail shot her a menacing look.

"That's a lie! You know how Dad felt!"

"I'll give you a copy of the will. The rest is up to you two," Bill smiled in Abigail's direction.

It was the last time Lydia saw Abigail.

Eight months later Lydia graduated from school and with the amount of money in her possession, left Emmeth.

CHAPTER 10

After the will was approved and all proceeds paid out, Abigail left Emmeth with a backpack in hand and a purpose in mind. Her first stop in Harlingen was a short one, visiting three banks located on its main street.

"Do you have other branches nationwide?" she inquired with each and deposited a substantial amount into the one she thought would best serve her purpose.

Abigail decided to move slowly and check out the unfamiliar roads. She was now free to do as she pleased with no constraints to bind her to one place or one person.

Though unruly and unpredictable, Abigail was self-disciplined when motivated to do so. Placing most of the proceeds of her father's estate in a bank account provided her with a sense of financial security, a safety net she could always rely on in case of need. She had calculated things carefully and had kept only a small amount of cash to last her a few months, during which time she was determined to accomplish what she had set out to do.

* * *

She hitchhiked most of the way, though it had taken her several weeks with stops along its course. She didn't care where she slept or how many days she went without a shower. There were plenty of gas stations and small diners along the route with sinks and running water. Her mind was focused on reaching her final destination in the cheapest possible way without having to touch her savings. The money in her account was her ticket to a better future and the only thing that mattered.

Arkansas was where she first stopped for longer than just a night. Entering a small diner she glanced at the menu while taking a deep puff on her cigarette.

"What'll be?" a short waitress in her mid forties chewing gum with a pencil in hand stared at Abigail.

"D'you have sandwiches?"

"It's right there," the waitress pointed at the menu with her pencil.

Abigail was tired of the daily sandwiches and cold cuts but careful not to exceed her budget. Looking at the woman she said.

"D'you think I can have a juicy steak for the price of a sandwich?"

The woman rolled her eyes.

"Let me know when you're ready!" she walked away.

Abigail stared at her back.

"Is this how you treat an orphan?" she called out.

At the sound of her voice, the handful of cowboys who sat at the bar, turned around and stared at her. One man wearing a stetson walked over and asked.

"Mind if I sit?"

"Suit yourself!"

"So…you're an orphan, are you?" he stared at Abigail.

"Yeah."

"Hungry?"

"Yeah."

Motioning to the waitress he ordered a steak and French fries.

"Wanna drink?"

"Beer."

"Make it two, Betsy."

"So…what's your name?"

"Abigail."

"Wanna know mine?"

"What for?"

"'Cause now you owe me …and you're gonna have to pay me back… somehow…" his eyes rested on her breasts.

"Fuck you!" Abigail responded.

"If that's what you wan."

She burst out laughing despite herself.

"Name's Rick…they call me Ricky."

"Hi Ricky."

"When did you last eat?"

"Ten days ago…I've been eating sandwiches…"

"How would you like to have some fun?"

"Doing what?"

"We'll talk 'bout it later…"

Turning to the bar he called out.

"Betsy, where the fuck's the steak?!"

Abigail liked Ricky sensing he had something exciting up his sleeve. It triggered her curiosity and turned her on, though she wondered how long it would take him to ask the usual.

"Is that from an accident?" strangers would always point a finger and ask her that question with pitying eyes.

"Nah, it's the lord's blessings handed me at birth," she'd respond leaving them speechless."

She waited anxiously for her food wondering what Ricky had to offer. He kept staring at her saying little with a fixed smile on his foxy-looking face. He seemed to enjoy her anticipation for the food. As soon as it arrived she cleaned out her plate disregarding the chewiness of the steak and the greasy fries. She then drank the last bit of beer, burped loudly and said.

"Ok, Ricky, what'll be?"

He laughed.

"You a businesswoman or somethin'?"

"I don't have time to waste."

"You in a hurry?"
"Yeah."
"Where to?"
"The only reason I'm telling you I'm headin' for Chicago is 'cause you bought me food."
"What's in Chicago?"
"None of your fucking business."
"So! The woman's got spite!" he kept staring at her eyes.
"What d'you wan', Ricky?"
"See this small package?" he took out of his jeans pocket a cloth.
"What's in it?"
"Open it and see."
She moved slowly unraveling another wrapping then another until she found the white stuff.
"What the fuck d'you want me to do with this?" she stared at him.
"Repay me for the meal."
"How?"
"I wan' us to have fun…" he opened his mouth half way wiggling his tongue sideways.
Abigail visualized a snake.
"We can do it without the stuff…"
"Thought you'd like it…" a smirk on his unshaven face.
Abigail asked for another beer.
"There's plen'y over at my place."
"Let's go," she smiled.
Abigail trailed behind Ricky watching him tip the hat in Betsy's direction and wave a hand to the four men left sitting at the bar. As soon as they were seated inside his shabby car, Ricky moved in Abigail's direction.
"I thought you were takin' me to your place?"
"This is it."
Abigail burst out laughing.
"You're kiddin' me?!"

"You owe me... now it's pay time," he grabbed her breasts with both hands.

Abigail found it amusing.

"Never done it in a car-house before...guess I'm gonna have fun..." she unzipped his pants.

As far as Abigail was concerned, Ricky was just an ordinary horny guy looking for a free fuck. She didn't mind Ricky or the fuck, but she didn't enjoy the acrobatics involved throughout the night.

The next morning Ricky again asked.

"How 'bout tryin' some of this stuff?" he pushed it in her direction.

"Need a clear head."

"What for?"

"I told you... it's none of your business."

"Fuck off!"

"Fuck off yourself!"

Stepping out of his car and slamming its door Abigail walked over to the main street looking for a fresh ride.

* * *

Determined to make her dream come true and feeling confident of its success, Abigail kept moving from one car to another never thinking twice about hitching a ride with strangers. Believing she could bend circumstances and reshape situations to get her way, Abigail ploughed on stopping in small towns that offered little other than a one-night stop. After spending two nights in Missouri, drinking and joking in the company of a group of homeless men, it was time to move on again. She stood on a side street trying to find a ride.

The sun felt like a whip. Drowsy and thirsty she decided to make her way to the nearest gasoline station, a few blocks away.

"D'you have any iced water?" she asked.

A heavy-set man in his thirties, with straw colored hair fastened in a pony tail and tattoos covering his arms kept staring at her.

"What you staring at?" she asked.

The man kept chewing his gum without moving his head.

"Wan' a picture?" Abigail stared back at him.

"Where you headin' to?" he asked.

"None of your business unless I can hitch a ride with you."

"Fine by me," he said.

The man paid for his drink and walked over to the eighteen-wheeler parked on the side.

"Get in," he said and climbed at once into the cabin.

Abigail struggled up the laddered steps.

"Got a cigarette?" she looked at his unshaven face.

"Don't smoke."

"Shit!"

"Want one?" he handed her a beer can.

"Thanks."

"Duke's the name. What's yours?"

"Abigail." She took a long swig.

"Nice name," he moved his finger along her arm.

"Can we move?"

"Don' it matter to you where I'm goin'?"

"Don't give a shit as long as it's in the direction of Illinois."

"Where you from?"

"None of your business."

He laughed.

"I like 'em rough."

Abigail took another gulp.

"Can we move? They'll be plenty of time for that later."

"I wan' it now," Duke moved closer.

Abigail stared at him.

"You think I'm an acrobat?!"

Again he laughed.

"Plen'y of room in the back."

"I'm kind of tired. Mind if I rest some?" she shut her eyes and leaned back.

Duke's eyes roamed her stained T-shirt. The large breasts reminded him of overly ripened melons, squeezed together like a tray above the overflowing stomach. He looked at her face and burped.

The country music was loud.

"Get out. I don' need this kind'a shit."

* * *

By now well experienced with men and their ways, Abigail took for granted their touches and demands as if nothing else could possibly be of interest to them. Having learned how to appease each one, she toyed with the idea of opening a bordello, cutting short the road to riches.

Improvising was Abigail's way of surviving each day. She never knew where she might end up or with whom, a fact that rather appealed to her. As soon as she'd get to a new town, Abigail would look for the nearest bar or cheap diner, order a sandwich then move on to find a quiet corner for the night. She liked meeting new people as long as they weren't police officers or do-gooders who always messed things up. Forever curious she liked to hear other people's reasons for staying on the road. No two were identical and none were like hers. Once a week she'd allow for a layover in a cheap motel where she'd wash her clothes and take a long hot shower.

Dropped off late, one night, in a remote town on the outskirts of Illinois, Abigail looked for the closest place to have a drink before settling down for the night. Scouting her surroundings she spotted what looked like a road diner not far from the only gasoline station. Tired and thirsty she headed in its direction, walked in and sat at the bar.

"Hi," she turned to the only person around, tilting her head to his side with an unlit cigarette between her lips.

The dimly lit place reeked of beer and smoke and a sleaziness that matched the stale air. A screechy ceiling fan rotated lazily above the handful of tables and jukebox. Without as much as a wink, the man responded.

"It's better to be dead with a fart face like yours!"

"Speaking to me?" Abigail was spiked.

"Yeah. You're ugly!"

"Look who's talkin'!"

"You callin' me ugly?"

"I was born this way, ass hole!"

"Callin' me an ass hole? I'll show you one!" grabbing her shirt he pulled its stretchy cloth forward exposing her overflowing breasts.

"Keep your filthy hands to yourself!" Abigail screamed into his face.

The barman approached.

"Want some privacy? Over there!" he pointed in the direction of the rest rooms.

Still holding onto her shirt, the man dragged her forcefully into the corridor, a dark narrow space that smelled of urine. With one twist of his hand he pinned both her hands to the wall behind her, with his other he unzipped his pants, lifted her skirt, ripped off her underwear and forked himself into her. Abigail screamed. The man let go of her hand and slapped her across the face. Grabbing her again, he pulled the long hair and slammed her head against the wall.

The music, seemingly louder than before, blared throughout the empty bar. Pained and covered in blood, Abigail struggled to get out of his grip, but the more she kicked the stronger he pulled her hair.

"Looks like fun…mind if I join?" the barman approached.

"Wait 'till I'm done…I'm done… I'm done…" he forced himself into her over and over until Abigail didn't feel a thing.

"She's all yours!" he finally let go of her, pulled up his pants and walked away, leaving her to the barman's mercy.

She woke up on the pavement semi-conscious and barely breathing. The breezy air held an early morning haze, with soft rays of a fresh daylight. Abigail felt groggy and her mouth tasted of blood. It took her a few seconds to make out where she was. Her sore body ached all over but especially around her pelvis. She felt a burning sensation and was at once overwhelmed by the horrible ordeal of the previous night. Looking at her legs she saw bloodstains and felt wetness between her legs. She moved her hand under her skirt only to realize she was naked. Her hand was bloody. She needed to wash herself and take care of the blood that was still oozing from her insides.

Amazingly, her backpack was still straddled onto her back containing the full amount of money in her possession. She dug inside, found a pad with a pair of clean underwear. She knew it required medical attention. The pain was now worse. Scrambling to her feet, Abigail stared at the blood left on the pavement then turned her head and recognized the gasoline station. She decided to go there for help.

The guy in charge was watching TV.

"I need help. Someone raped me," she told him.

He looked as if he'd been slapped on his face.

"When?"

"Last night. I just woke up…got hurt pretty bad down there," she pointed to her lower part.

"Oh…Oh! Sure! Right away!"

He reached for the phone.

"Is there a roadside clinic around here?"

"Well…no, I'll need to call it in…"

"How far is it? I can't pay for a hospital…"

"Oh …they'll take you there…no need to worry. The station's ain't far but Hank will take you. Don't you worry now."

"Hank?"

"Yeah, the sheriff. Gets lots of calls out here… drunken drivers, you know, and trucks…" he dialed.

Abigail didn't argue. She felt the blood oozing and it hurt.

Hank arrived within minutes, took one look at her and inquired briefly.

"See who'd done it?"

When Abigail shook her head he asked.

"Wanna file a complaint?"

Abigail declined. Hank was relieved.

Once inside the clinic, a small booth like structure that housed a paramedic and a nurse, Abigail was checked and told she needed antibiotics and rest.

"I'm an orphan. Got no money or home to rest in."

"Where you from?" the paramedic asked.

"Texas."

"Ah," the paramedic responded then looked at the nurse, "Just a minute."

The two conferred in another room then returned.

"Well, we can take care of the medications and there's an extra room over here," he pointed to the side, "it's for emergency cases, you know, where we can keep a patient until the ambulance arrives. You're welcome to stay here for the day but tomorrow you'll need to leave."

Abigail's eyes welled.

"Thank you," she lowered her head with gratitude, "thank you for taking care of me."

"It's ok. We understand your situation."

The paramedic and nurse exchanged glances.

Abigail wanted to tell them that they couldn't possibly begin to understand her situation but that she understood their pitying looks. Then she remembered Bill's advice and decided not to linger over it. Instead, she tried to convince herself that she was lucky to have a twisted face for people to pity.

The following day she felt better and was soon on her feet again.

But the cruel words of the man who had assaulted and raped her kept churning in her head adding to her sharp sense of vengeance and heart-filled hatred of life.

"Bastards!" she muttered as the memory of her sister and her deceased parents flashed through her mind, "fucking bastards!"

She continued moving, changing towns and cars and men and at one point had even thought of continuing past her target destination.

"Maybe one day…after I get what I want…"

CHAPTER 11

The car came to a stop. Abigail stretched out her tired body and stepped onto the wide pavement, meeting the city's bright air with a smile.

It took her a while to gather herself, before setting out in search of a job. Curious as always and new to the city of Chicago, she looked around enjoying the skyscrapers and noisy streets, aiming to roam the city and get a feel for it.

It was early afternoon by the time she'd spotted the restaurant, lightly populated at this time of day and rather small with two narrow windows overlooking a side street. When Abigail saw the red bold letters of 'Casa Mia' over its green-framed entrance, she was reminded of the diner on Emmeth's main drag. Looking once more at the 'Waitress Wanted' sign taped onto the window, Abigail pushed open the door and stepped inside.

"I'm here for the job," she told the mustached man who stood behind the counter wearing a white apron.

He kept staring at her.

"I'm orphaned and I need a job to eat."

Abigail was used to the stares and the questions but she tired of the explanations.

"I'm a good worker, don't mind long hours, work hard, smoke fast and don't eat much. How's that for a deal?"

She could tell by the smile at the corners of his eyes that the man was amused.

"I'm Carlo. When you can start?"

"How about right now?" she returned his smile.

They shook hands and Carlo showed her around.

Initially he thought she had momentarily twisted her face; he couldn't believe it was a permanent thing, but then he considered the way she spoke. He liked her spirit and he also liked her figure. It made him think of a cuddly toy with a cushioned belly and pretty boobs. He could have fun with them.

"Where you stay?"

"I just got here. I don't know the city and I don't have a place. Can I stay here until I find something?"

His eyes were fixed on her orphaned face.

"For tonight is ok, then we see."

"Ok."

He showed her the back room next to the small toilet and its adjacent bathroom.

"Dis to clean every day," he told her pointing at the bucket and mop set near the cleaning materials

"Ok."

"And here," he moved next to a cot sized bed with a pillow and a blanket, "is for you. Ok?"

"Ok."

He later told his wife.

"I feel sorry for her…you have to see dat face …and dat body. Maybe she don' have no more chance."

Abigail didn't really mind spending her first night in the back room. It was just a resting place for her tired body and by far better than some of the weird places she'd stayed at over the past two-and-a-half months.

The next day Carlo said.

"Now I show you place."

The back door of the restaurant, just behind the room where she'd spent the night, opened into a small alley. Carlo led the way, turned the corner then climbed up the emergency stairwell to the first floor. A tiny room overlooked a giant knot of railroad tracks that serviced freight trains day and night. Darkness turned the sluggish moving shapes into titans adding eeriness to the unending sound of the clanking cars. But Abigail couldn't care less, using the room as a mere resting place for the night. Blind to its peeling walls and patched up gas range Abigail concentrated solely on saving money to attain her goal. The room's proximity to the restaurant would save her the bus fare.

Although she'd been on the road for over two months and experienced many difficult situations, Abigail found it hard to recover from the violent rape she'd experienced only weeks earlier. The physical scars had healed and the pains were gone, but her scarred soul continued aching. She felt a deep sense of anger and frustration towards her assailant and found it hard to accept the fact that she had been unable to fight back and punish him for what he did. It was hard to face the visions that kept floating at her like a movie stuck on replay; but it was even harder to accept the notion that she'd been raped by a monster who got away with it. There was no other way to define the creep who forced his sickening penis into her against her will. It made her angry. Furious. Ferociously mad. Her sense of frustration kept feeding itself. She was trying to cope with the notion that she hadn't been able to stop him.

Yet at the same time she wanted to erase the ordeal from her memory all together, put an end to the sights and smells and touches and…oh, to the pains she endured that were now scorched deep inside her head. She tried to move a step further from just coping, and to acknowledge the fact that she was raped, confront the horrific details every step of the way, relive the horrors that happened so that she could change their terrible outcome in her imagination. She wanted to replay the scene from the beginning but be able to change its ending, to alter her reactions and slam the bastard a hard one in the groin, kick his penis to damnation, make it bleed, shriek her head off and get the help she deserved. She was only nineteen years old but felt as though she'd lived and experienced several lifetimes.

Without realizing it, Abigail was undergoing internal changes. Her mind and soul were reshaping themselves faster than those of other teenagers who had never known hardships. The painful experiences had changed her internally and made her aware of things she hadn't noticed before. Recalling Bill's words about taking control of her life she was now more attentive to the 'why' and 'why not's' surrounding her. Wasn't taking control part of moving away from her past? If she had control over her thoughts, she could move away…

It led her into thinking about her brain. It belonged to her and she was its master. If she could make her brain move her arm or leg, she should be able to make it work for her in other ways; she could control her thoughts, choose her priorities, and make her own decisions.

In a way she'd allowed her brain to get out of control, and had stopped thinking for herself. What if she played back the horrific ordeal then changed things along the way? Like using several layers of paint on a blank sheet of paper? The more layers, the brighter and more pronounced the colors. What if she then did the reverse, and peeled off the layers one by one until all colors faded away? Maybe she could repeat the details of the rape in her mind, go over them again and again until they'd crumble into miniscule particles that wouldn't have the power to hurt her? Dilute the painful events the way she'd dilute the layers of colors, take control of her memories and weaken them until they'd fade and couldn't hurt her any longer.

But thoughts could also be sneaky and tricky: They lead you somewhere and then extended their tentacles turning into giant octopuses each stretching further than the previous one. Abigail's flexible mind was beginning to expand and without realizing it she was starting to undergo changes. She had long ago learned to take care of herself but failed to consider the effects of her own words and behavior on others. The awful rape changed her perspective. She kept rehashing in her mind the short conversation she'd had with the violent man and had come to recognize the fact that her own words were just as rude and sassy as his. After accepting this fact, she was able to shift her thoughts to the act itself. The rape made her sick. No one could ever justify or make any excuses for such a loathsome act. There was no justification or forgiveness for rape. None! Nothing! Absolutely nothing that could be used in defense of forcefully penetrating someone else's body against their will. Absolutely nothing!

Using her intuition Abigail found a compromising solution to help her come to terms with her traumatic experience. She kept replaying the degrading dialogue over and over in her mind until she was able to admit to herself that she could have been spared the ordeal altogether had she simply walked away from the scummy place and the creep who had hurt her, and taken better care of herself. Acting cautiously and politely would be helpful and get her what she wanted. Acting on impulse would get her into trouble.

Her eyes welled.

"I was wrong... but that doesn't justify what he did to me... he had no right to do it to me..."

Then she settled on accomplishing her newly aimed target by practicing self-discipline and restraint. She knew how hard she'd have to work to control herself but it was a worthy challenge, something she really needed to do if she wanted to accomplish her ultimate dream.

She recalled a saying her mother used to quote from the Scriptures:

"If I am not for myself who will be for me?"

At the time her mother explained that they were the sayings of the Desert Fathers, wise stories that described the experiences of the early Christians. But when she'd asked her mother for more details, Mable grew uncomfortable and impatient.

"We'd have to ask the priest about that," she said.
Jasper was quick to interrupt.
"That's enough!" he shut her up.

Abigail's first work day at Casa Mia was the hardest, but one that marked a changing point in her life.
"You eat spaghetti, yes?" Carlo asked her during her first lunch break.
"No, only salads...need to lose weight."
Carlo tilted his head sideways and let out a sigh.
"Why you wanna' be tin?"
"I'm sixty pounds overweight."
"No...no...twenny...maybe..."
She laughed, wishing it were true.
"I need to think thin."
"Eat someting," Carlo placed a steaming plate of spaghetti under her nose.
"I can't, Carlo. I need to lose weight."
"Ah! You ok."
"I'm not gonna' touch it!" her mouth watered.
She smelled the vapors of the meat sauce spiced with oregano, thyme, basil and marjoram, topped with melted cheese and grated Parmesan. When she got a whiff of the sweet rosmarine she was forced to swallow again.
"I need to lose weight...I need to lose weight..." she kept repeating over and over in her head.
"Jus' a taste," Carlo begged.
"I want to lose this," Abigail repeated tapping her stomach.
"Ok if you dow wanna' eat dis good spaghetti..." Carlo dipped his finger in the sauce then licked it, "but don' get too tin. Not nice for young girl. You need to show your..." Carlo caged both arms under his chest as though cradling his breasts.
"You rascal! I bet you wouldn't mind some..." she let the sentence linger in the air smiling coyly and moving her head sideways.

Carlo's eyes rested on her breasts. His laugh sounded like a growl. "You say someting?" he winked.

Abigail lowered her head and smiled knowing she had him where she wanted even if it meant using the back room from time to time. She had just won her most difficult battle by practicing self-control, one of many things she had never experienced before. It felt great. Handling Carlo was much easier by comparison. It could help her earn extra wages and allow her some free time to do the things she really wanted.

"Maybe…" she changed her voice to sound small and shy though inside she felt stronger than ever.

She'd decided to leave that part for later, give herself the extra time to dilute any leftovers of her ordeal. Only then would she deal with Carlo.

The smells would hit her nostrils the moment she'd enter the restaurant at nine sharp.

"Oh, shit… my stomach hurts," she'd rush to the bathroom sit on the toilet and repeat.

"I'm gonna make it… I'm gonna make it … I wanna lose weight…"

By the time she's return to the kitchen to pick up the orders her mind would switch from food to notions of thinness.

But it wasn't always easy.

"I've got to have some," Abigail devoured the cannelloni with her eyes.

She held the plate away from her face as far as possible repeating silently.

"I've got to lose weight… I'm strong… I'm strong…I can do it…"

"Here we go… enjoy your cannelloni," she smiled placing it in front of the customer.

"Mmm…this smells great! I'd like some extra Parmesan…"

Abigail felt like grabbing the plate and licking it clean. Her mouth filled with spit and she could actually taste the melted cheese and the softness of the pasta with her eyes.

"I'm strong… I can do it…I can do it…" repeating the silent mantra in her head.

"Here we go, sir… extra Parmesan."

Three months into her new job, Abigail stood in front of the mirror and stepped on the scale. She noticed the bagginess of her panties and the new hint of a waist. Sucking in air, she imagined herself wearing delicate lingerie or a bikini. She giggled.

"I'm gonna do it… I'm gonna do it…" she smiled at her thinning body.

The following day while serving platefuls of pastas Abigail found herself thinking about things that had nothing to do with food and at once realized she had stopped craving for it. Her mind, filled with dreams and hopes was busy elsewhere.

A month later Abigail smiled as she stood on the scale calculating she had shed forty-one pounds since her arrival. She was beginning to feel the rewards of her self-control and knew it was a matter of a few more months before being able to move ahead.

"Another twenty pounds to go…then I can do what I want," she spoke out loud staring at the mirror.

That night, in bed, she lay quietly with her eyes shut. She thought of the long trail she'd had to cross before achieving the strength she now felt. Taking control of her own self and her own body, made her feel more powerful than she'd ever felt before. She could now do anything she wanted. Climb as high as she wished. Go as far as her imagination stretched. She was now free, totally empowered by her own sense of accomplishment and the endless possibilities that lay ahead. She was in control of who she was, in control of herself, in control of Abigail.

She fell asleep that night totally fulfilled, smiling with content and comforted by the softness of teary droplets rolling down her cheeks.

The following day she told Carlo.

"I'm leaving early …"

"But is only two…"

"I need to be someplace… you'll manage…" she walked out.

It was one of the privileges she had demanded. Everything had its price.

Abigail enjoyed seeing how jealous Carlo had become, watching her narrowing waist against the shapely breasts.

"You find new boyfriend now, eh? Your body is…bellissimo… getting more pretty…" he moved his hands over her stomach where once was a mountain of flesh. "I like dis," he moaned moving his own heavy body to meet hers.

She began taking care of her hair, by now back to its original color, well trimmed and shiny. It had once hidden her bright eyes and was now held up in a simple bun.

"Is smelling good," Carlo liked the smell of her hair, even when she wore it up.

"What you don?"

"What's wrong?"

"Noting. You look pretty!"

Abigail smiled. Her hard work was finally beginning to pay off.

***

The special arrangement she had established with Carlo allowed her daily freedom as of mid-afternoon leaving ample time for her library visits. It was crucial she continue her tutelage guided by Ms. Nora Carlisle, the chief librarian she'd befriended on her first visit to the library. She had noticed the elegant way with which Ms. Nora moved swerving through air in a lady like fashion, her thin figure held proud and tall walking with a purpose to respond efficiently to everyone's questions.

"Excuse me," Abigail approached the oval desk surrounded by countless books.

"May I help you?" Nora looked up.

Abigail took in the small silver bun held fast by two elegant pins and the kind smile over the carved lips, and at once realized Nora could be very useful.

"I need to find books about Ivy League schools and universities," Abigail spoke softly.

"Let's see," Nora pointed to the different sections within the library.

Abigail assumed she had responded nicely to her out of pity, the same reason others always did. Pity made people act that way.

"Oh, that poor ugly thing," Abigail could imagine the words though she seldom actually heard them spoken.

She had learned to use it to her advantage and in Ms. Nora's case, even welcomed the pitiful look realizing it could be of enormous help to her.

"It's nice to see someone interested in such a topic," Nora had commented on their way to the various shelves scattered throughout the large room.

Abigail was quick to respond.

"I want to see my mom's school…and my dad's…"

"How nice of you to want to do that," Nora moved her head slightly as though approving Abigail's choice.

"I'm an orphan…I'd like to see where they went to school…"

Nora stopped in her tracks. Staring at Abigail with shiny eyes she said.

"I'm so sorry…I really am…I had no idea…"

"Yeah…well…"

"Do you come here often?"

"Actually…I'm new in town…only been here a short while…"

"Welcome to Chicago," Nora smiled.

"Thank you. You're kind," Abigail forced out the words.

"And you're a very nice young lady."

Abigail smiled shyly.

"I hope you'll frequent our library."

"I love books."

"That's wonderful. We encourage young people to read."
"Yeah… I know what you mean."
Nora smiled again.
"Do you live far from here?"
"No, not really."
They continued chatting until Nora excused herself.
"I'm so sorry… I'd love to continue our conversation but I've got to return to my desk. It was a real pleasure…and please, do stop by again…any time."
"I also enjoyed it…Ms. Nora," she looked at her tag and added quickly, "I'm sorry…I'm Abigail," she offered her hand.
"Nice to meet you, Abigail," Nora smiled broadly.
"I'd… I'd like to come again this week."
"Oh, that would be wonderful…"
"You see…I don't know anyone in town and it was so nice talking to you."
"Well, I'm glad. I dare say… would you like to join me for a nice cup of English tea?" Nora released a small giggle.
She hadn't planned on it but the girl was so pitiful looking and probably very lonely, one couldn't just stand around and not try and help her. At once she felt warm all over.
"I'd like that," Abigail grabbed the opportunity, "That would be nice."
"Yes, it would," Nora kept smiling.

The extraordinary relationship, that of a mentor and friend between the manipulative Abigail and the elegant Ms. Nora, soon developed into a tight bond with Abigail spending the weekend with the 59-year-old widow and former wife of Lord Carlisle who, several years earlier, had chosen to put a bullet through his head rather than sober up to life. His suicide had left the childless widow to fend for herself in the big city removed from her native country.

Nora, or Lady Carlisle, as was her formal name and title, was a qualified librarian born and bred in London until she'd moved with her husband to Chicago. Following his tragic ending, Nora was offered a full-time position in the public library.

Her chance meeting with Abigail had proved beneficial to both of them. The sophisticated Nora felt she could be of guidance to the poor girl and contribute to her upbringing. Abigail's compliance awakened within Nora suppressed maternal inclinations and infused her dull life with a new invigorating challenge. Over a cup of tea, only weeks after their initial meeting, Nora, who had come to appreciate Abigail's brightness of mind and had introduced her to the classics, commented.

"I would love to see you grow up to be a real lady."

"I'd like that," Abigail answered with a sincere smile, imitating Nora's intonation and softness of speech.

Abigail spent every spare moment in Nora's company, watching her move and laugh and converse in a manner only a true lady could appreciate. In turn, her days were now filled with a new purpose, as were Nora's. Going out of her way to give Abigail all the love and attention she had held back over long and lonely years, Nora seemed to blossom.

Besides Nora's daily company, Abigail began following the 'who's who' of society by flipping through fashion magazines and reading society columns with tidbits of informative gossip. It was important to get to know the faces involved in the social hubbub. She forced herself to learn new names, get acquainted with new places and social events, making mental notes of those who repeatedly appeared in charity balls, public affairs and various other high-profile gatherings.

Though brittle and coarse, at times, as a country maid, Abigail was clever enough to realize that the only way to get what she wanted was by changing her style and behavior. She had learned a lot from just sitting in fancy malls watching women pass by and following the various dressing styles. Noting the ways in which they spoke to each other, to the sales staff in the fancy stores and to the men who accompanied them, sharpened her sense of social mannerisms and helped her develop a keen sense of what and how to say and do. It was amazing how much she was able to pick up by just staring and making small mental observations.

The city of Chicago with its beautiful shopping malls and exclusive stores offered the most elegant luxury items money could buy. Displayed in front of her eyes like bountiful trays of riches waiting to be noticed and appreciated, Abigail absorbed the smallest of details and the finesse of each precious ornament. She collected important designer names, read all references pertaining to men's and women's fashions, looked closely at shirts, dresses, shoes, ties, cigarette lighters and wrist watches, registering the latest hairstyles, perfumes, jewelry, cars, and even cigars. She went on to expand on the arts and the latest exhibits and upcoming artists and theater shows and couldn't stop appreciating the bountiful riches around. Studious and well organized, she listed all her findings in her neat handwriting as if she were planning a shopping spree. It was a question of memorizing and learning how to recognize each and every item.

Sharp eyed and sensitive to her surroundings, Abigail understood how important it was to keep her dream alive by feeding it with added details and elaborations. Visualizing its outcome she imagined herself in beautiful surroundings wearing stunning gowns and courted by handsome men. In her dream she lived a glamorous life and was accepted by society's elite, people who were truly important and influential.

Nora's presence made it all the more interesting, shedding light on the small particulars, tiny detailed elements that made the final difference between a look-alike lady and a true-to-life lady in manners and in speech.

***

Determined and strong willed, Abigail concentrated her efforts on the daily tutelage drilled into her by Nora, and was soon amazed at the changes. She had come to new arrangements with Carlo, who had learned to appreciate the very capable waitress she had become, and allowed her to use her after work hours as she saw fit. Abigail was no longer bored, nor did she count every minute of every passing day. Rather, having begun noticing new things, she looked forward to learning as much as she could, absorbing the smallest voices and insights offered by Nora.

Her voracious appetite for reading enabled her to devour books and magazines related to and motivated by her new interests. Encouraged by her fast learning, Nora began tutoring Abigail in French, explaining the basics of a menu, and teaching her how best to make light conversation, paying attention to the small mannerisms that counted.

"French is the most important language, a language meant for socializing and making small talk…you know, getting ahead in society where it really counts… and it's the language of love…" Nora blushed.

Abigail responded with a shy smile.

"Don't worry," Nora spoke gently, "You'll see…there'll come a day when you, too, will find someone special. I know you will…and when it happens, I hope you'll remember my words…"

"I'll always remember you," Abigail responded, "and help you the way you've helped me, I'll never forget it…"

Nora placed her hand on Abigail's shoulder and shut her eyes briefly.

"French will come in handy. All you need are a few words and sentences. It's fun!"

Abigail took it very seriously. Standing in front of the mirror, she repeated the foreign words and watched her mouth as it moved to intone the proper accent.

It was amazing how sexy and coquettish words sounded in French.

Feeling as though she'd spent time abroad tasting and experiencing foreign lands, Abigail was ready to tackle her next goal. But deep inside, things remained the same and Abigail never failed to say her nightly prayers.

"I hope you rot in hell, Mommy and Daddy …and I can't wait to see you suffer, little Sis…"

Externally, though, she was able to hide it under layers of new masks; there were simply too many novelties that required many hours of practice.

Now that her figure was trimmed and defined to perfection, Abigail was forced to concentrate on her long bulbous nose, protruding ears and ugly twisted mouth even more so than before. She kept dreaming of another face. Beautiful women had no idea what life truly was for the likes of her. She would be happy to have Nora's features and the overall plainness of her face in exchange for her own twisted features.

Abigail, who had envied the simplicity of a normal face for so long, was now getting ready for her next big challenge, the one that would be the hardest of all.

It was time to make the move.

Recalling the name from a magazine article she'd recently read, she found the number and made an appointment.

The following day she decided to make a clean break that wouldn't require any explanations or tears. It was better that way, preventing any and all unpleasantness.

* * *

Her abrupt disappearance was as sharp as a butcher's knife, its incisiveness matching only her sudden arrival in Chicago some two-and-a-half-years earlier.

As was his habit, Carlo waited for her in the back room, wondering where she was. It was ten, and the regulars were already waiting for their morning cappuccinos and beers. He had called the apartment but had gotten a recording saying the line had been disconnected. Rushing over he found the place empty.

Abigail Gray had vanished overnight leaving the key on the gas range.

Carlo was stunned. After all, she'd worked with him for over two years, and by now he was used to the ugly girl, the one that drove him crazy in bed. She was willing to do anything he asked for and he'd gotten used to her. He even liked her. More than just liked her; he even thought of telling her so.

Now he stood empty handed, thinking she had cheated him, wondering what he'd done to deserve it.

Carlo returned to the restaurant depleted and frustrated as though he'd been robbed of something, but he couldn't quite figure out what exactly.

Pride never crossed his mind.

Shortly after Abigail's disappearance, Nora lost all interest in life as though someone had shot her through the heart. She became depressed and within a month was unable to get out of bed.

She died three months later, convinced Abigail had disappeared victimized by circumstances beyond her control.

CHAPTER 12

The tall building could easily be mistaken for a luxury hotel set in the midst of a well manicured park surrounded by lawns and gardens. Located in one of Chicago's plushest northern suburbs, it was heralded as one of the nation's best medical facilities with a newly added wing specializing in corrective surgeries related to craniofacial congenital malformations. Abigail again looked at the address then spotted the sign 'Northwestern Hospital Reconstructive Clinic'.

Stepping inside with a pounding heart Abigail knew it was her ticket to a better life.

She arrived ten minutes early and waited to be called in to consult with Dr. Feinwald, head of the department. He was a short and slimly built man with a good-hearted smile who welcomed her into his office.

Extending his hand he smiled at Abigail.

"Hi, I'm Joe Feinwald. Please take a seat," pointing to the recliner, "I'd like to hear your medical history before we start with assessments and measurements…"

Abigail had prepared herself for the long journey ahead. She'd read a lot about the procedures involved and the time it took to recover after each stage. It had been on her mind for so many years that it felt only natural to begin the ride of her life from its early stages. She knew what the process involved and was willing to dedicate an entire year to its completion. She was now strong enough to go through with it though anything shorter than a year would be welcome. Abigail shared with Dr. Feinwald the countless medical procedures and follow ups she'd been through and the hardships she'd endured since childhood growing up with her deformity.

Dr. Feinwald listened intently and asked few questions. He understood that Abigail's treatments were paid for by charity care and didn't include the aesthetic follow up procedures. Her congenital deformity was a classical case that distinguished between those who could and those who couldn't afford private medicine.

"Ok, now let's proceed with the measurements…"

Abigail knew by heart the key words of 'proportions' and 'symmetry' that defined beauty and could even recite the exact formula of facial ratios that underpinned it. It pointed to precise calculations that measured the distance between the various facial parts amounting to immaculate proportions of a classical divine looking face.

The old adage of 'beauty is in the eye of the beholder' infuriated her; she viewed it as a simpleminded cliché spoken lightly for the purpose of pacifying all.

Having grown up with the knowledge that she was ugly and therefore unloved, Abigail found herself in an emotional state that negated any notion that she could ever be loved by someone. It seemed that the two were looped together. Her acute mind was capable of processing the fact that, if she didn't love herself, she couldn't expect others to love her, but it was only in theory, a notion she could comprehend and rationalize only in her mind. But it wasn't a concept she could internalize emotionally. Nor could she translate what her mind understood into emotional understanding. She seemed to be torn between her mind and her emotions, separated by two very different spheres.

Dr. Feinwald used special instruments to scrutinize and measure every millimeter of Abigail's face under powerful lights. He checked her skin, which despite everything, was very smooth and clear with a porcelain-like complexion. It was ironical in a way given the rest of her oddly misplaced facial features. He checked her eyes, probed into her mouth, measured her teeth, looked closely at the gums, assessed every angle of every part of her face, peered inside her nostrils and ears, estimated every skin fold and even smiled at her dimple.

"Well, I think we can now sit and chat. Would you like something to drink?"

Abigail's eyes welled.

"It didn't hurt, did it?" Dr. Feinwald looked concerned.

Abigail didn't want to tell him it was his small gesture of kindness that made her tear up.

"No…oh no… sorry," she said then wiped her eyes.

"No need to apologize. I understand…you've been through a lot since birth."

He handed her a glass of water with a tissue box then smiled at her.

"You're lucky to have such beautiful eyes," he pointed to the side of her nose, "and this is a well structured angle…the frame of your face is very nice… the rest…well, it's mostly excessive scar tissues… " he explained what he meant by elaborating on the changes he'd planned.

"You see," he asked her to look in the mirror, "This skin fold is twisted sideways so it gives the impression of being part of the facial structure but it's only skin…yes, it's thickly layered skin… with a lot of scar tissue and there's a nerve crossing over here… and muscles with different layers of skin… but it's not something that requires an entire restructuring of your facial bones…they did a very fine job in both surgeries, really fine… so the structure is not the problem…it's mostly esthetic…the ear will need some extensive work," he pointed out to her with his finger and explained how it could all be done together.

After twenty-eight years of reshaping human faces to look prettier than what nature intended, Dr. Feinwald was well experienced with the likely outcome of each surgery. He'd estimated that Abigail's case was less severe than he'd initially thought. Surgery would undoubtedly prove satisfactory given her startling eyes and unblemished skin. He was also well acquainted with the psychological effects of pre and post-surgery, and had acquired the tools for handling even the most difficult of cases. From the minute she had entered the clinic, Abigail impressed him as being astute and very smart and psychologically ripe for the lengthy procedures awaiting her, in terms of having thought through the complex surgeries.

He then quoted her the price.

Abigail stared at him pitifully.

Though she could afford it, she insisted on paying less. It was another goal she'd set up in her mind to accomplish. She'd come to realize that the only way to advance in life was to cut short those who intended fixing things that belonged to others, be it other people's wants, other people's minds or even other people's faces, anything at all as long as it wasn't their own misshaped ills. By hesitating momentarily she'd found the perfect opportunity to make Dr. Feinwald feel pity for her and rethink his price.

"There's a lot of work that needs to be done here," he moved his fingers along her face pointing to specific elements as he detailed what needed slicing and stitching.

"But then I'll still need some work on my teeth…" she lowered her gaze.

Dr. Feinwald took a deep breath.

"Yes, you'll need to have some periodontic work done and consult with a specialist …but if you choose to go with Dr. Penn our own excellent periodontist across the hall from here, we could work out a deal …"

A small voice whispered in her head.

"Go for it!"

For the first time in her life Abigail found herself following instructions gleefully. They were Dr. Feinwald's, the finest plastic surgeon in Illinois.

Abigail consulted with Dr. Penn who explained that part of his work would involve procedures that intertwined with those of Dr. Feinwald's.

"Some minor work would have to be done prior to Dr. Feinwald's procedures and others later on. It's going to take a while but it won't involve major surgery…they did a good job aligning your teeth and jaws during your surgeries…really good…"

"Great! I can't wait for the miracle to happen."

Dr. Penn smiled when he heard Abigail's reaction. He liked her attitude.

Having read the brochure and inquired ahead of time about the facility, Abigail was able to negotiate well in advance the price for a prolonged stay at the clinic.

"We have a small place for our out-of-town patients… it's on a monthly basis so if you'd like we can arrange for you to stay there…"

Having followed Bill's advice and handled her savings carefully, the money that had been stashed in the account was now paying off and put to good use.

Abigail Gray had entered the clinic only to vanish forever behind its white doors.

* * *

Dr. Feinwald coordinated his efforts with Dr. Penn along with the teams of specialists each in his own area of expertise. Abigail found the physical pain easier to sustain than her emotional aches that tugged at her heart relentlessly. As she continued to wrestle with the demons of her previous life, Abigail's face was being reshaped to look very different from the way it was originally designed.

She had no idea what time it was. The room was partially dark with only the vital sign monitor dimly illuminated. She felt the need to pee. Moving her hand she pushed the button and the nurse appeared instantly.

"How are you feeling?"

Abigail couldn't speak. Her lips felt very swollen. She moved her finger and pointed to her mouth.

"Yes, they've taped it together but it'll soon come off. Can I get you something?"

Abigail pointed to her lower abdomen.

"D'you need to use the bathroom?"

Abigail couldn't get a sound out. Her eyes welled.

The nurse was quick to grasp. She dried her tears and placed a bed pan under her robe.

"You can use the pan for now…we don't want you out of bed … you might get dizzy… there'll be plenty of time as of tomorrow…"

After relieving herself the nurse cleaned her bed and changed her gown. It was then that Abigail began feeling a strong burning sensation as though her face was on fire scorched with live flames. She pointed to her face and looked at the nurse with pleading wet eyes.

"Do you need something for the pain?"

Abigail winked. It was so painful that all she could think of was sprinkling cold water over it. The nurse readjusted the ivy drips.

"You won't feel a thing in a moment."

They were the last words Abigail remembered.

She woke up the next day feeling all swollen and bloated. The nurse helped her to the bathroom but there was nothing recognizable when she saw her ballooned and partially bandaged face in the mirror.

"Remember Dr. Feinwald's words? You won't recognize yourself for the next few days… the swelling is totally normal but right now you need to rest and take care of yourself. It's gonna take a while…"

Abigail had prepared herself for a long recuperation period. She was just very anxious to see her face free of the swelling but knew it would take a long time. She took a deep breath. It was another test to prove her determination, one of the many tests she'd invented over the past two years.

After two weeks had gone by with most bandages removed, Abigail noticed a drastic change. The swelling had subsided considerably, though it was still very puffy in some places. Her teeth felt as though they'd been squeezed together and held firm by silver colored brackets cemented to them. She noticed her face was taking on a new shape with a changed volume.

It was uncomfortable and felt strange yet very fascinating to watch.

At one point her face resembled a war zone with wires, gauzes and tapes in various sizes, and a rich palette of colors dotting her face. There were black looking bruises all over edged with green and purple blotches. The size and shape of her mouth looked like a small croissant cut in half with short strips of tape glued over its different parts.

"How long will the tapes stay?" she pointed to her lips.

"Depends…" Dr. Feinwald replied.

"It looks so bad…what if the swelling stays?"

"It won't! I promise you'll love the end result!" the doctor repeated.

"Are you sure?"

"I'm sure. You really won't recognize your mouth…you see over here?" he pointed to an entire area of her face, "this was all covered by thick scar tissues but now it's all gone and the skin is healing beautifully…we've taken quite a lot off …"

Her fears spoke out in her dreams, as she imagined herself bloated and swollen with a nose larger than the one she had before with four ears attached to her head, and lips resembling those of a gorilla's.

"Once the swelling goes down… we'll be able to assess the entire procedures…" Dr. Feinwald smiled, knowing the final results would be superbly better than his wildest expectations.

* * *

Four months later Abigail came out of the clinic feeling as amazing as she now looked. They were the longest sixteen weeks of her life and the most expensive ones but they were worth it.

"Dr. Feinwald," she looked him in the eye after he'd finished checking her face for the last time, "I don't know what to say... I... thank you..." she couldn't control her tears.

Dr. Feinwald returned her hug.

"You're beautiful... amazingly beautiful...," he grinned.

She smiled and stared at her mirrored image gazing at the strikingly beautiful woman who smiled back at her.

Again she hugged him.

"Thank you... thank you so much," she held his hands in hers, bent her head and kissed them.

"No need for that... it's my profession."

She shot one last look at herself and smiled. It all seemed so incredible.

"It will take at least another six to eight months to heal completely," Dr. Feinwald said, "These scars will eventually disappear. Don't mind them," he pointed to different places on her face, "Meanwhile you can use make-up ...they won't be noticeable at all... and the puffiness will subside... it takes time..."

When Abigail saw Dr. Penn for the last time he handed her two custom-made clear aligners that fit over her teeth.

"I've given you an extra set...but don't forget to use it nightly... it must stay on your teeth for at least seven consecutive hours each night ...that way you'll be able to retain the alignment we did. You'll need to keep it up for a while...it's important..."

"Thank you Dr. Penn," Abigail was overwhelmed with happiness, "thank you for everything..."

Looking taller than she had ever seemed, given her added confidence, Abigail Gray left the clinic and headed to the airport.

Six hours later she landed in New York as Miss Carlene Ridge, daughter of the deceased Hugh R. Ridge, former British CEO of a large conglomerate.

CHAPTER 13

Finding the right residence was crucial. Insisting on the best money could buy, Carlene, once again, followed the advice of Bill McKinney who had jokingly told her how he would go about changing his identity if he ever wanted to disappear. They were at his office resting after some stormy love making and talking about Bill's fear of losing Kayla's financial support in case of a divorce.

"Maybe I should just disappear for a while… become somebody else and have some fun… remember the fire in Harlingen seven years ago? Well, this guy vanished… just disappeared like he'd never had a wife and kids… I know 'cause I was involved … but they never found him. I bet you he lives someplace else… probably having the time of his life… meanwhile his wife claimed the money from the insurance company and everyone's happy…" resting his hand on Abigail's thigh.

"What d'you mean vanished?"

"Gone. No trail. No history. Gone with the fire except there was no evidence he'd actually been in the fire."

"Neat! Never thought of that!"

"See… if I did that, Kayla wouldn't find me and I could just be a free man."

"But then you wouldn't have her money either, goon head!"

Bill laughed.

"Let's imagine you had to change your identity. What would you do first?"

"You'd need money to do it…" he went into a detailed elaboration.

Abigail had the money.

Now standing inside the beautiful apartment walking around the spacious rooms, she smiled.

"Do you know any of the other tenants?" she asked the real estate agent who kept staring at the beautiful face.

"I can assure you, Ms Ridge, they're first class and well respected…like yourself…" a long list of names followed.

"And is this the monthly rental price…plus expenses, of course?" Carlene pointed to the number that appeared on the rental contract.

"That's correct, Ms. Ridge."

Working out the details and calculating her money, Carlene decided to take the apartment for the duration of six months, allowing herself ample time to adjust and find what she was looking for.

Signing the contract freed her for the next step.

***

The first person she met in New York was Anita Maria Joree, named after her grandmother and nicknamed Margie, an attractive young woman who carried her long neck with pride, giving the impression of a queen in procession. Most notable, besides her well manicured red nails and manner of speech which resembled that of a parakeet pecking its seeds, was her ability to make things happen.

Carlene took an immediate liking to her. She'd encountered Margie during her first days in the city while visiting an art display at the Met. Reaching stardom and becoming part of the social élite was Carlene's ultimate goal but it was crucial to be introduced to its intricate pathways. Carlene noted how quietly Margie conducted herself allowing her presence to do the work. Medium height and slimly built with a near flat chest that gave the impression of a young girl, Margie moved among the giants of society with an elegance and stardom equal to theirs. When she spoke people listened, for she knew the ins and outs of society as one might know the way around one's own frame of mind. Margie was someone to be reckoned with, part of the crème de la crème of society and the magician who could make Carlene's wishes come true.

"Margie, dear… we're having a small dinner…week after next… the Mayor will be there, of course… and a senator or two … would you like to join?"

By knowing when and where to be seen, Margie was able to pass on the information to those she favored and pave the way into the parties and events that really mattered. Nicknamed a social queen, Margie took to Carlene like oil to fire and before long the two were inseparable. Carlene needed Margie for her knowhow and connections. Margie was captivated by Carlene's incredible beauty and intelligence and her willingness to accept her as a mentor.

Carlene began spending more time with Margie and was astonished to find out that, like herself, she too had left home at an early age. Relaxing somewhat, though never really letting herself be caught entirely off-guard, Carlene felt comfortable in Margie's company, having found a new person with whom she could share herself openly albeit with some reservations.

"Keep an eye on that tall blond…the one with the flowing Dior… she's very useful when it comes to organizing bodies for fundraising activities and that sort of thing…" Margie tipped off Carlene pointing to the ropes pulled by the various social puppeteers.

It was a fascinating rich world that promised to be profitable for those able to move fast in the right direction. The name of the game was 'watch and catch' with an overly bountiful number of hunters chasing after a goal named Fame. It was up to people like Margie to keep up the chase by padding its trail with an assortment of goodies.

***

Sharing their pasts was something Carlene and Margie did not do easily. Having learned from an early age not to trust anyone, it took them a while to find themselves seated in Margie's stunning apartment overlooking the park.

"So…you're definitely not a New Yorker," Margie exclaimed.
Carlene shot back.
"And where are you from?"
"I'm not into games, Carlene."
Carlene hesitated briefly.
"You're not gonna laugh, are you?" her voice somewhat defensive.
Margie waited patiently.
"I'm from the deep woods of Texas…a shit hole in hell."
"Why's that?"
"What if I told you it's where I've spent two years in a loony bin?" she waited for a reaction.
Margie burst out laughing.
"What for?"
"My Dad…he put me there …said it would do me good."
"What did your Mom say?"
"She was a nothing…scared of her own shadow. The kids were nasty to me and…anyway… my Sister and I…we had this thing, still do…we hated each other. My Mom always took sides …my sister's of course…"
They were quiet for a while.
"Good thing I didn't have a sister." Margie said.
"Why?"
"My Dad…he would have done the same to her…at least I got away …"
"What about your Mom?" Carlene reached for the cigarettes.
"She got away before I did…left me with the creep."
They drank their beers in silence.
"How did you end up here?"

"Long story," Margie took a deep puff, "I've done my share… two years behind fucking bars."

"What for?"

"Armed robbery."

"No shit!"

"Yep! In a fucking state penitentiary."

"I won't hold it against you."

Margie's smiled.

"Thanks."

She lit another cigarette and inhaled deeply.

"Let me tell you about my loony bin years," Carlene said, "But you've got to promise not to laugh. Promise! No… I won't tell you unless you promise!"

"Ok…ok…I promise."

"There was this cute assed male nurse called Bobby, a black guy with a jabber the size of an umbrella. No kidding. His pants looked like he was carrying a tank with him. This gal, Sue, she swore she'd seen it dangling to the floor. I was curious so I decided to see for myself. Bobby would always come in the morning to give us our drugs…yeah… he'd wheel this cart with cups full of pills. Three times a day they'd feed us this shit… fuck up our brains. So one day, when he came near me, I took a cup of water and splashed it on his face.

'What d'you do that for?!' he screamed.

"I was real scared… thought he'd call the head nurse but Bobby had that special look in his eyes, know what I mean?"

Margie giggled nervously and lit a fresh cigarette using the tiny butt left over from the last one.

"He had that look in his eyes… like he was undressing me, know what I mean? I dow know…men always look at me like that. So anyways… I looked back at him and said.

'I did it 'cause I want you to fuck me but I didn't know how to tell you.' I made it look like I was…you know, kind of shy…"

Margie roared.

"So what happened?"

"I told you not to laugh!" barely able to suppress her own smile.

"Ok...ok..." Margie puckered her lips displaying a serious face. "Go on..."

"So he smiled and moved closer until I felt his jabber on my thigh. Then he kind of ...winks and says.

'Wanna meet me there?' looking sideways.

'In the bathroom?' I ask.

'Yeah'

'Ok.'

"So I wait for him inside the stall. When he comes in I want to open his zipper but he slaps me."

'What d'you do that for?' I ask.

'Don't touch my stuff. I'll tell you when you can touch me.'

Margie couldn't help herself and rolled laughing. Carlene's face remained serious.

"He pulled down my panties and pushed his hand into me. I tried moving but he was so strong ... I couldn't. He kept turning his fucking hand inside and it hurt. He was done in two minutes. His face looked like he was going to faint with pleasure. That's when I reached over and unzipped his front and ...this huge thing, a long foam rubber just like the stuff we used for arts and crafts, it just flew out...sort of...jumped out like a spring. He was so stunned that he couldn't even move. He grabbed hold of my hair but someone had just opened the door and I ran out screaming for help."

They held their stomachs and laughed so hard that at one point Margie began sounding small sobbing sounds.

Later, Carlene went on.

"Bobby helped me get out of there," her voice softer than before.

Puffing on a fresh cigarette, she continued.

"I was waiting for the review committee. Bobby said he'd speak to my Dad but ...my Dad wouldn't listen so Bobby said I could walk out and he'd help me. I was fifteen when my Dad put me in there and I just wanted to get out so I ran away...and when they found me, a week later, they fired Bobby, said he'd messed up with a young girl. When I turned seventeen they released me but I didn't feel seventeen. I felt much older…"

"Oh fuck, Carlene… you're so fucking beautiful! How's that possible?! Don't you ever see yourself in the mirror?!"

She reached over and wiped Carlene's cheeks.

"My Dad was a piece of shit. He smelled so bad even the dogs ran away from him. Honest. We had this small house near Venice Missouri… wasn't much bigger than a barn. My Mom left when I was seven, came home one day and she was gone… so there was only me and my Dad. I don't remember when it started… but he messed up with me and stuff…" Margie's eyes misted over.

"He said we needed to stay together… that there was only him and me and that it was ok to hug him and be near him. I remember crying for my Mom but he said she's better off not being with us. Then one day he told me I had to dress real nice, he was going to take me out for dinner. We went to the local diner and he told me I could taste his beer. I was kind of sleepy by the time we got home and my head was spinning. I don't remember exactly what happened but when I woke up and saw the blood I cried. It was bad. It was real bad…couldn't move for a coupla' days…" Margie was silent for a long time before she went on.

"I was placed in a foster home. There were two other kids there and it was ok, I guess, but it didn't feel like home. I knew my Dad was locked up and I didn't have anyone else. He was my only family. I started lifting stuff from shops…small things…then more. After they caught me the foster family didn't want me back so I ended up with social services until they found me another home…then another …and when I was fourteen I teamed up with these kids, a group of losers. We were like a gang, you know. Social services moved me to a place for juveniles with problems. When I came out, three years later, I had nothing. No family other than my creepy Dad and I didn't wanna' see him… and no money. I met this real handsome guy. He didn't do much drugs but… enough to mess him up. He told me it wouldn't be risky and all I'd have to do is sit in the car and wait. So I sat. Didn't even see the police patrol… they came from behind. I told them I didn't know anything so the judge let me go but I was stupid and got involved again. I moved some stuff… when I got caught a second time I was thrown in the slammer for two years."

"What d'you mean you moved some stuff?" Carlene asked.

"White stuff…?" but when Carlene shook her head, Margie added.

"You're joking, right? Don't you do this?!"

Taking out a small package from a nearby drawer, Margie eyed Carlene.

"Nah! Never cared for that shit! I stay away from it! But go ahead…I don't mind."

"This is the ticket to everything you see here," Margie moved her arm to include the entire apartment.

Carlene seemed baffled.

"I thought the money was…"

"This is it!" Margie held up the small package, "There's nothing else that'll get you as much as this 'heavenly snow'…" she went on detailing the vast amounts made from dealing white powders and pills.

Probing further Carlene tried to calculate the huge amounts that could be made. It sounded too good to be true.

They stayed up the entire night talking and laughing and crying and being honest with each other as they had never been before.

But after that night they never spoke again about their pasts.

* * *

"We need to dress you up real pretty…and special," Margie called up Carlene the following day.

"Where and when?"

"I'll pick you up…there's this outlet…"

Carlene was stunned as they entered a hangar sized area filled with racks of clothes in every size, shape and color. The sheer size of the place was mind boggling.

"How… I don't… where…"

Margie giggled.

"I know… it's crazy, right? Well, we only need to look at evening gowns today so let's take the shortcut," she ploughed between the racks taking endless short cuts.

"Ok, this is it!" Margie announced, "Now let's look for a few nice gowns."

She walked ahead of Carlene crisscrossing countless racks with long, beautiful evening gowns in every conceivable color and cloth. Carlene kept touching the silky dresses adorned with trimmings and the richness of rhinestones. It was all like a dream, a confusing illusion.

"Here," Margie filled the basket with several gowns, "Let's go have fun and try them on."

Carlene was glad to have Margie at her side. The world around her was overflowing with riches and glowing in ways she'd never known before. It was good to have someone to share it with who knew the ins and outs of the things that counted.

At one point Carlene tried on a long gown in royal blue. Stepping out of the small cubicle and staring at the large mirror, she found herself encircled by several women all glaring at her.

"What d'you think?" she turned hesitantly to Margie.

"You still need to ask?!" one woman released sarcastically before moving away.

"Sold!" Margie smiled, "It's stunning!"

"I can't believe how beautiful this dress is," Carlene kept saying, "I've never seen such beautiful dresses…"

"Stick around and you'll see many more!" Margie chuckled.

Carlene mumbled.

"It's like…as if…I just can't…like it's been tailored especially for me…"

"What's wrong with you?!"Margie sounded angry, "I'd kill to have your body and face. Don't you ever **look** in the mirror?!" she turned around leaving Carlene in total disarray.

There were so many confusing images brewing inside Carlene's head. The physical transformation she'd undergone recently was only now beginning to seep in. But accepting it on an emotional level was harder. Her physical transformation was so swift and so extreme that she hadn't internalized it completely. Carlene had been struggling in her previous state for so long, that the change hadn't quite been absorbed. Her instinctive reaction to everyday situations and to anything that was said by anyone was still based on her innate reflexes prior to the surgery. Her mind was conditioned to function as before, thinking and acting the way it had been over many years. Surgery, for now at least, was merely a brand new and fabulously beautiful physical mask, one she would need to adjust to quickly.

But there was something else missing from the emotional healing process. Carlene didn't have anyone with whom to share her transformation, stand by and reflect her changed mask, a trusted person who could help her confront the outside world. She'd even kept it away from Bill careful not to unravel the changes she'd undergone. Nora was no longer in her life and she could only muse at the notion of Carlo seeing her new face. There wasn't a shred left of her past that could attest to her changed appearance, nothing to back up her terrible childhood and give her some perspective or comfort for the newness of her face. She was left totally to her own thoughts and conclusions.

Margie, who wasn't aware of Carlene's past, was angered by her friend's seemingly nonchalant reaction to the comments she received. How could someone as stunningly beautiful as Carlene act the way she did? Maybe it was Carlene's way of demanding constant attention and additional adulations but Margie was beginning to get fed up with it.

Following their shopping spree, Margie drove to a different part of town. Carlene gazed at the display window and let her imagination run loose. She saw herself in a crowded ballroom dressed in a long evening gown adorned with the diamond necklace and matching earrings that stared at her from Tiffany's display window. She planned one day to own them.

Margie was the one who kept track of things.

"You've got three months to make it or leave it," she told Carlene then went on to explain.

"When you land in a new place you need to catch on quickly or someone else will take your place. Know what I mean?"

Carlene was trying to learn as much and as fast as she could. She joined Margie to some of her social events but made sure to stay in the shadows sensing that Margie preferred it that way. The long hours spent with Nora proved worthy. Familiar by now with French dishes and wines and the bubbly chitchats and smooth conversations practiced by those worthy of them, Carlene became well acquainted not only with the latest fashions, restaurants, clubs, and gatherings but also with the men, those suitable for the likes of her. An eager learner, she was also quick to pick up Margie's techniques of moving white stuff. Things were done differently amongst the very wealthy: elegantly and discreetly.

"This can be your future…so don't overlook any detail…" Margie encouraged Carlene to take part in her exclusive circle of distribution.

"Besides, it's always more fun doing it with friends."

Margie kept stressing the importance of attending social events.

"But only those that matter."

"You really need to know the ropes here," she went on, "otherwise you can find yourself ousted faster than wind. Puff!" she clicked her middle finger against her thumb then went on. "Remember, once you're out, you're out for good!"

Cautious by nature and careful not to fall into unfamiliar entrapments, Carlene stepped slowly and hesitantly. The most important element was the social bonding and getting to know the who's who.

The day following each event she'd list the names of the people she'd met, adding personal details pertaining to each one. It was fascinating how eager people were to talk about themselves. All Carlene had to do was learn how to probe and ask the right questions. People wanted their stories to be heard if only to distinguish themselves from others. Carlene's sharp memory enabled her to register the smallest of details then note them in her diary. It was amazing how descriptive people were, releasing long trails with unique details without giving it a second thought. One only needed to listen attentively in order to gather information. Carlene's lists were growing longer by the day as she added nicknames, birth dates, favorite colors, past places of residence, additional family members, childhood anecdotes, past incidences, and on, and on.

Shortly after joining Margie, though still somewhat hesitant, Carlene was well on her way to establishing herself as an independent distributor for those willing to pay her prices. She never asked for Margie's permission. She simply acted as per her temperament. Her personality had remained the same as before though she'd gained self-confidence to match her beautiful new mask. She no longer wasted her days crying over her ugliness. Her days looked beautiful and full of newness and the further she moved from her surgery, the less she thought back on it. Her ugly face was stashed deep inside her memories, condensed into the curlicues of her childhood reminiscences. She wanted them locked up with a key and lost forever.

But there was one basic fact that Carlene failed to recognize: no one can escape their own past. People can only change their future if they take the time to acknowledge their past and react differently in the present.

Proclaiming herself as the best dealer in the city, Carlene preached the proverb.

"What you get is only as good as its price."

Then she upped her prices. Considerably.

Carlene's extraordinary beauty went a long way.

The two remained friendly, but Carlene was beginning to distance herself from Margie realizing the dangers involved in peddling powders with another person.

"I can't trust anyone... not even Margie... I better do this on my own..."

Margie, who up until three months ago had moved around with confidence, was beginning to wonder who Carlene Ridge really was.

"That fucking beauty! At least I know about her past... in case she ever tries anything..."

They kept up their friendship but didn't lose their wariness of each other.

* * *

With time ticking fast and her mind set on reaching her next goal, Carlene organized her daily routines in a way that enabled her to attend all the important galas and parties in town. It wasn't an easy task showing up uninvited to any glamorous gathering but was easier by far for a beautiful woman such as herself. Keeping a close tab on the social activities, she decided to take the plunge on her own and attend an event in one of the city's prestigious private clubs. Choosing the perfect gown from the several purchased with Margie, was a fun and easy task.

Entering the club Carlene smiled at the doorman.

"How are you?" she touched his shoulder lightly with her fingers.

Fitted to perfection over her shapely figure, Carlene's silhouette in royal blue proved a stunning sight turning her azure-colored eyes into a breathtaking ocean. Convinced he'd been touched by a movie star, the stupefied doorman failed to ask for the invitation. Once inside Carlene looked around. No one could have imagined the fast beats of her heart. Remembering Nora's instructions, she took a deep breath and brushed against the first man who came her way.

"Oh… I'm so sorry…"

"Not at all… my pleasure. Allow me," he signaled to the waiter and took two glasses off his tray.

"Dan Sharp," he handed her a glass and smiled waiting to hear her name.

"Carlene Ridge. I'm new in town."

Operating smoothly, it took her less than two hours to make the rounds and be introduced to everyone. It was the art of mingling; those small maneuvers and senseless words that force a person's attention to the speaker rather than to the words spoken. Though Nora's teachings didn't name it "social climbing" it was now Carlene's goal, which she practiced daily by manipulating her mesmerizing looks to her advantage. It didn't take her long to reach its summit and get the attention she craved.

Within four months of her arrival in New York, Carlene Ridge had met all the eligible bachelors in town that were of interest to her. She knew their names and catalogued them in her mind according to their potential bank accounts. Bubbly and charming, Carlene was soon at the center of Manhattan's affluent society.

Assuming the identity of a rich daughter born and raised by a now deceased British father, Carlene was able to spin tales about her growing up days spent in schools around the globe.

It was time to claim her trophy.

* * *

Of all the names frequently mentioned in the various society magazines, Prof. Dr. Glen Wilmore's was by far the most attractive, if only for the fact that he was much older than her and looked totally harmless.

"It'll be a piece of cake," she told herself.

Carlene's choice of the famed Prof. Dr. Glen Wilmore was only partially due to her wish to live a life free of financial burdens and limitations. Having spent two years at Cedars Home, Carlene's pick was sure proof of poetic justice at its best. With New York's finest psychiatrist as her husband, she'd secure her position as someone sane and free of any emotional turbulence, as though the marriage could attest to her emotional stability and well-being.

Detailed and methodical, she set out to acquire the heart and bank account of her future husband.

She had mentioned his name casually to one of her acquaintances, a society hen by the name of Denise who was only too happy to hear that the beautiful Carlene Ridge had found Prof. Dr. Glen Wilmore, her own husband's caring psychiatrist, an attractive man.

The very next day Denise called up Glen.

* * *

Though the two continued speaking on a daily basis and even joked with each other about men and romances, Carlene's free time was now dedicated to Glen. Margie felt let down by the friend she'd taken to heart. After all, she'd entrusted her with the secrets of the trade and had been hoping Carlene would eventually replace the family she'd never known. So how could Carlene neglect her now? They had been best of friends until Carlene had turned her interest to someone else.

Jealousy mingled with a strong sense of disappointment fed into Margie's frustration. Carlene owed her. How could she be so ungrateful and neglect the one person who taught her all the tricks of the trade?! Margie's head and heart were filled with a deep sense of loss and mistrust touching on a feel of betrayal. Losing Carlene to Glen was like losing, once again, the one true friend she had only recently found. It wasn't meant to happen. Margie went as far as blaming Carlene for choosing the wrong side and being ungrateful.

"But I thought you wanted me to meet someone…it doesn't mean I'll stop being your friend," Carlene tried soothing her.

"You know darn well what's gonna happen, so don't try your games on me."

"What's wrong with you?!"

"As if you care!"

"Your choice, Margie."

"You're fucked up, Carlene Ridge!"

It was then that Carlene was glad she hadn't revealed her true identity to Margie. It only strengthened her cautious behavior.

She could never trust anyone again. Never.

***

Three weeks later and well into her hot relationship with the famed doctor, Carlene showed up at the Nostrums' grand mansion in the Hamptons with Glen at her side. It was a noisy event, with a large crowd of guests enjoying the poolside and sprawling gardens of the estate. Sipping her favorite drink Carlene spotted Margie at the far corner of the pool wearing a stunning dress in bright reds and pinks. Moving closer to Glen, she whispered in his ear.

"Presch...I'd like to circulate some. Don't run away... I'll be right back."

Glen beamed and kissed her cheek.

Carlene headed in Margie's direction but was interrupted on the way.

"How are you, Carlene? You look radiant with that gorgeous hat. Where did you get it?" one of the social peddlers who never missed a party, moved her cheeks to meet Carlene's in mid-air.

"I'm fine, thanks ...and yourself?" Carlene smiled and hurried on but by then Margie had disappeared. Carlene looked around. Scouting the entire grounds and past the covered porch, she decided to enter the house with the hope of finding Margie.

Entering the large foyer her eyes stared at the marbled checkered floor in black and white with the stunning décor and opulence of its interior. Straight ahead was a large room that looked inviting. As she crossed its wide double doors Carlene came face to face with a wall-sized tapestry in heavy burgundy and winter greens depicting a hunting scene.

"Someday I'll own one just like this," she thought admiringly recalling some of the paintings Nora had shown her.

Mesmerized, her eyes surveyed the heavy furniture all around and oil paintings that stared at her from the walls.

"Is Renoir," the voice behind her sounded.

Carlene turned around meeting a smiley looking face of a rather short bald man. His finger was pointing at a painting.

She extended her hand.

"Jean Nuellic for your servis," he said with a slight bow, kissing her outstretched hand.

"Carlene Ridge," she answered adding a wide smile.

"More bootiful dan de picture."

"Mercie."

"French?"

"No… mais … juste un petit peu…"

"You like French, yes?"

Carlene let out a coquettish giggle like the one she'd practiced under Nora's tutelage.

Walking around the room appreciating its marveled beauty, Carlene felt like a grand dame being escorted through a museum.

"Anoder drink, perhaps?"

"Perhaps later, thank you. I need to find a friend."

"Avec plaisir, madam," he bowed again.

Carlene enjoyed the company of foreigners, hearing different languages and being treated like a lady. French men, in particular, seemed to know the secret paths to a woman's hidden wishes and heart.

Returning to the foyer and choosing another corridor Carlene found herself inside a library room. Covering its walls were countless mahogany shelves well packed with leathered books in all sizes.

The sight took away Carlene's breath. Moving slowly, she touched the books and breathed in the scent of the spectacular volumes exhibited in front of her.

Nora's image sprang to life.

"Oh... the smell... the delicious smell of books...you should see me now...in my dress...with Glen..." Carlene giggled at the mere thought. "You'd be proud of me, Nora darling. I haven't forgotten anything you've taught me... you wouldn't recognize me if you saw me now..."

She heard a faint swish and caught a glimpse of the unmistakable dress as it turned the corner to her left then disappeared swiftly behind a tall shelf of books. She followed silently and reached its end. Margie, who had just emptied a wallet, threw it on the floor and was about to head for the door.

"What a surprise!" Carlene came face to face with her.

Like a cornered bird unable to move or twit, Margie waited for the snake's bite.

"How much did you get this time?" she stared at Margie's chest where the money had been stashed.

Too stunned for words, Margie simply stared back at Carlene.

Not a word was spoken between them until much later, after Carlene had returned home. Picking up the phone she smiled then forced herself to sound serious.

"Hi Margie."

"Hi."

Carlene waited for the effect to seep in. When the silence became too heavy she went on in a decisive tone.

"I have a favor to ask. I'd like you to back me up on something."

"What do you want, Carlene?"

"I've just returned from my outing with Glen. I told him I couldn't meet him tomorrow because I've already promised to go shopping with you."

"I'm busy tomorrow."

"Fine by me. I only need for you to back-up my story."

"Go to hell, Carlene!" she cut her off.

Carlene burst out laughing. Picking up the phone, she re-dialed then waited patiently for the answering machine to pick up. Using her sweetest voice she said:

"Margie, pick up the phone …I know you're there…you leave me no choice but to tell the Nostrums about the sad affair in the library…"

"What do you want, Carlene?!" Margie cut the silence.

"Just like I said…I want you to back me up,"

"If you think you can black mail me…"

"Of course I can! And that's precisely what I intend doing, Margie dear."

Margie was silent.

"Now! Am I going to get some cooperation?!"

Margie remained silent.

"Damn it Margie! I expect a reply!"

"I'll back you up… bitch…"

That day marked the beginning of Margie's altered status as Carlene's puppet. Pulling the strings, Carlene forced Margie to serve as her permanent alibi every time she needed one. With their roles now reversed, Carlene was able to maneuver Margie into the very same spot she herself had occupied only months earlier.

* * *

It took Margie only a couple of months to pack up and move away from Carlene's reach. Interestingly, she had chosen Texas as her retreat, as if wishing to retain the memory of the Texan friend she had left behind. The once inseparable friends had become silent enemies with Carlene's threatening hand pointing at Margie's head.

Within a month of her arrival in Dallas, Margie was able to secure herself a position much like the one she had occupied in New York thanks to her previously established contacts.

Carlene, who by then had already conquered Glen's heart and married him, kept in touch, demanding Margie's assistance whenever the situation called for it.

Despite her new status as the wife of the famed Doctor, Carlene remained cautious. She refused to neglect her thriving business, rationalizing that one could never predict the future. Things happened and circumstances changed. People could easily find themselves in needy situations due to unexpected events. Having experienced hardships throughout her earlier life and remembering only too well the bitter taste of a penniless existence, Carlene decided to open a separate bank account under her birth name. Her well-earned money would allow her peace of mind and a sense of security regardless of what the future might bring.

But as much as Carlene tried to change her old way of thinking, most parts of her remained the same. It was impossible to rid herself of the emotions that brewed within or hide her thoughts. Deep inside she remained the cautious little girl she'd always been, forever wary and suspicious of being found out. Life for Carlene was as tedious and as lonely as it had always been for little Abigail. She couldn't let go of anything that might endanger her position, never able to trust another soul. Now, more than ever, it was crucial for her to keep her small business all to herself. Glen could never know about it, though he willingly and gleefully took part in Margie's wild parties. But that was in the past. Glen would never approve of such conduct now that she was his wife.

CHAPTER 14

"Do you have a moment?" Glen was standing in the entrance to Kalb's office.

"Sure…come in, come in."

Their offices, located at two ends of a shared corridor, served as a junction between the Medical School and the Psychology Department. Similar in size and shape, they both enjoyed identical views of old oaks and maples surrounded by luscious lawns.

Kalb looked at Glen and forced a smile.

"So…how's Carlene? I haven't seen her around lately."

Glen looked tired and distraught.

"Well… actually… not too well," his voice cracked.

Kalb didn't know how to react. Reaching into his desk drawer, he pulled out a flask then got up and poured a glass for Glen and a smaller one for himself.

"Doctor's orders," he placed the drink in front of Glen.

"It's bad, Kalb… it's bad."

Glen took a large gulp.

"Why don't you start from the beginning?" Kalb asked gently.

"Beginning? There was nothing at the beginning. Now it's there all the time."

Glen kept drinking. Kalb kept his eyes on Glen.

"I can't do it…I can't do it with her."

Kalb wasn't sure he had understood.

"You mean…you can't …"

"I can't fuck my own wife!"

Kalb re-filled his glass.

"Have you gone to a sex…"

"It's me…ME…not her. I'm the fucked up one."

"I see…"

"I tried to ignore it…" His voice was choky, barely a whisper. "She doesn't say anything…but I feel I'm losing her… I love her, Kalb, and I know she loves me. It's just that…I can't…I can't do it…"

Kalb was lost for words.

"Have you considered seeing someone? Dean Klein is a top…"

"No, no. I can't do that. I can't go to anyone."

"But impotence is curable in many cases…come on, Glen… you of all people…"

Glen shot him a strange look.

"It's not impotence. It's that…it's that …I can't do it…"

"Why?"

"Because of her…"

"What do you mean?" Kalb was confused.

"She's seeing someone…I can't think of her with someone else… she's hiding it from me…"

Kalb felt hot all over.

"Are you sure?"

"Yes… I'm sure."

Kalb moved uncomfortably in his chair. Too overwhelmed to respond, he listened to Glen's words as though from a distance.

"Can you maybe…maybe…talk to her…make her understand…?"

"Make her understand what, Glen?"

"That she's hurting me…" he choked on his words.

"It's really not… Glen…I don't think it's fair…"

"But you're the best shrink… I trust you…"

Kalb took a deep breath then cleared his throat.

"I really don't think it's…."

"I consider you as a friend…my trusted friend…"

"So let me get this straight: you'd like me to talk to Carlene! Any suggestions?"

"You know her …you've spent time with her… she'll listen to you… I'm sure…"

Kalb took a long sip. He couldn't begin to imagine what it would be like to try and talk to Carlene on behalf of Glen. He had seen her only the week before at Tony's with the other staff members, and had smelled her familiar perfume when she offered him her cheek. How could he now turn to her with a message from her husband? It meant, once again, playing a game behind Glen's back and carrying on the charade. But then…he owed it to Glen…he simply had no choice.

"Ok…if you're absolutely sure that's what you want."

"Yes, would I ask you if I wasn't?!"

"When would you like me to meet her?"

"As soon as possible. I'm leaving for a conference the day after tomorrow."

"Is tonight too soon?"

"No, it's fine. Today's…" looking at his wrist watch he added, "it's Monday. She should be home."

Kalb felt confused and overwhelmed.

Needing to think things over, he remained seated long after Glen had left his room.

Later on that day Kalb called her up.

"How are you, Carlene?"

With hand over his tightly shut eyes, Kalb tried to visualize the beautiful face at the other end of the line.

"Well, well…what a surprise!"

"How have you been, Carlene?"

"I've said my last word to you!"

She hung up.

Clearing his throat as if preparing for a long speech, Kalb redialed the number.

"Glen knows about us," he spat out quickly wanting to catch her attention.

He did.

"What the hell are you talking about?"

"Meet me tonight and I'll tell you."

"Is this your way of coercing me to meet with you?"

"I've got a message from Glen which I'm sure will interest you."

Carlene was silent.

"Carlene? Are you there?"

She took her time before replying.

"This better be for real."

"It is."

"Ok. Where and when?"

"Tonight… my place at seven."

"I'll be there."

Dressed in his customary casuals, denims and a white designer T-shirt wearing tanned loafers, Kalb glanced at his wristwatch then hurried, once more, to the mirror, eyeing the silvery crew cut and clean-shaven face. Moving his head sideways, he brushed the back of his hand in a masculine gesture over his shaved cheeks.

It was now 7.15 p.m. Kalb took a deep breath and answered the doorbell. Standing in the doorway wearing a light coat was Carlene.

"Nice to see you again," he moved towards her cheek.

She turned her head and met his lips.

Still pained and too stunned to move, Kalb complied. Using her special voice Carlene whispered.

"Aren't you going to invite me in?"

"Sure…come in …" he felt embarrassed and somewhat giddy.

"Can I take your coat?"

"No…I'm fine."

She stepped inside.

"A drink?"

"Sure. Make it large."

Kalb was confused. Walking in the direction of the bar he tried to understand Carlene's unexpected move.

"So...how are you?" he turned around holding both glasses.

Carlene stepped forward, opened her coat and dropped it to the floor.

She wasn't wearing anything under it.

Kalb's initial shock at seeing her naked body was soon replaced by the familiar and uncontrollable passion.

"Oh...Carlene...I've missed you..." his hands searched her body.

Blinded by ardor and an uncontrollable fervor, they found themselves on the thick carpet next to the love seat tearing into each other frantically as if wanting to make up for lost time. Mounted over Kalb's strong body, Carlene stared into his now darkened eyes.

"Touch me, Kalb...I want to feel you... I want you..." her tongue roamed his body.

His head was swooning. Carlene moved lower, circling his nipples with the tip of her tongue nibbling all around and pecking plumes like a budgie. Kalb felt he was about to explode. Her light hands moved teasingly up and down, reaching his ribs and the masculine curve below. Feeling a strong urge, Kalb embraced her as she moved herself to meet his yearning body.

"Kalb...I want you...Kalb..." Carlene called out just before her body shuddered.

They held each other tight.

Afraid to open his eyes and find himself in a dream, Kalb lay still, trying to relax his breathing.

"Why did you walk out on me?" Kalb asked softly.

They were sprawled on the rug, still warm from their stormy lovemaking.

"I was scared...scared of having my emotions out of control."

"I still love you, Carlene," he kissed her gently.

"Let's' change the subject..." she replied.

"Why?"

"Because I want to hear about Glen."

With the sharp pain of loneliness still fresh in his mind, Kalb didn't dare argue, fearful of loosing, once more, the softness of her touch.

"Glen knows about us."

"What does he know?"

"That you're seeing someone."

"That's it?!"

"Isn't it enough?"

"And how do you know about it?"

"He came into my office today and asked that I speak to you… he's in bad shape, Carlene, he's hurting real bad."

"What d'you mean?"

"Don't you realize what this is doing to him?!"

"But he hasn't said a word to me!"

Kalb had thought about it earlier. It occurred to him that perhaps Glen had wanted Kalb to know that he had found out about him and Carlene. Maybe it was his way of telling Kalb to let go of Carlene. But the more he thought about it the less it made sense. After all, he and Carlene had stopped seeing each other three months ago, which meant that Carlene was seeing someone else now.

In some ways it was easier and took the load off his conscience. He hated having to lie to Glen and pretend that Carlene was just a casual friend. Hell, it drove him crazy and nearly messed him up. But would Carlene be truthful and tell him if she was seeing someone else? His head was making him dizzy. What kind of nonsense was he thinking about? Of course she'd never confess to him. Why would she? It wasn't as though he and Carlene were a real twosome; what they had lasted only two months, the two most incredible months of his life. No, it was no use; she was just using him again. She wasn't interested in him; she just wanted to hear Glen's message and he, Kalb, happened to be the messenger…only the messenger…

Kalb's head was swirling with thoughts and assumptions.

Looking at Carlene he tried to guess what lay deep inside behind those beautiful eyes of hers.

"I wish I could trust her," the painful thought shot through his mind, "I just want to hear her say that she cares about me… just for once…"

Carlene smiled. Kalb placed his hands on both sides of her face and kissed her eyes. He knew it wouldn't matter if he asked her about it. She'd never tell him and even if she did say something, it wouldn't be the truth. That was the part that bothered him, and yet… it was the very same part that took his breath away. Carlene was so… so elusive and unpredictable, captivating and evasive. One moment he'd feel she was his and the next… she'd refuse to acknowledge his existence. He couldn't even think about it, he'd have to pretend and go along with whatever she was willing to dole out, he'd be forced to be satisfied with morsels or tiny crumbs, anything was better than being out of her life altogether.

Looking at her, he said.

"Don't you know husbands are the last to know?"

"Still…I would have expected him to at least mention it to me."

"I didn't know you were **that** close!" he released sarcastically.

Carlene smiled.

"Well…you'd be surprised."

"Am I missing something?"

"It's just…well… I wonder why he chose to tell **you** about it…"

"I was wondering about that myself."

Kalb tried to understand the situation, but the more he turned it in his mind, the more confused he became.

Carlene seemed as if she couldn't care less one way or the other, leaving Kalb to his own thoughts and conclusions.

"So…how's life treating you?" he asked after a long silence.

"I'm ok…how 'bout you?"

"Miserable. I've missed you…" he hated himself for choking on his words, but couldn't help it. How many times had he lay in bed saying those words out loud as if by mouthing them she'd hear him and come back? He'd promised himself that he wouldn't say it to her again, but the agony of being away from her…it hurt so much… why couldn't she love him? Why?!

Kalb put his hand over his mouth and coughed again.

"You'll get over it," Carlene tapped his back lightly.

Kalb knew Carlene couldn't be trusted. He'd heard her lies and witnessed her manipulations and sudden irrational outbursts of anger but he still loved her despite everything. As he lay still next to her nakedness trying to imagine what it would be like without her touching his face, his chest, his craving body, he dreaded the awful pain. Maybe he should try to do something…follow his plan…it might work…at least it would make him feel better…but it had to be done slowly…and he needed to sound casual… very casual…

"I thought about you last night," he said.

"Mmmm,"

"Funny…I remembered a story you once told me…something to do with your school in LA …"

"Mmmm"

"And I couldn't remember the name of the school…"

"Greenhill?"

"Yeah…that's it…strange how some things get stuck…got me thinking about all the traveling you did in different places …"

"Ok…I've got to leave," and she was out of the apartment faster than Kalb could think of an excuse to keep her there.

Any excuse other than the fact that he was still very much in love with her.

* * *

Now all alone, having kissed Carlene good night and seen her to her car, Kalb sat up thinking about what he had recently come to understand. Piecing together the information he concluded Carlene was now seeing someone else.

But why not admit it? Why did she pretend to still care about him? And why make love and pretend to enjoy it? Maybe…just maybe…she did love him… obviously she had someone else but … maybe she still loved him. But did she? Carlene loved flaunting her adventures even in front of Glen. Maybe Glen didn't care but … it hurt… it hurt so much….

Shutting his eyes Kalb covered his face with both hands letting his mind churn over the endless possibilities. If felt like a dagger inside his heart, but he was determined to get to the truth. He wondered what it was that Carlene had hoped to gain by jumping into his arms again. After all, there was no need for it now, not after the way they had parted.

The more Kalb thought about it, the more confused he became and the more illogical things seemed. It was obvious Carlene was hiding things not only from Glen but also from him.

Taking a long gulp from his fresh drink and writing down the name of her school, Kalb made up his mind to find out everything there was to know about Carlene Ridge.

Wearing a long chiffon gown in light skinned beige, Carlene's divine figure floated amongst the guests with an air only a goddess could exude. Nearing Glen in his impressive tuxedo and green sash, she hooked her arm into his and dazzled the ring of scholars who stood utterly transfixed staring at the divine image fronting their eyes.

"But that's still within our jurisdiction…." Glen raised his voice as he argued a frivolous point.

Standing to the side sipping a drink, Kalb watched the glamorous beauty and registered the piercing eyes that roamed her silky shoulders. Oblivious to everyone's presence, Glen kept lecturing to the polished marbled floor with his hands flailing sideways. Dangling in his left hand was a large shrimp hooked into a toothpick splattering pink sauce all around.

Within minutes Carlene detached herself from Glen and was now scouting the crowded room. Saul Rose, a senior lecturer in psychology who was famed for his sharp-tongue and concubine conquests, smiled at Carlene.

"You've got quite a place here," he looked up at the walls decorated with original paintings.

"Mmmm"

"Which do you like most?" his hand moved in a wide circle to include the entire room, "the modern or the classics?"

"Mmmm"

He moved closer.

"May I guess what mmmm means?"

"Be my guest." Carlene returned his smile.

"What d'you say to that, Glen?" the deep voice trumpeted in Glen's direction.

"I'd say we need to change the definition, get the legislator to agree to redefine sanity, have them approve …."

Saul Rose raised his voice.

"Glen! Your wife here said I could be her guest," his tallness staring down at Glen.

Too pre-occupied with his thoughts Glen ploughed on.

"…so as the situation now stands, it would virtually be impossible to render someone insane unless proven…" Glen's left arm flew up into the air unleashing the shrimp and sprinkling its pinking sauce all around.

"Wilmore!" Robert Danziger, a sought-after guest in New York's most fashionable circles, and a Professor Emeritus of Harvard, called out.

Kalb bit his lip as he watched Danziger.

An elegant man in his late sixties wearing a black tux and tie, the distinguished professor stood with his mouth slightly open staring through lenses smeared with cocktail sauce unaware of the crustacean that landed on his head. Glen's eyes were now leveled with Danziger's. It seemed to Kalb that although Glen was staring straight ahead, he didn't really notice Danziger. Glen's fingers touched his own right eyebrow. With his gaze still on Danziger he plucked off something, stared at it then proceeded to pluck another.

Carlene's face reflected shock. Moving quickly in Glen's direction she whispered something in his ear.

"Sorry… sorry… I must have forgotten myself…shall we drink to sanity?" Glen called out.

There was momentary laughter all around.

Carlene eased her way over to Robert Danziger who remained totally flabbergasted. Now next to him, she motioned to a uniformed man who hurried over with a white serving towel draped over his arm and began cleaning off Danziger's mess.

"I don't know how you did it, Glen… but I've got to hand it to you…" someone remarked loudly.

"I say… I say! Chop that hand!"

More laughs.

"I'm good at working wonders with my hands, right darling?"

Kalb watched Carlene's steely eyes.

"Only when you aim!" her voice razor-sharp.

The roar was louder.

"You should see me…" Glen went on but the group had already turned to face Carlene who kept tracing her upper lip with her tongue.

With the vision of last year's anniversary celebration still fresh in his mind, Kalb now realized that Glen was totally helpless when it came to Carlene despite his incredible brilliance, or perhaps because of it.

Comprehending Glen's predicament yet still vacillating over his own, Kalb tried to figure out the situation.

Once back in his apartment, he dialed Carlene's number but got the answering machine and hung up. A moment later he reconsidered and redialed.

"Hi Carlene, it's Kalb…please return my call as soon as you get this message. Thanks."

* * *

Shortly after he'd stormed out of Kalb's office suspecting that Carlene had not kept to their agreement, Glen hurried back home feeling hurt and dejected. He found Carlene in bed, still asleep. Moving closer he crouched beside her and lay his head down on the pillow next to hers.

"Hi Presch," she snuggled into him, "Thought you were at work…what time is it?"

Taking Glen's hand, she placed it on her breast.

"I missed you …so I came home."

Carlene stretched her body.

"Then let's not waste time," she moved her hand to his crotch.

"Honey…we need to talk about something." Glen moved her hand away.

Carlene was at once fully awakened.

"What about, Presch?"

"Remember our agreement?"

"I've never let you down, have I?"

"Are you seeing someone?" his eyes misty.

"How can you even ask me such a question?!" Carlene burst out crying. "Don't you trust me? I love you…" she sobbed.

"I'm sorry…I'm sorry…it's …sorry… I love you, Carlene. I really love you."

"I know that…"

"Would you tell me …if…if you…?"

"I wouldn't do it to you, Presch…"

"We promised each other…"

"And I'm yours forever," Carlene cried harder, remembering the pre-nuptial agreement she had signed, promising to stay faithful as part of the overall deal.

She had no intention of falling off the ladder she had worked so hard to climb. Speaking slowly, she began to mouth out the words Glen loved to hear while placing her hand over his flat crotch waiting for its momentary awakening.

Glen's sexual encounters were unlike anything Carlene had known before. He seldom ejaculated. Rather, he seemed to enjoy mere teasing. He loved to hear Carlene use crude words, run him down as a piece of shit, slap and spank him, enforce light physical pain on him, brush his lower body with a peacock feather that would drive him insane, stick plaster on his hairy chest and remove it slowly, oddities she'd never known with others. But sometimes she could get him to cum immediately. He liked the messiness of body fluids, the feel of spit and the smell of blood. Nothing repulsed him. He could get a hard cock from smelling her armpit or sniffing her dirty underwear. He was unpredictable in his sexual desires as he was in his everyday conduct.

Now after he had been satisfied in his own weird way, Carlene asked.

"Presch, are you still upset with me?"

"Not anymore."

"I love you," she kissed him.

"You know I don't mind some things… as long as you keep to our agreement."

"I always have!"

"And you know I enjoy hearing you tell me about…"

"I know, Presch. Would you like me to tell you again?"

He smiled.

"I'll tell you again…" she began. "I once fucked this guy…he had a huge cock …he liked me to touch him…like this…" moving her hands while mouthing the words Glen adored.

* * *

After Glen left the apartment, Carlene called Bill McKinney, the only contact she still retained from her previous life in Emmeth. She was in the habit of calling him every so often, whenever she felt bored or wanted to gossip and talk things over.

"How's your cock these days?"

"I miss fucking you, Abigail."

"D'you still fuck every woman you see?"

"Try to…I pretty much do the same…Kayla's still hoping I'll shape up one of these days…"

"Tell her not to hold her breath."

"How 'bout holding mine?" Bill responded.

They laughed like two wild kids.

"So how's life?" he asked.

"Fucked up…nothing's changed…"

They spoke some more until she felt bored and yawned.

"Ok cocky…I'll call you again sometime…"

Smiling, Carlene hung up and moved outdoors to the large veranda. She enjoyed talking to the one person with whom she was utterly honest, the one she felt she could trust…well, almost trust…

though not completely, which is why she hadn't shared with him her new identity or newest goal. She had mulled over it for quite a time, ever since he'd casually mentioned something to her several months earlier. But then a thought occurred to her and she decided to hold off a while longer. Things could always get worse for those who deserved it… Perhaps had she discussed it with him, she would have realized how powerful and self-consuming opiates of hate and vengeance could become.

Now sitting on her veranda surrounded by a blooming garden, Carlene dialed Kalb.

"You left me a message?" she asked coolly.

"Yes, I think I understand what …"

"Me too. So don't call me again!"

Kalb was left with a silent phone in his hand.

Wondering what to do next and how to go about it, he reached inside his drawer and brought out a small notebook. He scouted the pages and searched inside until he found the name then dialed the number.

"Hi Jeff, this is Kalb Gales, how are you?"

CHAPTER 16

"Hello?"
"Hi…Margie…this is Glen."
"Glen?"
"Glen Wilmore."
"Glen Wilmore!"
"Well… yeah…I wasn't sure about the number."
"The number's right… sure…this is Margie…"
"So…how are you Margie?"
"Fine…just fine…and yourself?"
"Great…great…"
"What a surprise!"
Silence.
"Are you looking for Carlene?"
"No, no…actually…no ….I'm not looking for Carlene."
"So… how's New York these days?"
"Great, great."

After another long silence, Glen cleared his throat and spoke hesitantly.

"Eh…eh…. there's something I'd like to ask you, Margie…" he half whispered.
"I can't hear you…"
"Eh… I'd like to ask you a question."
"What is it?"
"Well…it's …"

"Are you ok?"
"Yes… yes."
"Is Carlene ok?"
"Oh yes! Yes…she's ok…it's nothing like that…"
"What do you mean?"
"Nothing."
Margie's eyebrows went up and down.

Glen had never called her before except when Carlene was visiting Dallas. Now out of nowhere and without prior notice, he suddenly calls her.

Unsure of what she should say next, Margie merely listened.
"Are you busy?"
"Well…let's see…I'm conversing with you and…"
Both forced a laugh.
"I…I need to … ask you something," Glen's voice was barely audible.
"I'm listening Glen."
Margie held the phone against her ear.
"Well…it's …it's about Carlene."
"What about her?"
"Do you …do you think she's happy?"
"What?"
"Did she tell you she was happy?"
"Well…yeah…I guess…not in so many words…but…"
"Could she maybe be …unhappy?"
"Glen, are you trying to tell me something?"

His voice sounded thick as if he'd choked on something. Margie kept silent trying to understand what was going through his mind. Following another long silence Glen spoke again.

"I'm sorry, Margie…please forgive me."
"Are you ok?"
"Yeah…yeah…it's just…"
"Is there something I can…?"
"No…no …I didn't mean to… I guess…"

"I'm kind of lost, Glen."
"Yeah, me too…"
"What are you talking about? If there's something bothering you, just spit it out!"
Too mortified to speak out his thoughts, Glen blurted out.
"We miss you, Margie. When are you coming for a visit?"
Margie stared at the phone.
"Is this a joke?"
"No! I mean it. Carlene and I haven't seen you in a while…"
"Cut the crap, Glen! What is this all about?"
"Like I told you…"
"Did Carlene put you up to it?"
"No! I wanted to talk to you and…"
"And what? Invite me to New York?"
"Yes!"
"You must be joking!" she slammed the phone in his ear.

* * *

Still holding the receiver in his hand and looking as though he'd been hit on the head, Glen was shocked to think about the useless conversation he'd just had with Margie. Adding to his sense of insult were Marige's last words before cutting him off.
"What should I do?" Glen spoke out loud.
He was standing in his office next to his desk. No other words came to his mind.
"What should I do? What should I do?" he kept chanting.
All at once he moved away from the desk. Nearing the leather armchair he hesitated momentarily then moved across and sat on the chair reserved for his patients. Staring at his own empty armchair he kept repeating.
"Dr. Wilmore, what should I do? What d'you think I should do, Dr. Wilmore?"

After several minutes, he got up, returned to the desk took a deep breath and redialed.

"Hi Margie this is Glen again."

"What are you trying to do… harass me?!"

"No, no…goodness Margie, I would never harass you. I'm sorry…"

"Then cut the crap and get to the point!"

"Well…I think …is Carlene seeing someone?"

As soon as he had spoken the words, Glen was sorry. It had come out as an accusation, though he had not intended it that way.

"Is this one of your sick jokes again?"

"Oh no! No! I'm just…I'm asking you…as her friend.…"

Margie was silent. She was unprepared for Glen's question.

"Why ask me? Ask Carlene!"

"Because you're her best friend …so you'd know."

The silence lasted longer than Glen had hoped for, hushed seconds that ticked away the unspoken truth. By the time Margie had recovered her train of thought and voice, Glen had understood the answer. Yet realizing his question had put Margie in an awkward position, he quickly added.

"Of course… if you prefer to take the fifth I'll understand."

Margie cursed under her breath. She felt doomed regardless of her answer. Remembering Carlene's threats she knew she must remedy whatever suspicions may have settled in Glen's mind but found it impossible to accomplish. She had come to hate Carlene.

"I'd appreciate that."

Glen now knew for certain that his suspicions were confirmed.

Well versed in human reactions, he had understood Margie's dilemma and her attempt to circumvent a direct reply. It meant she was trying to hide the truth from him. He wondered how much more there was to it. Trying not to rush into hasty conclusions, Glen decided to wait until he'd calmed down to absorb it all and reflect.

CHAPTER 17

It had been a long day at the office followed by four private sessions with patients and topped by an emergency case at the hospital. Kalb was looking forward to a hot shower and a cold beer. Taking off his jacket and loosening his tie he punched the button and listened to the messages. The first three didn't faze him. By the time the last message began playing, Kalb was already nude and on his way to the shower.

The voice stopped him in his tracks.

"How you doin', Kalb, this is Jeff Vinsen. Ah…I'd like to continue our discussion where we left off…please give me a call. Thanks."

He smiled then stepped into the shower.

Twenty minutes later, with a large towel wrapped around his waist and a cold beer in hand, Kalb dialed Jeff.

"Jeff, this is Kalb. It's now 8:30 p.m. I'd appreciate hearing from you as soon as you can. Thanks."

Kalb took a swig of beer then spread himself on the love seat. He opened the TV and stared at the images not really absorbing what was playing on the screen. It was just relaxation, a passive pastime following a very demanding day listening to other people's problems and helping them sort out complex situations. Doing nothing was precisely what Kalb now wanted to do.

The phone call, an hour later, woke him up. Forcing his eyes open, he looked around realizing he must have fallen asleep.

"Yeah?"

"How are you Kalb? This is Jeff."

"Hi…"

"Did I wake you?"

"Nah, I kind of snoozed…"

"Sorry, your message said…"

"No, no…it's fine… really."

"I've been thinking about what we'd discussed…and I'd like to take a shot at it."

"Great…that's great!"

"Where and when can we meet again?"

"The Spicy Pub tomorrow at 3 p.m.?"

"Hold on…let me check…yeah, that's perfect."

"Great. Thanks."

"See you then."

Kalb hung up. He was hoping to be proven wrong but his gut feeling told him he was about to pop open a can of worms.

* * *

Kalb strode briskly into the Spicy Pub, a thriving though rather smallish establishment packed with students and teachers. It was a very popular place and a crowded one with the tables practically falling over each other. But most importantly, it was central to all the administrative facilities on campus. With Jeff as head of security on campus and with his own office nearby, Kalb felt at ease.

"How are you, Jeff?"

"Good to see you, Kalb," they shook hands.

"Pretty hot outside, eh?"

"Yeah. Calls for a couple of beers," Jeff smiled.

Kalb scouted the place.

"I'd say it's more crowded than usual. How did you manage to get this table?"

"Twisted some arms."

Kalb laughed. Jeff signaled the waiter.

"Two beers and …" moving his head in Kalb's direction, "have you had lunch?"

"You bet… but please go ahead, Jeff."

"Ok. I'll have the… tuna salad on rye…low on the mayonnaise and no onions. Thanks."

"So!" Kalb said.

"You've got me hooked!"

"Glad to hear it."

Jeff smiled wryly.

"So where do we go from here?" Kalb looked serious.

"First I'd like to know who's interested?"

"I am."

Jeff puckered his lips in a silent whistle.

"Am I looking at a love triangle?" he asked.

Kalb felt his face redden.

"No… not really… it was just… an easy catch…."

"Can you flesh it out for me?"

"At this point I'd be doing the lady an injustice."

"How so?"

"It's complex …let's just say I suspect it's real messy once you start digging."

"How messy?"

"Very."

"Here you go," the waiter placed the plate in front of Jeff with both beers on the side.

"Thanks."

"Enjoy it."

Jeff's mouth watered at the sight of the salad then took a bite and looked at Kalb.

"Well…the only thing we have going for us is the lady's name… or her presumed name. I've tried piecing together some information on her but have come up with nothing so far. Zero."

Jeff shook his head.

"Where was she born?"

"England… that's her version," Kalb said.

"D'you think Glen knows more?"

Kalb's shoulders went up and down.

"She has this pitiful story that she tells everyone," Kalb went on.

Repeating the words told to him by Carlene made Kalb feel uncomfortable, as if he were betraying her trust. But he knew he had no choice. It was something Jeff needed to know. It wasn't like Kalb to repeat stories, especially not ones told by women and certainly not by a woman he had once loved…. and was still in love with. But there was something odd about it…and for some reason Carlene's words felt insincere. It was just a gut feeling, a hunch, and the sort of thing that has guided him over so many years in his profession. His reputation as one of the finest psychologists in town was solid. Kalb knew the secret to his success. It was his inner intuition, which he had come to rely on and respect. It rarely failed him.

Now seated across from Jeff he couldn't help but feel the familiar tingling inside his guts, a confirmation that his suspicions were correct.

"Ok, so we know her name and place of birth." Jeff kept eating.

"Something did happen three months ago," Kalb said cautiously weighing every word.

"I'm listening."

"I'm gonna have to back up a little…otherwise it's not gonna make sense."

"Go ahead," Jeff took another bite.

"This is strictly off the record…and very…very discreet," he stared at Jeff's eyes.

Jeff shook his head.

"Carlene and I… we… we were together and… had some fun… you know… anyway…it ended abruptly three months ago…we didn't exactly involve Glen…" lowering his head, Kalb felt the heaviness of guilt.

"I understand," Jeff said.

"She's not exactly the virtuous type…"

"How long did this…togetherness last?"

"Only a couple of months…"

"Go on."

"It was weird… she switched from one day to another. It was unbelievable."

"What d'you mean?"

"One day she claimed…" Kalb found it hard to mouth out the word he had longed to hear from Carlene.

Merely mentioning her name made him aware of the heaviness in his stomach, accompanied by a sharp pain that lingered between his head and heart making him feel worse than before. How could he bring himself to talk about her… and to confess he was still in love? Should he explain how it ended? And should he admit that she had dismissed his love…simply turned away and cut it abruptly? He couldn't possibly share with Jeff how he felt about her…it was wrong…it came close to cheating on her… but it wouldn't be fair not to tell Jeff…make him run in circles knowing he wouldn't get anywhere….

Kalb couldn't think straight. He knew what he had to say but the words simply wouldn't come out.

"Are you ok?" Jeff asked.

Kalb swallowed and looked up at Jeff.

"I'm sorry…what did you say?"

"Is something wrong Kalb?"

As though he'd been slapped on the face, Kalb shook his head and said.

"It was love one day… and hate the next…"

"Women, right?"

"No…not in this case."

Jeff noted Kalb's serious face.

"Ok, Doc. What are you saying?"

"It was very striking. You could say we were… well… I just fancied a bit of her," Kalb lowered his head.

Jeff didn't react.

"One day she walks into my apartment and says. 'It's time out. Don't call me anymore.' I thought she was kidding… I actually had to …well…she made me grovel…" Kalb twisted his face.

"Sounds like an itch," Jeff cracked a smile.

"Yeah!"

Kalb took a deep breath. He was hoping to sound casual, real cool and non-involved.

"Then she turns around and says. 'Did you really believe me when I said I cared about you?' I knew she didn't mean it…like I said…the woman's been around. I put on a face like I was hurt and asked for an explanation…that's when she got angry, fidgety and irritable. I called her up the next day but she turned vicious … said she never wanted to see me again."

"And that's when you called me?"

"Nope. It gets better."

Jeff wiped his mouth with the napkin, pushed away his plate and picked up his glass.

"It …it took me a while…I was … she messed me up quite a bit…."

"I understand. I'm a man…remember?" he smiled.

For Jeff, who had seen and heard many love stories in his professional lifetime, it seemed that Kalb still cared a lot about the woman he was trying to pass off as a mere casual love affair. He watched Kalb's hands, the fidgety fingers and the hesitant mouth, quick movements of lips and occasional cough. He didn't have to hear his confession. He already figured out the story behind the words and understood Kalb's predicament.

"Anyway…a few days ago Glen calls me into his office all broken hearted and says he knows she's having an affair. Now it's strange, because we haven't been together for over three months …but he's claiming she's seeing someone now and to top it all, he wants me to speak to her and tell her how he feels about it!"

Jeff's face twisted.

"Let me get this straight: you fuck her, she leaves you. Three months later her husband calls you and asks for your help 'cause she's seeing someone?!"

"Right!"

"So where the fuck's the husband?!" he stared at Kalb, "Are you telling me he's too chicken to do anything about it?"

Kalb shook his head.

"So you're actually asking me to help this… husband of hers? Glen?"

"But I'd like it kept between us."

"What are you gonna do after you find out about her?"

"Depends on what you dig up."

"And how will the husband know?"

"I'll eventually tell him…when the time is right and when I have all the information."

"That's what I call one hell of a fuck up."

Kalb was relieved to release a giggle.

"Ok. Let's take it a step at a time. What exactly are you after, Kalb?"

"Carlene is hiding something and I think it's more than just a lover."

"Do I hear a vindictive tone?"

"Oh no! Absolutely not! It's not what you think it is."

"Isn't it?" Jeff's eyes were glued to Kalb's.

"I think Carlene's playing with Glen, tossing him to the dogs and the poor guy is totally lost."

"So what you'd like me to do… is find out about her for the sake of her husband, correct?"

"It's more than that, Jeff. After Glen asked me to speak to her, I called her up. We met in my apartment. She walked in wearing a coat and by the time I'd turned around and handed her a drink, she'd dropped it off."

"I'm listening…"

"She wasn't wearing anything underneath."

"Save me the question…"

"Hey…I only did what any red-blooded man would have done!" he laughed softly.

"Then what?!"

"Nothing! That's exactly it! I asked her why she'd left me and why she pranced back again, after three months. I didn't get an answer, only excuses, like… she was curious about what Glen's message was… but once I told her, she wasn't interested anymore."

"I don't get it," Jeff said.

"It's strange…going so far just to hear what I had to say…basically deliver a message from her husband. Her reaction was strange. She could have come fully dressed and…"

"I get the picture. You suspect she was trying to manipulate you …"

"Exactly. But why? What for?"

"If she felt threatened…"

"That's it! That's what I was thinking."

"But what is she afraid of?"

"Precisely! The "What" is the question. Finding out the "What!""

Both men sat quietly a serious expression on their faces.

"You see," Kalb finally said, "her extreme reactions …they tell me there's something going on."

"Ok. You've got me hooked, Doc. Would you like me to tell Glen or would you like to tell him yourself?"

"I don't think…"

"It's your shot, but I think he should know what's going on."

"Even if it's only suspicions?"

"Your suspicions got me here."

It was something Kalb had feared but something that was unavoidable. He felt that as Glen's colleague and friend, though it now seemed ironic to call him by that title, he owed it to him.

"I'll sleep on it… need to think things over…"

"Let me know if you need help."

"Thanks."

"Meanwhile, I've got some digging to do."

"Right."

"See you, Doc."

He shook Kalb's hand.

* * *

"Damn, damn, damn!"

Kalb was back in his apartment.

"Coward! You damn fucking coward!"

He threw down the pillow in frustration. Who was he trying to fool? Of course he knew there was more to Carlene than just suspicions. He'd listened to her stories about her childhood and life prior to landing in New York. Hell! He knew she wasn't telling the truth… on two occasions she'd gotten some details wrong then tried to correct them… he pretended not to notice … as if he didn't catch on… she talked about her days in Wellesley College… he knew she was lying. Why didn't he stop her then? And why did he keep it from Jeff? It was useless going on… telling lies… beautifying the facts to make them seem other than the way they actually were … he was alone now. Why was he doing this? Why was he protecting her? Why?!

Hours later curled up in bed with both arms hugging the pillow, Kalb muttered:

"Damn it Carlene! I love you … I love you…" he then shut his eyes.

CHAPTER 18

Glen's unexpected phone call left Margie irritated and confused. When asked about Carlene she'd chosen silence and basically admitted to hiding the truth from him. With all his oddities, Glen was a brilliant psychiatrist and as such able to spot a lie from a distance. Margie realized she'd fallen into a trap and wanted to ensure that Carlene didn't suspect her of betrayal.

"You're either with me or against me," was Carlene's way of keeping Margie on her toes and in compliance with her demands.

Spending hours thinking about how to solve the problem, Margie began to entertain several options. For the past two years, since Carlene's marriage and her own move to Dallas, she'd been burdened with Carlene's presence, feeling threatened every time Carlene requested her help. Margie was looking for a way out, a path that would lead her out of the trap. If Carlene disappeared, simply ceased to exist, Margie's worries would vanish with her. She wouldn't have to lie to Glen or take a cut in deals in order to pay for Carlene's fixed percentage. The more she thought about it, the more the idea appealed to her.

"If she'd only disappear …I'd never have to be afraid again…"

Margie hadn't suspected Carlene of spying on her until it was too late and by then there was little she could do to stop her from meddling in her affairs. Margie had experienced several small thefts, crooked deals masked by misunderstandings, and a blackmailing attempt gone sour. She realized too late that Carlene was dealing behind her back, infiltrating her territory and closing large deals that were starting to infringe on her own business. Margie was motivated to think of a way out. Maybe if she teamed up with Glen who was obviously angry and frustrated with Carlene, she could somehow force her downfall. Margie was tired of constantly worrying about her and liked to imagine Carlen's beautiful face as it dropped in slow motion from her plush apartment building smashing full force on to the pavement below.

It wasn't easy for Margie to start all over again in Dallas and had taken her several months to build up her clientele, put down roots, settle in and get to know the right people in the right places. Unlike New York with its very old money and traditional ways of cutting discreet deals, Dallas was more of a transient place, a crossroads filled with gaps along its unpaved paths, offering opportunities for eager folks willing and able to cut fast deals. Having gained a few extra pounds with an added blush and a longer styled haircut, Margie's face resembled that of a worry free woman fortified with confidence. She liked Dallas with its vibrant vibes and warm weather; everything seemed larger and faster in Texas as were the endless merriments of everyday life. Texan men with their unquenched appetites for her unique services were no exception.

A go-between for those willing to pay a hefty price to satisfy their lascivious desires and those dishing them out, required more than just a pretty face and a feminine body. By now well versed and in great demand in the intimate matchmaking industry and its extensive derivatives, Margie seemed to have a natural knack for it. Investing in her connections was her priority. She relied on her former reputation as New York's grand lady of society. Using masterful cunning to ensure a constant growth of clientele, she spun intricate social networks within the top echelons of Dallas' ritzy-glitzy society. Having chosen Highland Park, one of the most affluent towns in the entire nation as her private residence, Margie was able to fortify her sense of security.

But things were starting to change.

The town of Highland Park located within the city of Dallas was spread over two and a half square miles. It had a reputation as the epitome of luxury living with exorbitant real estate prices, thanks to the brilliance of the local administration and the battalions of devoted gardeners able to preserve its natural beauty. Though she'd enjoyed a life of opulence within her seven thousand square feet palatial space with its magnificent swimming pool and tennis court, Margie was now unsettled and somewhat concerned. She knew how dangerous Carlene could become and resented the fact that at any given moment, Carlene could decide to put an end to her enchanted life. Convinced it was only a matter of time, and realizing the unpleasantness of living with constant fear, Margie decided to make the first move and dialed Glen.

"Hi Glen, it's Margie."

"Well…hi, Margie."

There was a strange silence followed by Margie's cough.

"Are you ok, Margie?"

"Yes, I'm ok. Thanks."

"So, what…?"

"There's something you should know, Glen. It's important. Can you meet me here?"

"Where?"

"Here in Dallas."

Glen released a nervous sound.

"Why? What's so important?"

"I can't talk about it. You've got to trust me."

"Does this have anything to do with…."

"Of course! Why else would I call and ask you to come to Dallas?"

"Are you telling me you want me to fly all the way to Dallas just to tell me something about Carlene?"

"I don't want to tell you anything. I want to show you something."

"What? Show me what?"

"Once you'll see it, you won't have any more questions."
Glen was hesitant.
"Well…when would you like me to come?"
"As soon as you can."
"I'll let you know."

Following Margie's phone call, Glen hurried into Kalb's office but found it empty. He rushed back into his own and tried reaching Kalb in his apartment.

"Hi Kalb, this is Glen. Please call me ASAP at the office. Thanks."

Pacing the floor, Glen waited anxiously to hear from Kalb.

Glen's next phone call was to Lionel T. Fitch, Harvard's Dean of Humanities.

"Fitch! Wilmore! how are you?"

"Glen…Glad to hear. We're looking forward to seeing you tomorrow."

"That's why I'm calling… I can't make it."

"What's up?"

"It's my wife…she's not feeling well… I'm afraid you're gonna have to do it without me."

"I hope it's nothing serious…"

"No, no…just a bad case of the flu…"

"Hope she's better soon," Fitch said, "better now than next month. When is your first lecture of the series…on the second or third?"

"The second."

"We're planning quite an audience."

"Glad to hear."

"I'll let you know how the meeting went. Hope your wife is better soon."

"Thanks."

"Take care."

Still feeling tense, Glen remained seated waiting for Kalb's call.

His head was swarming with thoughts about Margie and what she had told him. Though it was difficult to guess her motives, Glen sensed that she was goaded by something other than good intentions. He was sure she had something important to show him about Carlene but couldn't quite make up his mind or pinpoint what it could possibly be or the reason that propelled her to do it. Did it have to do with her covering up for Carlene? Of course it did! What else could it possibly be? And why would she want him to come to Dallas? Surely if it were that important she'd have already told him over the phone, explained things to him…he'd understand even if it was something involved. Maybe Margie was afraid of something? Or simply wanted to tease him? He remembered the wild parties she'd organized while still in New York with all the white puff floating around and the beautiful girls as part of the décor. Was she perhaps planning a surprise? Well, he was sure it couldn't possibly be for his birthday…that was only in November so it must be something else. Whatever she had in mind, he suspected it wasn't something pleasant. And the longer he thought about it the more nervous he became. He couldn't wait to hear from Kalb, the one person he felt comfortable with… Kalb would know what to do…he was good at figuring out stuff like that.

Waiting to hear from Kalb, Glen recalled his own teachings, those he was in the habit of reciting to his first-year students. He now found them soothing and inspirational and a way to divert his mind away from his problems.

"Sufferings of the soul are the worst kind…unlike a sore or an open wound where the pus can ooze out…our profession strives to heal the intangible…the hidden…the mystifying sufferings buried within the deepest capillaries of our hearts and minds…"

He'd never faced such a situation before and had never been in need of someone's help. He was perfectly capable of helping himself, of course… but having a close friend would be nice…someone to trust and confide in. Maybe if he had one, it could help him to understand certain things…yes, maybe he could understand Carlene better. Of course it's obvious that he's the awkward one…it definitely isn't Carlene…that's how it was from the start…but she's the one who always makes him feel so… inadequate, yes, fucking inadequate! Why does she keep reminding him how fucked up he is?! every time he looks at her beautiful face he's reminder of his fuckups… his dick is so fucked up! He can never count on it to get a move on…always so…so hesitant…and weird! and right now it feels even worse… like a tree…a fucking gnarled tree with its roots sticking up into the air… that's how his dick feels now… plain fucking weird… But he can never discuss it with anyone… and certainly never with Carlene…she's normal …he's the fucked up one… his mirror never lies …all he has to do is stare back at the tiny ugly man …anyone can see how fucking twisted he is… with his….

He pounced on the first ring.

"Hello!"

"That was quick…I didn't even hear it ring…" Kalb said.

"I did! I'm so glad you called. I need to see you right away. It's urgent."

"Sure! Are you ok?"

"Sort of…something's come up and I'd like to discuss it with you. NOW!" his fingers tapped the leathered desk.

Kalb was trying to calculate his free time.

"Well I'm busy right now preparing for a lecture at four… then I've got an urgent counseling session …so I should be free around six-thirty or so…"

"Great."

"Where would you like us to meet?" Kalb asked.

"I'll be at the Pierre Hotel for the next couple of days…why not meet me there?"

"At the Pierre?!"

"I'll explain when I see you."

"Ok, what time?"

"As soon as you can get there. How about straight after your session?"

"See you then."

Kalb wondered why Glen was staying at the plush Pierre and what was on his mind but couldn't really focus on anything other than his own problems. Knowing he would, one day, need to confess to Glen about his illicit relationship with Carlene was causing Kalb sleepless nights and extreme agitation.

"Maybe Glen found out about us," the thought had crossed Kalb's mind but only briefly.

"He probably wants to talk about Carlene …maybe she left him?" the question consumed him as he leaned back in his chair trying to sort out his emotions.

Her beautiful face refused to leave him, though he tried to let go of the memories. Looking at his watch, he cleared his throat, shut his eyes and forced himself to concentrate on the lecture only hours away.

"I better get this straight!" he spoke out loud.

* * *

By the time he was done with the lecture and the private session, Kalb felt the need for a brisk walk. He was somewhat agitated and apprehensive about his meeting with Glen, and knew that a long energetic walk would help reduce his anxiety. He cut through Central Park enjoying the freshness of air and greenery. It cleared his head and boosted his strength. He kept up the pace until he couldn't hold it off any longer and strayed from the path anxious to find what he needed. Stopping at the first newsstand he purchased a pack of cigarettes.

CHAPTER 19

After calling Kalb, Glen dialed Carlene.
"I'm sorry, darling…but I don't have a choice…I can't postpone Harvard… I was hoping to be able to move it but… it's an important lecture…part of a series, you know … I hate to have to leave you alone over the weekend…but I've got to be there…"
"That's ok, Presch…I'll be thinking of you…" she smiled.
"I'll be back on Sunday…"
"Don't worry…I'll keep myself busy…I'll miss you…"
"Me too…"
Relieved to learn of Glen's plans and wishing to take advantage of his absence, Carlene reached for the phone. She started dialing Tierry's number but was at once swamped with doubts and hung up. It was something that had to be thought through carefully. She could easily fly over to Dallas and surprise him but it was too risky, even under the pretext of visiting Margie. She had seen him only ten days earlier and knew how happy he'd be to see her but there was something else… a tiny inner voice that signaled it was best not to risk anything and remain in New York… at least until she was able to quench Glen's suspicions…she should try to rebuild his trust in her … make him feel like she cared for him… he was so weird…but she didn't really mind…after all she too was weird… ugly weird…it was just that… she had on this beautiful mask…fuck! No wonder she ended up with him…'cause deep inside she was so ugly… so fucked up and ugly! All this hatred

stored within…hatred and jealousy…she could feel it bubbling inside her head…uncontrollable hate…percolating ceaselessly like magma on the verge of eruption.

She smiled. It was the only way to cover up for the weird stuff that was brewing inside her mind…all those thoughts…God! Keep smiling and no one will suspect… how she hated her family… and her righteous sister… Oh! She couldn't wait …

The phone rang. She released her finger on the first ring.

"Hello! Hello? Anyone there? Hello! Hello? Hello!" Carlene screamed into the void, "You mother fucker! Creep! Is that you weirdo? My fucking weirdo of a husband! I hate you! I hate your touches… and your fucking hands! Can't bear to touch your skin… you fuck up! fuck you… they should lock you up… lock you up and throw away the keys… fucking creep… screw head…" she realized she was raving but couldn't stop until her voice turned hoarse.

Having exhausted herself, she poured a tall drink and, once again, considered the situation. It was too dangerous to give Glen cause for new suspicions, but what if Tierry…what if he pushed her too much…or demanded that she leave Glen …he was now very vulnerable …all he needed was a tiny prod…a slight push in the right direction. He'd do anything she asked of him…Anything! Maybe she could push harder…make him leave his wife sooner than she'd planned. It was all a question of timing…. she mustn't miss the perfect timing…

She toyed with the idea of inviting Tierry to New York instead of traveling herself to Dallas, but didn't really feel up to it. Never having known a true love, despite countless lovers and an even longer line of mere passers-by, Carlene couldn't care less if Tierry truly loved her or not. What mattered was his willingness to leave his wife and child for her sake…and hers alone. It was a challenge, a game she had learned to play from a young age, which gave her a sense of control. Now thinking about it she decided to tighten the cord around Tierry's neck. It might prove to be the last straw, the final one that would force him to leave home for her sake.

She dialed his number. In her huskiest voice she spoke into the receiver.

"It's me, darling…"

"I've missed you…" Tierry replied.

"I've missed you too…I can't wait any longer…"

"Where are you?"

"I'm in the tub soaking… Glen's on his way to Harvard…"

"I can't wait until you get here…or stop thinking about our room at Le Château…with the champagne …"

Carlene faked a cry.

"What's wrong? Are you ok?"

"No…I'm not…"

"What's wrong, darling?"

"I…I can't see you…"

"What do you mean?"

"I can't come to Dallas."

"Why not?"

"Glen…he won't let me…" she cried harder.

"That son of a…"

"Please…don't be angry…I just wish…I miss you so much…if we could only be together…"

"Why won't he let you come here? You said he left for Boston…"

"Yes, but he's retuning on Sunday…"

"So why can't you come here?"

"He… he told me… he'd…I can't even say it…"

"He'd what?"

"He'd…divorce me…" she let out bitter cries while her eyes followed the muted TV screen.

"I love you…I don't care if he divorces you…I want to spend the rest of my life with you…"

"Me too…but…but I can't divorce him…not yet…"

"We need to do something about it…I can't have you stay with him…"

"I've been thinking about leaving him…but you're still with…"

"I want to tell her about us…"

Carlene yawned.

"What if …"

"I only care about us. I want to spend the rest of my life with you…"

"We should do this gradually…" Carlene sniffled.

"I'll speak to her this weekend…I've… I've decided to move out of the house…"

"Oh… I'm so happy…I love you …" she continued whimpering.

"Oh…Carlene…"

"I love you more than anything else in my life…"

"I wish you were here…beside me…I'd soap your back and legs…lick your nipples…move my fingers slowly…slowly down …"

"I want you…I want you in bed with me…I want to feel you inside of me…I…I need you…"

"Don't…please don't…I can't bear it…"

"Hurry darling…please speak to her…I can't think of you in the same house…in the same bed with her… I want us to be together…"

"I will…I promise you…"

Carlene smiled. Achieving her goal now seemed closer than ever.

* * *

Hanging up, Tierry found it hard to control his emotions. He wanted to throttle Glen and even toyed with the notion of speaking to him.

"Maybe I should call him…have it out with him and simply scoop her out of his reach."

He was now angry. Very angry.

"You bastard! You damn bastard! You're not fit to have her as your wife… I'm gonna take her away from you…away from that darn place of yours…"

Debating on what to do next, Tierry sat at his desk with both hands over his face. He planned on telling his wife about Carlene and moving out of the house... but he should first work it out with Carlene. He'd be willing to marry her immediately and start a new life with the woman of his dreams. But then again, maybe he should wait, take the time to think and make sure... but he was already sure! He knew he was doing the right thing so why was he still hesitant? He loved Carlene and she loved him but what if...what if she changed her mind? What if he divorced his wife and then she didn't go through with her own divorce? No! He refused to think about it...it was too terrible to even consider. She loved him, he was sure of that. He knew he wasn't wrong about that...he couldn't be...it wasn't even something that needed any consideration...but... but what if he was wrong after all? Could he possibly be wrong about her? She was so devoted to him how could he be wrong? With a love like his...so intense... surely they were meant for each other. She loved him the way he loved her...she even told him so ...and came over to see him. There was no reason to reconsider anything...it was just ...normal hesitations of a true love. Oh! That face! That beautiful face of hers smiling and telling him how much she wanted him...she definitely loved him with those maddening lips of hers. And just touching her skin...

Tierry's insides began rattling. He shut his eyes and could almost feel what is was like touching her all over, moving inside of her and...oh! He could barely stand it and the longer he kept it up the more acute he felt the pain brewing within him. The mere thought of moving his hand over her skin teased his cock into an erection. He was getting horny and felt it coming again. Forced by an uncontrollable urge, he rushed to the men's room, entered a stall, unzipped his pants and moved his hands wildly on his steaming erection until he exploded. With his eyes still shut, he let out a heavy sigh.

After settling back in his office, he smiled, picked up the phone and made the arrangements.

***

The plane was on schedule. Landing at LaGuardia on time, Tierry held onto his small carry-on and walked out to hail a cab.

"Any luggage?"

"No. Just this one."

"Where to?" the driver asked.

"The city…between Fifth and Park."

Too excited to think of anything else, Tierry imagined Carlene and her beautiful face. She was smiling at him …and her body…all warm and soft and…Oh! He couldn't wait to touch that body of hers… she won't believe her eyes…she'll think it's a dream. Imagining the surprise on her face he broke into a smile. It was now 6:45 p.m.. In just under an hour he was planning on being with her. In bed.

"How's the traffic into town?"

"Smooth ridin.'"

"Don't mind if you step on the gas…"

"Gotcha!"

***

Undressing in front of the mirrored wall covering the entire southern section of her bedroom, Carlene studied her body. She moved closer to examine what looked like, from a distance, a blemish, but as soon as she moved close enough to be able to count her eyelashes she realized it was no longer there.

"Must have been a shadow," she spoke to the nude woman in the mirror. "What should I do? I'm bored…fucking bored…"

Wearing only black pointy stilettos, Carlene swung her hips sideways gesturing with her hands as she paced along the length of her bedroom.

"I hate you Glen Wilmore….I hate your fucking face…and your screwed up brain…with your ratty little cock…what a waste…oh… what a waste…"

Moving sideways, she switched on the CD swaying her nakedness and twisting in small gestures around and around as if mating with an invisible ghost. The music raged. Walking to her night table she took out a tiny box unscrewed its top and popped two pills into her mouth then reached inside again and pulled out a whip. Swinging to the rhythm of the music and throwing her hips around and around she returned to the mirrored wall.

"I hate you," she lashed out holding the whip and flogging the mirror, "I hate you…"

The music screamed above her voice. With blazing eyes she kept whipping the mirror, disregarding the wounds on her hands as the rough handle cut into the flesh. Her wet face was twisted.

"Fucking ugly… you fucking ugly bitch…" she grabbed her hair and pulled it sideways, "You need to go back to the rat hole… the rat hole… you belong in the rat hole… the fucking hole… take off your mask… grab it… grab it… " she pulled out hands full of hairs.

Covered in sweat and smudged with blood, her wet body jerked and shook. She moved her hands in wild gestures trying to stay in rhythm with the roaring music. With eyes still shut, she moved her head as if trying to shake off a hat. Her breathing was coming faster than before, causing her body to vibrate and spin uncontrollably.

At once she fell to the floor, her face streaked with tears and her head exploding with pain thinking about the one thing she'd never known.

Love.

CHAPTER 20

Walking briskly in the direction of the Pierre hotel, Kalb wondered what Glen had in mind. It had to do with Carlene, he was sure of it. He only hoped Glen hadn't found out about them. But what if he had? And what if Glen asked him about it? How should he react? He couldn't even begin to imagine what it would be like… it was too awful to imagine… but what if … what if Carlene had already told Glen about their affair? Confessed what had happened? No! She wouldn't do that! He was sure of it, just a gut feeling he had about her… but what if he was wrong? What was she hiding and who was she besides the most beautiful woman in the world? He loved her despite everything… so why think about it? The thoughts were poisoning him, forcing weird notions into his head.

Kalb lit a cigarette and inhaled deeply.

"Oh, I missed this shit!" he shut his eyes then took another puff.

He was nearing the hotel.

Glen had been pacing up and down the lobby totally consumed with his thoughts and anxiously awaiting Kalb. Again he glanced at his watch. It was already 7:30 p.m. His eyes moved to the entrance door. He hadn't even noticed the security guard or the front desk manager who surveyed the well-dressed bewildered looking man and decided to approach him.

"May I help you sir?" the security guard asked.

"Help?! I don't need help."
"Are you waiting for someone?"
"Yes."
"There's a bar over there…"
"I'm not looking for a bar. Who do you think I am?!"
"I don't know, sir, that's why I'm asking."
"I'm Professor Dr. Glen Wilmore… Columbia… Harvard…" reaching into his coat pocket he brought out his driver's license.

"Sorry, sir… eh… professor Wilmore… we don't take any chances… you know…" apologizing on behalf of the hotel and its management, the security guard headed in the direction of the front desk.

Just then Kalb entered the Pierre spotting Glen as he stood in the center of the lobby facing the front desk.

"Hi, been waiting long?" he smiled at Glen.
"No!"
"Anything wrong?"
"No!"
Glen sounded angry.
"Are you sure you're ok?" Kalb asked.
"Yeah… yeah… how about a drink before dinner?"
"Fine by me."
"Good. Let's get out of here."
"I thought you were staying here?" Kalb eyed him.
"I changed my mind. I'll explain later…"

Kalb shot him a quick glance wondering what was going through his mind. Knowing it was pointless to ask him again, Kalb waited. Glen needed to relax and feel more at ease before he could talk about whatever it was that he wanted to talk about.

Keeping up the pace and on their way to the restaurant, Kalb's head was swarming with words that he couldn't let out of his mouth. He tried to keep his mind focused on what Glen was about to say but the darn words kept popping up.

"I fucked your wife," he tried to imagine how Glen would react to his confession. "And I enjoyed it."

Hell! How could he even think of it now? Was he turning into a monster? What was wrong with him? But the more he tried to hush the words from within, the more they insisted on sounding out loud and by now they were out of control, gathering strength and flooding his mind .

"Carlene and I…I was Carlen's … Please understand, Glen…I'm in love with your wife"…it all seemed so…ludicrous… incredibly out of place. Grotesque! They were playing tricks on him… flooding his head… trying to drown him…

Kalb lit a fresh cigarette

"I thought you quit!" Glen said.

"I did… for a while. Now I'm hooked again."

Kalb knew he didn't have the guts to mouth out his thoughts and words. He couldn't possibly bring himself to confess his deeds and even less how he felt about it. Keep moving, keep up the pace, one step at a time… her face… lips, eyes… her smile…her body …oh… she made him feel so powerless… he'd do anything just to see her smile at him…or feel her fingers touch his body…

"Watch it! Wanna get yourself killed?" Glen grabbed Kalb's arm and pulled him off the street.

The yellow cab swung sideways. Kalb jumped back just on time.

"Ass hole! Fucking ass hole!" Kalb screamed.

"Are you ok?" Glen was visibly shaken, still holding onto Kalb's arm.

"Yeah, I'm ok."

"Jesus! You nearly got yourself killed."

"Nearly doesn't count!"

"You're upset…it's understandable…"

"Wouldn't you be?!" Kalb felt his voice was getting out of control.

"How about…"

"Look…look over there…it's the fucking cab again! It stopped!" Kalb hurried in its direction.

"That's my building…" Glen called out trailing behind Kalb.

"I'll show the fuck…"

"Hold it, Kalb, hold it! Don't do anything.…"

But Kalb was already closing the distance. Another eighty yards or so…getting closer… he'd soon grab a hold of him. The bastard! He saw a man pulling a carry-on out of the cab, tip the driver and enter the building. Kalb was out of breath… another thirty yards… his hand was stretched in front of him.

"Son of a bitch!" Kalb screamed as the car swerved leaving a trail of hot air behind.

It took Glen a while to catch up with Kalb. Breathing heavily he asked.

"You ok?"

Kalb was bent in half, hugging his stomach with both arms. He breathed deeply.

"Yeah…I'm…I'm fine!"

"Sure?"

"Yeah," Kalb said. "I need … I need a drink…a long …fucking drink."

"There's a quiet place over there," Glen pointed to a bar across the street.

"Just what … the patient needs… Doc."

They crossed the street still shaken from the ordeal.

* * *

"Two tall Chivas!" Glen ordered then turned to Kalb. "How are you feeling?"

"Like a jerk."

"Lucky you weren't killed."

"Am I?"

"Come…come now, Kalb, it's only a…"

"Right! Coming from the famed psychiatrist!"

"Get a hold of yourself, Kalb."

"A hold? You want me to hold something?" his head spinning with images of Carlene.

"Straighten yourself out, Kalb. It was only a cab."

Kalb bit his lower lip. He knew Glen was right but he felt so hurt, so utterly wretched. Taking deep breaths, he decided to leave his confession for another time. He couldn't handle it now, not with his head drumming and Glen trying to make him feel better.

"Damn Carlene, to hell with everything… I'll let Jeff handle it from now on…" Kalb decided. "I'm not going to think about it… let Jeff dig in the dirt… let him find whatever there is out there … to hell with it all…"

Amazingly, as if by magic, the mere thought of having someone else take control, calmed him down. Taking another deep breath he shut his eyes.

"Sorry, Glen, sorry…it's …there's a lot on my mind, I really didn't mean to…"

"Cheers! Take a big one!" he held up his glass to Kalb.

"Yeah…cheers."

They sat a while longer, each holding his own turmoil and thoughts until Glen said.

"Ready to eat?"

"Do they have anything in this joint?" Kalb looked around.

The place was a small bistro with a pleasant bar at the front. Too distraught to notice its interior when he came in, Kalb now scouted the surroundings and found it invitingly warm. The wooden tables matched the décor across the bar with its large windows overlooking the street. He ordered the house salad with extra sauce to go with a roast beef sandwich. Glen chose a club sandwich.

The background music, a velvet-like voice of a nameless singer, eased the wait for the food. Kalb kept sipping his drink but it only added to his gloomy feel. Another gulp. And another cigarette. They were seated in the smoker's section with another couple across from them. He didn't really crave a smoke… it's just that, right now he was nervous and needed to occupy his hands while waiting for Glen to say something. Kalb decided not to help him.

Let him figure out what he should or shouldn't say. Another sip and by now his thoughts were less painful… less confusing… he didn't even think about anything…

"One club sandwich… for you sir…"

"Thank you."

"And the roast beef…"

"Thank you," Kalb added.

"Enjoy your meal," the waiter smiled.

"That's Carlene's favorite," Glen pointed to Kalb's plate, "I…I wonder about her…"

"What about?"

"I'm not sure…I…this is embarrassing…" Glen lowered his head. Kalb swallowed hard and waited.

"I have this feeling but I'm not sure…I'm not sure I can trust her…" his eyes were shiny. "What should I do, Kalb?"

Kalb exhaled. He couldn't think of anything to say, not one single word, any kind of word. Nothing made sense anymore. Glen continued.

"I got a call from a Margie Joree… in Dallas… she's Carlene's friend… worked here as a social gal…you know what I'm saying? She asked me to fly over …said she had something to show me…"

"You mean…fly over to Dallas?!"

"That's where she lives and every time Carlene visits her I get these strange vibes…"

"What does she want to show you?"

"Actually…I…I called her first and asked her if Carlene was seeing someone…"

Kalb felt his heart was about to explode. The sudden gush of blood to his face caused his mouth to feel dry. He placed his fork on the plate.

"Calm down…get a hold of yourself…" he repeated silently, "I mustn't show anything…just stay cool…calm down," but the more he thought about it the more nervous he became and the more swollen his tongue felt. He moved in his chair then took a deep breath. Trying to control his voice he asked Glen.

"Why did you call her?"
"Because they're good friends and I thought she'd tell me…"
"Did she?" Kalb held his breath.
"She didn't exactly answer…"
"Did she deny it?"
"No…she didn't deny it either…"
"So why does she want you in Dallas?"
"That's just it! I don't know!"
Kalb felt his stomach sink.

Motioning to the waiter, he ordered another drink then lit up another cigarette.

"I lied to her… lied to Carlene. I told her I was going to Harvard…I think I wanted to catch her with a man…and …and…" Glen chocked on his words.

"That's understandable," Kalb said in a tone slightly louder than intended, "any man suspecting his wife of…seeing someone, would want to catch her in the act."

"They would?"
"Sure! It's only normal."
"I can't…I can't think about it…"
"Try shifting it…as if it's happening to someone else…it can help…"
Glen moved his head up and down in agreement.
"It's what you'd tell me if I were in your shoes, right Glen?"
"Are you…are you telling me I should surprise her?"

Kalb considered the situation. His entire involvement was absurd. He never should have agreed to meet with Carlene in the first place. Now he was in the middle, between Glen and Carlene. It was unbearable. He'd give anything to catch Carlene with a lover… heck! What the hell was he thinking about?! He couldn't watch her with anyone else… what was wrong with him?! Of course he knew she wasn't his but he was still hoping… hoping to … what was he hoping for? Was there any hope of him and Carlene? He was just raving… the drink was getting to his head and he was … he couldn't organize his thoughts… they were swarming … filling his head with all kinds of weird thoughts. Why was Glen asking him about Carlene? Didn't he know they had fucked? Hold it Kalb! Hold it! If Glen was asking him… then maybe, just maybe he didn't know anything about him and Carlene, maybe he was safe… at least for the time being until…

"I need another one," he raised his glass in the direction of the waiter.

"Take it easy…I never saw you drink so much…"

"Never felt this way," Kalb wanted to scream out the words.

"So what d'you think, Kalb?"

"I think you should do what you bloody well want to do!"

"Are you angry?"

"No…I'm not angry. I think you should follow your gut feeling, you know?"

Glen shook his head.

"Look Glen, if you think she's …she's fucking someone else as we speak then go in and surprise her!" he nearly gagged on his words.

"Your drink…"

"Thanks."

Kalb reached for the fresh glass. He felt woozy, slightly dizzy… things weren't as clear anymore… Glen suddenly seemed different, kind of … with it, at least he had Carlene…

"So…what d'you think?" again he looked at Kalb.

"I don't know…maybe…"

Silence again.

"What happens if I come home and she's alone?"

Kalb smiled.

"D'you really need my advice on that one?!"

Glen shook his head. Kalb smiled wryly.

"And if she's not alone?" his eyes shone again.

"Kick the bastard and tell him to go fuck himself!"

It was past 10:30 p.m. by the time Glen felt it was safe to return home.

Looking at Kalb he said.

"Are you sure I should do this?"

"I think you're entitled to surprise your wife… like you said, you're not committing a crime; if you're wrong, she'll never know you had a room at the Pierre and if you're right, you'll have where to spend the night…"

"I hope I find her in bed…asleep…"

"I hope so too," Kalb said thinking about Carlene's breasts.

Carlene's image refused to leave him. Kalb was beginning to feel obsessed as if there was something the matter with him. He focused on Glen and sensed his fear. He too was afraid. Afraid of breaking down and confessing his love for Carlene.

"Ok… time to brave it. Let's go…." Glen walked ahead.

"Yeah!"

Both men crossed the street again.

"You sure you don't want a night cap?"

"No thanks, Glen, it's late."

"Thanks," Glen patted his shoulder.

"Thank you," Kalb returned the pat.

CHAPTER 21

On his way to the lair, as Jeff liked to refer to his former place of work, he thought about his colleagues within NYPD's special tactics unit hoping they could lend a hand with the task at hand. He knew he could always rely on their help and had no doubt there was something odd about Carlene Ridge; but the question was where to begin since he had so little to go by. The hardest part of the game was always where to begin, but it was the part he enjoyed most. It reminded him of a puzzle and the importance of finding the first piece of the outward frame which could help solve the rest.

Nearing the unassuming building with its external look resembling its neighboring buildings, Jeff recalled some amusing incidences from the past. He was used to visiting the guys, though not on a regular basis and usually only when a situation was called for. Moving through the various security zones, he smiled in front of the hidden cameras then used codes and gadgets to identify himself.

Once inside he called out.

"Hey Joey…long time no see," Jeff extended a firm hand with a friendly slap on the back.

"What's up, buddy?" Joey returned the same.

It was the manly thing to do and something that was expected, a practiced routine and a gesture they all felt good about every time he'd stop by.

"Nothing's changed," he looked around the room with its large window and steel bars framing its outer shell. "Same shit, ah?"

"Yeah! Same crap only the ..."
"Players change!"
They mouthed simultaneously then laughed.
"It's been...how long?"
"You tell me, Jeff."
"I think two years to the day."
"No shit!"
"Flies, doesn't it?"
"Sure does."
They all knew Jeff had opened his private investigation practice following his retirement two years earlier but no one really counted. It only meant something when one of the guys returned for a visit. Then it was time to reminisce and bring up past times.

Jeff sat down.
"So...what brings you to this rat hole?"
"Eh...a woman...as usual..." Jeff smiled.
"Must be something special?"
"Sure is."
"Shoot. What is it, Jeff?"

Jeff was now seated in what was once his office, a small room inside New York Police Department's special operations unit located on the east wing in a relatively quiet neighborhood. The room, the largest among five others, had been, at one point, a living room of an apartment overlooking an empty parking lot. Scouting the mustard colored walls with the framed citations for outstanding merits and congratulatory letters, Jeff shifted his eyes to the glass cabinet with its assorted trophies.

"I need to find a woman."
"That important?"
"Yeah!"
"Place of birth?"
"None. No address no place. No history."
"Face?"
"Beautiful but without a past."

Joey smiled.

"You always liked hard cashews."

"Still do. Get a kick out of breakin' 'em open."

"Social security number?"

"The only clue. Here it is," he said, handing him a small piece of paper.

Joey sneezed as he moved his fingers on the keyboard.

"Bless."

"I'd say it's an omen."

"Oh yeah?"

"Yeah. Last time I sneezed I split open a big cashew."

The laughed.

"Is Sandy in?"

"You can check. I saw him earlier on."

"Thanks," Jeff left the room.

Moments later he returned.

"D'you find him?"

"Nope."

"Here's for starters," Joey handed him a printed paged. On it was a name.

"Interesting…" Jeff said.

"Need help?"

"Not sure."

"Thanks, Joey. I have a feeling this ain't the end. Tell the boys I was here."

"Will do."

Leaving the building, Jeff cursed behind clenched teeth.

"Fuck!"

***

Back in his office, Jeff dialed Kalb.

"Call me when you can. Thanks."

Jeff was hungry. Crossing the street he entered a small diner seating himself next to the window. He was basically out of clues wondering how to proceed. If at all.

"Beer …and …a double cheeseburger with fries on the side," he ordered.

It could go either way but there was basically nothing more to go on. He couldn't invade Carlene's privacy or question her. She probably had her reasons for making up those stories and inventing her own past like so many other women. And men. He'd met a number of them while still on the job, people without history. It was weird. But they each carried their own reasons for wanting their pasts left behind.

He'd seen Carlene a few times on Columbia's campus, her slim figure tiptoeing next to Glen's. He'd recalled thinking that the two didn't look like a couple though she had her arm reaching down to his and sort of leaned on him. He did remember her stare, towering above her husband and scouting men that happened to pass her way. It was strange, as if she wanted to swallow every male passer-by with her eyes. There were also lots of jokes and rumors spread around, which Jeff didn't really care for. Maybe the way to solve the mystery was simply to approach the lady herself.

"Ok, dimwit, how d'you approach her?" he tried to imagine a conversation with Carlene Wilmore.

"Thanks," he swallowed at the sight of his burger and beer.

Tucking the tail end of his tie in between two buttons and attaching the paper napkin to the top of his shirt, Jeff was hoping not to mess it up with the ketchup. At least this once.

* * *

Thirty minutes later he was back in his office hoping to hear from Kalb. He went through his paper tray, signed two letters and made a few phone calls. The ring caught him on his way out of the room.

"Jeff speaking."
"It's Kalb. What's up?"
"I'm just on my way out."
"Can you stop by?"
"Give me ten minutes."

Jeff had chosen to locate his office within the safety of the Morningside Heights neighborhood on the city's upper west side in close proximity to the campus. It was something he'd done out of consideration, a courteous move for his unique clientele. Kalb's office was also a mere walking distance from Jeff's.

Entering Kalb's office, Jeff went straight to the point.
"Ok, this is the situation. I've got to speak to the lady."
"How come?"
"I checked out her social security number."
"And?"
"Carlene Ridge is all I got."
"What does that mean?"
"It means that she's what she claims to be until proven otherwise."
"You mean to tell me you can't check…"
"Kalb, trust me. There's no place of birth, no links to anyone or anything except a driver's license and the usual stuff. The woman's clean. At least from what little info I have."
"What else would you need?"
"You mean besides fingerprints and questioning?" Jeff said with a smirk on his face.
"Ok, ok… I'll try to think up of something…"
"Great!"
"Hold it! There is something else. About three days ago the husband got this phone call from a Margie Joree…another lady…but in Dallas."
"Dallas Texas?"
"Right. Turns out she was a social lady…you know the kind…? She was also Carlene's best friend."

" I'm listening…"

"She called up Glen and wanted him to come to Dallas… said she had something to show him …that he'd understand once he saw it, something about Carlene…"

"And?"

"Glen didn't really give her an answer… said he'd think about it…."

"Why?"

"Don't know."

Jeff's lips puckered.

"He's kind of… different, you know? you can't really tell with him." Kalb added.

"What do you mean?"

"Well… he didn't exactly fill me in with details…"

"At least we now have another name. But it's out of town… getting complicated…" Jeff said.

"There's also a name of a school that I checked out …"

" Carlene's School?"

"One of them, supposedly."

"I'd like to see it."

Kalb's stomach was doing funny things. He felt nausea rising within and wasn't sure anymore if it was right to do this, check out and spy on Carlene. How could he do it? But then he remembered her refusal to answer his questions, avoiding giving names and other details. It was better this way; someone needed to check her out.

"Any other ideas?" Jeff asked.

"No. Not really. Can you go with it?"

"I'll see what I can do and let you know."

"Thanks Jeff."

Waving his hand in the air, Jeff turned around and walked away leaving Kalb to his own thoughts.

CHAPTER 22

Tierry stepped out of the cab feeling slightly tipsy from the wild drive and the anticipation of seeing Carlene. Pulling behind him the carry-on he entered the lobby wearing a broad smile on his face.

"May I help you sir?" Tony, the uniformed guard looked him over.

"I'm here to see Mrs. Wilmore."

Tony smiled and dialed the apartment. There was no reply. Concentrating on the number he tried again. He couldn't remember seeing Mrs. Wilmore exit the building. In fact, he was sure she was up there. Alone. Her husband wasn't with her. Definitely not.

"I'm sorry… there's no reply."

"That's impossible!" he stared at Tony.

"Mr.…?"

"I'm a family friend … I've just arrived here from Dallas. I came to visit Mrs. Wilmore… she's expecting me."

"Sir, I'm sorry, there's no reply. I can't let you in without permission."

"I understand… can you try again?"

Tony shook his head.

"Come on… come on… pick up the phone…" the words vibrated in Tony's head.

Tony knew Mrs. Wilmore never picked up the phone except when the housekeeper was out. Several hours earlier he'd seen the housekeeper in the lobby. He even remembered tilting his hat in her direction.

She smiled.

"That's it? Done for today?"

"Got the rest of the day off…"

"She must be in a good mood, eh?" Tony winked then added, "Have a good day."

She returned his smile and walked out.

Now looking discreetly at his watch Tony realized that it was over four hours ago, which meant that the missus was definitely inside her apartment.

"Sorry, sir, but there's no one at home."

Tierry felt like screaming. In his urgent desire to be with Carlene he had come unannounced wanting to surprise her. Now after having acted on impulse he found himself in an infuriating situation unable to see the woman for whom he had planned the surprise.

Standing in the plush lobby with the guard staring at him, Tierry was lost for words. He wanted to push away the uniformed man and storm into her apartment. Carlene's cell had been switched off shortly after their earlier conversation in the morning.

"Can you maybe try another number?"

"No… she doesn't have one…"

Tony knew that wasn't the case but he couldn't say anything. He had been given specific instructions never to use any of the private numbers belonging to the Wilmores except in case of an emergency.

"Only if the building's on fire and we're asleep, only then can you call us on our private phones." Dr. Wilmore had instructed Tony.

"So what do I do?" Tierry asked Tony.

"Sir?"

"What should I do? Are you suggesting I return to Dallas just because you won't let me in?"

"I can suggest a hotel, sir…"

"Right!"

Covering his face with both hands, Tierry let out a deep sigh. He felt frustrated and weak. No! This can't be happening. He had to see Carlene…he just had to … the situation was absurd.

"Merde!" Tierry released silently, "Merde!"

"Try again! Please!" he insisted.

Tony was hoping someone would finally pick up the phone and free him of the embarrassing situation.

It rang endlessly. Tony kept his head lowered.

"Can I order you a cab, sir?" he dialed once again staring at the wooden desk.

When he looked up Tierry had already stormed out of the building pulling his carry-on behind him.

***

Carlene's naked body lay still on the floor. The phone kept ringing as the music played on.

"Stop it …stop," she muttered.

The ringing stopped only to resume a moment later.

"Shut up…" her voice was hoarse.

The phone kept sounding.

Placing both hands over her ears Carlene moaned.

"Stop the noise… the fucking noise…"

She rolled onto her stomach then scrambled slowly to her knees in the direction of the sink.

"I don't … don't want to be… alone… all alone…" she sobbed.

Holding onto the cabinet frame her fingers moved inside the drawer searching for the bottle. It fell to the floor. She fumbled to find it, unscrewed the cap and stuffed a handful of pills into her mouth.

"Sleep… I want to sleep… just sleep …" she held her head with both hands, "Sleep…"

She stumbled in the direction of the large spa with its automated release system of aromatic lavender oil. Crawling on all fours with her tearful eyes all puffy and blurry, she felt for the CD button then slid her naked body into the bubbly waters still wearing her stilettos.

The opera Lakmé roared all around her.

"Alone… just to be alone…" she cried.
The phone kept ringing.

* * *

It was late and nearing the end of Tony's shift by the time Dr. Wilmore strode into the lobby.

"Evenin' Dr. Wilmore."

"Good evening, Tony," he walked towards the elevator.

"Dr. Wilmore…" Tony stepped from behind the reception area, "your friend…the one from Dallas was here, but I didn't let him in."

"What friend?"

"A man… said he was a family friend… Mrs. Wilmore was expecting him…"

"When was this?"

"About two hours ago… maybe less, he came with a cab straight from the airport …had a carry-on with him…"

"Is he up there now?"

"Oh no, sir, like I said… I didn't let him in… there's no one in the apartment."

"What about Mrs. Wilmore?"

"There was no reply, sir. I would never let anyone in …"

"What did he look like?"

"I'd say…about…forty…a big guy…looked ok type…serious, you know?"

Glen remained standing trying to digest Tony's words. Picking up his head he said.

"Thanks… Tony."

"Sure thing Dr. Wilmore."

***

Exiting the elevator on the top floor, Glen used the special key to unlock the side door then walked quietly up the staircase and into his workroom. Spacious yet densely furnished with antiques and oil paintings and what seemed like an endless array of assorted ornaments alongside over-heaped book shelves, the room looked its usual serene and quiet yet well organized and collected. Glen took off his shoes and stepped into his leathered slippers.

It was more than just a workroom. It was his escape, a world apart from his patients and the demanding writings imposed on him by his position at Columbia. If anyone thought a professor's life was quiet and calm, Glen was only too happy to point out the constant demands for research papers and updated articles. It was an exhausting task but one that Glen loved doing and did well. Now in his world apart, away from the daily clamors of life, Glen sat and thought of how he should proceed.

His initial reaction was to call Kalb even though he'd just parted from him. Tony's words made him feel uncomfortable, as if he were trying to hint at a secret. A terrible secret.

"What's going on?" he muttered to himself. "Who could it be? Someone from Dallas… how strange… Dallas again…"

After what seemed like eternity, Glen relaxed somewhat in his leather armchair.

"What should I do? What should I say to her?" he kept muttering. "Should I ask her about him… or just ignore it, yes, ignore it… he'd already left… went away… ignore him… yes…"

Unsure of what to do next, Glen reached for the receiver.

"Kalb will know…he'll know what I should do…" but a second later he changed his mind again.

"Maybe I should check it out first… just like Kalb said… she might be home… maybe in bed… sleeping… alone…"

The thought made him smile.

"Yes… sleeping… she's probably sleeping…"

Tiptoeing quietly as if preparing a surprise, he opened the door that connected to the rest of the apartment. The lights were on and the music was loud. He smiled recognizing Carlene's favorite Flower Duet aria.

"Darling?" he called out.

There was no reply.

Crossing the long corridor Glen cut through the music room with its silk padded walls and into the waiting room that served as the entrance to her suite. It was empty. The music was everywhere pouring out of the audio system throughout the apartment.

"Maybe she's in the tub?" Glen spoke out loud entering the large room.

"Darling?" he called.

The air smelled delicious reminding him of Carlene after she'd soaked herself in one of her special bath oils. He stuck his head in the doorway and tried again.

"Darling are you there?"

He kept calling her name.

"Where can she be? All the lights are on… music's blaring… where is she?"

Looking around he tried to imagine where she could possibly be but his head swarmed with strange thoughts all of which he was quick to dismiss.

"Where the heck are you?" he called out, "in the shower? Dressing? I know you're in here…someplace…"

Returning to her suite, he decided to check out the dressing room. Holding his breath he reached for the doorknob.

"Anyone there?" he called.

He was now inside Carlene's boudoir, her most secretive room. Constructed out of the finest cedar wood, the place could be mistaken for a plush boutique stocked with shelves and drawers and what seemed like miles of hanging spaces loaded with clothes and fur coats and…It was endless. Glen admired the craftsmanship of the wood. Moving his fingers over the finely trimmed drawers he smiled.

"Nice job…"

He opened some, looking at the color coordinated lingerie. He liked going through it from time to time, touching the delicate Coco De Mer lacy bodysuits, seductive little pieces barely visible against the silkiness of Carlen's skin. His fingers quivered over stringy thongs, playful shreds of satin adorned with sequin that made his cock tingle. He looked admiringly at the La Perla brassieres and the rose colored Fleur of England coordinated underwear, picked one up and placed it on his face. Shutting his eyes he scratched his balls. It was appetizing especially with the tag price still attached to it. It filled him with pride. Not too many husbands could afford such delicacies. He went through countless shirts and skirts and dresses next to drawers full of Hermes scarves, Chanel, Burberry, Gucci, Dior… too many to count in all colors and designs followed by an entire section reserved for belts and small accessories apart from the section of handbags and shoes. It reminded Glen of the new boutique recently opened at the Waldorf.

Adjacent to Carlene's most precious of rooms was their own bedroom decorated with contemporary art works hand-picked by Carlene and complemented by the breathtaking view of the park below.

Glen continued his search.

"Where are you, darling?" his voice louder now, "What the heck is going on here? Maybe I should check the extra rooms."

Returning into the connecting corridor Glen eyed the doorknobs. He spoke to himself debating the different options.

"What if she's hiding here with someone? What if she's seeing someone else… someone who's with her right now? Not the guy from Dallas… maybe Tony is wrong… no one's perfect… heck… I should know…so what if I find them inside one of these rooms? Should I say something? Should I walk out? What if she screams and starts cursing and goes wild?"

The thought sparked his imagination. He smiled.

"Maybe it's her way of wanting to play a new game? Maybe she's hiding and I'm supposed to find her then she can have a reason to…" feeling encouraged, Glen placed his hand on the first doorknob and stepped inside. The room was dark. Taking a deep breath he switched on the light. The king sized bed with its beautiful bed spread stood perfectly still with a large painting depicting a magnificent bouquet of red gladiolas hanging above it.

"Fuck!"

Occupying only four out of the eight bedrooms, allowed their out of town guests to enjoy luxurious comforts within the spacious rooms each equipped with its own private bathroom and dressing room.

Glen enjoyed roaming the empty rooms, stopping by to admire a painting, an armchair or one of the rare tapestries, as part of his own favorite collections. The blue room with the Flemish paintings dating back to Rubens was one of his favorites. Another, the smallest of all, held a collection of Easter eggs, part of which resembled the famous Fabergé eggs exhibited annually at the Met museum. A set of five glassed shelves hermetically sealed and framed against the entire back wall housed an exceptional collection of Monarch butterflies displayed inside the orange room marking the end of Glen's inspection.

"Where are you, Carlene?" he called again.

He then decided to try the bathroom once again.

"Maybe she's hiding…"

Turning around he headed back in the direction of her room, then turned left into the large space.

"Are you hiding in here darling?"

With a smile on his face, he tiptoed into the spa room.

"Darling? Is that you hiding under the bubbles?" he called out over the music as he stepped inside.

He moved closer then crouched next to her noticing her submerged body. Only her head showed above the suds.

"Is this a new game?" he whispered in her ear.

Glen noticed her eyes were shut and her head tilted backwards.

"Darling… wake up … wake up darling…" he touched her face.

"Oh God!" he let out a shriek, "Oh God! What have you done?! Carlene…talk to me…what's wrong?" he grabbed her arm and placed both fingers on her wrist.

"Wake up…wake up, darling, what's wrong… you're cold… wake up…open your eyes…"

He reached for the phone.

"Help! It's my wife…she's dying! I need an ambulance! NOW!"

He spread a large towel on the floor. Pulling her carefully out of the tub he laid her on the towel then pulled off her dripping shoes and bent over to listen to her breathing. It was shallow matching her pulse.

"Darling," he slapped her face gently, "you've got to stay awake, darling…they're on their way…they'll soon be here…open your eyes darling… you've got to open your eyes…"

It had taken the emergency team less than ten minutes to enter the apartment and by then Glen had covered her nakedness with a bathrobe

"She's in there…still wet from the bath…careful…I took her out but…"

"Dr. Wilmore?"

"Yes?"

"Could you please wait over there?" realizing Glen's condition the paramedic held his arm and led him to a chair.

"Ok, but…"

"We'll be very careful…you can join us later on…in the ambulance…"

"Ok…ok…"

Glen fumbled with the phone.

"Sorry to wake you up…I thought you'd want to know…there's been an accident…it's Carlene," Glen's voice was thick and choppy.

"Where are you?"

"Mt. Sinai."

"On my way…" Kalb jumped out of bed.

It took a while before Dr. Hicks, the cardiologist, was able to assess Carlene's condition and by then Kalb had joined Glen.

"Looks like she OD'd…is she on any medication?"

"No! Absolutely none!"

"Look Glen as one doc to another… for Carlene's sake… let's cut the bull…I need to know."

Dr. Hicks kept staring at him.

"I…I…"

"It's for her own good…surely you realize how important this information is… we need to know if she's on something…"

"She's not on anything. Why are you insisting?"

"Because of her blood pressure…and pupils!"

"Shit! I told her not to… She must have taken the …"

"She's in bad shape, Glen… I need to know the name…"

Glen mumbled the name of the pills then turned to Kalb.

"Thanks for coming, Kalb," his eyes were red and swollen.

"What happened?"

"They're not sure…still thinking it's the heart but also checking…you know…"

"Yeah…OD?"

Glen nodded.

"I'm sorry …"

"I still can't believe it…probably the heart… but they're checking…"

"Where did you find her?"

"In her bathroom, she was in the tub…"

"What tub?"

"She's got this huge spa…it's like a small pool she likes to soak in."

Kalb moved his head. He could see her image floating in the water.

"She loves to soak… does it everyday…"

"Yeah, I know."

"What?!"

Kalb hadn't meant for his tongue to slip off like that.

"She'd mentioned it once…besides…don't all women like to soak? It's something of a pastime."

His reply seemed to pacify Glen who kept shaking his head.

"I just can't imagine…"

"How is she now?"

"Still unconscious…but they're hopeful."

"I need a cup of coffee. Feel like joining?"

"Ok."

Glen's shoulders looked heavy. Dragging his feet he kept muttering.

"How could she do this? Why? Why did she take those fucking pills? I don't understand…what's wrong with her? She loves me… and I love her… what's wrong Kalb?" staring at him with pitiful teary eyes.

Too overwhelmed to respond Kalb only listened. It felt stuffy inside the waiting space. Kalb got up and paced the length of the room. Every so often Glen wiped his eyes. Checking his wrist watch, Kalb said.

"Why don't you go in and see how she's doing?"

"Yeah…I guess I should…"

"Unless you'd like me to… to join?" Kalb asked.

"I insist."

They entered a white corridor leading into the trauma unit where they met with the nurse.

"Sorry… but you're not allowed inside …"

"That's ok… I'm Dr. Wilmore and this is Dr. …"

"I'm sorry…" the nurse shook her head, "you know the rules…"

"Is Dr. Hicks in?"

"Yes he is…he's busy inside the unit."

"Could you please …?"

Just then Glen spotted him.

"Dr. Hicks… John… over here…" he motioned with his hand. "Glen…"

"John …this is my associate Dr. Kalb Gales…how is she doing?"

Dr. Hicks acknowledged Kalb with a nod.

"I'm glad to deliver some good news. I think the worst is behind us…she's showing signs of waking up…moving…turning…it's a process…"

"Can I see her?"

Dr. Hicks looked at his watch.

"I'll make an exception …but only for a minute …it's nearly two…we'd like her to rest as much as possible…"

"Sure… sure… I understand…"

"Follow me."

They entered the large room with green drapes engulfing each of the cubicles. Dr. Hicks led the way to the far corner.

"Carlene…I'm Dr. Hicks…can you hear me?"

She looked like a beautiful figurine. Overwhelmed at the sight of her, Kalb felt an urge to bend down and kiss the penciled lips. He imagined his love was strong enough to wake her up. She looked so calm and peaceful.

"Carlene can you hear me? Open your eyes if you can hear me…"

They remained standing next to her bed for another minute or so.

"I think we should let her rest."

Just then Carlene moved her head and let out a sound.

"Did you hear that? Did you see how she moved her head?" Glen smiled.

"She still has a long way to go… she's not completely out of the woods…let's give it another twenty-four hours before we're sure…"

After leaving Carlene in Dr. Hicks' care, Kalb drove Glen home.

"You sure you're going to be ok?" Kalb asked Glen for the fifth time.

"Yeah…I'll be ok."

"See you tomorrow… I mean… in a few hours, Glen. If you hear anything please let me know. I'll be home 'till two."

"Will do."

* * *

"Hi Glen, this is John Hicks."

"How is she, John ?" Glen was still in bed.

"She's remarkable…"

Glen chuckled.

"I know…that's my Carlene."

"Yes…well…" Dr. Hicks released a short chortle.

"What time is it John ?"

"It's nine."

"That late?!" Glen sat up in bed. "I've been out for six hours…"

"I wanted to let you know …"

"Is this good news or …?"

"It's good…Carlene's fine…"

"I knew it…I knew it!"

"Hold it Glen. She's fine in the sense that …she'd regained consciousness… and physically…"

"Oh…you don't know what this means to me, John …"

"Glen, I'm trying to tell you that Carlene's not fully recovered yet…"

"Yes…but she's physically…"

"But not emotionally. She'll need help…"

"Don't worry about that. I'm a shr…"

"That's just it, Glen. I'm glad we're both physicians…I can talk to you freely. What Carlene needs is…"

"I know what she needs, John . I appreciate what you're trying to do but…"

"I don't think you understand, Glen. She tried to commit suicide."

"I know! Don't you think I realize that?!"

"I can have our chief psychiatrist…"

"Don't even think of it! If anyone's going to take care of my wife it's going to be ME!"

"Glen…please listen…Ben Feldman…"

"I know the joker and I'm telling you right now I won't allow it!"

"But why? He's an outstanding psychiatrist. I don't need to tell you… you shouldn't treat Carlene, it's not…"

"Are you trying to tell me what I should or shouldn't do?! Don't you think I know?!"

There was a long silence before Dr. Hicks finally said.

"I'm sorry. I assumed that as a psychiatrist … well…that you'd understand…"

"Thanks John . I'll keep it in mind."

An hour later, Glen was in the hospital next to Carlene's bed.

"How are you darling?" he reached for her hand.

It felt dry and powerless like the dangling hand of a rag doll.

"Do you know where you are?" he smiled.

Carlene didn't react.

"You're in Mt. Sinai…you were saved…I saved you darling… fished you out of the tub…"

Glen noticed the wetness of her eyes. Plucking a tissue from a nearby box he dried her tears. She squeezed his hand. Glen's face broke into a big smile.

"Just listen to the doctors…they'll take good care of you…"

"Home…home…" Carlene mouthed.

"I'll take you home soon…I promise darling…you'll soon be home…" his voice broke down.

***

Carlene's recovery over the next several days was slow but steady. Refusing to leave her bedside, Glen flooded her private room with flowers in every color, a nursery-like room with beautiful bouquets placed in large vases and huddled next to each other to create a colorful flower bed all around.

"I ordered your favorites," he pointed to the orange lilies.

Carlene smiled.

"Thanks, darling," she kept wiping her eyes.

"What's wrong, Carlene?"

She shook her head and shut her eyes. Glen looked at the door. There was no one in the corridor. Moving closer Glen spoke in her ear.

"I want to know…were you expecting someone that night? Someone… a man…just before getting into the tub?"

"No."

"I think you're lying, darling," he whispered.

"No! I'm not."

"So why are you crying? There's no reason to cry…is there?"

"It's not …" she said in the tiniest of voices.

"Really! You sure you weren't expecting any visitors?"

Again she shook her head.

Dr. Hicks opened the door.

"How are you, Glen?" Dr. Hicks shook his hand.

Glen smiled.

"Glad to see you're awake Carlene… you've been up for quite a while. How are you feeling?"

"She's coming along just fine. Great!" Glen announced.

"Glad to hear it."

"You did a great job, John . Thanks."

Glen patted his shoulder.

Dr. Hicks smiled in return and signaled with his thumb to step outside.

Glen turned around and said to Carlene.

"I'll be right back, darling…don't worry about a thing."

Outside, Dr. Hicks didn't waste any time.

"I'll be frank with you, Glen. Your wife will need constant supervision. She's showing signs of severe depression…we've stabilized her but she'll need…"

"That's why I'm here…lucky for my wife she's married to me…" he chuckled.

"As her treating physician, I need to share with you…" they had reached Dr. Hick's office.

"If this is more of the same… don't even bother!" Glen said.

Dr. Hicks shut the door behind them.

He wanted to make sure Glen understood the severity of Carlene's condition.

* * *

Later on, Kalb called Glen.

"How's Carlene?"

"She's doing great! John Hicks thinks she'll soon be released."

"That's great news! I'm so glad to hear it."

"Yeah…can't wait to have her back home with me…"

"I can imagine," Kalb answered.

"Jealous?" Glen snickered as if reading his thoughts.

"Absolutely!"

Glen chuckled then added.

"By the way…before I forget…there's something I'd like to discuss with you…it's about the other night…can I call you later on? How late can I call?"

"As late as you want. Always at your service," he laughed.

"Thanks Kalb.

It was nearly nine thirty by the time Glen had left the hospital, returned home and called Kalb.

"Hi Kalb…I just walked in the door…"

"How is she?"

"Asleep…is this too late?"

"No…no, not at all. How about a drink?"
"I'd like that." Glen sounded relieved.
"Where?"
"How about my place?"
"I'll be there shortly."
Kalb was eager to hear about Carlene's condition.
"Thanks Kalb."
Glen hung up and checked the list.
He needed to make only one more phone call before Kalb's arrival.

Glen's secretary for the past eight years was a fifty-six year old widow who was efficient as a Swiss clock and didn't mind late night phone calls. She answered on the second ring.
"Yes?"
"Hi Barb, I…"
"Dr. Wilmore…I'm glad you called. How is your wife?"
"Fine… fine… I'm going to be busy for the next few days … I'd like you to hold off all my calls …let the answering service know… all patients should be referred to the usual …"
"I've already spoken with Dr. Jackson…" Barbara said.
"Good. Good."
"But what about the emergency cases?"
"Yes… that's why I'm calling…that Cox kid, Brian Cox. If he calls they should put him through to me no matter what. He's Jacob and Felicia's son and he may need urgent hospitalization… he's not well balanced now…"
"Sorry to hear that."
"Yeah…unfortunately…"
"Ok, I'll take care of it immediately and make sure they have his name. Anyone else who should be put through?"
"No, only the Cox kid."
"Will do. I hope your wife feels better."
"Thanks Barb."
"You bet."

CHAPTER 23

"Come in…come in…" Glen stood next to the elevator waiting for Kalb. "Thanks for coming."
Kalb placed his hand on Glen's shoulder.
"How is she doing?"
"Great! She's …she seems fine…tired but fine…"
"Glad to hear it."
Glen poured two glasses. Handing one to Kalb he seated himself across from him.
"Cheers."
"To Carlene's health!" Kalb held up his glass.
"To my Darling."
"So… what's the verdict on her situation? Did she ….?"
"Hicks says she'll be fine…she'll have to adjust, of course…"
"What d'you mean?"
"She won't be able to run around like before…she'll have to rest a lot."
"Why? Is she on any medications?"
"She will be…as of now…"
"When are they thinking of releasing…"
"Probably within a couple of days…maybe even tomorrow afternoon…"
"Great! That's good news!"
Kalb forced a smile.
"Yeah…I hope so…"

"What's the prognosis?"

"She'll need someone…someone to talk to…"

"She's got you…what could be better?" Kalb wanted to scream out but instead he clenched his jaws.

Glen helped himself to a refill.

"Want some?" he held the bottle in Kalb's direction.

"I'm fine… thanks."

"Of course I can't handle it…she's…she won't…"

Kalb felt like shouting, telling Glen he should call him day or night in case Carlene needed someone to talk to, but he knew he couldn't really say such things, not until he had revealed his secret to Glen. His damn secret. Why did he have to keep it a secret? Why couldn't he let the world know how much he loved her? Maybe he could explain the situation to Glen…ask him to consider Carlene's needs. Fuck! They were his needs! His head was spinning, it was crazy to even think about it … but what if Carlene did care for him after all? No, it couldn't be…or she would have stayed with him …she wouldn't have left him after two months…oh…all these thoughts… they only confused him more….

Lost for words, and feeling utterly confused, Kalb changed the subject.

"So…what else is happening?"

"Like I said…she won't' go to just anyone…"

"Why not Ruth Wardings?"

"Ah! You must be joking!"

"Why?"

"If Carlene wants someone, she'll get the very best."

"Hold it…hold it!" Kalb raised both hands. "You know darn well Ruth is one of the best…"

"One of the best isn't good enough. I want **The Best!**"

"And who might that be?"

"**You**, my friend! **You!**"

Kalb felt he'd been punched in the stomach.

"I'd like some more, please," he held up his glass.

Glen refilled Kalb's glass.

"Well…at least you found out the truth…she was alone when you got home, right?" Kalb released cynically.

Glen stared at him.

"What?! What's wrong?!"

"Sometimes people say stupid things!"

"Sorry…I didn't mean to… I just wanted to say that I couldn't possibly see Carlene. Professionally, that is…I can't talk to her…it wouldn't be right…"

Glen didn't reply. He kept staring at Kalb. Then as if he'd suddenly remembered something, added:

"Oh! I just remembered! That's it! The cab driver… remember?"

"It's ok, Glen…don't worry…I'm fine"

"No, no! It's not about you, Kalb. It's about the man we saw getting out of the cab…the one that nearly ran you over the other night."

"What about him?"

"This is kind of strange… After you'd gone home, I saw Tony the security guard. He told me there was a guy who'd stopped by a couple of hours earlier and asked to come up to our apartment."

Kalb was listening intently.

"Said he was a family friend … and that Mrs. Wilmore was expecting him."

"Do you know him?"

"No! But he insisted she was expecting him."

"Did this …Tony…did he give you any details?"

"Well…let's see…said he was about forty or so… looked ok…a serious looking guy…I think those were his words."

"Anything else?"

"That's it…oh…yeah…said he came from Dallas…yeah…he said that he came all the way from Dallas…"

Kalb stared at his drink. Somehow, it clicked familiar.

"Are you sure you don't know anyone in Dallas?" he eyed Glen.

"No!" Glen shook his head, "I don't."

"What a coincidence. I'm thinking about Margie's call…the one you told me about…"

"Sounds like two different things to me," Glen said.

"Doesn't to me," Kalb emptied his glass.

"What are you saying?"

"I don't know what I'm saying…I'm just trying to find a thread…a lead…"

"To what?"

"To Carlene!"

Glen stared at Kalb in total confusion.

"What are you talking about?!"

"I think Carlene has some explaining to do."

It was then that he realized how angry he'd become. His head swarmed with thoughts and words he couldn't voice out loud.

"Glen…there are things that we're going to have to discuss…not now…not immediately, but you've got to trust me on this."

"I do…I do…" Glen shook his head.

"You can't discuss it with anyone…not even Carlene…it might upset her…let me get back to you on this, ok?"

"What do you mean some explaining to do?"

"Think about it, Glen. First, you get this strange call from Margie whom you haven't spoken to in…"

"But I called her!"

"But Margie wanted to show you something, right?"

"Yeah, but…"

"And now this guy shows up from Dallas…"

"It's probably a coincidence…"

"I suppose it could be…but it's not very likely, is it?"

Glen lowered his head.

"What are you trying to tell me, Kalb?"

"That maybe… just maybe…Carlene isn't who she claims to be…"

Glen covered his face with both hands. In the silence that followed, Kalb heard his sniffling.

"How about another drink, Glen?"

"No, I'm fine…it's just…I can't believe it…"

"That's why I stressed the maybe, Glen. It's only a possibility but…"

"I can't imagine…" Glen's voice broke again.

Kalb's thoughts were elsewhere, on the words that were now at the tip of his tongue, those he wasn't brave enough to spit out.

"How about some fresh air?"

"No…I'd rather stay here. I'm ok, Kalb. Really."

"Sure?"

"Yeah."

"Ok…then I'll see you tomorrow."

With shoulders drooping and head lowered, Glen walked Kalb to the door looking shorter than usual.

Kalb was relieved to be out of there.

* * *

It was a sunny Sunday when Glen stepped out of the reception lobby onto the paved entrance next to the parked limo pushing the wheelchair in front of him. Larry jumped out of his seat and opened the back door.

"It's so bright," Carlene called out.

"Here," Glen handed her sun glasses.

"Larry, could you…"

"Sure thing, Dr. Wilmore, right away…" he took Carlene by the arm and helped her slowly into the back seat.

Glen followed.

"Are you ok?"

"Yes, I'm fine. Stop treating me like an eggshell."

Glen hushed.

He couldn't forget Kalb's words and kept hearing maybes. Maybe, his head chimed…maybe…just maybe…Carlene isn't who she claims to be…

Turning to Carlene he stared at her profile.

"What's wrong?"

"Nothing."

"So stop staring!"

"Are you hungry?"

"Do I look it?!"

They drove in silence. Having reached home, Glen helped Carlene out of the car.

"I'd like to rest…"

"Sure. That's a good idea."

Glen tried to concentrate on what Carlene was saying, but his head was throbbing with Kalb's maybes.

"I'd rather be alone," Carlene said after settling in bed.

"Right. I'll be in my room if you need me."

Unable to resist himself, Glen bent down and kissed her forehead.

He felt his eyes sting.

CHAPTER 24

At eight-thirty the following morning Kalb entered his office and at once dialed Jeff.

" D'you have a moment?"

"Sure thing, I can be there in a few minutes."

"Thanks, Jeff."

For the past two days, ever since he'd heard about the stranger from Dallas, Kalb tried to figure out who it could be. Convinced he was a personal acquaintance of Carlene's and curious about his connection with Dallas, Kalb was determined to untangle the knot.

"If anyone can figure this out it's Jeff."

Ten minutes later Jeff walked into his office.

"Early Monday morning… what's up?"

Kalb placed a cup of coffee in front of him.

"Black?"

"Sure thing. Thanks."

"Our lady's had an accident…" Kalb shot out.

"Accident?"

"And was rushed to the hospital…"

"OD'd?"

"Yeah."

"Shit! How is she?"

"Much better. They released her yesterday."

"Good."

"It's very good… considering what could have happened."

"Right."

"But…you're not going to believe this."

"Try me."

"I saw Glen two nights ago… spent time with him away from the hospital. Turns out he had an unexpected visitor."

"I'm listening."

Kalb updated him about the man from Dallas who'd come to see Carlene.

"Interesting!"

"Thought you'd enjoy it…"

"Very interesting…"

"Are you thinking what I'm thinking?"

"I'm not gonna make you blush!"

Kalb laughed though he felt a pinch in his heart. Still smiling Jeff asked.

"Is there anything decent to drink in this academic joint?" looking around Kalb's room while eyeing the rows of framed honorary citations.

"The bar doesn't open 'till noon." Kalb winked.

Jeff laughed.

"These are all fake, right?" Jeff moved his arm to include all frames on the wall.

Kalb noticed the faint smile on his lips.

"Over twenty years of hard work, man."

"And all for the sake of frames, right?"

Both laughed.

"I'll be glad to sell you one."

"How much, Doc?"

More laughs and smiles.

"So? What'll be?"

"I'm going to find out what the fuck is going on. You got me hooked. Can you give me Glen's address and the name of that security guard?"

"The name's Tony, he works at…" Kalb wrote down the address and handed it over to Jeff.

"Right. I'll get back to you as soon as I have something."
"Thanks Jeff."
Waving his hand, Jeff turned around determined to find out who Carlene Ridge really was.

* * *

As soon as he was back in his office, Jeff called Sandy.
"Joey speaking."
"Hey. It's Jeff. How come Sandy's not answering?"
"He's kind'a busy…. what's up?"
"Great! Is he there?"
"Yeah…hold on."
He heard Joey holler and a minute later his voice was on again.
"Must be out. Wanna' leave a message?"
"What d'you mean he's out? It's only nine!"
"He's taking a crap! What's the difference?"
"Ok…ok…tell him it's urgent."
"Will do. Sounds interesting."
"It is."
"Same woman?"
"Different."
Jeff decided to stay put and wait for Sandy's call.

He sat in his room and held the unlit cigarette in his hand. Knowing the entire area was smoke-free only aggravated his craving for a smoke and added to his nervous habit of biting his lower lip. Ten minutes later, unable to contain himself any longer, Jeff stepped away from his desk and peeked into the distant corridor listening to any footsteps.

Re-entering his room, he locked the door, opened wide the window and quickly lit up a cigarette wondering when he'd hear from Sandy.

* * *

Kalb couldn't stop thinking about the stranger from Dallas. It was obvious that he was connected to Carlene, probably the man she was now seeing. But why from Dallas? There were plenty of men in New York, he thought bitterly. Why Dallas? Unless… maybe it was someone she'd been seeing for a much longer time. Maybe they'd been friends in the past and he only… no! That didn't make sense. Why would he come all the way from Dallas? And how did he know Carlene was alone at home? Unless… unless Carlene told him she'd be alone…

Covering his face with both hands Kalb took a deep breath. It didn't make him feel any better. He still felt a lump in his throat, a big stone-like obstacle that reminded him of the tangle he was now involved in. How could he be so stupid? Why did he allow Carlene to make love to him? Why? Darn it! He should have been smarter… and not given in to her. But seeing …and smelling and… touching her body…

Kalb realized he was moving in circles but couldn't help himself. He wished he could stop thinking about her. But he knew he couldn't stop loving Carlene.

CHAPTER 25

Sandy, an accomplished police officer and head of NYPD's special operations unit was one of a kind. Exceptionally tall and impressive looking with a short crew cut leaving only gray spikes on his handsome head, Sandy looked younger than his fifty two years. The steel metallic eyes were just as bright and alert as when Jeff had first met him some thirteen years earlier.

Sandy's real name was Tadoosh Sandomirsky Varlovsky, shortened for Sandy when he first started school at the age of five having been spotted as a prodigy. By age twenty he had graduated from Columbia with master's degrees in physics and mathematics. A first generation born American to Russian immigrant parents, Sandy was drawn to the navy and to the police. He chose the former for fifteen years then changed his mind and switched to the latter. The police force was only too happy to see him join its special forces. He was placed in charge of the most delicate and complicated of cases and had become somewhat of a legend. Besides his brightness and wry sense of humor Sandy had his own way of solving problems and getting results. A man of integrity and enormous charm with a stunning gray stare and a boyish smile, Sandy was much more than just Sandy.

Jeff and Sandy had taken to each other immediately and became good friends spending days and nights planning sting operations. Their war against drug lords was fierce and nerve-wracking, relying heavily on inside information. It seemed to strengthen Sandy's already hardened core as well as his bond with Jeff. But there was one snag and one snag only: Rene Dortmund.

Jeff had begun dating Rene after divorcing his wife and spending the next three years alone. Rene, a sergeant within the unit, was a short brunette with a plain-looking face who appealed to Jeff from the moment he first set eyes on her. It took Jeff four months to dare ask her out, and when he finally did and she had agreed, there wasn't a happier man in the unit. But Rene, unknown to Jeff, was still in love with Sandy, who had dated her years earlier; and though he had left her and had moved on with his life, Rene had never quite recovered.

Hoping to make Sandy jealous and win his heart over to her again, Rene agreed to date Jeff. It all came to a head and fell apart when, Sandy, having bumped into Rene in the corridor, one day, asked her.

"So…how's it going with Jeff?"

"Who's asking?"

"Me. Your boyfriend."

Rene blushed and chose to interpret his response her own way.

"Dream on, lover boy…I'd never take you back…"

"Are you sure?"

Rene's split-second hesitation gave her away. Well-versed and experienced in feminine logic, Sandy burst out laughing.

"What would you say if I'd ask you out?"

"I'd tell you to go fuck yourself! Creep!"

Sandy moved his shoulders up and down.

"Enjoy your new boyfriend. He won't last long!" Sandy turned his back and walked away.

It only aggravated her more. Unable to contain her emotional upheaval, Rene didn't think twice before splashing the two cups of coffee held in her hands, on Sandy's back.

"Shit!" Sandy let out.

Without as much as turning around, he moved fast in the direction of the bathroom passing Jeff on his way.

"Your girlfriend is nuts as usual. I'd watch her if I were you."

Jeff saw Sandy's tall figure disappear inside the men's bathroom. Infuriated by his words yet bewitched by Rene, Jeff went in search of the man who had dared bad mouth the woman he loved and caught up with him.

"Son of a bitch!" Jeff kicked Sandy's rear with his boot.

Acting instinctively, Sandy turned around and boxed Jeff in the stomach with a fist that caused Jeff to fold in two and gasp for air.

Nothing remained the same after that incident, though Jeff did apologize to Sandy who reciprocated. Rene, who was transferred out of the unit shortly thereafter, had left her two former boyfriends behind without as much as a blink of an eye.

Now sitting in his office and waiting to hear from Sandy, Jeff was tense.

The five-man team headed by Sandy was the tip of the spear within the special operations unit. It was up to Sandy to prioritize his cases.

* * *

Now back in his small cubicle Sandy called up Jeff.

"What's up?"

"Long time no hear, man!"

"Miss me?"

Jeff laughed.

"Yeah…kind'a. Have an interesting twist for you."

"Age and size?"

"You ain't heard nothin' yet!"

"I'm drooling."

"Actually…I'm…" Jeff was trying to calculate when he could squeeze a meeting with Sandy. He really needed one but wasn't sure if Sandy could manage it.

"Do I hear you're busy?" Sandy asked sarcastically.

"Well… can we meet later?"

"Can you at least give me a hint?"

"I'd like to interest you with a beautiful lady."

"Is this one of your bad jokes?" Jeff could almost hear the smile in Sandy's voice.

"If I won't be able to make it, I'll let you know."

"When and where?"

"*The Rogue* around eight."

"Done."

Jeff smiled. It was the usual Sandy with his wry, laconic air.

CHAPTER 26

Carlene lay in bed thinking about Tierry. Her head felt heavy and she couldn't remember when they had last spoken but knew it must have been several days earlier. She wondered if he had called her then remembered she hadn't been home to answer the phone. Where was she? It was someplace quiet without music and people. A very quiet place filled with beautiful flowers. It was a garden… probably her own. She forgot. She didn't recognize it…it was different… very different.

With her head still fuzzy and somewhat dizzy, she tried to focus on the large painting in front of her eyes, wondering where she was. Then all at once, in a split second of lucidity, Carlene remembered who she was and realized it was dangerous for Tierry to call her. Glen, now constantly at her side, took care of her needs making sure she wasn't alone for a second.

"I wonder what day it is," she spoke out loud.

It was difficult to concentrate with her eyes always staring at the same painting with the same small figurines skidding in the snow. Her heart was overflowing with a sense of emptiness. She lay perfectly still in her bed. There was something wrong with her body. There were moments when she tried to recall events from the past but soon realized that her head wasn't as clear as before. Her memories were playing tricks on her, rushing teasingly back and forth like sea waves. Why did they flow so unevenly? It made her think of her conversation with Tierry but then it might have been with someone else, she wasn't sure anymore. Didn't he mention something about his wife? But why? He'd promised to marry her but...no, she must be confusing him with someone else...someone who didn't have a wife. But did it really matter? Maybe. Maybe not. Those pills... those darn little things were mixing her up and making her forget what she needed to remember. How she hated them!

"I'll do what I did at Cedars Home," she thought but then remembered Glen's face.

"Damn him...damn Glen...always here to make sure I swallow them ..."

Carlene could still recall the feel of it all, the senseless monotonous existence inside the tiny room curled up on her narrow bed without a shred of privacy. It was strange how some things refused to leave, like the smell of the place, a repulsive stench of unwashed bodies and disinfectants mixed with cigarette smoke and the musty putrid air of chlorine and Lysol. She could see the filth and hear the screams that filled the darkened corridors, overwhelmed by a sense of total helplessness. Moving her tongue she imagined the tiny capsules inside her mouth. It was Bobby who had told her how to avoid their effects.

"Put them under your tongue...swallow the water... get rid of 'em as soon as you can...they'll only mess up your brain..."

It didn't take long for the nurses to catch on and when they did she cursed Bobby for having suggested it. Three times a day and against her will, she was strapped up and forcefully medicated. Things turned fuzzy again and her eyes misted over. She tried to remember and forget at the same time. It only made the world spin faster in front of her blue eyes with Tierry stuck deep inside her head. She needed to focus, talk to him, it was important...she was close to something...so very close...

"I remember! I remember! I've got to speak to him..." she said out loud, "I can't lose him now...not when it's so close."

She thought she heard the phone ring and moved her arm sideways. A strange man kept asking for Mrs. Wilmore. In her confusion she couldn't understand why they insisted on Wilmore. Didn't they know her name was Abigail?

She picked up the phone.

"Fuck off!" she spoke in a small, hoarse voice.

But the man kept wanting to speak to the other woman.

She tried sitting up in bed but was overcome by dizziness.

"Maybe later…" she shut her eyes, "maybe later…"

* * *

Looking at his wristwatch, Glen got up and walked in the direction of Carlene's room. It was time to wake her up.

"Food, medicines and fresh air…that should do it," Glen was convinced he could make Carlene better. But his thoughts were elsewhere; unable to rid his mind of the last conversation he'd had with Kalb.

How could Carlene be someone other than the beautiful wife he now took care of? He loved her too much to cause her any pain or harm, but it was only fair that she, too, should love him. He'd never let anyone or anything get in the way of their love, even if it meant keeping her away from others. She'd be much happier living quietly with him… only with him.

Glen's beeper sounded. He read the message.

"Urgent message. Brian Cox needs help. Requests to speak with Dr. Wilmore urgently."

"You'll have to wait, screwball!" Glen said and switched off the beeper.

Carrying a food tray, he approached Carlene's room.

He tapped quietly on the door.

"Mind if I come in?"

Entering the room he tiptoed to the bedside and stood nearby watching Carlene's beautiful face. His eyes stung. Placing the tray on the night table he crouched beside her.

"Do you love me?" he whispered in her ear, his hand moving gently over her hair.

Carlene groaned and tossed.

"I love you more than myself," his face was streaked with salty tears.

"What d'you want?" Carlene muttered.

Glen's face looked drawn.

"Go away! Just go away…I hate you!"

"Why?" he whispered.

"Leave me alone…don't touch me!"

"Would you like to eat?"

"Away!"

Things were swirling and moving faster than she could focus with her eyes. She felt a thousand hands touching and tearing at her body. Her tongue felt strange, too big inside her dry mouth.

"Don't touch me!" she screamed.

"How about some fresh air?"

Carlene's eyes remained shut.

"I'll bring your pills…"

"Out! Don't touch me!" she forced her eyes open but was unable to keep them from shutting again.

"Ok… rest some more…I'll return in a few minutes…"

Carlene didn't react.

Glen blew his nose shut the door behind him and returned to his own room. Locking the door he crossed the oriental carpet past the Louise XIV oval shaped desk and moved in the direction of the heavy wooden table standing against the far wall with the beautifully hand carved crystal Waterford vase in its center. Reaching into his pocket Glen took out a tiny key then moved towards the painting hanging on the wall next to the table. Using one hand he tilted the frame to its side inserting the key to reveal a safe filled with small flacons and vials. Picking one up he muttered.

"This should do it…this should definitely do it…"

He turned the key again and locked the safe then entered the bathroom, picked up a syringe from the cabinet and walked out in the direction of Carlene's room.

CHAPTER 27

Tierry tried calling Carlene from his room at the Ritz hotel, but got no reply. He found it very odd, especially after having spoken to her only hours earlier. Was his memory playing tricks on him or did she really say she was considering leaving her husband? If it were only up to him he would have already left his wife. Maybe he should do it anyway… just tell her he's found a real love, the love of his life. He'd be willing to leave her the house, their sprawling mansion with the pool and the tennis court and…no! Not his daughter, he'd definitely want to have visitation rights. Maybe he could see her over the weekend or during the week…Carlene will love her… his beautiful little girl…and maybe he and Carlene could have another kid or two together…

The thought forced a smiled on his face but then he changed directions and imagined Carlene under different circumstances. Could he be mistaken about her? Looking at her face she was as pure and as beautiful as an angel. Surely she couldn't be toying with him…they were serious about each other…and in love…why was he even doubting it? Maybe it was her husband's fault… Carlene had told him how weird he was…what if…what if he found out about them and went crazy? Tierry couldn't stop churning the thoughts in his mind. He'd never forgive himself if anything happened to her. Oh, Carlene, I can't live without you. I miss your face…your smell…your body…your being… Please Carlene, please give me a sign you're ok.

He felt a confusing turmoil from within. Here he was, a senior vice president of one of the world's leading banks, a successful international banker capable of sealing deals involving billions of dollars across the globe, a tall handsome husband and father who was able to provide his beautiful wife and daughter a luxurious life filled with joy and opulence, yet he couldn't explain how or why the woman he loved had disappeared into thin air. How could he, Ralph T. Huber of Franco Swiss Credit Bank, have found himself in such a predicament? And why was he, despite his many virtues and well cultured background, why was he denied Carlene's love? Surely he was worthy of her beauty and mind at least as much as her husband? He'd earned his MBA from Harvard and spoke French fluently and…

The longer he thought about it the more confusing things got. If he could only understand her sudden disappearance… she was probably in trouble…maybe even at risk… but there was nothing he could do about it except… go to the police and report her missing. But what about her husband? And how would he explain it to the police?

Tierry was lost for answers.

He had once asked Carlene about friends and relatives, but never really got a reply. Now lounging on his bed with dead-end thoughts occupying his mind, Tierry found that he actually knew very little about the woman he loved and adored.

"But I love her so much," he kept repeating over and over. "She's so beautiful…I must see her."

The more he thought about it, the more determined he became to find Carlene and take care of her. He would figure out the rest later on, there'd be plenty of time to sit and get to know her family and past.

"I need some fresh air," he muttered aloud then stepped out of the hotel for a walk.

Tierry was born to a French father who worked as a car salesman at the Mercedes Benz showroom in Paris. He knew how to charm ladies and potential buyers with his good looks and spun-out tales.

Each year he won the Top Salesman Award of the Year that added to his bank account and thrilled his ego. Tierry's Belgian mother, a seamstress by profession, was a brunette beauty from Namur who met his father by chance while touring Brussels and its Grand Place.

"Avez-vous déjà vu le Mannequin Piss ?" his father to be asked his mother to be as both happened to mill about the antiques booths in search of the small statue of the peeing boy.

She responded with a smile and captivated his heart. They were married on a whim and within a month moved to Canada and settled in Quebec where they enjoyed a lustful love affair that lasted seven years. Tierry was six-years-old when his father dropped dead from a sudden heart attack leaving him and his mother with inconsolable broken hearts. Over the years Tierry wanted to leave the house from under his mother's protective wings but when he got accepted to Harvard, the two decided to move together to Boston. Shortly thereafter his mother met someone else and remarried.

Throughout his childhood and years of growing up, Tierry was spoiled by his mother who felt the need to compensate her son for the death of his father by being overly protective and preventing his every fall and slip. Though well-meaning, she failed to appreciate the importance of allowing her child to blunder from time to time within the safety of their home. By always fixing and mending matters for him, she denied Tierry the experience needed to overcome failures in life. Her behavior resulted in her son's deeply rooted insecurities though he had learned to camouflage them by displaying overconfident behavior. Tall and very good-looking like his late father, Tierry was a born charmer with charismatic brilliance. He dated every girl and woman who came his way but proved a self-centered egotistical partner. He enjoyed young beautiful smiles and delicate feminine odors but shied away from any emotional commitment. Life for Tierry was one long spin on the carousal of carnal love, with rapid rides that never lasted long.

By age 40 he began feeling somewhat uncomfortable at work, with occasional hints and humorous remarks about his marital status. As a successful international banker he understood the innuendos and knew that his bachelor days were numbered.

Though surrounded by countless beauties who tiptoed around him trying their best to placate and fulfill his every whim and wish, deep down Tierry was hoping to encounter a very different type of woman, a strong-willed beauty who could protect him in case of need.

He met her a year later and introduced her to his mother who liked the fact that despite her twenty one years of age she was already making a dent as a talented interior designer. Their courtship was a very short one given the fact that they were both eager to start a family of their own. Five months after the wedding they celebrated the birth of their first child, a little baby girl that made Tierry smile sheepishly and promise that he'd never fail her in any way.

But their marriage soon turned into a lukewarm affair because of Tierry's overinflated expectations of the woman of his dreams, his constant travels and his wife's acceptance of his impetuous behavior. Judgmental of his wife, he evaluated her from his shallow perspective and badgered her constantly about actions and decision making. It didn't take him long to see her very differently from what he'd imagined her initially. He had hoped for a stern woman with a rigorous character who would basically keep him in line as did his mother, yet still hold him above all as a shining star. To his disappointment he found a person who basically allowed him ample space to continue his impulsive behavior. There were never any harsh exchanges between them and very few conflicting moments. They seemed to stay within their personal boundaries, sharing little of each other's spheres. Things were smooth. And at times, boringly smooth, as far as Tierry was concerned with seldom any upheaval, excitement or more than just a casual feel of romance. And at times it seemed that neither one knew the meaning of passion.

Until… Carlene's spectacular jolt into Tierry's arms.

* * *

It was past one a.m. when Tierry, having returned to his hotel room, tried dialing Carlene's number again.

"Come on…answer the phone…it's one in the morning…you must be at home…" he spoke to the silenced receiver.

By four a.m. he was beginning to juggle other notions in his mind. What if… what if he surprised her at home? He could just stop by for a casual visit…

He fell asleep despite himself with the TV still on and the lights bright. By the time he'd opened his eyes, he realized it was already past nine in the morning.

He reached for the phone and dialed.

"Hello?" a man's voice answered.

Tierry quickly hung up. The husband was home! I should have asked for Carlene, just demanded to speak to her. But what if he suspects…it would only add to Carlene's difficult situation. Wondering what to do next, Tierry decided to call again. After all, he was sitting in a hotel room only minutes away from her home… so close yet so far. He couldn't very well return to Dallas without having seen her…he had come to New York especially for her…he couldn't go back empty handed.

Inhaling deeply, he shut his eyes then opened them and reached for the phone.

"Hello?"

"Is Carlene in?"

"Who's calling?"

Tierry hesitated a second longer than was necessary and by then he felt the blood gushing to his head. He slammed down the receiver and shut his eyes wishing he'd have been brave enough to demand to speak to her.

He waited out the day calling every so often but always getting the same masculine voice, until he decided that it might be the butler or another house help and not necessarily the husband. Feeling somewhat braver, he dialed the number without needing to look it up.

"Hello?"
"Is this the Wilmore residence?"
"Yes it is."
"Is Mrs. Wilmore in?"
"Who's asking?"
"This is Dan Partly...I'm calling from Stylisimo."
"Can I help you?"
"And you are...?"
"I'm Dr. Wilmore, can I help you?"
"I really need to speak with Mrs. Wilmore. She'd called me a week ago and asked to be fitted..."
"What is this all about?"
"A dress she'd ordered..."
"I see."
"If I could just speak to her for a moment..."
"I'm sorry... she's not here."
"Will she be in later on?"
"I'm afraid she's not too well. Can she call you back?"
"Do you know when she'll be well enough to..."
"Listen Mr. ....?"
"Dan...Dan Partly."
"Right. Dan Partly, I don't know what this is all about... but I do know that Mrs. Wilmore isn't well and she can't come to the phone, so if you'll excuse me..."

He hung up.

"Damn you, damn you, damn you!" Tierry screamed as he slammed his fist into the pillow.

* * *

The following day around lunchtime Tierry tried the number one last time, just as he'd finished packing up his belongings. He was on his way to the airport.

"Hello?" a strange voice answered.
Tierry wasn't sure who the speaker was.
"Mrs. Wilmore?"
"Fuck off!"
The phone went dead.
Tierry assumed it was the wrong number and redialed.
"Yes…"
"Is Mrs. Wilmore in?"
Someone laughed. Tierry thought it sounded like Carlene…but surely she'd recognize his voice….
"Hello? Is someone there?"
Silence then that voice again.
"Abigail…this is Abigail…"
Hanging up he left the room, checked out and decided to wait for Carlene's call. He deserved some explanations.

On his return flight to Dallas, Tierry kept hoping he'd be able to resist the urge to call her again.

CHAPTER 28

The background music with the dimmed lights felt relaxing. Jeff spotted Sandy, his tall chest peering above the bar counter.
"Sorry I'm late," Jeff extended his hand.
"Is that unusual?" Sandy showed his beautiful white smile.
"Give me a breather!"
They slapped each other on the back like old buddies. Jeff took a seat.
"Same?" Sandy held up his glass.
"What are you having?"
"Does it matter?" he signaled the bartender, "The usual, Troy. Make it a double for the old man."

A hangout frequented by police officers and those wishing to share discreet words, *The Rogue* provided a pleasant, intimate atmosphere with what some considered the best drinks in town. Located near the campus *The Rogue* had been transformed by a retired police officer named Troy from what was once a small warehouse into a bar with an adjacent diner. The inside décor with its warm wooden panels reaching halfway to the ceiling alongside western paraphernalia and photographs covering the walls created an air of nostalgia and a sense of home away from home. Though well filtered and aided by ceiling fans, the air, thick with loud voices over soft music, held trails of smoke and the comforting aroma of strong coffee and beer.

Troy placed the drinks in front of them. Jeff lit up a smoke.

"Thanks, Troy. How's it going?"

Showing a thumbs-up sign, Troy smiled and nodded his head.

Jeff sipped then turned to face Sandy.

"I heard you had a nasty case the other day on campus…"

Jeff's face lit up with a smile.

"Yeah…I guess two years away from the unit makes one forget that nothing moves around town without you".

"You bet!" Sandy smiled.

"Sir!" Jeff jumped to his feet and saluted.

They chuckled.

"Good to see you, old man."

Jeff slapped Sandy's back.

"So!" Sandy's face turned serious. "You have something for me?"

"A beautiful woman. How's that for starters?"

Sandy shot him a gray stare.

"Any day or night…especially night."

"That's what I thought."

They sipped their drinks.

"Why would I be interested?"

"Ever bump into a dead-end person?" Jeff smiled.

"No history?"

"Nope. Nothing."

"Is she really that beautiful or are you leading me on?"

"Oh no! She's beautiful all right…incredibly beautiful…but uneven…like those we've had to dig up…those undocumented zombies we used to chase…"

"Umm."

Another sip and another cigarette.

"Name?"

"Carlene Wilmore previously Ridge."

"Any relation to the Doc?"

"Know him?!"

"You kidding me?!"

Jeff raised his eyebrows.

"This guy has a kinky taste and a history to match…likes badgering teenagers…not your usual stuff…he jerks off to the tune of howls and whips."

Jeff's jaws fell open. Staring at Sandy he asked.

"How kinky?"

"As kinky as they come… straight out of the zoo."

"Any charges?"

"Pending. In the past."

Sandy motioned Troy with his hand, signaling another round of drinks.

"So!" Sandy said, "What's the scoop on this Wilmore woman?"

"Let's just say it's a hunch. A strong hunch."

"Keep going…'"

"She's not what or who she claims to be. How's that for starters?"

"Got proof?"

"That's just it! Strictly a gut feeling and a few weird coincidences."

"Go on. You're doing this like an old man."

"Doing what?"

"Spitting it out! Are you getting rusty?" Sandy twisted his face.

Jeff laughed. They both saluted to their pasts before settling down to a serious conversation and an exchange of petty cash, Sandy's term for inside information.

"So what have you got?"

Troy placed the fresh drinks on the counter.

"Thanks Troy."

"A beautiful woman half the age of her husband, carrying a false name with a false background. I've checked that part, and she's definitely not a diplomat's daughter."

"Nice story," Sandy chuckled.

"Yeah!"

"What else?"

"Husband asks a colleague of his, a shrink, to talk to his beauty and ask her why she fucks other men. Our man gets a near cardiac arrest 'cause he's fucked her too, on the side.... So he joins the husband in the biggest quest of all: finding out the truth. A few interesting twists and turns with mysterious visitors from Dallas Texas. End of story."

"Is this the part where I should say 'wow'?"

Jeff laughed. It was catchy. For the next ten minutes all they did was laugh like a couple of teenagers.

"Let me fill you in," Sandy began. "Our Doc ain't so cozy as he'd like to seem. Five years ago we get called to the rescue. Our kinky guy hooks with a seventeen-year-old diplomat's daughter during one of those fancy dinner-cocktail parties. Girl plays hard to catch and loses herself in one of the rooms. Doc follows and falls to his knees begging her to whip him so that he can jerk off. Gal turns into stone and Doc panics. When she finally spits out her tale, kinky boy offers parents a large settlement in return for silence. A year later, same gal visits town again and bumps into Doc who accuses her, in front of a large crowd of dignitaries, of blackmailing him. The involved parties reek of alcohol and we get called again to hush matters at the direct request of the guys down in DC. That's when Doc gets pending charges. Turns out our Doc keeps doin' it over and over, only the gals keep getting younger. So as far as I'm concerned, he's got what he deserves."

"But what if it's more than that? What if this gal ain't for real?"

"Who the fuck cares?" Sandy held up his glass.

Jeff was silent, wondering maybe he, too, should just drop it. But there was something troubling in the story...something he couldn't quite put his finger on.

"What if I told you that some of the players are as straight as a ruler and that this gal is screwing them all?"

"Hope she enjoys it!"

"Look," Jeff's face turned serious, "There's something fishy about it...this shrink...the husband's colleague I was telling you about, he's the one that filled me in. He's a straight guy who thinks likewise. Then there's a Margie Joree, a social bird and Carlene's closest friend who left the city and moved to Dallas shortly after Carlene got married. A week ago she calls up the husband and tells him she has something to show him."

"In Dallas?"

"Yeah."

"What did she show him? Her ass?"

"He never went."

Watching Sandy's expression, Jeff added.

"Don't know why."

"Anything else?"

"How about giving it a shot? I have this feeling…"

"Like when you thought you were in love?"

Jeff smiled.

"It's a hunch. A gut thing."

Jeff cuddled his drink, his eyes set on Sandy.

"Did you say Carlene Ridge?" Sandy's eyes stared straight ahead.

"Yeah! Goes by Wilmore now."

"Ok you son of a bitch! Now beat it. I'll call if I need you."

"Thanks Sandy."

"Uh huh!"

Left sitting by himself at the bar, Sandy wondered about Carlene. Rumors had it she wasn't such a refined lady as she liked to seem, but one worthy of her weird husband. Two weeks earlier her name surfaced in connection to selling and distributing refined powders among the city's elite. Quite an assortment of powders and purchasers, especially those on the Who's Who list of New York's rich and famous who occupy mansion-like apartments in Manhattan's center.

Sandy was curious to find out for himself.

CHAPTER 29

"Darling… I have something special for you," Glen whispered in Carlene's ear.

She tossed kicking off the light blanket. Knotted around her body was a thin white bathrobe.

"Mother fucker…you son of a bitch…ah…leave me alone…I hate you…ah…"

"You're turning me on," Glen lowered his head to her chest.

"Creep! Leave me alone!" she shrieked.

"I'll take care of you…don't worry," he stroked her forehead with one hand while injecting her arm with his other. It was done with such swiftness and precision that she hadn't realized what was coming.

Carlene turned still.

"Please go on dear…I feel hot and …I want to hear you say words to me…" he kissed her lightly on her forehead.

Glen untied the knot revealing her nakedness. His eyes traveled slowly down her long languid body admiring the sculptured-like figurine. Then he lay down on his side, placed his head on the pillow next to hers and watched her slow, rhythmic breathing. His hand moved to her left breast rotating it slowly and perking up its nipple into a quivering peak.

"Oh…yes…yes…" he moved his hand over her right breast.

Her naked body looked as though carved out of stone, a statue with only its breasts heaving shallowly.

His hands squeezed her stomach.

"This is so good…I want to feel you…touch you…like this," letting his hand travel over the tanned body.

"I better take these off," he muttered.

Undressing wildly he kicked off his shoes and pulled down his pants making sure not to crease them.

"Let's hang you up, guys," he chuckled and straightened the creases of his pants then placed them carefully on the chaise not far from the large mirror reflecting the bed and Carlene's body. As he neared the mirror, Glen kept his eyes on her, taking in the long nakedness sprawled helplessly on the white sheet.

"You're beautiful darling…do you want me to fuck you?"

Unbuttoning his shirt Glen kept gazing at the mirror admiring her body. Carlene tossed again. Hurrying to her side Glen touched her leg.

She released strange incomprehensible sounds.

The big blue eyes suddenly opened wide then shut again.

"I want you to touch me…here," he climbed naked into bed taking her hand and closing it over his shriveled penis.

"Come on darling… touch me…make me horny…" he stroked himself up and down with her hand.

Glen saddled himself over her stomach placing his bent legs on each of her sides.

"Tell me you want me darling… fuck me…fuck me now," he kept moving up and down checking his instrument.

"I'll have to slap you if you don't fuck me…" he moved his left hand over her face.

Carlene remained very still.

"You asked for it, darling," he slapped her face, "I warned you… now fuck me bitch! Fuck me!" he forced himself into her.

Glen didn't dare move, amazed at having penetrated her. His body stiffened then shuddered several times.

A second later he felt the familiar relapse.

"I'm growing small...I can't believe I did it...I did it darling... and all because of you."

He kissed her lips. Her body remained still.

Glen crawled to her other side and spoke quietly into her ear.

"Sorry I had to give you the injection...you should have taken your pills like a good girl," he gently stroked her head and kissed her again.

Getting out of bed Glen took a shower then returned with a towel draped around his waist. Less anxious than before, he neared Carlene.

"I'm going to dress you, darling ...no need to worry... first I'll wash you... I'm not going to hurt you..." again he kissed her cold lips.

* * *

He picked up on the first ring.
"Hello?"
"That was quick!"
"Who's this?"
"It's Kalb. How are you Glen?"
"Fine...fine..."
"And how's Carlene?"
"What?"
"Carlene? How is she?"
"Why are you asking?"
There was a slight pause before Kalb responded.
"Excuse me?"
"Why are you asking about her? She's fine!"
"Are you ok, Glen?"
"Yes... I'm just tired."
"I'm sorry...I'm really sorry...I didn't mean to intrude... I should have..."

"No, that's ok. I should apologize… I didn't have to lash out."
"That's fine, Glen, I'll call another time."
"No! I insist!"
Another untimely pause.

Kalb waited thinking Glen was about to say something, but when the silence grew and it became apparent that Glen wasn't going to speak, Kalb took the lead.

"Glen, would it be ok that I come visit Carlene? I promise…I won't stay long…just to say hi and hope she recovers soon…"
"She's asleep…you can't disturb her."
"Glad to hear she's resting," he felt a heavy disappointment.
"Best medicine in the world."
"Right…well…sorry I couldn't visit her… I'll let you go. Maybe you can give her my regards."
"I'm sure she'll be happy to see you some other time…."
"Ok…then I'll see you around."
"Yes."

Glen was relieved Kalb hadn't come for a visit.

"We don't need anyone around… right darling?" he spoke out loud while dressing Carlene up.

"Should I order Chinese darling? I'm so hungry after my hard work…" he chuckled to himself admiringly.

* * *

Kalb wondered about the strange conversation he'd just had with Glen. It wasn't like him to speak crudely using such tones. Could it be because of Carlene's condition? Or maybe Glen had found out… no, it couldn't be… why would he suddenly become suspicious? And how was Carlene feeling? Did she even want visitors?

Playing different scenes in his mind, Kalb imagined Carlene's happiness at seeing him. That beautiful glowing face of hers would smile at him.

"I was only kidding when I said I didn't want you," her incredible blue stare begged him to believe her.

"I love you… I've never stopped loving you…did you really think I'd let you go?!"

As if awakened from a dream, Kalb shook his head then turned away from the window.

"I'll visit you tomorrow…my love…I promise…"

CHAPTER 30

The Dallas Special Operation unit occupied a Spanish style structure located in a quiet neighborhood. The front part of the original house, constructed in 1881 as per the engraved copper plaque hanging above its entrance door, was transformed, a century later, into a public library forming a natural passage between both entities. Few readers were aware of the back stairwell leading up to the annexed addition and fewer still knew the identity of its occupants.

Felix Drexel served as head of the unit in Austin until his promotion and transfer to Dallas where he soon gained the reputation of a solid fighter and a first-rate police commander. Within a few short years he'd become known as one of the best team heads in the nation. His impressive achievements were compared to those of Sandy Varlovsky, his counterpart in New York, who was as equally respected in his own right. The two had met during special operations involving criminal activities in their respective territories that eventually called for mutual collaboration. As soon as the two met they took to each other and established an open line of communication based on mutual trust. It allowed for a smooth and productive flow of information between both centers that was further strengthened by a direct line of trafficking drugs and night birds, as the hookers were called. For the southern traffickers, New York was considered a haven for fast global distributions of weeds, powders and the glories of the sex industry. Dallas was padded with riches but New York was where it all came together with the big bucks and the glory attached.

Their acquaintance proved worthwhile professionally and personally.

Appreciative of his professional performance and thankful for his cooperation, Felix had written a letter of commendation to New York's chief of police, elaborating on the facts and on Sandy's exemplary assistance. Sandy received an honorable citation which he later hung in his room along with the others, and kept in touch with Felix on a regular basis. Several get togethers followed, some related to professional matters others for pleasure. Sandy and Felix had become more than just colleagues. It was only natural that Sandy now turned to Felix for additional information relevant to his probing. He had planned a long weekend, something he enjoyed doing when work didn't get in the way. Curious to follow Jeff's lead, he decided to combine the two.

Felix was only too happy to assist.

"Let me know your flight details and I'll come pick you up."

Landing on a Thursday night, Sandy was met by Felix and scooped into the city in an unmarked car.

* * *

Sandy spent Friday with Felix and his unit and was later shown the alleyways of the city alongside other tourists who flocked to its downtown area, clicking their cameras at the various sights. Dallas was a beehive of action.

It was past six when they finally made it into Mia's, a Tex-Mex restaurant off Lemmons known for its outstanding Mexican-style food.

"Howdy guys, nice to have you with us," the waitress' smile was the whitest Sandy had ever seen, resembling a toothpaste commercial. "Anything to drink?"

"I'll have what you're having," Sandy blurted out still gazing at the white against the beautiful dark complexion.

The restaurant, one of the most popular joints in town, was established by Jose Lupid and his wife Juanita 52 years earlier and has since remained within the extended family. Employing 32 family members over three generations, the Lupid family was reluctant to hire outsiders.

Felix kicked him under the table forcing Sandy to shift his smile and gaze back at Felix.

"Is that ok with you, buddy?" Sandy returned the kick.

They burst out laughing.

"Would you like more time?" the waitress asked.

Sandy swore he could see her blush.

"Nah, we've made our choice. Two Margaritas for starters. Thanks."

"Thank you," she stole a quick look at Sandy.

"Boy! Can't grow up, can you!"

"Just following nature's calling." Sandy winked.

"Any news on the prick who shot you?"

It had made headlines in New York four months earlier. A man hiding a gun inside his coat pocket walked into the building housing the special operation team. Entering the empty lobby, he climbed the flight of stairs and found a locked door. Joey, who'd spotted him earlier on one of the camera screens, saw him ring the bell but decided to ignore him. When the goon finally caught on that he wasn't welcome, he took out his gun and shot the lock and door several times. Joey and a fellow officer jumped out of their seats and prepared to close in on the perpetrator who entered the inner corridor unaware of its final destination. Sandy had just stepped out of the elevator and spotted the bullets in the door. Pulling out his gun he advanced cautiously towards the corridor. He kept walking with his gun aimed until he came face to face with the man holding the gun. It took Sandy less than a second to disarm the guy and force him into a submissive position, but by then the man had taken another quick shot, later determined as a normal reaction to a shocking surprise, and had managed to scrape Sandy's crew cut hair. Handcuffed and kicked in the groin by Sandy, the stunned man was dragged inside and handed over to the officers in charge.

"Last I heard he's still enjoying staring at iron bars," Sandy answered with a smile.

One of the things that attracted Sandy to Dallas was the size of everything in sight. Felix theorized that big men felt more comfortable in Texas because life in The Lone Star State was tailored to fit their size. Sandy released a heartened laugh.

"Nah, it's only a joke," Felix added, "but things are bigger and taller in this fucking state. It's part of who we are!"

"Really!" Sandy who towered over Felix by several inches responded with a wink.

"Have you ever seen a Texas sized steak or cheeseburger?"

They laughed and Sandy had to agree that there was some truth to it. Looking at the elephant-sized margaritas balancing on tall legs Sandy was in agreement with Felix.

"No comment!" Sandy capitulated.

"Have you decided?" the girl with the stunning whites returned.

"Anything you suggest!"

"That can be dangerous," she smiled at Sandy.

Felix kicked him under the table. Sandy returned the kick.

"Ok. Let's see…"

"Would you like a few more minutes?"

"No…no, we're hungry…how about it, buddy?"

"I'll have…fajitas with chicken…and maybe some tacos with chili sauce… enchiladas…tortillas…this is just too much…can you help us out?"

"Sure, looks like you might like to try a bit of everything. Yes?"

"Yeah…yeah…that's it," Felix licked his lips.

Smiling at him, she suggested an assortment fit for two hungry kings to which they both agreed.

"Thanks," she collected the menus.
"So…how's shitty life in the big one?"
Sandy laughed.
"Shitty!" they both mouthed out loud.
"Anyone interesting?" he winked at Sandy.

With all his charm and good looks that went so well with his gray stare, Sandy remained a loner. Not that he ever lacked the company of women whenever he felt the urge to be with one. It was just part of who Sandy was, despite his externally impressive frame. He had learned to hide his complexes and insecurities, stash them deep inside so they wouldn't bother him too much. He'd been through too many painful experiences to dare risk vulnerability again. But he was used to being asked if there was anyone interesting or special in his life. He guessed it was part of human nature to assume your external mask reflected the condition of your heart and the thoughts that filled your head.

"Nothing earth shattering."

To which Felix reacted with the expected response.

"Fill me in, buddy. Recharge my dead brain with some exciting news."

Felix was waiting for the juicy stuff, the small gossip and the intricacies that were part and parcel of every special police unit. It was the same shit everywhere - only the players differed.

The spicy hot food arrived. Two girls carrying enormous trays placed them on two small stands that appeared from nowhere. Pointing to the different sizzling dishes they left the men with a near mountain of food.

"Wow!" Sandy let out.

"Yeah!" Felix exhaled. "Where do we start?!"

They laughed and joked and emptied their large glasses.

"So what d'you have?" Felix finally asked.

"A gut feeling and two names."

Felix laughed.

"Yeah… I'm familiar with that gut of yours. It's a good one."

"I'll drink to that!"

They raised their re-filled drinks.

"Shoot!" Felix burped.

"Margie Joree… rings a bell?"

Sandy was waiting to hear the usual 'what is this? A who's who quiz?'

To his surprise, Felix didn't say a word. He simply stared at Sandy.

From the expression on his face, Sandy knew he had landed on something big.

CHAPTER 31

"It's a long story but an interesting one," Felix began.

They had cleaned out their plates. Sandy felt heavy but in good spirits thanks to the margaritas. He was in the mood for sharing some professional gossip.

"There's a community not far from here called Highland Park…a plush place where you can eat off the pavements. They have rich schools and palaces like you've never seen anywhere else and some of the world's richest people. The police department employs thirty-eight officers round the clock with an average response time of less than two minutes per call."

"Fairytale, right?" Sandy asked.

"This ain't no fairytale," Felix' face turned serious before he went on.

"One day we get called in. It sounded strange, 'cause like I said, they have their own guys doing their own jobs cleaning out their own shit. I take Edi with me; he's a no-nonsense, big black guy. We drive into the neighborhood…slowly you know…they really hawk you on every street corner, kind of feels like you're in Beverly Hills. We're snailing along this fancy wide Lake Avenue that borders with a creek. We drive real careful, 'cause they're these clanking birds and ducks running all over the grass and crossing the street. Suddenly this swan jumps at us and Edi swerves to the left to avoid hitting it and ends up kissing this big Rolls-Royce right smack on its face. Big commotion, lots of noise and bad stares. The guy in the Rolls doesn't wana' open the window. He immediately calls the local guys.

So here we are a crowd of five or six cars blocking this street with kids and mothers and strollers... get the picture? Turns out this guy's a big shot, a real big, big shot, not just your usual one..." Sandy joins Felix and their laughter rolls throughout Mia's.

"So we finally sort things out and the big, big-shot gets what he wants and we're escorted to the station. We pass this real fancy avenue lined up with houses...unreal! You have to see it to believe it...called Beverly Drive...like I said...looks like it too. We end up at this beautiful Spanish looking chalet with the fire trucks all lined up in front and the police cars... looks like a permanent fourth of July parade. But now we get the black carpet treatment 'cause they're as angry as hell that we touched this guy's car. Now we're inside... walking into the chief's office way in back.

'Heard you developed a taste for kissing big asses,' he says.

'Tastes good,' Edi blurts out.

'Ooh! Nigger boy has somethin' to say...'

Edi stands up and says.

'Got a color problem?'

'Yeah!"

'Are you a clan member?'

"Edi knows what he's talkin' about. See, that's where those KKK mother fuckers started their business... at the local university next door to that fancy community. But Edi figures... we're already in 2018 and he can demand a different attitude ..."

'My grandpa barbecued guys like you,' the prick says.

'You either turn color blind or I'll have your white ass stripped publicly,' Edi spits back.

"The chief looks him in the eye, but Edi's taller, much taller and the other guy has to hold up his head.

'Ok...let's call it truce just 'cause you're so nice,' the chief says.

'I demand an apology,' I stand up, 'otherwise I'm joinin' Edi here in stripin' your ass.'

"You should have seen his face. He almost dropped dead the mother fucker."

"Would you like a dessert?" the smiling waitress asked.

"What've you got?"

"Quesadillas…it's Mexican cheese squares…delicious…with Turron, like almond candies and sopapillas, Mexican beignets, square fried puffs with cinnamon, sugar and a drizzle of warmed honey…"

"I'll take 'em."

"Which ones?"

"How 'bout a bit of each?"

"Great. And you?" she turns to Sandy.

"Sounds fine by me. I'd like another beer to go with it."

"Sure."

"Thanks."

"So?" Sandy looks at Felix enjoying every minute.

"The guy did everything except kiss Edi's ass. He was so well behaved that I offered to have him come visit us."

They were laughing so hard Felix wiped his eyes.

"Now, this is the interesting part. A couple of months later this chief, Ryan's his name, he calls us in 'cause he wants us to look into a certain lady by the name of…" Felix gestured with his hand as if offering Sandy a tray.

"No shit!"

"Yeah!"

"Margie Joree?! I don't believe this! What've they got on her?"

"That's just it…nothing! Absolutely nothing…except! Except that this lady is very influential within the community and deals in the oldest tricks in the world, but on a scale like you've never seen. Like I said, this is Texas…you wouldn't see that kind of scale anywhere else!"

"A fancy madam?!"

"Fancy? Uh! You ain't seen fancy if you ain't seen this one!"

"Kidding me?!"

"Nope!"

"Why d'they call on you guys?"

"'Cause, like I said, they don't have anything on her. But we've got the big stuff so we can dig 'till China if needed."

"So?"

"So we dig and come up with shit. Lots of it. The woman's done time in a state penitentiary. Now she's playing the grand lady, does a lot of charity stuff, doles out money…the whole nine yards."

"Where is she now?'

"In her palace organizing treats for guys who can afford it. Mind you, she doesn't take the usual kind only the very heavy loaded ones, and I'm talkin' heavy…real heavy…"

"Texas weight?"

They laughed.

"Here we go," the desserts arrived and with them, on a small side plate, a few after meal candy mints.

"Looks delicious!" Felix' eyes rested on Sandy's plate.

"Yours too, here…want some?" Sandy moved his plate towards Felix.

"Enjoy," the waitress revealed her amazing whites.

"Thanks."

"End of story?"

"Nope. No one can touch the lady. She operates from her home, from her palace and they can't get their hands on her."

"So you guys are just standing by?"

"We're working on it…" he smiled like a cat hiding cheese.

"I smell a trap."

Still smiling, Felix picked up his glass of water and took a sip.

"Saluda!"

"When is the shit hitting the fan?"

"Sooner than you can imagine. We've got four working on it right now with bait the size of a whale."

Sandy loved the intricacies involved in the planning and setting up of decoys and traps. It was the most interesting part of the job played out by the special operations unit. It meant that all the information had already been gathered and analyzed and the players were assigned their roles. They were the best professionals in the business, the type he liked working with. The atmosphere and tension preceding each sting operation was skintight charged with adrenaline. It was the part Sandy enjoyed most.

By the time they had finished dining it was already nearing nine.

Sandy was impressed with the upcoming operation and even discussed some of its finer details with Felix.

"I'll fill you in on the rest tomorrow."

Dropping him off at his motel just off Central Expressway, Felix continued home.

Sandy was intrigued. Things were becoming interesting by the minute. He now wondered how this Margie could possibly be connected to Carlene.

"Jeff's gut is right on target," he smiled and decided to give it more thought later.

It had been a long day. Felix was expecting him the following day for a family barbecue in Lake Highlands a quiet neighborhood around White Rock Lake. They'd have plenty of time to chew on it.

* * *

The next day Sandy tried piecing together all the details. The easiest part was the obvious one: Carlene was part of Margie's larger business operation. But why would a famed psychiatrist's wife, who had everything she could possibly wish for, be involved with someone like Margie? Unless! Unless…indeed, she wasn't whom she claimed to be. Or there might be an easier explanation, one that claimed total disconnect between Carlene and this Margie. But if that were the case, why Margie's sudden phone call to Carlene's husband asking him to show up in Dallas? There were too many unknowns with loopholes and unanswered questions to solve. Sandy was beginning to feel a deep interest in the case.

He decided to prod Felix further and share with him his doubts.

He arrived at the one-storied red-brick house just on time for the barbecue. Johnny, the Great Dane welcomed him, sniffing his legs and wagging his tail.

"Hi Johnny." Sandy patted the calf-sized dog.

"Hi Sandy," Betty smiled.

He responded with a warm hug.

"Come in…come in…how are you?"

"Great! How are things over here?"

"Fine, fine. Felix is already outside…let's join him…"

"Thanks for having me, Betty…it's been a long time," he said as they crossed the large living room into the back yard.

"Glad you could come, Sandy."

Cathy zoomed by wearing a bathing suit.

"Hi, Cathy," Sandy smiled at her.

She smiled back then ran in the direction of the pool.

"Mushrooming by the day!" Sandy turned to Betty.

Just then his eye caught the diving board.

"Is that you, Brandon?" Sandy called out.

"Hi, Sandy," Brandon waved just before diving in.

They moved past the deck and the colorful zinnias.

"This is lovely…I really love it here," Sandy looked around.

"I wouldn't replace this for any luxury house in that community I was telling you about yesterday," Felix came towards him laughing while holding a glass in his hand.

"How you doin'?" he slapped his shoulder.

"Great! Slept like a log."

Scouting the pool and the surrounding garden, Sandy said.

"This is nice… it's really nice."

"How about something to drink?" Betty asked.

"Got ginger ale?"

"Maybe something stronger?"

"No…no, thanks. I'm fine."

"I'll be right back."

"Thanks Betty."
"Food will be ready in 20 minutes. How's that?"
"What time is it?"
"Barbecue time. Hungry?"
"Yeah."
"So how d'you like your steak?" Felix moved to the fire holding the long tongs in hand.
"Medium rare. Thanks"
"How's it going?"
"I've been thinking," Sandy said.
"What about?"
"About what you told me… and how it's connected to what I need…."
"What d'you need?"
"To dig into Margie's friend… a mysterious lady without a history or a past."
"So… who's this lady?" Felix asked.
"Name's Carlene…Carlene Ridge. Ring a bell?"
Felix took his time before answering.
"Nope. Absolutely not."
"Any chance of extracting this bit of information from your guys?"
Felix looked serious. He kept quiet for a few minutes then said.
"Are you sure she's from Dallas?"
"Nope! Like I said…she's a real zombie without a past."
"Social security…"
"We've already done that and she checked out."
"Why d'you think she's a phony?"
"Just a hunch…a strong one."
"I can try and help… but only if she's from my neck of the woods."
"What d'you need?"
"Fingerprints will help. Can you deliver?"
Sandy hesitated.
"It can be arranged."

"Ok, we're getting someplace."

"How about digging around this grand lady of yours?"

"Margie's? From what you've told me, it might be easier if Doc keeps his appointment and agrees to meet with her. All he has to do is show up and meet her here."

"I'll work on that as soon as I'm back home."

"Let me know."

"Will do."

The enormous steak with baked potato and coleslaw was enough to satisfy someone twice the size of Sandy. After Betty had gone in to clean and tidy up, both men sat down for beers and cigarettes.

Seated on the deck overlooking the pool with two ceiling fans rotating above their heads, the men continued talking. It was time for the smallest of details, those last-minute items that made each operation so special. Sandy offered to help from his turf, if and when circumstances could connect Margie Joree to his territory back home. Felix knew he could count on him.

Later that evening, Sandy said his farewells and flew back to New York.

CHAPTER 32

"How's my darling this morning?" Glen moved slowly towards the bed.

He was nude.

Sprawled on the wide surface with the same transparent nightgown barely covering her body, Carlene lay very still her head partially hidden under long strands of unkempt hair.

"Aren't you going to say good morning darling?" he looked carefully at her legs, arms and face, the beautiful fairy-like angel that lay perfectly still barely breathing.

"If you're not going to say anything…I'm going to fuck you," Glen stroked her head then kissed her lips.

"I don't think you need any more injections right now…looks like you're fast asleep, right darling?" his hand brushed over her leg.

He kept staring at her then turned away reached into a drawer and drew out a peacock feather. Holding its stem he brushed the beautiful eye with its loosely knit barbs against her inner thighs.

"You're giving me a hard-on," he spread open her gown and moved his fingers along her lower stomach, "I feel it again…here it comes," he mumbled as he let go of the feather and moved his fingers into her holding his penis in his other hand.

Eager to prove himself capable, he kept rubbing his lifeless cock into submission.

"Fuck you Carlene… fuck you… it's all because of the beautiful feather…fuck you…" his movements became more forceful.

Carlene groaned as she tried to move her legs.

"Are you enjoying this, darling? Fuck you, bitch!" his hand moved faster and faster.

Glen's face was red and sweaty.

"Fuck me back!" he screamed into her face, "Fuck me! Whore! Fuck me now!"

He kept at it relentlessly.

Moments later he drew out his fingers and stared at them. He noticed a few spots of blood on the bed.

"Ok...you tired me out, darling...you really did...I'm leaving you now...I need to be at the office but I'll be back later on, darling."

He got up slowly, kissed her lips and moved to the bathroom.

After he'd washed and dressed up, he walked over to the door, held the doorknob then turned around one last time and looked at her before shutting the door behind him.

* * *

It was Monday again, the one day of the week Kalb really hated. It meant making a switch in his head, thinking about work and long hours, instead of being free to read and write and make his own choices. It also meant getting up early and coming to the office and lately, seeing Glen and being forced to contemplate unpleasant thoughts.

With his eyes still shut, trying to prolong the last remnants of sleep, Kalb thought of Carlene.

"I've got to find out how she's doing... I'll call her as soon as I get to the office..."

It took him a while to fully wake up, get in the shower, dress, eat and read the newspaper, then leave for work. Entering his office, he glanced at the clock and saw it was past nine. He placed his briefcase and went in search of Glen and a fresh cup of coffee.

"Good morning," he smiled at Pam, the department's secretary.

"Wow… look at these newly shining shoes …" she eyed his sneakers.

Kalb released a wry smile.

"It's Monday today, right?!"

"Absolutely. So how about a cappuccino?"

"Thanks, Pam. How are you?"

"Don't ask, and I'll tell you no lies."

"That good?"

"Yeah. I had a very tiring weekend."

"Sorry to hear."

"Well… we all have our problems. So how 'bout that cappuccino?"

"Right… I'll bring you one … I'm heading in that direction anyway…"

"Thanks, Kalb."

Stepping into the corridor, Kalb thought of Pam's troubled life and her recent divorce.

"Pam's right… we all have our share," he thought as he entered the men's room on his way to the coffee machine.

He heard it as soon as he stepped inside. Then he heard it again and stopped in his tracks. A small groaning noise like that of a person breathing hard, a heavy rasping sound that came from the third stall. Kalb thought it sounded like Glen but dismissed it .

"Am I nuts?! It can't be! Glen can't be jerking off in here!"

Entering the adjacent corner booth, Kalb shut the door quietly thinking it was his imagination but then he heard the mumblings.

"Come on…touch me…oh…oh …that's good…come on darling…touch me… here…fuck me…like this…oh…keep going…"

Kalb felt hot all over. He didn't want to embarrass Glen by making his presence known so he remained silent until the stall door opened followed by footsteps. He heard Glen approach the sink, wash his hands and walk out.

Kalb waited another minute before exiting the men's room in the direction of the coffee machine. Returning to his office balancing a cup of cappuccino in each of his hands, he approached Pam.

"There you go," he placed a cup in front of her.
"Thanks, Kalb."
"Say, Pam…have you seen Glen by any chance?"
"Yeah, he just passed by…returned from the end of the corridor…" she winked.
"Thanks, Pam," Kalb turned in the direction of Glen's room.

Though aware of Glen's strangeness and social inadequacies, Kalb had never thought of him in terms of intimate situations or sexuality, and could never imagine holding a man-to-man talk with him. Glen was someone who always busied himself with theories and lectures and was very active in his thriving clinic. Considered a genius in his field of expertise, he never failed to stress the importance of openly addressing issues pertaining to masculine sexuality and its mechanical malfunctions. It was a delicate subject that affected millions of men worldwide and consumed their thoughts. By openly speaking and writing about it Glen had acquired the reputation of a very open-minded psychiatrist who never shied away from sensitive issues pertaining to men's sexual performance. Kalb wondered about Glen's public persona, the one he shared with his admirers and followers, and how different it was from the real Glen.

Now walking towards his office Kalb felt embarrassed, as though he'd peeked through a keyhole.

"Morning Glen, how's Carlene?" he stood in the entrance to Glen's office.

"Hi, Kalb. She's doing much better. Thanks. I left her sleeping like a lamb."

"I'm glad to hear she's doing so well. What time does she usually wake up?" he remembered other mornings with her beautiful head next to his, sharing the same pillow.

"She went to sleep very late last night so… I guess I'll wake her up when I return home."

"But today's Monday, you're here 'till five…"

"None of your business!" Glen cut him short.

"I...I'm sorry...I didn't mean to..."

"I'm ...I'm also sorry...I shouldn't ..."

"Would you please tell her I inquired about her and hope she's feeling better?"

"I will. Thanks."

Kalb felt like a total idiot. Once back in his office he shut the door.

"How stupid of me! How could I have said such a thing to Glen? I should forget about Carlene, just stop thinking about her... she's Glen's wife, it can never work out..."

But as much as he tried and regardless of what he said or did, Kalb couldn't get Carlene out of his mind. Two hours later, still sitting at his desk wondering about her, Kalb imagined a sudden flash of her face and decided to call her on a whim. He dialed her home number and counted the rings.

Someone answered on the fifth, just as he was about to hang up but it didn't sound like her. The voice, that special voice that made him do crazy things for her, was different, distinctly different. He wasn't even sure it was hers. But what shocked him was what the voice whispered.

"Help...help..."

Without thinking twice Kalb shot out of his room.

* * *

Determined to check things for himself, Kalb decided to visit Carlene. He rationalized that Glen was either too busy or simply unaware of Carlene's call for help. It wouldn't harm anyone if he just showed up and asked to see her. Maybe introduce himself as her physician... no, that wouldn't be necessary since the doorman would probably recognize him. Not that he'd been a regular guest there but he'd visited the Wilmore's a few times so he'd probably be allowed in. Besides, the housekeeper had seen him several times... he could always remind her, it wasn't as though he was a stranger.

With an unsettled gut feel, Kalb entered the lobby.

"I'm Dr. Gales to see Mrs. Wilmore," he showed Tony his ID.

"Morning Dr. Gales," Tony smiled, "I'll need to call the housekeeper."

"Sure."

Seconds later Kalb entered the elevator then rang the doorbell.

"Mrs. Wilmore is expecting me."

"Right this way, Dr. Gales," the housekeeper led him to Carlene's suite. "Dr. Wilmore mentioned someone might stop by from the hospital..."

"Right... right..." Kalb moved his head.

His heart was pounding like mad.

"How's she doing?" he asked.

"She's been in her room for the past three days. Dr. Wilmore's been taking care of her."

"Right."

"She needs the rest."

"Right."

They entered a long corridor.

Kalb feared his heart would explode. He was anxious to see Carlene but was just as scared. Like a teenager eager to see his sweetheart, he imagined Carlene's smile but then he remembered what she'd said to him and he wasn't sure anymore... maybe she really didn't want him or maybe she'd meant something else. But surely she'd appreciate the man who rushed over as soon as he heard her whispers for help... Kalb was hoping she'd at least allow him to tell her how he felt ... she had to know how much he loved her...cared for her...

"Mrs. Wilmore," the housekeeper called out then knocked on the door before opening it.

"Thank you."

Kalb stepped inside.

"I'll be downstairs in case Mrs. Wilmore needs anything."

"Thank you."

Kalb glanced at the large room taking in Carlene's body, lifeless looking on the bed, her breathing barely visible from a distance. He walked over and sat next to her.

"Carlene...Carlene..."

She moved her head and twisted her face then burst out crying.

"Don't... leave me alone... no more...stop it...don't ...no more injections... please...no injections..."

"It's me, Kalb. I'm here to help you..."

"Go away! Don't touch me!"

"I'm not going to hurt you...please open your eyes..." his hands supported her head.

He saw a tip of blue peeking from under the swollen lids.

"Carlene, it's me... Kalb...can you hear me?"

She shook her head slightly.

"I came to help you...can you hear me?"

Her eyes were trying to fight the heavy lids. When they finally opened, Kalb knew for certainty why he had come to her rescue. Those beautiful blue eyes of hers were always in his dreams whenever he thought about her and imagined the woman he loved. But now those blues were empty, void of any expression like two pieces of metal.

"How are you feeling?" he removed the strands of hair from her face.

"Thirsty... I'm thirsty..."

"I'll be right back," moving quickly to the bathroom he returned with a glassful of water.

"Here...drink this..." he supported her back with pillows, "I just came by to see how you're doing. I'm not here to hurt you."

She drank slowly, taking tiny sips and by the time she had emptied the glass, her eyes were wide open.

"Feeling better?" Kalb asked.

"My head...it's fuzzy...I don't want the injection..."

"What injection?"
"Medicines…"
She shut her eyes and leaned back.
"I'm bleeding…it hurts…"
Kalb was confused.
"Why didn't you call for help? Did anyone hurt you? Speak to me, Carlene, I'm here to help …"
But she had already drifted off, her puffy eyelids tightly shut.
Kalb removed the light blanket strewn over her. The sheet was spotted with blood. He was shocked unaware of Carlene's medical condition or usage of drugs, but seeing the blood he wasn't sure how to react to what Carlene had just told him and decided to call Glen.
"He'll know how to handle the situation."

Kalb reached for the phone.

CHAPTER 33

Sitting on the deck of her Beverly Drive home overlooking the pool and tennis court beyond, Margie was considering the situation. The fact that Glen hadn't returned her call and had not confirmed his visit to Dallas worried her. She had called him four days earlier. He should have returned her call by now or at least shown an interest. But what if she was wrong? What if he wasn't interested after all? Maybe he'd sorted it all out with Carlene and wasn't interested in coming to Dallas and hearing her out? Somehow she doubted it.

While living in New York she'd witnessed their marriage arrangements and routines from close by and got to hear about Glen's bizarre behavior. They didn't have a normal marriage and their intimate relationship was kinky and full of twists. Besides, Glen was the one who had called her initially asking if Carlene was seeing someone else. No! There must be another explanation for his silence.

What a jerk! What a weird fucking jerk of a man! And a shrink! It sounded like a lousy joke. If he'd only known how his dear wife felt about him…how she'd manipulated him into marrying her. It was all pre-planned … a fucking circus act…a joke.

Margie stared at the azure pool, sinking her thoughts deeply into its cool waters. Then at once she decided to check things out for herself.

Imagining Glen's face, she reached for the phone and dialed his number.

***

In his splendid Maplewood Avenue home, seven-minutes walking distance from Margie, Tierrry was having similar thoughts. Though they resided in the same community and neighborhood, neither was aware of each other's full name and address. Carlene had gone to great lengths not to expose any identifiable details about her lover. Knowing Margie only too well and using her as an excuse for her frequent visits to Dallas, Carlene retained a deep mistrust towards her and had given plausible explanations for all of Margie's questions.

"Tierry and I are staying at Le Château on Turtle Creek," was the way she presented it to Margie.

When Margie asked where Tierry was from and where he lived, Carlene had a well-prepared response.

"He's from out of town and travels quite a bit. That's why we meet there... he likes to take a couple of days' rest... loves the city..."

But Margie didn't believe Carlene.

After losing her business in New York and having been effectively forced out of town by Carlene, Margie had used her extensive connections to build herself a life in Dallas. As soon as her business had picked up again, Margie had employed a detective to find out about Tierry. She kept the information to herself knowing that, one day, it would come in handy.

Tierry now found himself in uncharted territory, unable to figure out what had happened to him only four days earlier. His feelings alternated between anger, worry, and love, the last the strongest of the three. The more he tried to think rationally about his aborted efforts to spend the weekend with Carlene, the more frustrated he became with anger rising inside him. But it was soon displaced by images of Carlene's beautiful face floated by, filling his heart with anguish and pain.

His talented young wife of two years, had left the baby with the nanny and was away with friends. It allowed Tierry ample free time to think about Carlene and feel his acute loneliness within the large house and its lush surroundings.

"Maybe I should try calling her? What if something happened and she can't…?" There were so many possibilities to hang onto, all kinds of ifs that threatened to drown him. "Should I say something if her husband answers the phone? How can I forget about her and just walk away? Maybe her husband became ill and she's now with him in the hospital? How can I possibly forget her? I've never loved anyone the way I love her…with her eyes, mouth, body…oh Carlene my love…I love you more than I love myself…"

Picking up the phone he dialed.

***

As Margie was about to call Glen she remembered her scheduled meeting at two over at Ball's.

"I'll just get this over and done with… then I'll be able to enjoy my meal," visualizing Glen's face she dialed his number.

"Hello?"

"Hi Glen this is Margie."

The silence was longer than Margie had expected.

"Glen? Can you hear me? It's Margie."

She heard groaning in the background, much like someone complaining of pain. Margie listened attentively.

"Wrong number!" someone finally said slamming down the receiver.

Margie was left with a dead line.

***

The line was busy. Tierry hung up and waited. His hands turned clammy with cold sweat. He knew no other way to sort it out other than talk to Carlene about it and tell her how he felt.

"She'll know how to straighten things out," he thought as he held the phone tightly.

Two minutes later he dialed again but the line was still busy. He wiped the small valley between his nose and upper lip and decided to wait a while before redialing. Staring out the window of his living room, his eyes caught a sudden movement. He stormed outside following the shadow in the direction of the large pool and witnessed the amazing landing of two wild geese on the large surface of water.

"I'll be darn!"

Rushing back into the house, he grabbed a camera and stood watching as they dipped their heads into the glacier colored surface gurgling, every so often, into the air with their elongated necks.

"She won't believe it when I show her the pictures…she'll want to come and see the pool…" his mind on Carlene.

As soon as he reentered the house he again tried reaching her.

"I'll simply demand to speak to her!" he spoke out loud trying to make himself feel stronger.

A woman's voice answered the phone.

"Wilmore residence?"

"Mrs. Wilmore, please."

"Who may I say is calling?"

Despite the long rehearsals and the many options he'd thought of, Tierry, the powerful international banker who'd been courageous enough to change the financial course and planning of large institutions, was stunned into silence.

"Hello? Hello?" the woman's voice asked.

Tierry hung up.

CHAPTER 34

Brian Cox sat on his bed looking frail and very upset. As a senior he'd planned to major in clinical psychology the following month, but had failed to submit two papers with a year-long pending thesis. The stress on his face was further accentuated by his curly shoulder-length hair and heavy framed glasses that suited his small physique. Wearing torn denims with an oversized T-shirt, Brian looked like a little lost child.

"Late papers will not be accepted," Prof. Dr. Kalb Gales had repeatedly warned his students.

"Dr. Gales, how about if I…"

"No exceptions, Brian. We've been through this several times. There'll be no exceptions. If you're late, you're flunking the course."

Brian was a problematic student. Besides carrying the burdens as single heir to the giant Cox Fashions, he had been diagnosed with Attention Deficit Disorder, and treated by Dr. Glen Wilmore for a variety of emotional problems. Depressed, and somewhat paranoid, he was taking an assortment of medications and had been subjected to intense therapy from an early age, visiting the famed psychiatrist twice a week on a regular basis. Though he'd been given special allowances to help him complete his exams and papers, it didn't seem to make much of a difference. Brian's teachers soon realized that it wasn't only his ADD that was holding him back.

It was never quite clear whether Brian used his problems as an excuse to get away with whatever didn't suit his wants, or whether his difficulties were truly responsible for his academic failures. His term papers, similar to his final exams, were brilliantly written when completed, but were never submitted on time. It wasn't as though he hadn't understood the questions or found the subject matter difficult to research. It was a question of attitude, rude behavior, and habitual procrastination on academic tasks that resulted in never turning in the required assignments on time.

As for the reading requirements for the course, they proved too much for Brian in terms of concentration over long periods of time so he decided to ask Dr. Wilmore for a change in prescription, and had called his answering service. But Dr. Wilmore had failed to return his call. Brian was in a state of panic. He tried to calm himself by using breathing techniques and exhaling slowly but it didn't really help. He felt desperate, but knew that it wouldn't do him any good to call again so soon. He'd give it another hour then he'd try calling again.

He now sat in the room he shared with Justin Meadows, a fourth-year med school student, trying to strike up a conversation.

"How's it going Justin?"

Justin, who was preparing for the Introduction to Hematology exam, was in another world. A dedicated student and one who studied long hours, Justin was always short of time, limiting his socializing to the bare minimum.

"I have this real important exam coming up," he told Brian, "Don't take it personally… sorry, I don't have anything against you…I simply don't have the time for small talk. Know what I mean?"

But Brian didn't know what it meant. He had always had difficulty connecting with other people who, for some reason, were always too busy to talk to him.

"You just don't wanna talk to me…I know your kind…you think you're too good for someone like me…"

"Definitely not!" Justin replied, truly sorry to hear Brian's words.

"So why don't you wanna…"

"Brian, Brian…hold it right there. We've been through this too many times before and I don't have the time to go into it again. Please! Would you please…just leave me alone and let me study?"

Having lost all patience and realizing he'd soon lose control, Brian acted impulsively and stormed out of the room. He had no idea where he was heading.

Justin was used to Brian's tempestuous outbursts and had managed to survive his presence until now, but refused to risk his end of the year finals. So a couple of days earlier he had approached his counselor and been promised another room.

"If Brian prefers to stay, I'll move out. If he wants to move, fine by me. I just want to study quietly."

"I'll take care of it," Steve, the counselor promised.

Now on his way to tell Brian he had found him another room, Steve heard the commotion and saw the crowded students talking in hushed voices.

It didn't take long for the rumor to circulate. By the time Steve had reached Brian and Justin's room, word had already spread that someone had lost his screws and was on his way to the rooftop. Steve was in a hurry to solve the problem of the room so that he could attend to the other matter.

He knocked on the door. Justin opened it wearing a T-shirt over shorts.

"How you doin' Justin?"

"Hi Steve…any good news?"

Looking around the small room he said.

"I see Brian's out."

"Yeah… he left earlier."

"Well…as a matter of fact…I do have good news! I've come to reassign Brian."

"That's great! I'm very…I'm happy. All I wanna' do is study, it's not like I don't care for Brian …"

"Yeah…I know…I know…he's a bit …" flipping his hand sideways.

"Thanks for understanding," Justin sighed.

"He'll be moving to the third floor...there's a room he can have all to himself...won't bother anyone..."

"Boy! I'm so relieved, you can't imagine what this means to me. Thanks Steve."

"My pleasure. Now go on...keep studying. If you see him..."

"Oh, you can count on it! I'll make sure he gets hold of you. Don't worry!"

Turning around Steve headed downstairs.

* * *

Standing in front of the elevator door with a key he'd snatched from the security room held tightly to his chest, Brian was overwhelmed by his own actions. He hadn't planned on stealing the key. He had simply reached a boiling point and exploded from within. He saw the open security door, jumped inside removed the key tagged 'ROOF' from the board and ran to the nearest elevator. He thought he could hide it under his shirt but just then the guard on duty returned to the room and saw him run out.

"Hey...stop! I'm gonna have to contact Security. Please don't force me to do that..."

But Brian had already disappeared inside the elevator and pressed the 'ROOF ONLY' button. Brian was panicky and felt things were out of his control. The pills weren't helping and he couldn't stop himself so he again called Dr. Wilmore.

The answering service took his third message adding:

"If it's that urgent he'll return your call. Dr. Wilmore always returns his patients' calls."

Brian couldn't stand the wait any longer. His stomach felt in knots and his mouth was dry. He had discussed it with Dr. Wilmore and told him about his anxiety attacks and the Doc said he needed to call his office the minute he felt one coming. Now he waited but the Doc wasn't responding. He felt trapped, as if he was choking, he needed to escape his own self. His skin was crawling with ants and tiny spiders burrowing through...his fingers tingled...he had to get away...he had to run or he'd get caught and trapped...he couldn't let it happen... his skin was itchy again...he felt it peeling away... everything was closing in on him... he was running for his life...he was losing air...he couldn't breathe...he needed fresh air...

Storming out of the elevator and onto the rooftop Brian found himself staring at the open space. He was terrified of heights and hadn't thought it through properly. He shut his eyes but felt dizzy so he opened them again and began shivering. What if he fell off the roof? Would it hurt? How long would it take him to reach the pavement below? The mere thought made him sick. He retched. Then burst out crying. He decided to lie down flatly next to the drainpipes to make sure his body didn't roll over the rooftop. The pipes would hold him firmly in place. The most that could happen is that he'd end up bumping against a pipe.

His thoughts were scrambled and confused. He kept retching even as the security team stormed the rooftop. When they realized he had soiled his pants they all came to a silent standstill. It had taken the paramedics less than fifteen minutes from the time the security guard had alerted them to reach Brian and medicate him. Jeff had been updated and was on his way to the hospital to check on things.

CHAPTER 35

Still holding the phone in hand, with eyes staring into the distance, Margie tried to guess who had answered her call. She had expected Glen, but instead heard an unfamiliar voice, someone who obviously didn't want to speak to her. The background noises… groaning…muffled…they weren't clear. Was it Carlene? Or maybe someone whom she didn't even know …could that mean that Carlene was now seeing someone else? Another lover? Had she stopped seeing that Tierry of hers?

In that case, she'd have nothing to show Glen if he had agreed to come over. She'd hoped to surprise him, take him on a special trip to see Carlene and her lover inside their love nest at Le Château. Surely that would infuriate him sufficiently to want to divorce her and get rid of the wife who'd cheated on him. Now it was all going to waste. Maybe she should call up Tierry and …no! Definitely not! Tierry was in another league, a man who wouldn't hesitate to call the police if he felt he was being intimidated or harassed. If he only knew they were neighbors…

Margie chuckled. All the what-ifs in the world now found their way into her head. She tried telling herself that she should forget about it and get a grip on herself. It was nearing two, and she couldn't afford not to be focused, not today and not with the person she was waiting to meet.

Sailing comfortably in her light blue Mercedes, Margie continued on Beverly then turned left on Hillcrest all the way to Snider Plaza. She parked her luxury cabriolet between a Lexus and a Rolls and entered Balls the popular burger joint. Wearing skintight blue denim with a button-down western shirt cinched at the waist by a leather belt and matching boots, Margie looked strikingly beautiful. With fashionable sunglasses used as a tiara to fasten her shoulder length hair in place, she knew all eyes were on her.

She scouted the place, and found a quiet corner where she sat down to wait for Jasmine. The large TV screen facing the diners, catered to the baseball fans scattered throughout the large room stuffing their mouths while glued to the screen. A large variety of video games stood against the far wall with tall bar stools for the older kids and teenagers. It was a place that allowed for a leisured pace and discreet conversation, which suited Margie's current needs.

She spotted her immediately as she walked through the door wearing a light green suit adorned by an elegant scarf to match the color of her eyes. From a distance Margie briefed her legs, breasts, posture and face like a merchant assessing his merchandize all within ten seconds. It was the first impression that counted, those first precious seconds that would determine her fate. By the time she was close enough to appreciate the smoothness of her skin and elegant hands, Margie knew she had found an exceptional jewel.

Their eyes caught each other's as she walked in looking around the small booths arranged to form intimate seating. She wondered if the woman now staring at her was the one she had spoken to on the phone only a couple of days ago. Noticing the slight tilting of the woman's head, she returned the nod.

"I'm Jasmine, nice to meet you," she extended her hand.

"Nice to meet you too," Margie replied, her eyes examining every curve and valley.

"Do you like what you see?" a white smile on her beautiful face.

"Looks like you've had some practice." Margie stared her straight in the eye.

"May I sit down?"

"I insist," Margie replied while sipping her drink with a straw.

"Do you always inspect your merchandize in public?"

Margie didn't care for her straightforwardness though she had to admit it was done with a degree of charm without even a hint of arrogance. Wishing to make her slightly less comfortable, Margie stared at Jasmine and waited. It took less than ten seconds for Jasmine to shift in her chair, long enough for Margie to know she had her where she wanted.

"I ask the questions. You only answer them. D'you have a problem with that?"

Margie's words, though spoken in a quiet voice and accompanied by a smile, wiped the grin off Jasmine's face.

"I'm sorry…I didn't mean to…"

"Glad we straightened that out."

"Yes," her head slightly lowered.

"Now! As for your question…Yes! I like inspecting what I buy before I buy it. Any objections?"

"None."

"Good."

Margie was trying to figure her out. Her beauty was exceptional, even among other beauties of her profession. Surely someone like her who obviously had the guts to speak out and ask pertinent questions, was also someone capable of taking care of herself, so why would she be interested in working for someone else?

Suspicious as always, Margie tried to read her out.

"So… tell me your life story…Jasmine? Is that your real name?"

"Does it matter?"

"If I ask, it probably matters."

"I'm sorry. I don't mean to sound…it's just that I was used to working…" looking up, Jasmine eyed Margie, "I've worked in places where the name was never an issue."

"Is that so?!"

Jasmine moved her head up and down.

"Where did you work?"

"At DeeDee's…and on Chestnut's …before that I worked in San Francisco."

"Where exactly?"

"The Flamingo."

"How long did you work there? I've heard it's a real harem…a pit of a place…"

"It sure is… which is why I left and moved here."

"Why Dallas?"

"I like it here. Weather's good."

Margie took another sip. She could tell Jasmine wasn't the usual girl. She was smarter and very discreet. It would take a while to get to know her real background.

"So why did you leave DeeDee's?"

"I was getting screwed."

"That's part of the profession, deary."

"No. I mean … with the money. The split was getting to me."

"What was it?"

"Sixty-forty."

"And what d'you think you'll get here?"

"I heard your split was seventy-thirty…for those who know how to work…"

"Who told you?"

"Tina…said she worked for you last year and it was good."

"Tina? Tina who?"

"I don't know… like I said…we all have different names…no one asks for the real one."

Margie thought about it. She knew who the so-called Tina was and remembered she had worked for a couple of weeks and had disappeared as suddenly as she'd appeared. There was something unusual about it. Margie's girls usually stayed with her because of the reputation and the added benefits which were calculated separately from the base earnings per client. At the start of her career, Margie realized that the more she invested in her girls, the better the results and the bigger the clientele that followed. Having worked as a hooker herself, at one point in her life, she knew exactly what the profession entailed and promised to make it as easy as possible for her girls. Her split was considered more than fair. Every hour one of her girls spent with a man, pocketed her an easy thirty percent of the total earnings. It amounted to vast sums, averaging fifteen thousand dollars a night, depending on the number of clients, the hours they spent with each girl and the usual side earnings attached to the powders, pills or vials, as per one's preference. It all helped fortify her business.

Margie's clients, selectively chosen and handpicked, were the wealthiest amongst the wealthy, ranging from oil sheiks to Japanese CEO's, which translated into impressive earnings. Tina had come looking for a steady base and was given a trial period of one month but had wormed her way out of fulfilling the customary obligations. Margie, who had found it very strange, had asked a private detective to find out what he could about her, but she had already disappeared without leaving a trace.

Now seated opposite Jasmine, Margie was not only suspicious, but also curious.

"So…you know Tina?"

"No… not really."

"But you just said she recommended …."

"Yes, she did… but indirectly …she knew someone at DeeDee's who told me about you…"

Margie couldn't stop staring at those stunning eyes. Besides their exceptional color, a mixture of green with blue and gray sparks, they were wide, as if penciled carefully with a purpose to create a frame for their slanted shape, and long, thick lashes over drowsy looking eyelids.

She couldn't make up her mind about Jasmine, though her story did sound convincing. The industry fed on gossips and rumors, especially those originating from competitive places referred to as agencies, the countless colonies of women whose business it was to provide sexual services. An Agency sounded professional, much more so than a whorehouse or a bordello, even if both were highly exclusive.

Margie's Agency employed anywhere between fifteen to twenty girls all dedicated to making money. There were different categories within each agency and a corresponding payment scale that depended on the girl's willingness to service the clients. There were those able and willing to 'chew it all', referred to those willing to perform all forms of sex, be it orally, anally or vaginally combined with added accessories such as chains and whips and its exotic expansions. There were those willing to perform strictly alone as opposed to those who didn't mind additional performers. It was a known fact that women who chewed it all were less selective, agreeable to take on the scummiest of scum.

Having formed a first impression of her, Margie assumed Jasmine belonged to the other category: those wishing to act more selectively, the kind that wouldn't agree to take on just any client. But only the girls, who were outstanding in beauty and brain, a selective few who had a special touch and were constantly in demand, could afford to be picky with their clientele and refuse to chew it all.

As she sat watching Jasmine smile and dazzle and showcase her goods, Margie was already thinking about the different possibilities and had made up her mind to approve her. The most that could happen was that she'd fire Jasmine and make sure she never showed her face in town again.

Now smiling at her Margie said.

"Ok, Jasmine. I'm willing to try you out."

"Thank you, Margie," Jasmine smiled, "I take it seriously and work very hard."

"I certainly hope so. Now let's get down to business."

Jasmine eyed her attentively.

"You get a split of sixty-forty for the first month. If all goes well I'll raise it to seventy-thirty. Do you chew it all?"

Jasmine' beautiful head turned sideways.

"Spell it out."

"I do the regular stuff... strictly classical and nothing kinky... no whips or cuts or anything like that."

Margie smiled. It seemed that Jasmine, or whoever she was, knew exactly what she was worth and what it was all about. She remained cool throughout which was a good sign and proof of self-confidence. Anyone who understood the jargon and the implications and kept her cool was a good performer. After all, dishing out sex for money required special talents, performing in front of a one-man audience even if an additional person was sometimes involved.

"You're on," she stretched out her hand.

"Thank you, Margie. You won't regret it. I promise."

"Good. When can you start?"

"As soon as you'd like."

"Let's see…" she held out a tiny brown-leathered calendar and turned it pages.

Jasmine smiled and waited patiently.

"Ok…I'm looking for one particular client…loves green eyed ladies… strictly ladies…no cheap stuff or talk, only the real classy stuff…"

"That's me!" Jasmine exclaimed.

"Here it is…a Japanese CEO…Chang Quow Di… not sure about the pronunciation. But before we go on, you'll have to give me your full details. Name… address…when you were last seen by a doctor… we monitor all our girls and check them once a month. You'll also need to be checked for HIV."

"Sure! I'm glad to hear you do this."

"I've got to otherwise I can be wiped out and my business ruined. You'll also need to visit Dr. Stroud over on Abrams and Mockingbird. Here's the address," handing her a small card. "How soon can you go?"

"I'm available right now."

"Great. After you're done with him, give me a call. I'll have the test results by then and we can start right away. How does that sound?"

"Great! Thanks Margie. I promise …you'll never regret this."

Holding the small card in her hand, Jasmine walked out with a broad smile on her beautiful face.

She had just landed a big promotion and was hoping to be successful.

Returning home, Margie checked her messages. There were eleven, all except for the last one, from established clients and her team of girls. Some required help; others sought advice or simple company. The last message, though unclear to the point of sounding somewhat garbled, was from someone named Mustafah Tawille, who spoke with a thick, heavy accent.

Margie loved to converse with the various clients. It was the exciting part of the job enabling her to touch the most intimate corners of their lives. She'd listen to their secret sexual drives and preferences while registering all weaknesses and fears. In return she received affirmation of her own powers. Every man had a fantasy he wished to fulfill and Margie's job was to translate the illusion into practical terms. The sheiks, the very rich ones, those who couldn't care less about the costs involved, were her preferred clients and usually the most conservative.

"I want a blond … or a brunette… no funny stuff… only straight…classical… you know?" though sometimes they'd ask for small additions.

"…with another girl… to watch us…" or a slightly different version of the same, "… have a lot of legs… eight legs in same bed… ten… is better…"

Other preferences were also available.

"I'll want to tie her up…smell her fear …" or even, "…someone to suck me dry…"

Margie enjoyed matching the assorted requests with the different girls. It was a matter of feeling out the buyers and knowing her merchandise inside out. Her ultimate goal was to sell a sense of trust in order to retain a high-quality clientele. It wasn't an easy task but one she excelled in. Using the phone as her main pipeline with the outside world, enabled Margie and her clients to retain anonymity throughout the intimate exchange of details, while ensuring their wishes were delivered. Margie's Agency was always only a phone call away regardless of the geographical location of her clients a fact that was worth a lot of money to those who could afford it.

Now sitting with a notepad next to her answering machine, Margie copied down the messages with the relevant names and numbers.

Then she dialed.

"Good evening, is this Mr. Tawille?" she spoke in her gentlest voice.

"Iz me."

"Hi Mr. Tawille, this is the Margie Agency returning your call."

"Yes…ello…"

"Well… hello to you too…" releasing coquettishly, "I'm honored to hear from you, sir…"

"Yes."

"Do you mind if I ask how you heard about my agency?"

Above all, Margie appreciated discretion. Well aware of the fact that the local police were interested in her activities, she went out of her way to take precautionary measures in order to keep one step ahead of them. Whenever a new client called, she'd chat with him and make sure he came well recommended. There was always a danger involved with unexpected invitees snooping around or making crank calls. She couldn't be too cautious.

"Maslem-el-Fahid."

The name was well familiar. For the past year, Sheik Maslem-el-Fahid, one of Margie's richest clients and a frequenter at the agency, was in the habit of giving out Margie's name to anyone willing to listen to his sexual escapades. This resulted in a long list of new clients added to the Agency by way of personal recommendation. Margie smiled and relaxed.

"How is Sheik Maslem-el-Fahid these days?"

"He good."

"I'm glad to hear. In that case, Mr. Tawille, I'm sure I can spare you the introduction to the Agency."

"What you say?"

"Mr. Tawill, I'm happy you chose my Agency. How may I help you?"

"I col you."

"Yes, you called. I'd like to help you."

"Oh, yes…I col…I wan' a woomen."

"Yes, Mr. Tawille, that's why I'm here…to hear your fantasies…yes?"

"Yes. But I wont speishal."

"Anything you wish, Mr. Tawille, our agency is known for variety and diversity …you can have whatever you want. Your fantasies…your dreams…"

"Speishal…speishal…you know what is mean?"

"Yes…Mr. Tawille…all our girls are special."

"Good. Good. Speishal."

"Do you have any preference…any special requests…?"

"Speishal, I wont speishal woman."

"Ok, Mr. Tawille…I'll get you a very special woman…she's beautiful beyond imagination. Her name's Jasmine…she's got green eyes…with sand color…"

"Ouw moch?"

"Would you like to hear more…?"

"Money…ouw moch?"

"Will that be…for one time?"

"Forr de night."

"Ten thousand plus expenses."

"Ok. I wont dat woomen."

"When and where would you like to see her?"

"De Château, yes?"

"Yes, that can be arranged. We can deliver services at Le Château."

"When she come?"

"When would you like her to meet with you Mr. Tawille?"

"Tooday. In night. I be in Dallas."

"What time?"
"In night."
"Is eight ok?"
"Nine ok."
The deal was sealed.
Margie had just netted an easy deal with one phone call.
"Not bad," she smiled. "Not bad for a Monday."

CHAPTER 36

"How you doin', Jeff?"
"All's good...that was great work on the rooftop!"
Jeff shook the security guard's hand.
"Thanks for helping out."
"Sure thing. That kid! He's one hell of a weirdo all right!"
"Oh yeah?"
"He tells this story... claims that Dr. Glen Wilmore's his shrink but..."
"Head of psychiatry here on campus?" Jeff moved in his chair.
"Yeah. The kid claims he's been under his treatment and supervision for years, he's on medications and sees him twice a week. We tried contacting this doctor but he's unavailable..."
"Thanks again, Cole. I'll take it up from here."
"Great. Thanks."
Now back in his office piecing together the many details he'd collected about Dr. Wilmore, Jeff knew there was something strange going on. He decided to call up Sandy.

* * *

Kalb returned to his office with a heavy feeling. His sensitive guts told him it was an omen of worse things to come.
While still at Carlene's he had called Glen.
"I'm here with Carlene...she seems ..."
"What do you mean you're with Carlene?!"

"I'm sitting here…watching her…"

"In her bedroom?!"

"I was worried about her so I stopped by for a quick visit. I haven't seen her in a while…"

"I told you to stay away! She needs the rest!"

"I know but I thought …since you've asked me in the past to talk to her …" he chose not to tell Glen about Carlene's call for help.

"Is she still asleep?"

"Yes…yes…she is…" Kalb looked at her lifeless body, "but she's …she seems restless and disoriented…she asked to drink …said something about…"

"Did you give her anything?"

"Yes, water."

"Yeah! That's fine!"

"I'm concerned…"

"She's fine! Don't worry!"

"But…"

"This is the Doc speaking, remember?" Glen tried to sound casual.

"Glen, she's not well…"

"Are you her treating physician?"

"Come on, Glen, you've asked me to…"

"You're not! So keep your nose out of it!"

Kalb was stunned.

"Fine. I'm leaving now. I'll see you shortly at the office."

"Ok," Glen hung up.

Following Glen's crude response, Kalb concluded there was something strange going on, something other than what he was able to gauge. He kept thinking about it, trying to put a finger on what precisely sounded strange, but couldn't quite figure it out.

Now back at work he decided to talk to Glen about it. The situation was getting out of hand and Carlene's condition was deteriorating.

Kalb returned to campus and walked over to Glen's office.

* * *

Following Kalb's phone call, Glen left the office and rushed home. He was convinced that Kalb had visited Carlene out of genuine concern for her well being, but he didn't need anyone snooping around, least of all Kalb with his radar-like eyes and intuition…the man was dangerous…he could blow this whole thing…he should be barred from nearing Carlene, at least for the time being.

When Glen reached home, he found Carlene in the same position he'd left her earlier.

"Kalb…that fool… who does he think he is…" he muttered while undressing and readying himself.

He hadn't planned on it… things simply got out of hand and someone needed to help Carlene understand that she couldn't go on…that she couldn't make a cuckold out of him. He was her husband and she owed him the respect. She was out of control…popping pills and flaunting her body…and all this time he had to keep quiet and pretend as if he hadn't noticed…act as though he didn't know what was going on. But of course he knew she was swallowing stuff and fucking other men but he never said anything afraid of scaring her off…but now someone needed to stop her and who could be better than a loving husband who just happened to be a psychiatrist?!

As he prepared himself for Carlene who lay still and just as pale as before, Glen smiled.

"Do you remember our wedding night darling? You were so beautiful… just like you're now…so quiet and …that body of yours…your legs…your stomach…your fucking cunt…" trailing his hands over her body.

He untied the loose string of her white negligee, the sheer gown that covered her nakedness for the past three days. Then he spread open her legs and checked to see if all was ok. He noticed the spots of blood. With trembling fingers, he began touching her again. Every so often he rubbed his cock against her lower stomach, trying to arouse himself at the feel of her triangle below.

"Fuck you…oh, how I want to fuck you, darling…can you feel how much? It wasn't so good this morning…maybe now you'll help me fuck you…" he slid up and down taking her hand in his, rubbing it against his flat pecker.

Carlene remained perfectly still.

"Come on, darling… NOW!" he roared becoming impatient with himself, "fuck me NOW, Carlene, NOW!" he kept raving as he rode her body up and down poking his dick in odd places all over her body.

Carlene moaned. Her head moved sideways and for a split second her eyes opened then shut again.

"What…" her voice slurred.

"Ah! Darling, my beautiful darling. Look, I'm fucking you! I'm fucking you!" he shoved his wilted instrument forcefully into her trying to accomplish what he'd started.

Carlene's face twisted.

"Like it?" Glen repeated, "Like it? Ah?! Say it, Carlene, tell me this is good, oh…I love fucking you…"

Glen was in a trance and out of control.

* * *

When Kalb reached Glen's office he found it empty. He turned to Pam who filled him in.

"He left a while ago…said he'll return later in the afternoon."

Kalb was glad he hadn't mentioned Carlene's call for help, especially in light of the somewhat strange tone of Glen's voice. Seized with a sudden inexplicable fear Kalb decided to call Jeff.

He'd know what to do.

"Jeff, this is Kalb, how are you?"

"Hi Doc, what's up?" sounding his cheerful self.

"Can't complain…"

"That's great. Anything new?"

"Yes…as a matter of fact, that's why I'm calling…"

Kalb proceeded to tell him about Carlene's pleas for help and the condition in which he'd found her.

"Interesting…" Jeff said.

"…and there was something else…while I was there the phone rang. It was Margie…"

Kalb filled him in on all the details and repeated his later conversation with Glen.

"Sounds fishy to me."

"I agree…that's why I'm calling you."

"Tell you what. I'll check it out and get back to you."

"Thanks, Jeff."

"You bet."

As soon as he was off the phone, Kalb felt a relief.

* * *

"Is the man there?" Jeff asked over the phone.

"How the fuck are you, old man?"

"No time for sweet talk, Joey."

"Boss!" Joey bellowed.

A second later Sandy's voice sounded.

"What's up?"

"We need to talk."

"That bad?"

"Yeah. Are you free?"

"Yeah."

"On my way."

"You've got to hear this ..." Jeff said as soon as he entered Sandy's room.

"I'm listening." Sandy replied.

"Turns out the rooftop weirdo is on medications and sees Kinky Boy, twice a week..."

"Nice."

"When the kid went nuts he tried calling the Doc but couldn't get through, says he felt an attack coming and needed to see him urgently. The answering service kept sending Doc messages but he didn't reply. That was the day after his wife returned home from the hospital...so we know he was home. Now! Just before I called you I got a call from our shrink, Kinky Boy's colleague. Turns out he'd called Carlene at home and heard her voice whisper 'help...help.'"

"Why did he call the Doc's house?"

"He knew Carlene wasn't well...besides, in the past Glen had asked him to talk to her professionally, remember?"

"Right. Go on."

"So this colleague, name's Kalb Gales, he rushes over to the house and sees the wife as white as a ghost and she's just lying there. She keeps crying to leave her alone, mumbles something unclear about medicines, injections and so on… then she turns into stone again never telling him why she called for help. Kalb calls the husband who reacts strangely and blows up like a torch. So by now Kalb's suspicious, he asks himself why would the husband get so upset, right? It's not like he's a stranger to either of them… now…while he's visiting her, the phone rings… Kalb picks up and Margie's on the line thinking it's the Doc himself. Kalb panics and hangs up. End of story."

"Nice saga. So where's Kinky Boy now?"

"At home. Checking on wife."

"Shit!"

"You thinkin' what I'm thinkin'?"

"Our boy likes to toy with bodies and drugs…let's go!"

Sandy reached into the safe, located behind one of the framed citations.

"This can save us in case we're wrong...which I doubt!" he held up a document.

"What is it?"

"A search warrant."

"Let's go."

Sandy reached the door.

"Wanna' join or do you prefer baby-sittin' Joey here?"

"Real funny!" Jeff moved quickly leaving the office in a hurry.

Now in the car, on their way to the Wilmore residence, Sandy updated Jeff.

"Had an interesting weekend in Dallas, spent some time digging inside dirty holes and got lots of juicy grime. Interested?"

"Sure."

"I talked to some people who got the scoop on this Margie. Turns out she's done time in a state penitentiary and is currently managing a successful prostitution ring... a very lucrative one with lots of coated sugar on the side."

"No shit!"

"They said they'd try and help... see if we can connect her to Carlene's operation ... but... we need to move fast. They're closing in on her..."

"What do we need?"

"Carlene's fingerprints. Can you handle that?"

"Sure."

"We'll also need to convince Kinky Boy to agree to meet with Margie. That way we can fill in the gaps."

"Right."

They kept planning how they would handle the situation once inside the residence, but both knew how unpredictable it could become; besides, some improvisation was always called for at the scene. Sandy's special license meant a pre-approved search warrant just in case they were prevented from entering. But it was not to be used lightly, only in extreme situations with firm evidence that a person might be injured or harmed unless rescued by the special unit.

Having discussed it with Felix over the weekend, Sandy had figured out most of the puzzle. There remained only one small question, something only Carlene could answer.

Sandy and Jeff were now trying to decide how best to proceed.

"We're basically missing two things: Carlene's fingerprints and her connection to Margie's operation."

Sandy eyed Jeff.

"I wouldn't put anything past that loony Doc…for all we know Carlene is in a precarious situation."

"I agree."

"Don't forget the fingerprints… they're real important …"

Having reached their destination they rang the doorbell and stepped into the elegant lobby.

CHAPTER 37

"Dr. Stroud, this is Margie from the Agency. Something urgent came up. Please call me as soon as you get this message. Thanks."

She hung up feeling somewhat euphoric, as if nothing bad could touch her. Thinking about Mustafah Tawille gave her the extra zest she needed on this first day of the new week. Oh! How she detested Mondays and their slow pace. Wednesdays were her favorite, that's when the action would start lasting through Sunday. Nothing was predictable in her areas of expertise, which was precisely what she liked. It left ample room for surprises fashioned by people who thrived on risky twists.

She'd tried to understand what drove a man to want to fuck a strange woman in a whorehouse. Was it the simple rush of excessive adrenaline? A sudden deluge of testosterone? What exactly triggered a man's prick to spark up in the presence of a strange woman? Was it the mere excitement of newness? Or the notion that he was being touched licked and catered to by a professional? Perhaps the desire to have his prickly ego handled by strangers? Was it merely physical enjoyment? Or the simple chance of a lonely man who sought the company of a strange woman? One thing she knew for sure: the spark that set in motion the repositioning of a man's prick, was ignited by thoughts that brewed inside his head. Men frequently scrambled their balls in public, releasing a chain of thoughts. As one thought leads to another, a man's prick turns pricklier arousing him to the point of losing control over his brain. Margie theorized that the powerful forces secreted within a man's ego were unveiled in bed. It had to do with the nudity of body spirit, and the lustfulness awarded all humans in Paradise. The performance of a man's prick was reflective of his psyche and soul.

Having worked as a fancy, high-class sex provider herself in several agencies prior to establishing her own place, she knew that life's circumstances usually forced young women into sexual slavery. Most girls ended up at her doorstep after having tasted the bitterness and brutality forced upon them early on in life. But there were some who actually enjoyed the excitement of being fucked every night by strange men, feeling an unknown man's skin touch their own or smelling the newness of his scent. It excited some, though they were the minority. Most did it for the money and though her girls were outstanding and could easily make several grand a week, their career span was short-lived despite their youth and beauty. They usually faded within a few years leaving behind their hollowed souls looking desperately to reinvent themselves. The trail leading from the sex industry to the pharmaceutical one was a sure and short one and in most cases, a combination of both.

She now wondered about Jasmine who impressed her as sharp, bright and incredibly beautiful. Why would she even want her body touched by strange hands? She could have the pick of any man, so what was it that got her started? Having experienced it herself, Margie was always intrigued by what propelled people, their choices and decision making. But she also understood that in order to achieve a profound understanding, one had to delve deep into a person's background. For some odd reason she was now reminded of Carlene's beautiful image.

Both of Margie's investments, her agency of pleasure and distribution ring relied on a regular flow of clientele who knew what they wanted and were sure to get it. Enjoying a favorable repute, more than anything else, was what counted for those interested in powders, pills or sexual favors. Margie's biggest desire, at the end of this long Monday, was to finalize the deal with Jasmine and prove her solid reputation to Mr. Tawille so that she could enjoy the sucker's money.

Margie viewed all men serviced at her Agency, as suckers.

"From the second they think of sex, their prick stands up and makes them lose control over their brain."

For the past two years, since her move to Dallas and the opening of her agency, Margie chose her own men with pride.

"I can afford to choose only what I want and like."

As for the girls whose job it was to dish out Margie's merchandize, they considered a man's cock as a mere stick, nothing more than a hard tool meant to be emptied every so often. They measured love by standards that differed vastly from any sexual encounters, and could be moved to tears if a man held their hand, offered to kiss their lips or just cared enough to sit and talk to them. Sex was a mere sellable commodity, nothing other than the sale of a smile, a rough touch followed by penetration and allowing their body to be manipulated in whichever way the client saw fit to gain satisfaction.

Margie, who liked strong-bodied men, didn't care for the rough types or the ones that smelled bad. She regarded a real man as someone who was physically strong and attractive yet soft enough to understand her tearful silences. Having had her share of sticks and screws, Margie was now in a position to do what she pleased. And for the past two years it had pleased her to stay away from anyone whom she did not hand pick herself.

Holding a glass in her hand she now sat at her pool deck waiting for Dr. Stroud's call.

***

Dr. Allan Stroud, a gynecologist with a clinic busier than a central train station, was a tall, lean man who couldn't care less about the women who came to see him and never failed to voice his thoughts out loud.

"All women are alike: They only want what's good for them. That's how I got rich – cleaning out what other men left behind. Show me one that's different and I'll bite my tongue."

Besides being methodical and well organized to the point of obsession, Dr. Stroud was a man dedicated to cleanliness. Hygiene, to him, was something that came closest to worship, a religion, practiced and rehashed to all the women who sought his help. Voicing opinions unrelated to the medical field in a somewhat lofty tone, his clinic was filled with patients willing to disregard the foul odors of his words. Considered by other physicians as a very competent professional, Allan Stroud made it his habit to repeat his philosophy to every new patient.

When Jasmine walked into his office, three hours earlier, he had preached the usual.

"You must take good care of yourself ...wash well after each time...soap hands and clean the area...never let foreign bodies into your own...unless, of course, you're familiar with them... use condoms...and come to be tested once a month for HIV... don't chew bubble gum while fornicating... when nude, never spread your legs wide open where there's a breeze..."

A lecture about Dr. Ignaz Philipp Semmelweis, the early pioneer of antiseptic procedures who'd saved the lives of birthing mothers, ensued.

"So... tell me a little bit about yourself," Dr. Stroud turned his head in Jasmine's direction.

"What's there to tell?"

"I'd say quite a lot for a beautiful woman like yourself."

Jasmine lowered her head.

"Don't tell me you've never heard it before!"

She smiled shyly.

"Margie knows how to pick her girls. I've got to hand it to her."

"Do you get to see all the girls in Margie's agency?"

"Every single one of them! Margie shares my philosophy. Cleanliness is the most important rule in life. A dirty person will act like one, don't you agree?"

"Well…yeah…kind of…"

"So I get to check her gals, but not before I've checked them for HIV and all the other tests, like I've done with you…"

"So what you're telling me is that I'm clean?"

"Certainly! We know you're free of viruses and sexually transmitted diseases and…basically, you can start working as of now."

"Thank you," she smiled.

"Tell me, how long have you been fucking men?"

"You mean…when did I start …"

"I mean… how long have you been a fucking whore?"

Jasmine wasn't sure how to respond.

"I've been in this profession for several years now."

"Why?"

"Excuse me?"

"I asked you why? Why do you sell your fucking vagina to men's dicks?"

"I don't think it's any of your business, Dr. Stroud."

"Anything and everything I ask you is my fucking business."

"I refuse to answer!"

"All I have to do is call Margie."

Jasmine hesitated momentarily before complying.

"Ok…I left home when I was very young…started as a simple rebellion… turned out into a longer one…"

"Lots of kids leave home when they're fed up. But not all turn out selling sex. Why did you choose to do it?"

"It was easy…and accessible… makes a lot of money."

"How much do you charge?"

"You'd have to negotiate that with Margie."

Jasmine thought she had finally understood. Dr. Stroud was probably trying to set a trap, check to see if she'd be willing to double cross Margie.

"Don't you fuck on the side?"

"Only when I choose my own man."

"How would you like to fuck me?"

"Is this a joke?!"

"Nope. It's part of the deal with Margie. I get to pick the cleanest and the nicest…she gets to supply the bodies."

"And what if I refuse?"

"Like I said, Margie would love to hear from me."

"Sorry to disappoint you Dr. Stroud, but I …I don't really fancy you."

"Sorry to hear that." His fingers dialed a number.

Frozen in her seat she tried to figure out what to do next.

Dr. Stroud's stony face was replaced by a smirk. He held onto the receiver then at once put it down and said.

"Looks like you've been saved by the bell. Margie's out."

"Do you make offers to all the new girls?"

"No. Only to those I fancy."

"I see."

"What d'you see?"

Jasmine looked baffled.

"I'll show you what you're missing…." Getting up from behind his desk, Dr. Stroud moved in front of Jasmine, kicked off his moccasins and pulled down his pants. Grabbing her hand, he placed it over his erection.

"Dr. Stroud!" Jasmine called out in a panicky voice.

"At your service!" he held her hand forcefully.

"Let go!" she raised her voice.

"Are you gonna let me fuck you or not?!"

"Please don't…" Jasmine faked tears, "Please don't…"

"What is this? Kindergarten?!"

"Please don't…"

"And you want to work for Margie? Is this a joke?"

Moving fast, Jasmine dug into her bag and flashed a badge. Holding it firmly in front of his eyes, she said.

"You're under arrest, prick!"

"What the fuck…"

"Don't even dream of moving! I've got you surrounded!"

Two plain clothed men barged into the room.

"So...Dr. Stroud, how about pulling up your stinking pants and getting your dick to cool down?" Felix pointed at his erection.

Dr. Stroud looked as if he was about to have a heart attack.

"I said dress up! Collect your stick and shove it back where it belongs! I'm not interested in having it dangle in front of me!"

Jolted out of his bewildered state, Dr. Stroud pulled up his pants and stepped into his shoes.

"Nice and easy, Dr. Stroud, don't even dream of breathing until I tell you to do so," Felix, dressed in a navy T-shirt with Special Police Force printed in large letters on its back, spoke rapidly and without as much as a smile read him his Miranda rights.

"Nice boy. Now let's get down to business...you have the right to remain silent..."

* * *

The call came an hour later when Margie had already dozed off on the lounge chair next to the pool. Several spotlights turned the place into an exotic-looking island. The air smelled sweet under the brilliance of hundreds of flowers planted throughout the large estate.

Graziella, the live in maid answered the phone.

"Is for you, ma'am," she stepped outside, "Is Dr. Stroud."

She handed her the phone.

"Yes?"

"Margie, this is Allan Stroud. You called me?"

He sounded so abrupt. Margie winced.

"Yes, I need speedy information. Did a gal by the name of Jasmine visit you today?"

Seated inside his clinic surrounded by Jasmine and two other policemen from Felix' team, Allan Stroud responded as directed.

"Yes she did, and she's already left."

"Are you alright?" Margie asked somewhat hesitant.

Felix moved his fingers across his throat in a motion of slicing it. Dr. Stroud was sweating in his chair.

"Yes, I'm alright. Just busy."

"You sound … edgy. Was she a good fuck?" she giggled on line.

Felix jammed his finger into Dr. Stroud's shoulder.

"She's something else… one of a kind."

Exhaling deeply, Margie smiled.

"Glad to hear you got paid."

"Yes. She was great," his face red trying to avoid Jasmine' piercing eyes.

Jasmine was enjoying every second. It had been a long and complex stakeout but one that had finally paid out.

"Then I take it she's clean?"

"Yeah… clean as a whistle."

"Great!"

Felix scribbled something on a piece of paper and placed it in front of Dr. Stroud.

"So when is she starting?" he asked Margie.

"Actually… that's why I've decided to call you. There's this sheik in town… wants a special gal…I thought of trying her out with him but I had to make sure she's been checked by you."

"As far as I'm concerned she's fit for a king."

"Great, Allan. Thanks. Hope it paid well."

"Yes. She was great."

Margie hung up feeling excited.

She could now close the deal with Mr. Tawille.

"You were cute!" Felix slapped the back of Allan Stroud's head. "Now move your stinking ass in the direction of the door," escorting him into the unmarked car parked outside his clinic.

CHAPTER 38

Tierry remained still. His eyes were shut as he held the receiver in his hand. He couldn't believe he had hung up on a housekeeper who'd asked him a simple question. He could have faked a name or even given his full name, what difference would it have made? After all, it was his intention to help Carlene through her divorce as well as his own … and then marry her. He wasn't trying to hurt Carlene; he only wanted to ensure she was ok.

Angry at himself for having reacted like a coward and frustrated with the situation, Tierry decided to think again before making another move. Perhaps it was time to speak to his wife and confess his love for Carlene…but what if Carlene had changed her mind and was now back with her husband?

The mere thought made him sick. Maybe he should return to New York, stay there until he met Carlene and finalized the situation with her once and for all, but what if…what if, once again, for reasons unknown to him, Carlene wouldn't meet him, just like the last time when he'd flown into town especially to see her?

Covering his face with both hands, Tierry wrecked his head trying to sort out the situation and decided his best bet would be to talk to Carlene on the phone.

With a fast-beating heart, he again dialed her number.

***

Leaning over her paled face, Glen kissed her lips.

"Please open your eyes for me, darling… I want to see your eyes … talk to me…" his head next to hers.

Carlene tossed.

"Leave …it hurts… leave me…"

"Never, darling… I'll never leave you…I love you too much to ever let you go.…"

Naked except for a pair of tight black underwear purchased especially for the occasion and sprinkled with perfume, Glen again seated himself next to Carlene.

Carefully, as if trying to avoid touching her, he opened her gown.

It smelled bad and was stained with blood. Carlene's greasy hair looked like a wet haystack strewn over her pale face.

"I love seeing you undress for me," he kept talking to her as though she were fully alert and able to comprehend.

"Let's move your arm…this way, darling…that's good…don't worry…it's ok…I'll take care of you…" his hands cupping her breasts.

Bending down he sucked on her left breast then moved to the right, circling her nipples and wetting them with his tongue.

"Come on you gorgeous little nymphs… stand up…make me wanna fuck you," his face turned red as he began steaming with satisfaction, "Darling, look what it's doing to me…" eyeing his erection.

Taking her hand, he led it inside his black shorts, tight by now and heavy with his newly aroused front.

"How do you like this?" he moved each of her fingers separately, "Are you enjoying this, darling? I want to fuck you…hard…"

Carlene turned and twisted in an effort to release her arm.

"Leave …let go…it hurts…" but the more she tried fighting him off, the more aroused he became.

"Keep going…I love this, darling…keep moving…I'm so hard… I can do it…keep talking…"

The abrupt ring caused him to freeze in place long enough for Carlene to get away from under his grip and roll over sideways. Confused and sexually aroused, Glen tried to understand why his front was suddenly flat again and his energies dwindled. The more rings, the flatter his front and the more confused he became. Reaching with his hand, he picked up the phone.

"Hello?"

Tierry listened carefully, trying to guess the voice at the other end.

"Who's this?" Glen spoke thickly.

"Is Mrs. Wilmore in?"

"She's busy."

"When will she be available?"

"Who the fuck are you?"

"My name's Tierry. I'd like to speak with her."

"I told you she's busy."

"And who the fuck are you?"

"Her husband."

Tierry hung up.

It was useless to continue the dialogue with a man who, obviously, had no intention of letting him speak with his wife. This entire situation was absurd. He'd have to speak with his wife and then return to New York again.

He wasn't about to let go of the woman he loved.

* * *

After slamming down the receiver Glen neared Carlene.

"Who the fuck is Tierry?" his face next to hers.

"Don't...don't touch me..."

"I'll touch you whether you want it or not!" he screamed into her face. "Who the fuck is he?" he slapped her face and shook her shoulders.

Carlene let out a howl.

"Leave …it hurts…"

"It'll hurt even more if you don't open your fucking mouth!" his face red with anger.

Carlene's eyes, barely open and confused, looked at him.

"Answer me! Open your mouth and answer me! Who the fuck is Tierry?"

"I…what…what are you…?"

"What?"

"Where am I?"

"Oh shit! This fucking injection is taking longer than expected. Let's give you something to wake you up…then you can answer my question!"

Sill nude, except for the stringy black underwear that formed a line above his pubic hair, Glen stepped into the bathroom to get a glass of water. Carlene tossed in bed trying to wake up. Her head throbbed and her stomach hurt. Placing her hand over her cheek she was hoping to calm the burning sensation. She felt cold and hot all at the same time. Moving her hands over her body she realized there was something wrong but found it hard to understand the situation.

"What…where am I…?" she spoke in a near whisper.

Glen returned holding a glass of water.

"No…leave me …it hurts…" Carlene kept whimpering.

As soon as he reached the bed there was a loud knock on the door.

Glen froze.

CHAPTER 39

The small room made Dr. Stroud feel very uncomfortable as though forcefully compressed inside a cubicle.

"I'm not saying a word without my attorney!"

"Which one? Seth or Dorsey?" Felix asked.

They had been on his tail long enough to know when and what he did and with whom. They also knew the names of his attorneys, both of whom were currently out of reach: Seth was in a special court session and Dorsey was out of town.

Felix had planned it thoroughly, leaving very little to chance. With only a couple of hours left, he was squeezing Allan Stroud into a tight corner. Sandy, who had shared with Felix some of the methods used in his unit during sting operations in New York, had added some tips used by the department.

"The shrink we work with is great. He comes up with all these psychological props. By the time a guy gets to call his attorney, we've basically squeezed out of him what we wanted…if we miss the timing it turns messy…"

Now putting Sandy's advice to the practice, Felix chose to attack Stroud by spitting out the names of both his attorneys. Allan Stroud's face was gaunt and gray looking. He was speechless.

"I have the right to an attorney," he repeated.

"You'll get him after you answer some questions."

"And if I refuse?" he swallowed holding up his head.

"I'll suck your dick dry 'till you throw up your answers!" his eyes burnt like those of a madman.

Allan Stroud lowered his head.

"Now! Tell me about your arrangement with Margie!" Felix, who'd been studying Margie's cleverly set Agency and ring of girls for the past year, knew all the answers. It was a question of getting a full confession out of Allan Stroud's mouth.

"This," he pointed to a camera, "is a videotape. We're now taping you. Anything you say can and will be used against you in a court of law. Is that understood?"

Allan Stroud moved his head.

"I can't hear you," Felix repeated.

"Yes." Allan Stroud's voice sounded small.

"Ok… let's move it," he signaled to the technician in back.

"This is Officer Felix Drexel, special operations…." Felix gave the usual introductions then asked Allan Stroud.

"When did Margie Joree first approach you?"

Standing behind a one-way mirror dressed in blue denims and a loose t-shirt, Officer Penny Links watched the taping of Dr. Allan Stroud's testimony.

"How are you?" Jessie joined her.

"Happy to be wearing jeans and sneakers instead of spiky heels and a wig."

They laughed.

"It's such a relief to see this skunk all shaken up," Penny stared at Allan Stroud knowing he couldn't see her.

"Yeah…I know what you mean. I've been with the Agency for a while…"

Penny giggled.

"I know, 'Tina' dear! Lucky you managed a clean break!"

The two officers exchanged words about their experiences at the Margie Agency.

It wasn't easy playing roles, and even less so being used as a decoy. For her last part, Penny had spent a month with the pros on the streets of Dallas, talking to and befriending prostitutes. As Felix explained, it was crucial to use their lingo and logic; one had to think like a prostitute in order to pass as one. When he had first approached her, Penny studied the information and understood she'd have only one chance to convince Margie. She had chosen the name Jasmine after a hooker who went out of her way to try and help her learn the ropes involved.

"That's a beautiful name. Where are you from?" Penny asked.

"Iran."

A long explanation followed about her background and circumstances of life.

Jasmine was destined from childhood and forced into the horrific trappings of the sex industry by her father. She was unlucky to be born a beautiful baby girl with light colored eyes. Enslaved to her father's sexual whims since she was first raped by him at age six, Jasmine knew she had nowhere to go but to end up working like her older sister. They were four sisters and two brothers but within the chaos of their house, they basically all slept together. They'd spread the small mats on the floor inside the two rooms and slept close to each other. But in the darkness of night things happened that couldn't be seen by all.

Penny felt sick when she heard Jasmine's painful history and took it as a sign of redemption, albeit a small and insignificant one, that pointed to her successful sting operation.

It worked.

Now standing and watching Allan Stroud shaking like a leaf, Penny appreciated tenfold the long hours and endless drills and preparations that went into the final operation. It was nerve wracking requiring a sharpness of mind blended with lots of common sense and humor, all in large quantities. And above all: Her dedication to the case and willingness to undergo an intimate vaginal check by the loathsome Dr. Allan Stroud.

"I want to hear more about the Agency," Felix repeated.

Allan Stroud tried to avoid answering the questions but was probed again and again. Felix believed in using a tactic called 'bombardment', literally bombarding the person with quick repetitive questions. Considered by attorneys as harassment not to be used during the initial questioning when it was most effective, Felix was racing against time.

Right now Allan Stroud was most vulnerable with no one to protect him.

"Answer me! Now!" Felix raised his voice.

"What do you want to know?"

"We've been through this shit so don't try dancing in circles or I'll make sure you get dizzy and throw up!" he slapped him on the back of his neck.

Allan Stroud was getting panicky.

Having someone slap him like that, though it wasn't too harsh or brutal, sent a frightening message to his brain, one of approaching terror. He knew he had a right to an attorney but somehow he wasn't sure they'd be able to find him. Maybe this guy had connections but then...maybe he wasn't for real? The police never used such practices but maybe they've changed tactics? He's been through questionings before, they didn't dare touch him so it must be someone else, maybe other people interested in getting a piece of the action? Maybe he should ask them about it? But what if they truly were police detectives? He'd only get himself into further trouble.

Allan Stroud's shirt was glued to his sweaty back. He was thirsty.

"Ok...ok...I started working with Margie two years ago, when she'd just opened up. She had this place on Knox but it only stayed open a couple of months then she moved to Highland Park. We struck a deal through a mutual friend..."

"Name!" Felix shouted in his ear.

Allan Stroud was visibly shaken.

"Guy Oleo."

"Then what?!"

"I went to see her and...we liked each other."

"Did you fuck her?"
"No!"
"I want details, fart face!"
"She told me I'd get to fuck the girls...and she'd pay me one grand each..."
"Doing what?"
"Checking them for HIV, venereal filth, patience, aptitude... should I go on?"
"I'll tell you when to stop!"
"Just ..."
"Don't!" Felix barked back. "Don't even try copping out!"
"Ok...ok...it was easy and I pocketed quite a bit... besides, I got to pick the lays...."
"How did she pay you?"
"Cash only."
"What did you do with the money?"
"Grocery shopping...cash payments ... clothes and other stuff..."
"How much did you gross that first year?"
"I'm not sure... it wasn't exactly.... reported... the situation was ..."
"Cut the crap! How much?!"
"I honestly don't know...something around... three or four grand..."
"Is that a day or a week?"
"A week."
"Go on!"
"I've said all there is to say...I'm not hiding anything..."
"We'll see about that!" Felix signaled with this hand and a cup of coffee appeared from nowhere.
"Coffee?"
"No, thanks. I'd like some water if..."
The coffee was scooped away replaced by a cup of water.
"So you start pocketing four grand a week..."
"Right."
"That's a lot of money...a very large amount..."

"Aha." Allan Stroud moved his head in agreement.
"D'you get to see her clients?"
"Never."
"Why not?"
"I don't understand your question…"
"Which part don't you understand?"
"Why would I get to see the clients?"
"Maybe 'cause her clients are interested in other things besides the girls!"
Allan Stroud's face was now visibly paling.
"What are you talking about?"
"You know damn well what I'm talking about! It's not only pricks that get bought and sold at the Agency, fuck face!"
Allan Stroud was quiet. He reached for the water.
"Were you ever invited to any of her pool parties?"
Allan Stroud bit his lower lip and swallowed. He got the feeling Felix knew everything there was to know about the Agency and was only asking for the sake of hearing him admit to it all. It was time to bail out, make the right moves while the going was good.
"I want to hear about the parties!" Felix whispered in his ear.
Allan Stroud's forehead was pearled with sweat.
"February nineteenth of last year…does that ring a bell, Dr. Stroud?"
"I…I don't…"
"March thirtieth…when that gal OD'd and we had to bust the place…"
"I…"
"May fifth…heavy duty clients come into town and you show up…"
"Ok…ok…"
"Ok what?"
"Ok…I'll tell you…only…"
"Only what, Doc?"
"I want a deal…"

"You prick! I'll consider giving you a deal if you spit out what we want to hear. Got it?!"

Allan Stroud shook his head.

"If you as much as forget to spell out one name you can kiss immunity goodbye."

"Ok...ok..."

CHAPTER 40

"Mr. Tawille? This is Margie from the Agency."
"Yes."
"I'm calling to confirm Jasmine's visit tonight."
"Yes."
"When exactly do you want her? What time…"
"After food."
"After dinner?"
"Yes."
"And when's that?"
"Nine."
"What room?"
"Five…zeero…one…one…"
"Five, zero, one, one?"
"Yes."
" Nine o'clock, right?"
"Yes."
"How would you like to pay?"
"I av box…one box."
Margie didn't respond. She needed to check the usual.
"Box? What box?"
"Box ov Maslem-el-Fahid."
"What's in it?"
The codes were often changed for security reasons. A person wishing to pay for the services rendered at the Agency with the contents of

a box, had to be approved by Margie. Drifters, specializing in moving from place to place without leaving any footprints or loose threads, handled the process itself using codes allocated to them by a third party. The only person allowed cross over information was Margie. Now looking at her private list, she waited for his reply.

"Meni sords and rozes."

It took Margie a second to translate the code. Mr. Tawille was getting impatient.

"I give stuff…"

"Yes, yes…I understand. I'll have one of my men escort Jasmine in and take the stuff out."

"Jasmine to come to tek."

"You'd like Jasmine to take the stuff?"

"Yes."

"That's fine. I'll tell Jasmine to bring it."

"Yes."

The deal was concluded. Margie could now afford to relax.

There was only one more matter to attend to.

Jasmine.

***

Dialing again, Margie cleared her throat and gave a small cough. She counted two rings. On the third, Penny answered.

"This is Jasmine, can I help you?" her voice soft and velvety.

"This is Margie from the Agency. I like your style."

"Thank you, Margie."

"I've got good news."

"I could use some."

The phone had been tapped and arrangements made for it to ring inside a small room within the department's special operations unit. As soon as Margie's number was identified, Penny was instructed to answer the phone. Two agents stood nearby, listening to every word and recording the conversation. Penny was hoping to convince Margie to give her a chance with one of her clients. It came sooner than expected.

"I spoke with Dr. Stroud. He told me your tests are ok."

"That's good news. I'm glad to hear it."

"He said you were great in other respects, too...that makes me very happy." Margie's voice sounded as though she was smiling.

"I promised not to let you down."

"You didn't. And now that you've passed the first test, I've got other good news."

"Thank you, Margie."

"Don't thank me yet. You may live to regret it..." she chuckled then added. "An Arab sheik...a heavy one wants you at Le Château tonight at nine."

"Le Château on Turtle Creek?!"

"We've got connections," Margie half laughed, "this isn't DeeDee's, remember? Our people are everywhere."

"What class! I'm impressed...glad to be working for you, Margie."

"Just make sure to dazzle him. Be there at nine ...room five zero one one... precisely at nine..."

"Ok. Anything else?"

"Yes...now that you've been assigned... there's something else you should know..."

"Yes?"

The agents surrounding Penny were hoping to get lucky. If they could only record a deal involving payments, they could present a closed case to the department head. Margie's Agency was trafficking and laundering drug money. By posing as a legitimate entity, Margie was able to smooth over problems and assist her best clients.

Margie's girls were known to be good carriers, non-suspected ladies that liked traveling to remote islands and romantic spots. It was not unusual for an Agency girl to find herself in Barbados for the night or in another exotic location within a moment's notice posing as hired help on behalf of the Margie Agency, Highland Park's Elite Work Force. Now trying to make it sound important but not to the point of alarming Jasmine, Margie went on.

"He might ask you to bring me a small package…or a bag. You do not, I repeat, **do not** ask any questions or open it. No matter what! Remember! We're very strict in the agency about privacy. You don't embarrass the client and you do as he says. Is that understood?"

"Absolutely, Margie."

"Good girl."

Margie then added the remaining details.

Mr. Tawille, a short blond guy by the name of Mark Angello sat with earphones across from Jasmine. Listening quietly he mouthed without a voice.

"Fucking bitch!"

His part was nearly done. There was only one more scene that needed to be played, much later, in the wee hours of the morning.

CHAPTER 41

They entered the lobby and approached the security guard. Flashing his badge, Sandy said.

"The Wilmores...what floor are they on?"

"Can I see your IDs?"

"Smart to ask," he handed it over.

Tony checked it out then shifted his eyes from Sandy to Jeff.

"I've got to get permission..."

"You've got mine. I'd like you to join us upstairs for a moment."

"I can't leave my position..."

"You can. I'm asking for your help ...you'll be back sooner than you think."

Hesitant and visibly shaken, Tony joined Sandy and Jeff. Once out of the elevator they entered a corridor leading to the apartment.

Sandy said.

"As soon as we go in, you're free to go downstairs."

Tony wasn't sure he'd live to see it.

* * *

The housekeeper was a short middle-aged woman with graying hair neatly collected into a small bun. She stood in the doorway wearing a white uniform with a pretty, well-starched apron.

"Yes?" she asked.

"Ma'am, I'm Officer Varlovsky, special operations unit NYPD and this here is Officer Vinsen." They flashed their badges.

She looked at both then glanced at Tony who stood poker-faced with hands dangling to his sides.

"How can I help you?"

"By telling us where we can find Dr. Wilmore and his wife."

"Dr. Wilmore is upstairs with Mrs. Wilmore. They've been there for a while… she's quite ill, you know…"

"Jeff, would you …please?" Sandy indicated the direction of the elevators with his hand.

"Sure, sure…" turning to Tony, Jeff said.

"Let's take a walk."

"I know the way," Tony looked terrified though he tried to sound casual.

"Let's go!" Jeff escorted him back in the direction of the elevators adding, "Thanks Tony. You can now go back to your post."

"How do you know my name?"

"NYPD special operations unit, remember?"

With Tony not posing any threat or alerting the housekeeper, Jeff ran back inside the apartment rushed up the stairs and joined Sandy who was listening behind the closed door.

They heard a woman's voice cry out.

"Don't…it hurts…"

* * *

Glen was still holding the glass of water in his hand when he heard the knocks on the door.

"Hold it right there!" a loud voice hollered as the door flung open.

The glass fell out of Glen's hand splashing water all around.

Glen remained standing as he stared at Sandy and Jeff.

CHAPTER 42

Felix was on his way to the storage room, a large wing off the central corridor of the main building.
"Mind if I join?" Officer Kyle asked.
"Shoot!"
"This sting…tonight…I'd like to join."
"Why?"
"It's… personal… I'd like to see this Margie's ass ripped apart."

The special unit was formed and built on trust with each of its six members contributing to its unity and to each other. For large operations, such as this one, Felix had requested and received assistance in the form of additional officers and technical specialists able to bring it to a successful wrap. Officer Kyle, a thirty-one-year-old graduate of Texas A&M in electrical engineering, was one of a team of four men and two women handpicked by Felix two years earlier to spearhead the war against drug trafficking in several affluent communities in Texas. It was part of a much larger scheme involving Federal Agencies such as the FBI and CIA.

As part of their rigorous training, Felix had demanded that his men share their most intimate moments with each other.

"A man who can't cry in front of other men won't become part of my team."

He claimed they needed to work as a one-man team and get to know each other to the point of being able to think for each other.

"If our mission calls for a rescue type operation of a stranded agent, you need to know how he's thinking and breathing otherwise the operation will fail. Imagine... just imagine the agent is hiding ...now we're circling around the bushes trying to get to him. If you don't know how the agent thinks, you won't know how he'll react or where he'll choose to hide. You've basically lost the game before it even started."

It made sense and became clearer when, during one of their training sessions, the unit practiced abductions of agents and had raised the issue of rape.

"Now that you've spent four sessions listening to me, I'd like to listen to your inputs," Dr. Salty, the unit's psychologist who had finalized a series of lectures on the posttraumatic aspects of rape, looked at the small group of six seated in a semi circle.

Felix cleared his throat.

"I was eleven when my twin sister...she was raped and murdered," his eyes shone. "We were very close...always played together... teased each other...I remember telling her I hated her but then...I remember kissing her good night when our parents went out and left us alone."

The room was silent.

"She was twelve minutes older than me," Felix smiled sadly, "but she died before me. We lived out in the country and on Friday nights my parents usually went to visit the nearby neighbors a mile or so down the road. We'd stay alone my sister and I and watch TV. That was basically all we did on Friday nights. This one last Friday we were watching a scary movie and Tammy, my sister, she was bursting to use the bathroom...couldn't keep it any longer so she ran out of the room shouting: 'Tell me what happened, Felix, I wanna' know what happened.' That was the last time she spoke."

It felt as though the air was sucked out of the room. No one moved. Felix swallowed several times then cleared his throat.

"He waited for her inside the bathroom...she...she never screamed...but when she didn't return I called out: 'Tammy, you're missing the best part.' The movie ended ... I kept calling: 'Tammy...what's taking you so long?' But she didn't answer."

Felicia, the young officer dried a tear. Two others coughed.

"I waited some more and...when she didn't answer and didn't return, I decided to go find her. Our house was kind of small, but my parents kept adding rooms to it enlarging it to fit the growing family. So at one point, we had a small corridor coming out of the bathroom with a fork like split into both directions: to the kitchen and to the bedrooms. When I went looking for Tammy I cut across the living room and into the bedroom. I saw her sitting there on the floor drenched in blood. She didn't say anything, just kept staring at me. Then the door moved and before I had a chance to get near her the man came towards me. I ran back into the living room shouting... like from out of hell.

"He kept yelling. 'I'm gonna get you too, little boy...I'm gonna get you...' He chased me all around and I kept shouting to Tammy to get out of there. But then I realized she'd bump into him if she ran out the side of the bed rooms... so I called out: 'Get out through your favorite room, Tammy, get out...' meaning the kitchen. Tammy loved eating. Sometimes, when mom and dad were out and before Barnie and Liz came along, we'd have these big meals of peanut butter and weird jellies...we'd compete to see who could eat more.

"It all happened very fast. It may have taken five...ten minutes... but it seemed like hours. Tammy, like me...we were confused, she thought I told her to go through the other door so I kept running and tiring him, like I said, I was eleven and he was much older, he kept huffing and breathing hard...I felt I was tiring him. I kept screaming and shouting for Tammy to get out: 'run to your favorite room...run Tammy...run...' I kept him in circles and he was beginning to slow, kind of stop every few seconds, he couldn't keep up with me. I wanted to make sure Tammy went out through the kitchen 'cause she had to pass there on her way out of the house, but I wanted to make sure she was out before I got out...but then she got confused, I guess…she crawled into the living room instead of to the kitchen like I told her to. He spotted her first, before I could help her, jumped on her with a knife and stabbed her once in the chest then ran out of the house. She died in my arms."

Felix' eyes were wet. He blew his nose and moved his hands over his face several times before going on.

"My sister could have been saved…I knew she could have gotten away without being caught…'cause I knew the kitchen was her favorite room…I guess she got confused…."

The silence was deafening. The agents remained seated trying to imagine the situation. No one said a word for a long time but they all wanted the story to end differently…

There wasn't an agent in the room who hadn't understood the point, regardless of its outcome. Felix had proved his point.

Now facing young Officer Kyle, Felix asked him.

"How come you never said a word?"

"I…it's not something…"

Felix stopped and looked at Kyle.

"Wanna' tell me about it?"

Kyle motioned with his head.

"Let's go through here," Felix led the way to a nearby 'exit' sign. Pushing the door handle outwardly, they found themselves inside a small patio adjacent to the left wing of the complex.

"Mind?" Felix crouched on the wide step and took out a pack of cigarettes with a lighter.

"Thanks," Kyle bent over to the lighter and inhaled deeply.

They were quiet until Kyle said.

"I …my sister …she ended up on the streets …working as a hooker…"

Felix' eyes were glued onto Kyle's.

"I…I can't talk about it… but I'm sure as heck would like to see Margie hang."

"What happened?" Felix insisted.

Kyle kept quiet for a long time. When he spoke Felix had to strain to hear him.

"She was three years older than me…would have been thirty-four next month," he took a long drag. "She was the smart one, the one who brought home the best school grades and…she was funny as hell, too…" he kept puffing. "She started dating this guy and soon thereafter came the pills then the shots…my parents claimed they never noticed anything wrong was going on. By the time she was seventeen she was already a pro… five months later she'd OD'd … just left us…"

Felix's eyes were as shiny as Kyle's.

"My parents never recouped. Dad had a heart attack shortly thereafter and my mom died six months before my graduation. You could say I grew up with my dead family's pictures staring at me from the walls …"

Felix put his arm around Kyle's trembling shoulders.

"Glad you finally got to spell it out…" he smiled at Kyle.

"Yeah," he smiled back wiping his tears again.

"I wish it were possible, Kyle…but I've already assigned you elsewhere…"

"I know…it's why I'm asking you to change it."

"Sorry, Kyle…it's all set."

"Can I exchange places with Rudy?"

"Like I said…it's all been set. I need you elsewhere."

"Can I at least join you later?"

"I hope we'll have a reason to celebrate. I'll let you know."

"Thanks."

Felix gave him a strong bear hug.

"Son of a …gun! You should have opened your mouth earlier!"

"Thanks Felix," Officer Kyle returned the hug.

***

For this particular operation Felix needed a small bag of white powder.

"Hey Greg, I need that one…over here…" pointing in the direction of a small cubicle stacked up neatly on the shelf.

Felix was inside the walk in safe, a huge structure with an assortment of drugs confiscated by the various police units. The place resembled a birding farm with endless rows of small cubicles sitting on shelves like bird nests. Inside each cubicle was a package catalogued and marked with identification numbers, specifying the name of the officer who had found it, the date, circumstances, quality and a bunch of other details all of which were now studied by Felix.

"I'll need it placed inside one of them fancy little pouches …" raising his eyebrows in the direction of a small utility wash bag, the kind used by visitors in fancy hotels.

"Sign here," Greg pointed to a specific line in the Inventory Booklet.

Felix signed and picked up the bag.

"Good luck," Greg called.

"Thanks…hope it'll come in useful!"

***

It was four in the morning when, Penny, dressed as Jasmine, sat in Felix's room drinking a cup of strong coffee. Next to her was agent Mark, the so-called Mr. Tawille.

"What time are you moving?"

"I'll call her at five and tell her what a great night I've had with you …" Penny poked her finger against Mark's chest.

"Wanna' play it out?"

"Maybe later…?" she winked at him.

"Aow much you want I pay madam…."

Penny and Mark laughed practicing their roles as Jasmine and Mr. Tawille.

"Now remember," Felix cut in, "We've got to squeeze the lady as soon as we're in...she'll have her attorneys all over us within five seconds... it'll have to be quick."

"I hope she buys my story," Penny turned to Mark.

"Good luck Penny," he squeezed her hand.

"Thanks, Mark."

The stage was set.

* * *

Everyone was in place, waiting for the clock to reach the digit five. Penny picked up the phone and, looking at the technicians, waited for the signal.

"Hello?" Margie's voice sounded groggy.

"Hi Margie, it's Jasmine... sorry to wake you up so early..."

"What's wrong?"

"Nothing...nothing...it's just that...Mr. Tawille had just left and asked me to deliver a small bag for you and..."

"Oh...what time is it?"

"Five ...I'm sorry Margie..."

"No...no...that's ok...let's see...I'll tell you what...maybe... wanna' bring it over?"

"No problem," Penny raised her thumb in Felix' direction.

"Actually...give me an hour or so and I'll send someone..."

"Sorry Margie...but I've already made arrangements to someplace...I'd like to come right away and deliver it, if that's ok with you..."

"Ok...ok...I don't usually..."

Felix had hoped Margie would ask Penny over to her house. It meant she'd be caught dealing on the premises and the local police could then get involved. Margie, who was well experienced with these types of deals, was always very careful not to be caught with anything even remotely related to drugs. Felix was counting on the early hour to throw Margie off balance. It worked. He'd had an agent near-by who reported Margie's lights had gone out only half an hour earlier. Felix was surprised to hear Margie's offer. It was an unusual move on her behalf.

"Let me give you my address…just make sure you're not followed…and come alone…"

"Of course…I understand…"

"I live on …" giving her the full address, Penny signaled to Felix with her other hand.

"Got that?" Margie asked.

"Yes, that's fine. I'll see you shortly."

"Let's go," Felix called out.

The team moved fast and was inside the car within seconds.

CHAPTER 43

"Move your ass over there!" Sandy screamed. Glen did as he was told. Jeff moved next to Carlene. Her stiff body resembled that of an older woman. Covering her up with a blanket, he helped her head onto the pillow.

"Can you hear me?" he spoke gently, his eyes on her face.

Carlene didn't move. Jeff removed a strand of hair from her face then looked around the room.

"Look at her," he said in Sandy's direction pointing at Carlene.

Leaving Glen standing at the far end of the room, Sandy cautiously approached the bed, his eyes on the ashen face. Leaning forward he examined the bare arms then shook his head pointing to the blue and green marks along the inner part of the left arm. They both stared at the thin face, black circles around the tightly shut eyes with two deep lines at the edge of each eyebrow giving the impression of someone in pain. Lying perfectly still, Carlene looked lifeless.

Sandy shot Jeff a quick look then turned to Glen.

"What did you give her?"

"I…I injected…"

"Just spit out the name or I'll make you talk!"

Glen released the name of the drug.

"Side effects!" Sandy's voice thundered.

Looking like a little boy who'd been caught playing a naughty game, Glen muttered.

"It affects everyone differently…you can't really…"

"Cut the crap or I'll give you a taste of your own medicine!"

"She's been out of it… somewhat…sleeps a lot…"

"You call this being out of it somewhat?!" Sandy gestured with his hand, "You nearly killed her!"

Glen lowered his head.

"Why? Why d'you do this?" Sandy's face was now an inch away from Glen's.

"She thought I was …she made fun of me…I couldn't …"

"You'll be lucky if she lives."

"She's not for real," Glen said.

"What d'you say?"

"I said…she's not for real…she's not as nice as you think…"

"You're her husband, right?"

"Yeah, but…she … made a fool …she…she slept with other men…"

"So you poisoned her?!"

"She…one of her lovers called me …"

"Name…give me a name…"

"Terrie…said he was Terrie."

"Know him?"

"No!"

"Anyone else?"

"She's always so…she wants men…can't get enough of them…"

Jeff, who had called for an ambulance, sat on the bed next to Carlene wondering how a person as competent as Glen could turn into such a monster. Being a physician, and a prominent psychiatrist, only made the situation seem more extreme, allowing him to misuse his medical knowledge for the satisfaction of his own whims.

Before covering her with the blanket, Jeff looked closely at the bruises, which seemed to have been inflicted with force. Large blotches covered her stomach with dry bloodstains on her thighs and lower legs. Looking around, he noticed a white gown on the floor next to the nightstand. Jeff wanted to air out the room. It reeked of semen and perspiration. He opened partially the window disregarding the heavy humidity outside then signaled Sandy to move nearer.

"Didn't anyone notice what was going on in here?" Jeff kept his voice low aware of Glen's stares.

"I was thinking the same thing," Sandy replied.

Shaking his head he added.

"He's an animal...nothing but a fucked up piece of shit with a license to kill."

Jeff kept looking in Glen's direction, trying to imagine how he could have done what he did. There was no explanation, just another case, another abused wife added to the list of statistics.

Turning to Jeff, Sandy said.

"I'm taking in the scum. You can stay here and wait for the paramedics."

"Ok. Will do."

Sandy turned around and walked over to Glen's side.

"Ok, Doc...move it...you better dress up unless you want to parade your prick in the county jail..."

Still shocked and moving slower than usual, Glen got dressed and followed Sandy into the police car.

"Carlene...can you hear me?" Jeff tried again though he didn't really think there was any hope.

It was then that he remembered the fingerprints.

"That's the easiest part ...wish it didn't have to be this way."

He spoke out loud as he held her fingers gently.

CHAPTER 44

"You ready?" Felix asked Penny.
"Yeah…" she took a deep breath, "as ready as I'll ever be."
"Now remember…speak clearly…and try to stall her with questions…"
"Right."
Moving away from the parked vehicle, a large van able to hold two technicians and their equipment, with reflective glass covering its windows, Penny walked briskly on her stiletto heels. Lowering her head she whispered.
"Can you hear me?"
"Loud and clear."
The air, heavy with July's humidity and the shrilly buzz of cicadas, was clammy. Penny recognized the house with its large, wrought iron gate.
"Here we go," speaking into her chest while placing her finger on the bell.
Looking around, she noted the tall trees peeking from behind the stone wall.
"Who's there?" Margie's voice sounded.
"It's me …Jasmine."
A buzz sounded as the gate unlocked. Crossing the wide terra cotta leveled steps Penny thought of the satchel inside her bag, while her eyes scouted the surrounding garden and the pool to her right. The Santa Fe styled mansion, with its rough reddish exterior and the wide

steps leading to its entrance, reminded her of a palace. It was simply beautiful. When she reached the door she rang the doorbell and a moment later Margie appeared dressed in a yellow terry-cloth bathrobe.

"Good morning, Margie… I apologize again…I'm sorry…"

"Come in…come in…" looking behind Penny as if to ensure she was alone.

"Oh! This is beautiful!" Penny exclaimed as she entered the large room.

"Thank you, Jasmine. Cup of coffee?"

"I don't want to bother you…really…"

"It's no bother…I'm already up…"

"Ok…I'd love some. Thanks."

Margie busied herself in the kitchen.

"So… how was Mr. Tawille?" she half smiled.

"A real gentleman."

"Is that so?!"

"Yeah…he even gave me a necklace… look…" she showed it to Margie, "said he liked me…"

Margie shot her a look.

"Nice present, but don't tell me you bought his story!"

Penny smiled.

"Well?" Margie asked.

"Do I really look that naïve to you?"

They laughed.

"I meant to say that…some men are generous…don't mistake it for anything else." Margie's face was serious.

"I know that…just thought of sharing with you."

"How come you finished so early?"

"Well…" Penny lowered her head shyly and smiled at Margie.

"What? I'm curious. How did you do it?"

"I didn't. At four-thirty he asked me to leave…said he needed a good night's rest…"

"Incredible! He paid a bloody fortune for seven hours. I hope you appreciate that."

"Yeah." They giggled.
"Did he ask for the usual or...?"
"No, no. Strictly classical. Conservative. He's kind of shy... no imagination... but gentle... well... as gentle as they come..." she smiled at Margie thinking of Mark only a short distance away with the other officers.
"So where's the bag?"
"When do I get paid?"
"Give me the bag first...then you'll get your share."
"The bag is...it's actually a small pouch...it's right here," handing it over to her. "What's in it?"
Margie laughed.
"What? What's so funny?"
"Try guessing what's in here," Margie held up the satchel.
"I ...I don't know..."
"How about sugar?" opening the small pouch, Margie stuck her finger inside then placed it on the tip of her tongue.
"Good stuff. Want some?"
"I don't do that," Penny looked serious.
"Couldn't live without it."
"That's a lot of sugar!" Penny pointed to the pouch, "So when do I get paid?"
"You're right! Just a minute...I'll be right back," Margie left the coffee brewing and disappeared into a corridor just off the living room.
"Ok..." Penny whispered into her chest.
She listened as Felix instructed her through the tiny mike planted inside her ear.
Margie reappeared. Handing Penny an envelope she said.
"Here you are... it's all there."
Penny counted carefully planning her next line.
"Thanks, Margie, thanks for paying on time,"
"That's how I run my show here."
Penny smiled shyly.

"You were saying…about the sugar…that's a hell of a lot of stuff…"

"D'you think it's all for me?"

"I don't know," moving her shoulders up and down, "Like I said…I don't do that."

"Well maybe it's time you tried," she smiled at Penny.

"I really don't care for it, Margie."

"How would you know if you've never tried it?"

Penny disregarded the question.

"What will you do with the entire pouch?"

"I use it from time to time…"

"But how long does it keep?"

"Are you kidding me?" her eyes on Penny.

"Honest… I stay away from stuff like that…don't want any part of it…"

"How come?"

"I just hate it."

Margie laughed.

"So … what happens if you don't use it a lot? Does it like… spoil? Rot?" Penny asked again.

"Silly…" Margie laughed, "It's not for self-consumption…"

"What d'you mean?"

Margie's face turned serious.

"Are you trying to sound stupid or are you just playing the part?!"

Penny returned the harsh look.

"Margie, I refuse to touch this kind of shit! OK?!"

Margie smiled. She felt relieved.

"Really wanna' know what I do with the stuff?"

"Yeah…"

"I sell the shit!"

"You actually sell this stuff?!" Penny's face looked incredulous.

"Of course! It's very profitable. Did you really think I could afford all this," gesturing with her hands, "just from selling pussies to very rich assholes?"

"Who buys it?"
"Does it matter?"
"No…I really don't care…just making small talk…" Penny replied casually.
"How d'you like your coffee?"
"Black. Plain black."
"I see you've got a lot to learn," Margie smiled and brought both cups to the table.
The doorbell rang. Margie shot Penny a look. Penny stared back at her.
"It's five thirty in the morning. Who the hell can that be?!"
The bell rang again followed by a loud voice.
"Police…open the door or we'll come in forcefully."
"YOU!" Margie pointed her finger at Penny.
Penny didn't move.
"This is a last warning… we're coming in…"
Margie jumped sideways as if ready to run. Penny's hand caught her shoulder.
"Leave me alone!" Margie screamed.
The door burst open. Felix, followed by two local officers, stormed in.

"Great job, Penny," Felix slapped her shoulder.
"Thanks," she returned the smile unlatching the tiny mike from her ear.
Margie, pale-faced and silent, stood at the far corner of the living room. Her face was expressionless, entirely deadpan except for her eyes that darted from one officer to the next settling on Penny. One of the officers approached her.
"I refuse to say anything without my attorney!"
"We can throw you in jail until doomsday!" the officer shouted into her face, "and even get a judge to approve it. Now open your mouth and tell us what we want to hear or we're gonna lose the key to your cell."

"I demand to call my attorney," Margie repeated.

Felix signaled to the officer in charge who joined him in the next room.

"We won't get a stitch out of her!"

The local chief of police was very eager to collaborate with Felix and see to it that the sting went down as smoothly as planned. It was a matter of mutual interest to see Margie caught dealing drugs, otherwise, they couldn't get their hands on her.

When Felix was called in for advice and offered help, he had made it clear that he'd be in charge of the operation itself.

"I'll need help for the final showdown... just let me do the planning."

Now standing with the local officers who've been instructed to give him their full support, Felix said.

"I have something personal that might shake her up...would you like me to try it?"

"Sure... go ahead."

Felix walked over to Margie who was now seated.

"Mind if I join?"

Margie stared at him as he sat down facing her.

"A cigarette?" he held out a pack, "Heard you're from New York."

Margie drew one out.

Lighting it, Felix stared at her face. She wasn't beautiful, but there was something very sexy and attractive about her. It had to do with the way she moved and carried her body, licking her lips every so often and touching her hair.

"Thanks."

She took a long puff.

"You're welcome. So! Tell me about New York."

"What d'you want to hear?"

"How long did you live there?"

"Long enough to want to leave it."

"Why did you leave?"

"None of your fucking business!"

"You know, Margie," Felix inhaled deeply before going on, "I'm the good cop. The one standing over there," motioning with his head, "he's a real bastard. Now! I know you've already had a taste of the slammer in your previous life...so why not save yourself another visit. You talk to me, maybe you can save yourself a return tour."

Margie kept puffing on her cigarette. She was in deep trouble and she knew it. Not only would she get time because of her previous history, but she'd also end up paying for the others...after all, the pouch was now in her possession. It took her a few minutes longer and another cigarette to re-think her position. If she wouldn't work out a deal now, she'd live to regret it later. She needed a deal. Right now. It was the only thing that might save her.

"What do I get in return?" she turned to Felix.

"I can try to work out something...but I can't promise."

"I'll tell you everything you want to know."

She was beginning to realize the full extent of her predicament.

"Like I said...I can only try," Felix could almost smell her fear. He needed to squeeze her fast, before she'd have a chance to confer with her attorney.

"I want a deal before I spill out the beans," she looked at Felix.

"You're really in no position to negotiate anything."

Felix noticed the change in her face, though she tried to cover it up by taking another deep puff.

"I asked you... why did you leave New York?" he spoke in a leisurely pace though time wasn't on his side. He had to make her sweat. There were still some missing details, important ones that could make or break a final deal. Right now Felix was pressed for details. Lots of them. It was up to him to push Margie into wanting to cooperate.

"So? Are you gonna tell me why you left New York?"

"Personal reasons." She sounded edgy.

"How personal was Carlene Ridge?"

Margie swallowed then took a short puff.

"Look Margie," he spoke evenly, "if you don't answer me now I'm walking out and you're basically on your own. There'll be no deal!"

Margie knew her chances were slim, even under the best of circumstances and the help of her attorney. She'd just been caught using and dealing drugs, a fact that was undisputed. Pushed against the wall, Margie was scared. Damn that Jasmine! She had led her right into a trap. She couldn't believe how stupid she'd been, trusting a stranger like that and allowing her into the house.

Sensing now that Felix was about to walk out, she said.

"Ok...ok...I'll tell you about New York."

"I'm not gonna ask you again..."

"I met Carlene when she first came to New York," Margie began, "we had some great times, spent days and nights together...like sisters, more than sisters. She told me she came from..." Stopping to think for a moment, Margie tried to remember the name. "It was something ... she called it the deep woods of Texas. She spent time in a hospital then came to New York."

"What kind of hospital?"

"The funny kind," reaching for another cigarette.

"Go on."

"We had a great time until she married that weirdo of hers...a real sicko...like a sick bat!" she released a whistle.

"What d'you mean when you say you had a great time?"

"What d'you think it means?"

"I'm the one asking the questions!"

Margie wet her lips with her tongue. She thought of all the things she had taught Carlene and the deals they had done together and knew that her only chance was to cooperate before Carlene opened her mouth. But then she realized it was Felix who had first asked her about Carlene. Could that mean that Carlene had already worked out a deal in New York?

"Didn't Carlene tell you all about it?" she looked straight at Felix.

"We're here to discuss what **you** know."

Margie puffed again.

"Ok, so we had some fun together."

"What kind of fun, Margie?"

"We tried some stuff…you know…"

"Like the stuff you hid in your room just now?"

Margie lowered her head. She guessed they already knew everything there was to know and wondered what Carlene had told them.

"What happened after she married?" Felix pushed on.

"She…she started seeing other men…drove him nuts but he also liked it…he liked hearing about it. Then she got hooked with this international banker…kept flying back and forth… she used me as an excuse… told her husband she's visiting me. A while back he suspected something 'cause she was late returning his call …"

"Who's the guy?"

"She calls him Tierry… I wasn't supposed to know about him but …I did some checking around …turns out he lives a couple of blocks from here…" Margie couldn't help smile when she said it.

"What's his name?"

"Ralph T. Schmidt…calls him Tierry for short."

"How come you agreed to cover up for her?"

Margie swallowed.

"She knew things about me…"

"What things?"

"About the time I did…"

"Try again!"

Her face turned red as she told him about the stolen wallet.

"That's it! It was only that once! There was nothing else."

Felix needed to move on. There'd be plenty of time to find out the rest of the details. Sandy would get Carlene to fill up the gaps.

"Did you deal in New York?"

She shook her head.

"Who d'you sell to?"

Felix glanced at the clock on the wall. He figured he could go on for another hour or so before extracting crucial information from her. The untold would, sooner or later, be told. He was now sure of it.

***

By nine-thirty, back in his office, Felix called Sandy.

"Got some interesting updates for you," he smiled resting his legs on his desk.

"Surprise me!"

"We went stinging today …"

"How did it go?"

"Better than expected. You were right about the lady. We got what we wanted."

"Got something' for me, too?"

"Yeah!"

"I'm listening!"

"Your woman originates from Texas and was hospitalized in a place called Cedars Home. Checked it out and guess what! There's no record of a Carlene Ridge, so it only reaffirms your theory. Carlene's probably a new name. Got the prints you emailed me but it didn't turn up anything. Also got the full name and details of her loaded lover… Ralph T. Schmidt. Turns out he's married with a kid."

Sandy wondered about the missing piece of the puzzle. He knew Carlene had gone to great lengths to preserve her relationship with her latest lover, but it wasn't love that drove her to him. A thorough investigator, Sandy was eager for the 'why's as much as for the 'how's. Now faced with a case lacking a motive, he wondered how long it would be before Carlene was well enough to stand up to questioning.

"How's Carlene?" Felix asked.

"In bad shape and so is fuck face. We nailed him bare-assed with only a pair of black strippers on his front. It was a sight to see," he laughed heartily.

"Will Carlene come out of it?"

"She's still under the influence, but doing better. I haven't been able to question her yet. Hope to do so later on today."

"Let me know. I'm gonna wrap things up here then touch base with you."

"Great."

***

Sandy wondered about Carlene, her incredible beauty and charm as opposed to the way she now laid, semi conscious in a hospital bed. People fascinated him. But it wasn't so much what they did as the why and how they did it.

Carlene's case was still a mystery to him. He was eager to find out the rest.

CHAPTER 45

Sitting in the living room waiting for his wife, Tierry kept thinking about the woman he loved. He had debated long about it and concluded that his life was worthless without Carlene. It was something beyond him, a passion he had never felt before, a kind of hunger that hit him in the stomach every time he thought about her. He wished it wouldn't have happened, but it had.

If only...

Tierry's mind drifted as he remembered the first time he'd met his wife at a banquet organized by the bank.

A talented young interior designer she was hired for a weeklong project due to take place in Horseshoe Bay east of Austin, Texas, in the beautiful hill country. The occasion, meant as an excuse to invite the bank's best customers and their spouses for a weeklong leisured entertainment under the pretext of lectures, was held in a large conference room removed from the pool and the ballroom areas. The bank looked for someone with spark and imagination to re-dress the ballroom's appearance on a daily basis, and turn it into a spectacular nightly sight for the enjoyment of its guests.

Tierry had reached the resort by early evening and had gone to meet some of the invitees. Later on, after they had dined and wined, he'd decided to have a late drink at the bar. He saw her sitting, holding a glass of white wine.

"Mind if I join?" he was taken by her beautiful smile.

Staring at her eyes he added.

"I just realized that your eyes are like almonds…in color and shape."

She smiled back.

They remained seated long after the others had left and hadn't realized how late it was until the bartender pointed to the clock.

"We close at five…"

He walked her to her bungalow. The weather was perfect with just a feathery touch of freshness. Entering the room with its soft music and crackling fireplace, the air was spellbound with magic and romance. They kissed and ended up spending that night, and the next five, together. They were married four months later.

"I want to know everything there is to know about you," Tierry said as they lay in bed looking into each other's eyes.

He couldn't get enough of the woman he'd met only the week before, as though they'd known each other their entire life and were meant for each other. There was something very special about her, a kind of strength and determination unlike any other he'd ever seen. And she was so young. Only twenty-one. Tierry, twice her age, didn't think she'd really want him. Why would such a beautiful woman, an upcoming star in interior design want to date someone his age?

She told him a sad story. Her family's life had been shattered by the unexpected death of her father. At the age of sixteen, eight months prior to her high-school graduation, she'd found herself all alone in the world with barely enough to survive on. Supported by neighbors and friends, she was able to graduate with exceptional grades and was accepted on a full scholarship to a fine university in Austin.

Her extraordinary talents in the world of the arts became apparent during the first term project competition, and earned her an immediate apprenticing job as assistant manager of a large chain of flower stores. She continued to excel both academically and in her job, and by the end of the first year had won the university's prestigious honorary Designer Prize award. This time she landed an offer from The Leather Inc., another prominent chain store for leathered furniture with fifty-eight locations spread nationwide.

"We don't expect you to come up with a totally new concept by year's end, we realize you're still a student, but we're aiming towards changing the image of our chain stores. We appreciate your talent, creativity and originality very much and would welcome your suggestions."

When she received the written offer, she couldn't believe her eyes. Not only did they take into consideration her studies and the fact that she still had a year to complete her degree, but they also ensured her excellent benefits with a salary to match. She had become a star overnight.

"I love you… you're everything I've ever wanted in a woman, I love your head and those almond eyes of yours… your kind smile…I love you and one day soon I'd like to marry you."

She hugged him and cried.

"I love you too and I want to share the rest of my life with you. I feel as though I've known you all my life…"

A month later, he chose a Saturday night to propose to her in their favorite restaurant. She agreed and they were married the following month with only his mother as witness, having lost his father as a child. She'd invited a few friends to attend the ceremony, old folks who'd come from afar to participate in her happiest occasion.

Five months later Tierry had become the proud father of a daughter, and the loving husband of his young adoring wife.

Now sitting in his lavish home and remembering it all, Tierry's eyes filled with tears, painful tears meant for another woman, the one that hadn't kept her promise. For the millionth time, he tried to imagine what could have possibly triggered Carlene's sudden disappearance but couldn't come up with a reasonable explanation. Regardless of the reasons, Tierry was adamant to speak to his wife as soon as she returned home

His daughter was asleep. Tierry felt a sudden pinch, knowing how much he'd miss her. Once again he tried to sort out his thoughts, but his emotions got in the way and kept reminding him of Carlene, her face and smile and…oh… how he missed her eyes, those incredible blues… His body ached for her. He shut his eyes and tried to imagine how his wife would react.

Their marriage, considered solid by his wife, seemed to continue as before, though Tierry did feel the difference and had found it hard to make love to her. His body craved another woman, his true love.

"There are times… periods in a marriage that aren't as smooth… maybe Tierry is busy, maybe he's working too hard…" his wife rationalized.

They hadn't had any fights or unpleasant arguments, simply a change of heart, as Tierry liked to think of it.

"I'm in love with another woman…I can't help it," Tierry told his colleague.

It had taken Tierry several weeks to make up his mind, debating back and forth on whether or not to listen to his heart or obey his vows. He now sat in the living room all by himself, waiting for his wife to walk in the door.

* * *

She walked in at nine with a smile on her lovely face. Nearing him, she bent and kissed his lips.

"How was your day, honey?"

"I have something to tell you, Lydia."

CHAPTER 46

"How are you feeling?" Sandy approached Carlene's bed.

Her vacant eyes stared back at him. Standing next to her, Sandy couldn't help but feel pity for the beautiful face. He knew she had played dangerously and was now suffering the consequences of her own deeds. But it didn't detract from the pitiful condition she was now in. Besides needing to extract information pertaining to drugs and its distribution among New York's elite, Sandy was curious on a personal level. He had heard rumors and stories, some of which, he was sure, were exaggerations based on hearsay and gossip.

Now eyeing the neglected looking beauty with her uncombed hair and white face, Sandy wondered how to approach her.

"Carlene?" he again called her name.

Her face didn't flinch.

"Can you hear me, Carlene?"

Her eyes stared back. Sandy turned to the treating physician.

"How long can this last?"

"I wish I knew the answer. She was injected with a very potent dosage of a depressant, same as taking an overdose of crack or a similar drug. It's a good sign that her eyes are now open and she's able to breathe on her own."

"Boy! I'd love to give her husband a dose!"

"Yeah…I know what you mean."

An experienced internist specializing in pharmacology and drug abuse, Dr. Elkins was used to seeing such cases on a daily basis.

Some were milder than others, but those requiring longer hospitalizations were usually quite complex leaving behind trails of permanent damage to some degree or another. Nothing surprised Dr. Elkins, not even the numerous cases of fatality. There was no way to predict the outcome. The sooner a patient had their system cleaned out, the higher the chances of their survival.

In Carlene's case it was a question of whether or not her body was able to sustain the prolonged chemical abuse and the brutal rapes she's been forced to endure over the past four days.

Though he had supplied them with all the necessary information, Glen himself was baffled about Carlene's condition.

"I didn't know she'd react this way… I expected her to wake up."

Sandy shot him a look from a distance and decided to let the other officers on the scene complete the initial interrogation. It was safer for Glen. What remained now were the 'whys'. Why did Carlene latch onto Margie? And why the obsession with Tierry? There were plenty of men in New York. Why did she specifically target Tierry? It must be connected, in one or another, to Margie. She was the key person to it all.

But …why? And how?

Sandy was looking for answers.

***

Carlene was kept in ICU for another two days and monitored carefully by the staff. Every so often she'd open her eyes and mumble something that didn't make any sense. Dr. Elkins kept a close check on Carlene before deciding to move her into a private room closely monitored by the staff.

It was then that Sandy came by again hoping to talk to her.

"How are you feeling, Carlene?" he smiled.

"Fine…I'm fine," she answered in a somewhat hoarse voice.

"Great to hear you're doing better."

She released an angelic smile. Sandy couldn't help noticing the tiny dimple at the side of her mouth.

"Let me introduce myself. I'm Sandy Varlovsky the officer in charge of this investigation."

Carlene's face registered surprise.

"Do you know where you are?"

"They told me... a hospital?"

"That's right. Do you know why you're here?"

"I guess... I guess I wasn't well...?"

"You were drugged."

Carlene stared at him. Sandy wondered what was going through her mind.

"Do you remember what happened?"

Carlene shook her head.

"You were injected with a very strong drug."

"Why?"

Sandy was glad to hear her question. It reflected clarity.

"That's what we're trying to find out. Why?"

"Who's trying to find out?"

"We...the police."

She was silent before asking.

"Where's my husband?"

"In custody."

"What?!"

"He's the one who overdosed you."

"I don't understand..."

"He injected you with a substance that knocked you out...you were unconscious for about three, four days ...do you remember any of it?"

Sandy noticed Carlene's slight movement of the mouth. She swallowed hard.

"Would you like something to drink?" Sandy asked thinking of the more complex questions he was anxious to ask her.

"Water...I'd like some, please."

Sandy poured her a glass.

"Thanks."

Seated on a chair near her bed, Sandy asked.

"Are you comfortable? Or would you prefer to sit on a chair?"

"Yes…actually, I'd like to get out of bed."

Sandy helped her slowly out of bed and into a chair. Then he moved his own chair across from hers leaving the small round table in between.

"Now I'm gonna have to ask you some questions."

"Ok."

"Do you know a Margie Joree?" Sandy kept his eyes closely on her face.

It remained expressionless, except for the lips. They moved lightly as if preparing to say something but then changed their mind at the last minute.

"I'm waiting."

"So what if I know her?"

"Can you tell me what you know?"

"Why?"

"Because I'm asking."

"She lived here for a while…we were friends…"

"Until the two of you split, correct?"

"We were only friends…"

Sandy knew from experience that he couldn't afford to be overly gentle with a person prone to lying. Carlene seemed physically and mentally frail, but it wasn't as though the conniving elements of her personality had suddenly mellowed or disappeared.

"Once a liar, always a liar!" was the adage he lived by preaching it to the younger officers within the unit. Then he'd go over his theory that a person's DNA didn't only refer to physicality.

"Think of a person's character as a DNA all by itself…sure, there are the blood samples, the fingerprints, miniscule human tissues and remains and so on that can point at a suspect's physicality; but then there are also thoughts…trails of mannerisms, emotions, logic and rationalization…patterns that affect one's behavior and serve as reflection of their true self. If you keep that in mind, you can always rely on your intuition when it comes to understanding the criminal you're up against. Character has a DNA all by itself and is as permanent as the original color of one's eyes!"

Now seated across from her Sandy knew that Carlene wouldn't hesitate to lie at the first opportunity. Her manipulative mind remained the same, constantly searching for escape routes while reaching out with her hands to grab the things she wanted.

Dismissing all leniency and sentiment, he responded:

"Bullshit! You were dealing and selling!"

Carlene's mouth remained open staring at Sandy in disbelief.

"I'm waiting for your reply, Carlene."

"I'm not gonna answer that!"

"You have no choice."

"I want an attorney."

"You won't get one until you answer."

"That's against the law…"

"What you did was against the law!"

Sandy let it sink a moment then went on.

"Glen's in detention. So is Margie… in Dallas. Are you going to cooperate?"

Carlene swallowed again. She was beginning to feel the pressure.

"Margie has nothing on me. I don't care what you say."

"Wanna bet?"

"You're bluffing!"

"You can take your chance. But there'll be no one to save you if you're wrong."

Carlene took a deep breath. She knew Sandy wasn't bluffing. How else could he have known about their deals while Margie was still in New York?

"What d'you want to know?" she asked meekly.

"D'you know a certain Tierry?"

Carlene moved her head slightly.

"I'm waiting."
"A guy I was seeing."
"Was?"
"Is…"
"But you're still married, right?"
"Yes, but…"
"But what?"
"Well, you know…marriage isn't always meant to be for life."
"So where is this Tierry?"
"I'm sure you can answer that."
"You betcha' but I'm the one asking the questions."

Both stared at each other until Carlene, knowing she'd been caught and wishing to minimize the damages, said.

"Ok, so I've been seeing this guy in Dallas."
"Why Dallas?"
"Why not? Is it outlawed?"
"You could have handpicked any one from New York. Why Dallas?"
"I like tall men."
"I asked you why him?!"

Carlene was becoming agitated. Sandy could tell. She was fidgeting with her fingers like small kids sometimes do when they're anxious.

"I fell in love with him."
"Why Dallas?" Sandy insisted.
"'Cause he happens to live in Dallas!"
"Nah! You went looking for the guy. Why?"
Carlene didn't respond.
"Why, tell me why, Carlene Ridge?"

Carlene wondered how much he really knew. She remembered the stories Margie had told her about the tricks played by the police investigators. She was now hoping he wouldn't ask her the whys again, because it made her nervous.

At once she spotted Dr. Elkins from a distance and was relieved to see him coming her way. She sighed.

"I'll let you know when I feel better," she again smiled.
Sandy could smell her lies, almost feel them brewing inside those magnetizing eyes of hers.
He kept his gaze on her then exited the room.

Sandy went to get a cup of coffee from the nearby machine. Thinking about Carlene he decided to try another tactic. He kept rehearsing the questions as he followed the long corridor totally oblivious to his surroundings. By the time he returned to the waiting room his head was throbbing with the opening question.

"She's all yours!" Dr. Elkins stepped out of her room.

"How is she?" Sandy asked.

"Getting stronger by the minute. She'll be fine. Just take it easy, ok?"

"Sure. I wouldn't want…"

"I know. Just slow down a bit."

"Fine."

He had no intention of honoring his word. Carlene had to feel pressured.

He strode into her room and approached her. She was back in bed, seated, with her head leaning slightly on the pillow.

"What's your real name, Carlene Ridge?"

"My name's Carlene Wilmore."

"That wasn't the name given to you at birth, was it?"

She swallowed and rearranged herself on the bed.

"Why are you playing games, Carlene? You'll end up in the slammer, if I have anything to do with it!"

"You have nothing on me!"

"Don't I? How about dealing in narcotics and selling it in fancy parties?"

"You can't prove anything."

"I'd hate to disappoint you."

Carlene was scared. She wondered if Margie had talked but didn't know how to ask. Not that it made any difference. If Margie had sold her out, then she was lost anyway, unless…unless he was just guessing and Margie hadn't said a word. Again she thought of what Margie had told her. They liked playing tricks on people during questioning. What if Margie hadn't told them anything and he was just fishing? But what if they ask Margie …will she tell them? In that case, maybe she should tell them first…cut a deal…maybe get leniency or whatever it's called?

Sandy wondered what Carlene was thinking about. It occurred to him she might be considering immunity. It was crucial he stay a step ahead of her.

"Are you thinking of cutting a deal?" he asked watching her carefully for any reactions.

"Maybe…"

"I'm the one you'll have to cut it with."

"So?"

"I don't cut any deals with someone who doesn't talk."

"Let me think about it."

"Sorry, no time. Tell me your real name and we'll take it from there."

Carlene bit her lip.

"Abigail. Abigail Gray."

"And why did you go after Tierry?"

"He's married to my fucking sister."

EPILOGUE

St. Helen's, the nickname given to Texas' state penitentiary, named after Miss. Helen Fallwell, the African American woman who'd left her fortune to charity, was constructed in 1974 as a facility large enough to house five hundred inmates. Just past the heavy Iron Gate, as one leaves freedom to enter the life of the incarcerated, is the large, bronze head of the old lady staring into the distance through gloomy eyes and a furrowed forehead. Rumor has it she had once served time in the original structure but had found a way out into a better world by repenting. The forlorn face copied and turned into a prominent statue and placed on a pedestal, allows inmates on their daily walk and those entering its gate to appreciate its impressive details. Wintertime turns the face into a tearful looking sight with large drops that nestle inside the wide open eyes.

Considered one of the most advanced prisons in the nation, St. Helen's is surrounded by green lawns and fields of flowers neatly spaced and weeded by the team of forty-seven inmates currently interned within its walls. The other three hundred and seventy two women couldn't care less if the place burned down or if weeds and poison ivy overran its gardens.

Carlene Wilmore née Abigail Gray sentenced to seven years, and Margie Joree to ten, are amongst those lucky team members now allowed outdoors to work in the flower beds.

But Margie wasn't as lucky initially, when she was first caught and charged with dealing and distributing drugs and sent to Hollow Springs, Texas' oldest prison with a much longer sentencing. She has since appealed and her sentencing was shortened. She'd tried cutting a deal with the authorities but Carlene had beat her to it. Both tried blaming each other and cutting the best deal, but neither one was ultimately fully willing to co-operate.

Glen Wilmore, whose height had been reduced by several inches since his shameful crimes were unveiled, was sentenced to twelve years for acting negligently in the capacity of a treating physician and ignoring his patients to the point of causing injury to others, raping his wife on several occasions and trying to murder her; yet to this day, has not grasped his wrongdoings and is still serving time at Turnpike in Tennessee. Tierry, who had requested a divorce from his wife and had realized his mistake as soon as Felix reached him, chose to go through with the divorce and has since relocated to Richardson in north Dallas. He has refused any and all contact with the woman who caused him heartache. Having aged overnight, Tierry has since quit banking and is currently employed as an insurance agent in a mid-sized company in Dallas.

Lydia visits Abigail occasionally with a promise to help rebuild her life once she's released. Every so often she takes out of her jewelry box the small velvet pillow given to her as a keepsake by her sister and strokes its softness.

Printed in Great Britain
by Amazon